The shining splendor of our Zebra Lovegram logo on the cover of this book reflects the glittering excellence of the story inside. Look for the Zebra Lovegram whenever you buy a historical romance. It's a trademark that guarantees the very best in quality and reading entertainment.

HEATED EMBRACE

Shivering, wet, and weary, Lark huddled against a tree. She'd ripped her chiffon dress into shreds to help bandage Logan's bullet wounds, and for over thirty-six hours, she'd nursed his fever.

Logan appeared to be quite snug and cozy now, protected by an oilskin slicker and wrapped in the only blanket. Tempted by the prospect of a little warmth and sleep, Lark stripped off her clinging wet under clothes and slid beneath the blanket. Shuddering with loneliness and fatigue, she pressed her body to his powerful frame for warmth, then drifted off to sleep.

The next thing she knew, Logan's hand was gliding smoothly along her body—his gentle, probing touch making her feel things she'd never before experienced. Arrows of pleasure darted through her as a fire of intense delight sparked in her belly. Through fluttering lashes, Lark's dazzled eyes opened to see Logan's handsome face moving closer to hers. She felt his lips on hers, and she thrilled to the taste of him.

Breathless, she felt him pull his lips away just enough to whisper words that made her gasp. "Skylark . . . you belong to me."

SURRENDER TO THE PASSION

LOVE'S SWEET BOUNTY (3313, $4.50)
by Colleen Faulkner

Jessica Landon swore revenge of the masked bandits who robbed the train and stole all the money she had in the world. She set out after the thieves without consulting the handsome railroad detective, Adam Stern. When he finally caught up with her, she admitted she needed his assistance. She never imagined that she would also begin to need his scorching kisses and tender caresses.

WILD WESTERN BRIDE (3140, $4.50)
by Rosalyn Alsobrook

Anna Thomas loved riding the Orphan Train and finding loving homes for her young charges. But when a judge tried to separate two brothers, the dedicated beauty went beyond the call of duty. She proposed to the handsome, blue-eyed Mark Gates, planning to adopt the boys herself! Of course the marriage would be in name only, but yet as time went on, Anna found herself dreaming of being a loving wife in every sense of the word . . .

QUICKSILVER PASSION (3117, $4.50)
by Georgina Gentry

Beautiful Silver Jones had been called every name in the book, and now that she owned her own tavern in Buckskin Joe, Colorado, the independent didn't care what the townsfolk thought of her. She never let a man touch her and she earned her money fair and square. Then one night handsome Cherokee Evans swaggered up to her bar and destroyed the peace she'd made with herself. For the irresistible miner made her yearn for the melting kisses and satin caresses she had sworn she could live without!

MISSISSIPPI MISTRESS (3118, $4.50)
by Gina Robins

Cori Pierce was outraged at her father's murder and the loss of her inheritance. She swore revenge and vowed to get her independence back, even if it meant singing as an entertainer on a Mississippi steamboat. But she hadn't reckoned on the swarthy giant in tight buckskins who turned out to be her boss. Jacob Wolf was, after all, the giant of the man Cori vowed to destroy. Though she swore not to forget her mission for even a moment, she was powerfully tempted to submit to Jake's fiery caresses and have one night of passion in his irresistible embrace.

Available wherever paperbacks are sold, or order direct from the Publisher. Send cover price plus 50¢ per copy for mailing and handling to Zebra Books, Dept. 3443, 475 Park Avenue South, New York, N.Y. 10016. Residents of New York, New Jersey and Pennsylvania must include sales tax. DO NOT SEND CASH.

Joyce Myrus
Desperado's Kiss

ZEBRA BOOKS
KENSINGTON PUBLISHING CORP.

ZEBRA BOOKS

are published by

Kensington Publishing Corp.
475 Park Avenue South
New York, NY 10016

Copyright © 1991 by Joyce Myrus

All rights reserved. No part of this book may be reproduced in any form or by any means without the prior written consent of the Publisher, excepting brief quotes used in reviews.

If you purchased this book without a cover you should be aware that this book is stolen property. It was reported as "unsold and destroyed" to the publisher and neither the author nor the publisher has received any payment for this "stripped book."

First printing: July, 1991

Printed in the United States of America

Chapter One

Lark McKay, wearing white practice tights and a gold-fringed, red silk shirt, stood gracefully nonchalant with her slippered feet set on the shifting haunches of a splendid Clydesdale mare. The girl kept her arms outstretched and knees slightly bent as her thick, yellow braid bounced down her back. Running along beside the colossal horse, who was moving at a slow even trot, a head-tossing, eye-rolling piebald pony moved at a full-out, ragged comical canter. His braided tail, yellow too, was held up proudly, and his long golden mane was streaming. The pony's mouth was wide-open in a whinnying horse laugh as he worked hard to keep abreast of the much larger equine just casually loping on massive hoofs around the single ring of a travelling tent circus, *Professor Gentry's Dog and Pony Show*, in which Lark shared star billing. It was just one of many small road companies crisscrossing America by wagon, boat and train near the turn of the nineteenth century.

Watching the rehearsal performance of the rider and mare and the clowning, slapstick antics of the pony were three leggy Russian wolf hounds, a fox terrier with his head intently cocked to one side, and a young woman perched atop a bail of hay. Charlotte McKay, Lark's co-star, appeared to be about the same age as the bareback rider to whom she bore an unmistakable resemblance. Both women were petite blondes with quick, radiant smiles and luminous eyes. Charlotte's were a velvet gray. Lark's, at some times the identical shade, could also turn silvery or pearly or even steely gray, depending on the quality of light they reflected and her own candid, and unequivocal, mood. Now, as Lark did her act for her discerning human and canine audience, concentrating fixedly on making difficult feats look easy, the color of her avid eyes was a bright, nearly induline lavender.

Her legs drawn up and clasped in her arms, chin resting on her knees, Charlotte smiled in silent approval before clapping her hands, the sound muffled by soft glove leather. To protect her delicate pale skin from the sun and other harsh abuses of prairie weather, she was encased in faded indigo-blue denim from buttoned shirt collar to pants cuffs, which were rolled up to exhibit patterned python boot shafts. Her hair, a shade darker than Lark's, was pulled back from her fine face into a ponytail that protruded from beneath a big hat, a deep-brimmed, high-crowned sugar-loaf straw sombrero.

At Charlotte's barely audible command, the pony, without hesitation, trotted right under the tall mare, adeptly avoiding heavy hoofs as all three — horse, pony and rider — made one perfectly synchronized circuit of the ring. When the bantam Shetland emerged from beneath the Clydesdale, Lark dismounted from the larger animal with a nimble flip in a flurry of flying gold fringe. She landed, standing, on the rump of the pony, who was still neighing and flinging his head, galloping along for all he was worth.

"Lark! You've got it, you have really!" Charlotte called, waving her sombrero above her head in a triumphant gesture before sliding down from her vantage site and landing amidst the dogs, who were as jubilant as she. The wolf hounds began to howl, and the terrier leapt and barked with delight. "Listen, Lark, do it again just once or twice before you have to go. Okay . . . ?" Charlotte called, trying to make herself heard above the keening wails and sharp yaps of the dogs, performers themselves for whom the flourished sombrero was a signal to emote.

"I could keep doing it all day long, Charlie, but I don't want to be late! It's not often I get to *go* to a show, now is it?" Lark trilled a laugh. She whoaed the feisty Shetland to a jog-trot and vaulted up onto the mare once more. The placid horse could serve both as a platform for a rider—in the circus trade called a "rosin back" because of the tacky substance sprinkled on to give the rider better footing—or as a "liberty" horse—a riderless equine dancer directed from the ground by voice and whistle. The gentle, intelligent white mare had been taught to stay parallel to the piebald pony despite the ever-present danger of a nasty nip from the mischievous smaller horse.

"A *show?* Is *that* what you call it?" Charlotte exclaimed. She leaned against the hay stack and gestured with a gloved hand for Lark and the horses to go around the ring once more.

The girl stood, again precisely placing her feet on her mount's broad rosined haunches. She clicked her tongue, urging the Clydesdale, Minnie, into a faster walk as Pumpkin, the pony, stretched his neck for a nip at the mare's exposed flank. For his insolence, he received a painful thump on the nose from a rear hoof that Minnie managed to raise and thrust without unsettling Lark.

"Well, isn't that what it *is*—a show—or leastwise what passes for one out here on the Arkansas border? 'Professor' Gentry didn't blow the stand—" Lark glanced quickly at Charlotte, who objected to roadshow slang—"uh, I mean, he didn't go and give us, the whole passel of monkeys and all twenty dogs this afternoon off for nothing, now did he? He knows there won't be anyone willing to pay a nickel to see us when there's a free necktie sociable goin' on just down the road a little. You know, Charlie, the whole town's goin' to the hangin'." As Lark talked, Minnie had worked up some speed again.

"Well, I'm not going with you. I couldn't watch such a terrible thing for fear it would call up sad remembrance. If you think a hanging is just another show, you're sorely mistaken," Charlotte said, looking askance.

"Fort Smith's infamous Gates of Hell, as I've heard the scaffold here called, are opening for nine men today, all at the exact same instant. Now, if that's not a show, Charlie, you just go on and tell me what is," Lark answered.

"I know only too well what the Fort Smith scaffold is called. How can you talk so glib and unfeeling when your own father himself stepped into eternity right from these very same gallows?" Charlotte shivered and closed her eyes for an instant, trying to block out a scene forever imprinted in her memory. "You *know*, Lark, I will *never* believe, no matter how much hell the man raised here on earth, that it was to perdition he got sent. It was the Pearly Gates, not those others, that opened for him. I know in my heart, no matter what they say he did, he was a good man — and innocent, of what they hanged him for, anyway." As Charlotte adamantly jammed her gloved hands into the pockets of her dungarees, her lower lip began to tremble. She pulled her sombrero low to hide her eyes.

"Oh, Charlie, don't you start in to cry now! I didn't mean to upset you! Remember, I never knew him, leastwise not like you did. I mean, if it hadn't been for that old Hangin' Judge, I might have got to know my daddy, too." In her hurry to make amends and comfort Charlotte, Lark dismounted the mare with a doubleback somersault, landing on the balls of her feet at the very center of the ring. As soon as she did, the Clydesdale pivoted and began to chase the pesky pony. The maneuver was a part of their usual act, one that always got roars of laughter and a lot of applause. This time was no exception.

Lark and Charlotte, thinking themselves alone and unobserved, looked up in surprise to see three people step forward out of the tent shadows into the ring. Two, business or professional men, wore starched white collars and waistcoats. The third was a cowboy or a prosperous rancher more likely, Lark decided, in one astute scan taking in his rugged, weathered good looks, the cut of his batwing chaps and the expensive boots with silver dress spurs.

"Young lady, that was quite a trick!" one of the businessmen, the tallest and youngest of the trio, began, his impressive thick, dark, drooping mustache moving as if with a life of its own. "That is as skilled and daring a bit of equestrian proficiency as I have witnessed, and I have been privileged to observe some of the very best."

"I've seen some fancy riding myself," the rancher said

in a warm mid-south drawl, the crow's-feet at the edges of his eyes deepening when he smiled, "but I've seen nothing to compare exactly with what you just did. A move like that—it would come in mighty handy at roundup time—or win you a prize at a rodeo."

"I thank you both kindly, gentlemen, but unless you've seen Charlotte McKay perform, you haven't really seen the best, no sir. *She* taught *me!*" Lark's own smile seemed to light up the dim arena as she took a little bow. "To whom do we have the pleasure of speakin'?" she asked.

"That there tall feller is Mr. Al Ringling you've got the pleasure of flirting with, girl," the third man explained with a sly wink. A small, elfin, peppery person, he had close-cropped, tightly curling gray hair and shrewd, humorous eyes that gleamed blue through gold-rimmed spectacles. "Mr. Ringling picks the performers for the show he and his brothers operate, young lady. That's The Ringling Brothers Stupendous Great Double Show, Circus and Caravan and Trained Animal Exposition. The horse acts are his special area of interest and expertise. For him to compliment your riding is no small thing."

"I'm offering this talented young woman—both these beautiful women—" Ringling ruffled his mustache and flashed a smile to include Charlotte—"more than mere compliments. I'm offering them positions as artistes with what's rapidly turning into the greatest circus in America, greater even than the combined Barnum together with Bailey, especially now that old P.T. Ballyhoo Barnum himself expired April seventh past in this momentous year of 1891. Right now, we are expanding from one to three rings—got a real able twenty-four-hour man who goes in a day before, has all in readiness for our great bedazzling march into town that's led by our forty-horse hitch and ends with a big toot up on the calliope. Best parade in the business. Yep, I'm offering these ladies unequalled fame and fortune, their likenesses on posters printed special by the Erie Lithograph Company and displayed in every barbershop and hotel lobby in these United States *and* on most of the fences and walls, too. Besides all that, I am offering them a private living tent, too." Al's hand delved into his breast pocket. "My card," he said. "We aren't a mud show any more. Gave up wagons and took to the rails last spring. It's a lot more comfortable, I can promise you," Ringling added proudly.

"You from back east? You kick sawdust in New York? I've only been east far as St. Lou. It has always been my true ambition to go there, at least as far as Chicago!" Lark exclaimed excitedly. "Are you the Ringling brother who balances a wood plow on his chin? How do you do that?"

"I put a little chalk mark right here." The man pointed to his face. "We're doing a stand at Fort Smith in three weeks' time. If you're still in town, I'll show you then how it's done, if you'd like. That'll be our Home Sweet Home performance before heading back to our winter quarters in Baraboo. You could try working with us then, see if you like us. I'll introduce you to our snake charmer . . . show you our new HIDEOUS HYENA, the Midnight Marauding, Man-Eating Monstrosity, our mitt joint and picture gallery—that's a fortune teller's tent and a tattooed man," Ringling explained to the rancher. "And Home Sweet Home is the last show of the tour. We've got Arab tumblers—"

"Everyone'll see the barnside sheets you'll be papering town with, Al," his small and outspoken companion interrupted before going on with the introductions.

"That other fellow there in the eye-catching boots knows horses about as well as Al knows horses. Say howdy to Jake Chamberlain, ladies, owner of the JAK Bar Ranch, one of the biggest spreads in the Oklahoma Territory, out west of here a ways. He's in town today to see the show."

"*Our* little gilly show?" Charlotte asked as she extended her hand to each man in turn, lastly to the handsome rancher, who courteously swept off his high-crowned Texas hat revealing dark hair starting to pepper with gray. "Lark's always wanted to go east and see the civilized part of the world. I've no such interest. Since first leaving my Arkansas home for town life, I have missed the barn owls fledging and mockingbirds calling at midnight outside my window . . . pined to see wild horses pawing the earth under the moon, shaking their dew-spattered manes. Pardon my glove, Mr. Chamberlain," she added, her smile shy but vivid as she reached out to him.

"If you'll pardon mine, ma'am." He smiled back, friendly but formal. "I once heard Mr. Russell, the painter, say that if he had a winter home in hell and a summer home in Chicago, he'd spend his summers in hell. I, too, have always disliked cities. I only came on into Fort Smith today for that other show we couldn't help but overhear you ladies discussing. I'd no hope of finding so agreeable a diversion as a travelling tent circus featuring two such lovely and talented sisters. I'd be real honored to watch you both ride—after the hanging."

Chapter Two

"And we'd be honored to perform for you, Mr. Chamberlain, but we're not sis—"

"Charlie was about to say she is not planning on going to the hangin'," Lark pointedly interrupted. "But I wouldn't miss it for anythin'."

"Well, I suppose I *could* be persuaded to change my mind, Lark," Charlotte said, glancing at the rancher. "That's not what I was about to tell Mr. Chamberlain, though. I was going to explain to him that you and I are not sis—"

"Jake, ma'am. Call me Jake," Chamberlain insisted. "Soon as the hangman's shown us *his* tricks and set these rustlers dancing on air, why, we'll all come on to the evening performance of the Gentry Dog and Pony Show."

"Jake's got a personal interest in seeing this gang of outlaws swing. So do I," the small, fierce man added.

"Oh?" Lark lifted a brow. "Did they rustle stock from you, also, sir? You don't look like a cattleman, Mr. . . . ?"

"Parker's my name, and, no, they didn't steal anything from me, missy. I passed sentence on 'em, is all."

13

"You . . . are *Judge* Parker?" Charlotte gasped, looking stricken and wide-eyed.

"Uncle Ike to you, Charlotte honey. Have I changed so much in the years since you've been gone from Fort Smith you don't even recognize me?" he asked, removing his hat, then his spectacles, one gold-wire earpiece at a time, and carefully folding them into a hard-framed brass case. It snapped closed with a click. The small man with his gray hair and mischievous, shrewd gray eyes put one in mind not so much of Santa Claus as perhaps one of the North Pole's more impish elves.

"Uncle Ike! *Now,* without your hat and specs, I see the man I remember!" Charlotte proclaimed, bringing her hand to her face and peering over her finger tips in astonishment.

"I'd have known *you* anywhere, child. You are the spittin' image of your mother, my much lamented sister, when she was about the same age you are now. Besides, you don't hardly look one wit older than you did last time I set eyes on you, and what a sad day that was when—"

"When you hanged my daddy?" Lark asked, coldly accusative. "Charlie, you never ever said that the terrible notorious Hanging Judge, Old Man Isaac Parker, who did in daddy, is one and the same as the darlin' Uncle Ike you been telling me about since I was yay high." She held her hand low and parallel to the ground.

"It's like they were always two different men, to me, Lark honey, good-natured Uncle Ike and the Hanging Judge." Charlotte's expression was apologetic, her voice gone whispery.

"I just can't—I *won't* believe this!" Lark responded. She had been undoing her long braid, and now, as she shook her head emphatically, the gesture served the dual purpose of denying what she'd been told and sending a flood of flaxen hair to decorate her stubbornly squared shoulders.

"You damn well better believe it unless Charlie's got another Uncle Ike tucked up her sleeve I never heard of," Parker snapped, his lips drawing into a thin, hard line that turned jovial Uncle Ike into the Hanging Judge before Lark's very eyes. "Haven't you learned yet that our Charlotte is just full of surprises? Why, you yourself, young lady, was one of her biggest shockers."

"So I've been told," Lark answered, her tone brittle. "Now, I must ask you one thing, dear Uncle Judge. In the circumstance of a condemned man being my daddy, and his woman being my mama *and* your favorite niece *and* them so in love *and she* with an illegitimate child, how could you hang Mark Larken *before* he had the chance to marry Miss Charlotte McKay?" Lark's eyes were the wrathful cold gray of a prairie winter sky.

"I thought you would be far better off in life as a McKay than carrying a villain's name that was infamous all through the border states, just like Quantrill and James and Cook," the judge thundered, outraged by Lark's unheard of verbal assault on his integrity. "But just let me set the record straight; even feeling as I did about that, I did the right thing and you are no—"

"What's past is past, Uncle Ike. It doesn't matter any more." Charlotte stopped him, speaking with a raised hand and a pleading look. "My little girl needn't be burdened with all that old trouble now."

"You mean these two charming ladies are *not* sisters? That's even better," Al Ringling marvelled, more interested in selling tickets than in any mysteries of their past.

15

"Nope. I agree that's hard to believe, seeing them together, side by side, but they are really mother and daughter," the judge, looking bemusedly at his niece, explained. "Charlotte broke her father's heart when his only daughter ran off with that hellion, Mark Larken. Then Larken broke Charlotte's, running off with the riffraff dregs and offshoots of Quantrill's scoundrelly outlaw gang, leaving her with her apron high and that girl there under it." The judge turned to Lark. "But I did my duty, even if it broke *my* heart, darlin', sending your father to the hanging tree when you were just a few days old." Parker looked squarely into Lark's eyes.

She returned the look, coldly unflinching. "From what I've always heard, you never did have a heart to break, Judge. Well, go on, please."

"I am truly sorry Mr. Larken didn't get to see his daughter grown into a woman — a beautiful one at that. Nevertheless, I had no choice but to see him hanged. I'd do exactly the same again, for Charlotte's sake — and yours." Parker's chin jutted as aggressively stubborn as Lark's. He blinked.

"There's always choices, different ways of working things out," Lark answered, her expression as obdurate as Parker's, her voice, controlled and even, concealing strong emotions. "However, there's no need for you to take on and make excuses, Judge Parker, about doing your duty, and none for you to apologize to me. I'm a realist. I don't have to deny what's true for sentimental reasons of my own. You see, besides hearing you called heartless, I've also heard tell that Mark Larken was wild as a Kansas tornado and mean as a Texas rattler."

There was a stunned silence as the judge, rarely at a loss for words, gazed at Lark utterly speechless. The others looked intently at her, too, Ringling with puzzlement, Chamberlain with surprised admiration, and Charlotte a bit anxiously.

"Oh, but there were times your father could be so dear and tender, Lark. He was just a rambunctious boy, sewing wild oats like any normal young fellow, just kicking over his traces before he was broke to the bridle of domesticity. He suffered the ill luck of falling in with a bad crowd, is all. I'll always be grateful to Mark for leaving me one priceless, precious gift, Lark—you."

"Ill luck? Pshaw to that," Parker said with a snide laugh. "Larken was just plain lawless. He had the devil in his heart and soul and bones."

"Seems to me this here judge saw to it I was more a burden than a gift to you, Mama," Lark glowered. "Me and Mark and Ike here, all three of us together, got you shamed, abandoned, disowned, disinherited and driven from your home. We turned you into a gypsy, and you had to carry a baby on your back like a squaw woman. Judge, she took me right into the circus ring with her while she did her trick riding, to keep us both fed and warm in winter."

"We never got rich, Lark darlin', but we did manage to ease on by. Now please stop oppressing these gentlemen with our bygone plight. We came through well enough, didn't we?"

"Don't look so mortified, Mama. I know you prefer to think highly of just about everyone, except yourself, maybe. There's skeletons in lots more cupboards than you'd suppose."

"This is one outspoken, acid-tongued little female you've raised, Charlotte. She's a real clearheaded, cool customer." Parker took a step toward Lark. "So was your old man, sweetheart," he told her with a dubious grin. "You're like him in that way. I hope it's the only way. You may have heard it said, since you've heard so much else, that a carpenter is known by his chips."

"If it turns out I *am* more like my daddy than it seems, it won't be happenstance. It will be because I myself *choose* to follow in his footsteps."

"As your great uncle, I got an obligation to give you a word of advice and another of mild reproof, Miss McKay. Don't mess with the law; that's the advice. The reproof is this: Even if what you heard about Larken is actual, as I believe it to be, *you* are not one to be speaking of it. It's not family loyal, nor rightly fitting. Larken *was* your father in the eyes of man and—"

"Now, let it be, Uncle Ike. Don't go stirring up the past." Charlotte was quick, as always, to change that particular subject and come to her daughter's defense. Lark's gray eyes had the bright, dangerous glint of quicksilver.

"I do not welcome advice from a righteous, hard man who does not temper justice with mercy," she said coldly.

"What?" Parker sputtered. "And have a serpent sting me twice? Because that's what Mark Larken would have done to me . . . to your mama. . . ."

"Then, you shouldn't be asking me to be respectful and loyal to him. I do not give my respect to them who don't deserve it. I have never been a faint-hearted forlorn, self-deluded female inclined to be mooning over what I can't do anything about. Being an outlaw's illegitimate daughter is something I can't do anything about. Being a respectable rancher's *granddaughter—that* might be a different matter, though from what I can reckon, Rufus McKay is as wicked as Mark Larken, in a way. He may be upright; but he's also unforgiving, and that's wicked."

"Now, you just hold on one gosh darn minute, miss, and—"

"No, Judge, you hold on till I finish." Pale with anger, Lark planted her fists on her hips. "Rufus took about as much care of Charlotte, his only child, as Larken did of me. But then my daddy had a better excuse than Charlie's. You saw to that, didn't you, Judge? Dead men aren't real good at making amends, but I aim to see that Charlotte gets something from *her* daddy, leastways."

"If you think you can play the badger game—blackmail an old man in *my* jurisdiction—think again. Just what might that something be you plan to extort from Rufus?" Parker asked suspiciously.

"An apology is all we want," Lark answered with a chill, superior smile. "If he's still on this earth, Rufus owes us—owes Mama anyway—that much, don't you agree?" The spotted pony had come up beside Lark and thrust his velvet nose at her hand like a kitten wanting to be stroked. Sinking to one knee, Lark as usual indulged Pumpkin, glad for the excuse to turn away from Ike Parker's juridical, evaluating eyes. He was the first member of her mother's family she'd met, and she was more concerned than she'd realized about measuring up. After glowering at her awhile, the judge, apparently reaching a decision, harrumphed and almost smiled, if only with one side of his mouth.

"I think you should call me Uncle Ike, child," he pronounced, the half smile turning to a wily but warm grin. Ike Parker had never in all his sixty-odd years come upon so outspoken and opinionated a young woman, and though nettled by her, he couldn't conceal a grudging esteem and pride in his new-found greatniece. "Now, Lark, listen to your uncle; I agree with all you've been saying. I told Rufus back then all those years ago, he was wrong, driving your mama from his doorstep. She was only a willful child, like you," he twitted, "and about the same age as you are now, all of seventeen or so."

"I am nineteen," Lark proclaimed, sounding to herself like a bragging schoolchild. "Well, whatever happened to Rufus McKay? *Is* he still alive?"

"And kicking, same as ever. See if you can pick out your own grandaddy in the crowd this afternoon — at the hanging."

Chapter Three

Lark did pick out a man that day, one who would change her life, but it wasn't her grandfather.

"Do you see him, Mama, do you?" she kept asking Charlotte as they both peered about the crowd assembling at the Fort Smith stockade and jail. Every seasoned, graying, fatherly-appearing man Lark set eyes on came under her immediate suspicion and scrutiny.

"No, I do *not* see Mr. McKay, Lark darling," Charlotte answered with affectionate exasperation for about the tenth time in as many minutes. She had, to her daughter's satisfaction, accepted Jake Chamberlain's invitation to the "festivities," as he, like everyone else in town, referred to the hangings.

"Mama," Lark had whispered, "you *like* him! You could have let him suppose we were sisters—for a while, just in case he's lookin' for a wife. These ranchers like their women young with a long breedin' future in front of them."

"I am not good at deception, Lark," Charlotte had whispered back before explaining to Jake she would leave, or at least close her eyes, when the afternoon's grisly spectacle actually began. Then she had rushed off to put up her hair and change into her prettiest dress.

So far, despite Charlotte's trepidations, there had been no cause for her to close her eyes. The gathering was anything but grim. In fact, there was a holiday feeling in the air.

"I kept my promise, didn't I, ladies?" Chamberlain asked. "Isn't this more like a barn raising and branding party combined than like a hangin', with the finale of a big cattle drive thrown in, too?"

"It's a great day . . . great day for Fort Smith," the judge pronounced to everyone who came up to shake his hand. He spoke in the slow, growly judicial voice he used on the bench and for weddings and funerals. He accepted personal credit and congratulations for almost single-handedly bringing law and order to the unruly territories.

"I don't think this is a fittin' occasion for frivolity and a brass band," Lark commented, though she, like Charlotte, had also changed into a feminine, flattering ensemble. On that hot September afternoon, both wore dainty layered drifts of cool, ankle-length, white chiffon and wide-poke sunbonnets.

"The men being hanged here today are crookeder than a barrel of snakes, real bad actors. They been visiting harm on these people a long time, so the citizenry has a right to a little merrymaking," Jake answered mildly. "Most of those who are meeting their maker here today are horse-thieving bank robbers and killers. There's even a well poisoner in the lot. In this part of the country, there's nothing worse than a well poisoner."

"I know, but even so. . . ." Lark began to protest, standing on her toes, then jumping to get an improved view of the goings-on.

"There's no point, darlin', to your searching out Rufus McKay," Charlotte told Lark with a sigh. "Even if he *is* here and we walk right on up to him and say 'how do,' the man won't have anything to do with us. He swore he would not to speak to me ever again as long as he lived. He swore to that last time we were together, and he has never once in his life been known to go back on his word, never. He prides himself on that. Why, anyone who's ever met Father will tell you I'm right. Am I not right, Uncle Ike?" Charlotte asked the judge. "If you are also acquainted with Mr. McKay, Mr. Chamberlain, please tell this child I know whereof I speak," she appealed, peering out from under the scalloped edge of her parasol.

"Only if you'll call me Jake," he teased, pushing his wide-brimmed hat to the back of his head. "Your mother's right, Miss Lark, but not altogether. Rufus has the reputation of being a bona fide ornery curmudgeon. That propensity has got worse in him as he's got on in years, but also, he is known to be a right free-handed and kindly man when his neighbors need help," Jake explained. "I think, given half a chance, Mr. McKay would be deeply gratified and happy to make his peace with two such . . . such lovely women. Especially if they just happen to be his only daughter and his one grandchild. He is smart enough to have learned by now, as many do in their advancing years, that children and grandchildren are the true joy and consolation of a man's life Don't you worry your self none now, Miss Lark. Rufus McKay will be here for certain, though I don't see him yet," Jake added, looking around.

The rancher was a vigorous, ruddy-faced, good-looking man, strongly built and solid through the shoulders. He carried himself well and moved with an authority that made him appear taller than he actually was, but even at just five-feet-eight, he had a good advantage over Lark—even if one included the extra half inch she imprecisely tacked on to her own five feet when asked. For his own reasons, he, too, had been surveying the crowd that had swelled to a veritable sea of ten-gallon hats and straw bonnets.

People from the surrounding countryside had streamed into town for the historic occasion. Homesteading farm families arrived in mule-pulled buckboards. Well-mounted ranchers escorted their ladies, some of whom were also on horseback, though most availed themselves of the shaded comfort of surreys and summer buggies. Farm women were dressed in homespun and gingham, a few still with flour-sack aprons on. The frontier gentry, wives and daughters of bankers and cattle barons, wore pastel Sunday go-to-meeting dresses trimmed with lace collars and cameo brooches. Like broody hens, they kept watch over the scores of youngsters frolicking about the stockade, many of whom had actually put on shoes for the momentous occasion.

The saloons in Fort Smith remained open and were raking in profits, though most of the other shopkeepers had locked their doors to join in the general revelry. Even the bawdyhouse girls, rarely seen out and about in daylight, had taken to the hot, dusty street. Clothed in trade finery—store-bought gowns and heavy earrings, bands of yellow at their wrists and throats, some of it fools gold, some real—they received the open attention of what seemed a battalion of armed soldiers in Federal blue uniforms leaning wearily on their rifles in the scant shade, looking bored—except when the approach of a fancy woman brought them to attention.

Adding to the commotion, word had spread that there were strangers in town. Some were itinerant vendors and hawkers selling pins and pots and snake oil. There were journalists, too, correspondents from New York, Chicago, St. Louis, Omaha, even one from as far away as Sweden. Sent west to cover the Plains Indian Wars, they hoped to scoop their competition in the east by being on the scene for Fort Smith's big day. Included among their number was a new breed in the newspaper business, an artist-reporter. The man sketched continuously in rapid pencil strokes producing line drawings of the shifting, churning scene to which he would add dimension and shading at a more relaxed moment. Partial to faces, he produced very good likenesses and was particularly interested in capturing images of a silent, expressionless handful of Indians who in turn watched him. Pacified Apaches being taught the range cattle business, some of the braves wore cowboy gear while others were attired in frock coats and bent old hats, though they all had braids, but one. He sported a feather on a hat so big it covered his ears and the upper half of his face.

"Doesn't the young buck look just like the Indian on the new buffalo nickel? And the man with him in the big hat looks to be a natural clown. Do you think they would come work for my brothers and me?" Al Ringling mused aloud to Jake.

"There is something out of the ordinary there, Al," Jake acknowledged. "Apaches don't wear feathers. It goes against their tribal way." He frowned. It was a trivial matter, but it made the rancher more edgy than he was to begin with. He kept his thoughts to himself, though, reluctant to alarm his charming guests as Ringling went sauntering off toward the befeathered brave.

There were other new faces in Fort Smith that day, something that concerned Jake more than an overdressed Apache. Armed hard riders begrimed with trail dust had been drifting into town since sunrise. None was smiling or making idle chatter, and more significantly, none was seen to take a drink of hard liquor. Their presence and demeanor lent credence to hearsay that trouble was brewing.

Rumors that the hangings were not going to come off without a hitch had given Jake Chamberlain the grounds he thought needed to take Lark and Charlotte under his protection and make them part of his retinue. Actually, no excuse had been required. Both McKays were delighted with his company, and as the craggy, still-handsome cattleman made his way to the front of the crowd, followed by several of his armed ranch hands, he escorted a beautiful equestrian on each arm. The lovely blond mother and daughter appeared exotic and elegantly eastern, perhaps even foreign, to the assembled locals, who had no idea who they were. There was rampant obvious, though whispered, speculation about their business in Fort Smith, for they had yet to perform, and Jake, thoroughly pleased with the stir his guests were causing, leaned to Lark.

"Your grandfather is going to be real proud when he sets eyes on you," he said.

"Do you think he's really coming?" she asked. "Isn't it almost time?"

"Rufus hasn't missed a hanging since Mark Larken's and—" Jake cut his words short. "He hasn't missed one in near twenty years. I'll point him out to you when I spot him and introduce you, if you'd like so—Miss Lark, aren't you feeling quite well?" Jake asked, worried by a sudden rose-petal flush that had come to her cheek. "I'm sorry. I shouldn't have mentioned that, about Larken. Sometimes, usually when it comes to feminine sensibilities, I'm about as smart of as a box of rocks. I—"

"Never mind about all that, Mr. Chamberlain. Just tell me, who is that boy?" Lark asked the question with a flutter of her thick lashes toward the scaffold.

The guards had led out the prisoners. Hands tied behind them, they were climbing the thirteen steps to the gallows, each to take his place on the platform beneath his own custom-fitted noose ready and waiting with the hangman's requisite thirteen coils.

"Each man was measured for height and weight, and the length of his rope adjusted accordingly so that he'll drop quick enough and far enough, when the trap's sprung, to get his neck broke. I insist on that," Ike Parker said. "If it's not done right, a man can dangle as much as five minutes before the life is choked out of him."

The mood of the gathering changed from festive to somber as a dour, sallow-faced, hunched little man, George Maledon, the infamous Fort Smith hangman, went methodically about the job he professed to love. Maledon, with ghastly glee, already claimed the record for managing the greatest number of simultaneous executions on the frontier—six. Today, he had conceitedly boasted, he would be breaking his own record, doing for nine men what he'd done so well, in a jiffy and lickety-split, for those six. Maledon had considerable pride of craft and a penchant for quirky gallows humor which made him an oddly popular man, despite his trade, when he bellied up to the bar after a hard day's work.

At the moment, there was no laughter. The atmosphere had turned more than a little somber. The brass band went silent, and conversation fell to a low, tense hum so that when Lark repeated her question to Jake Chamberlain—"Who *is that boy?*"—it was clearly heard by onlookers and condemned men alike.

Chapter Four

The manacled men were mainly an inglorious lot—stumbling, dirty and unshaven. Their deportment revealed similar states of slack-jawed, cringing dread as they blinked, coming from prison gloom into the midday glare. Only one, the last of the nine desperados brought out, walked with squared shoulders and his head held high.

Alone among his fellow prisoners, he was clean-shaven. His was a handsome face, strong-featured with a determined mouth drawn thin and a hard jaw, defiantly set. At the sound of Lark's rich, low, fervent voice, he came to an abrupt stop, swivelled and met her appalled, unblinking, silvery-gray gaze with a fixed look of his own before he was shoved forward by a guard.

Tall and slender and tanned, the prisoner was obviously a man who worked out in the weather, for like his companions, a lurid white patch stood out where his shirt collar had been torn away and his neck shaved in back. It was the hallmark of a Maledon hanging, as if the executioner was going to use a guillotine on his victim instead of the noose. The young prisoner had slicked-back, short-cut chestnut hair, with little licks of gold showing in it like flickers of fire. Gold sparked in the amber eyes that riveted on Lark when he again faced the crowd. His gaze was hard, straight, unblinking, and unreadable.

Lark heard Charlotte beside her draw a low, gasping breath.

"Mama!" the girl whispered, unable to break the shimmering hold of the prisoner's stare, "I've never seen anythin' like him."

"Well . . . I sure have, Lark honey," Charlotte answered, her voice low and quavering. "That fine-appearing lad sure suggests your daddy. Oh, not in form and features, but in age and bold bearing. I shouldn't have come here today, I *knew* I shouldn't! I just can't bear thinkin' of all that sorrow of those years ago. But you know what?" Charlotte demanded. "I am glad still to this day, despite the outcome of my long-ago reckless rapture, that Mark Larken and I were so in love." Unaware of what she was doing, and drawing Charlotte with her, Lark had moved forward as if drawn by an invisible lariat.

"God, you *are* an incurable romantic, Mama," she declared. "I wouldn't care how much I loved a fellow, I would never in a hundred years . . . not in a thousand . . . take up with any outlaw." She was still looking straight ahead at the condemned man as she gently lectured her mother.

"Not even if you fell in love with one like him up there, that tall, slim boy who is surely more than just middling handsome? He's got such a fine grace about him, and a hint of the gentleman in his manner, doesn't he?" Charlotte asked in a dreamy voice, an earlier note of chiding skepticism gone as she and Lark both gazed ahead at the prisoner.

30

"I especially wouldn't let myself fall in love with one like him, slim and lank like he is, with those long cowboy bones. And, Mama, look at his eyes! Deep-set like they are, under those dark brows that are kind of edged with gold, why those eyes could haunt a girl's dreams forever."

"You are not telling me anything I don't know already, about the ache of loss and remembrance and such, Lark darlin', but *I* am telling *you*, you know nothing of love. If you did, you'd not be so silly as to say what you just said about not letting yourself fall into it—" Charlotte glanced down then, and the shadow of her bonnet brim darkened her swimming gray eyes— "as if you'll have a choice. I didn't. No one has a choice who's gloriously young and crazy in love."

"You and me are a lot alike, Charlie, but we're different, too. I've got *my* life planned out, not like you, letting things just . . . just happen. I'm going to play all the cards in my own hand, make the right picks and discards, no matter what. Want to know my next draw, Charlie? It's accepting Mr. Ringling's offer to join his show, even if you don't want to, even if you really do give up the performing life and stay on here like you said you would."

"Oh, I meant what I said—when I said it leastways." Charlotte shrugged, not taking her eyes from the young prisoner.

"Well, I will earn wide renown for my riding. I am going to follow my fame east to Chicago . . . to New York City. Maybe I'll get east as far as . . . England or France, even," Lark insisted with a touch of wonder in her determined whisper. "I will get us some money and have everything you never did, Mama," she added, she, too, looking directly at the

31

young outlaw all the while she spoke.

"I won't be with you, but I hope you do all that, darlin', because your happiness is all I've wanted for a *long*, long time." Charlotte sighed. For me. . . ." Her attention was diverted by the prisoner. He was having his last smoke. "For me it's too late — for the sort of happiness waiting for you."

"Thirty-six is not too late for anything, Mama. You could *still* find a man to share your life, give you more children. . . ."

"Think so?" Charlotte questioned speculatively. She glanced back over her shoulder at Jake Chamberlain, who was standing several feet away looking about, uneasy and watchful. "No, no. I should be a grandma by now, Lark. *You* are the one who'll find a feller," she protested, returning her attention to the handsome prisoner. "He doesn't at all look as though he belongs with those others, does he?" she asked, abruptly changing the subject. "He hasn't got the 'blue johnnies' like the rest, all of them drunk enough to be seeing pink spiders by now, or else missing some buttons — just crazy. No, he's definitely not like the usual horse-thieving, bank-robbing gallows bird somehow.

"Uncle Ike, what's this fine-looking boy done to deserve meetin' up with George Maledon here today?" Charlotte asked, stepping back and slipping her arm through the judge's.

"Logan Walker stands convicted of killing a well-loved maiden lady school teacher name of Miss Rachel Blue," Parker answered.

"He murdered a school marm?" Charlotte asked incredulously.

"Don't be fooled by his boyish and sincere good looks, Charlotte. You, of all people, should know better than that. Some of the most ruthless desperados ever to face me for judgment looked like they wouldn't do mischief to a fly."

"'Stands convicted,' you say? That's a curious phrase, Judge," Lark commented. With her eyes, dove-gray in sunlight, still on the prisoner, she, too, took a step back and rejoined the others, curious to hear about Logan Walker. "It sounds to me as if you've got some doubts about it, like you think he might not be guilty," she challenged Parker.

"Any last words? Messages? Confessions? Revelations?" Maledon, the hangman, asked the prisoners. Some blubbered, some snarled, others choked out a word or two of apology, and one asked his mother to forgive him the pain he'd brought her. Then Maledon stood before Logan Walker.

"Your turn to speechify, boy," the executioner said.

"I didn't come here to discourse, George. I came to die," Walker answered matter-of-factly as, with a gesture of his handsome head, he refused the hangman's hood. "No, thank you kindly. I intend to enter the next world with my eyes wide open and full of the beauty of this world. I mean to meet my maker while looking at the prettiest thing I ever saw or expect to see, here or in paradise." And then, Logan Walker, standing straight up on the notorious Fort Smith gallows, only minutes from meeting death at the end of a rope, winked right at Lark McKay, even as the noose was being placed around his neck. When he grinned, the hard sparkle of his white smile took her so much by surprise, she flushed and gasped aloud in a confusion of delight, admiration and outrage.

"Isn't he the brazen one," she exclaimed. "Where on earth did he spring from, Judge?"

"Call me 'Uncle,' will you, honey, like I asked you to?" Parker responded peevishly. "Logan Walker has been in the Western District of Arkansas only a short while. I do not know where he came from nor where he was goin'. Out here, we don't ask such questions."

"The boy signed on as a wrangler out to Matthew January's spread. No one in town hardly knew him to talk to, except Rachel Blue, the school mistress. Logan was known to visit with Rachel regular, every time he come into Fort Smith," Jake explained. "I know him better than some. He happened along once and helped me to cut a stray cow loose of barbed wire. After that, he used to call at my JAK Bar Ranch for a meal when he was in the neighborhood, which wasn't often. Logan, he's the sort of bold-eyed boy you notice right off, nice and easy in his ways, self-assured but no braggin' from him. I've heard tell he could do right good at just about anything he put his hand to. Yep, I thought Logan was just the sort of boy a man like me, being a rancher, would choose to have for a son, if a man *could* choose. I was thinking of hiring Walker away from January. Then this murder come up."

"Have you any sons, Mr. Chamberlain?" Charlotte asked.

"My wife passed young. She left me no children. And Logan—" Lark and Charlotte exchanged glances.

"And Logan Walker didn't have an alibi for the time Miss Blue was killed," the judge interrupted, sounding testy. "I said to him, 'Son, what is your alibi? Where were you when poor Miz Blue was robbed of what little she had and slain right in her own room.' She lived at the hotel where maybe a real lady like her shouldn't have been living, what with all the drifters and roughscuff passing through there. But the room was charitably provided free by Miss Ella, the hotel owner, to whoever was doing the teaching in town. Ella's Hotel and Boardinghouse was tolerable enough for the last pedagogue who worked in Fort Smith, a man name of Dario Heyward. 'Professor' Heyward was a bell maker by trade, wherever it was he came from. In a place like this, there ain't much call for bells, so he turned to teaching, for a time."

"That's all fascinating, but what about Logan Walker?" Lark pressed.

" 'I did not do it, Judge' was all the boy would say, and he said it only one time, like I was just supposed to believe him, like it was beneath him to plead for anything, even his own life. Well, you heard him yourselves telling the hangman, kind of arrogant and devil-may-care, to get on with it."

"You don't really believe he's guilty, do you, Ike?" Lark prodded, piercing Parker with a momentary fierce flash of her silver eyes.

"It doesn't matter what I *believe*, you saucy snip of a girl! I had no choice but to sentence Walker to hang. He'd been seen by reliable witnesses leaving Ella's Hotel in a big hurry just after the heinous deed was done." Ike Parker, literally hopping mad, reminded Lark of a cricket. She almost laughed, though she felt more like crying.

"No choice, Uncle Isaac Hanging Judge Parker? It seems I keep hearing that excuse from you Fort Smith people. It seems you are all afflicted with a bad case of helplessness, when it suits you."

There was a stir then in the crowd behind Lark, and she turned, as everyone else did, to see a woman dressed entirely in black make her way slowly and deliberately toward the gallows, only the outline of a pale face perceivable behind a long black veil. When the woman had taken a place in the front row of spectators, she stopped and looked up, not raising her veil. Logan Walker glanced at her for an instant, faintly smiling. Almost imperceptibly, he shook his head. Then he looked away.

"Who is she?" Lark asked, finding herself transfixed again by Walker's amber, gold-flecked eyes.

"That's Matt January's wife, Roe Ann," Jake Chamberlain explained. "She's been really broken up over young Logan. She even came to me asking if I had more influence with Ike Parker than her husband did. I told her old Ike was real ugly honest. I couldn't sway him. I wouldn't even try."

"Does anyone have any influence with the Hanging Judge?" Lark asked, finding herself greatly agitated. The hangman was cinching up Logan's noose. "What if I asked you, or Charlotte did, to commute this Logan Walker's sentence from hanging to life? Would you do it, Uncle Ike, as a trade-off like, for my daddy?"

"Try me," Parker answered, but before Lark, or anyone, could say another word, the stockade exploded in the roar and flash of gunfire. Instantly, Lark found herself beside Charlotte, both face to face with the ground, flattened by a strong shove from Jake Chamberlain, who was kneeling over them, a blazing pistol in each hand. She struggled to her knees.

"Don't kill him! Don't!" she cried out as Charlotte, also shouting, but something incomprehensible at first, tugged at her skirt. Men were falling all about them as half the remaining onlookers—the trail riders—fired at the other half—deputies and soldiers. Everyone else was lying flat, or gone.

Most of the strangers who had drifted into town over

the past few days were, as suspected, members of the Clarence Cumplin Gang bent on freeing their condemned accomplices.

"Get down, Lark, get down!" Charlotte kept repeating frantically. "They haven't killed him. It's only a flesh wound. Mr. Chamberlain will be okay!" Jake, hit in the shoulder and spun about by the bullet's impact, was writhing in the dirt.

"Your mama's right. Don't worry about . . . me," he choked. "Miss Lark, I . . . haven't met . . . a woman . . . a woman to care for since I . . ."

Lark, who quickly padded his wound with his pocket handkerchief, didn't hear a word he said. She squeezed his hand and stood again, completely unmindful of her own safety, to stare down at Charlotte as though her mother had gone daft.

"But, Mama, I wasn't talking about Mr. Chamberlain," she protested.

"Call me . . . Jake," Jake gasped.

"Jake. It wasn't Jake, I meant—" Lark, looking around her to search the crowd with urgent eyes, went speechless as a racing horse, a short-bodied black gelding, with a shaggy cow dog running at its side and a rider crouched low over the withers, came careening straight at her. Astonished, torn between protecting the downed rancher and darting to safety herself, she froze in place. Just before she was actually ridden down as she expected to be, she was swept off her feet and found herself clinging to the saddle horn of the tearing, wild-eyed jittery animal, her toes dragging in the dust. Using all her stunt rider's strength and agility, she managed to struggle to a less precarious position up behind the saddle, astride the runaway animal's flanks.

"Can't you control your damn horse, man?" she hollered, clinging to the rider in front of her. "Pull him in! I have to get down! I'm getting down!" For response she got a weak shrug.

"Saved . . . saved you from a bullet," he gasped. "Only a damn fool'd stand about spouting off . . . in the middle of . . . of a shoot-out." The rider made no move to control the runaway horse and determined to stop the animal herself, Lark uttered an angry expletive and reached forward around the man to grasp the reins. Something warm and wet coating the leather made it difficult to get a good grasp. She was about to complain again, even more vehemently, about the condition of the saddle leather and tack, but she stopped herself, realizing what the problem was.

"It's blood. You're hit!" she said instead. "Is it bad?" Again, there was no answer. Lark felt the body she was clinging to sag as the rider's strength ebbed. By then, she had the sticky reins firmly in hand and was pulling back with all her might, beginning to slow the horse's break-neck pace.

"Have to . . . get . . . have to get out of town," the wounded man coughed.

"Are you one of the lawbreakers supposed to be swinging by now from a George Maledon custom-fitted noose? I'll be damned if I'll help any desperado bank robber escape, you hear?"

But the man didn't hear. His long body was slumped against hers, and as he sank into unconsciousness, his head fell back onto her shoulder. With her slender arms extended, keeping him from what would most likely be fatal contact with hard ground, Lark finally got the horse under her control and drew the animal to a full stop. Only then did she steal glance at the face of the man in her arms, whose life she had probably saved.

"Logan Walker!" Lark whispered, stunned, elated and a bit confused. His lips were white, his face was peaked from loss of blood and he was losing still more from the two wounds she could see. A bullet had lodged in his thigh; another had creased his brow.

"Lark! For pity sake, get down off that horse and out of harm's way at once!" she heard her mother call. It took a moment to spot Charlotte in the chaos and confusion. When she did, Lark hesitated, but only for a moment.

"Don't worry about me, Mama!" she shouted above the din. "You know I've always been good at taking care of myself and of you, too, most the time! Now there's this . . . this person here needs some looking after from *someone*. And you," she addressed the unconscious stranger, "you aren't any rustler or even a bank robber at all, are you?" she asked affably. "No, no. You . . . you're just a murderer . . . maybe," she added with droll exaggeration before pressing the horse into a full gallop.

Chapter Five

Shivering and weary, Lark huddled against a tree. Though her favorite dress was in shreds, she tried, with characteristic ironic humor, to comfort herself with the thought that flimsy chiffon wouldn't have helped much anyway, to keep her dry and warm in a prairie storm. She had been without sleep for almost two days and nights, and though she fought it still, her eyes kept fluttering closed. When, dozing, she listed sideways far enough to be awakened by rain touching her face, she opened her eyes with a start, strengthening her grip on a small axe, the single tool she had. It was doing double duty as her only weapon as well.

She had built a fire, but it lasted only a little while before hissing out in the blowing rain. She had eaten nothing but wild berries and hard water crackers spiced with a few drops from a bottle of McIlhenny Hot Pepper Sauce. She had found the condiment and stale hardtack, along with the axe, in the gelding's scantily provisioned saddlebags which had also contained an oilskin slicker but nothing else.

Lark was tired, wet and cold to the bone. Worse, she was lonely. Logan Walker was unconscious again.

For over thirty-six hours she had nursed him unrelentingly. Almost all the while, he'd been either burning with fever or racked with chills or both. As she alternately and repeatedly bathed him from head to foot with cold river water or enfolded him in the single warming item in her possession, the gelding's saddle blanket, she had ample opportunity to study the man's face and form in fine detail. As she did, her misgivings about whether or not he would ever awaken again heightened. So did her worry that when—if—he did revive, he might not be of sound mind—or body—possibilities that increasingly grieved and distressed her.

The longer Lark nursed Logan, the more she came to admire his strong-jawed, sensitive face and lean physique. The more familiar—and appreciative—she became with his ample masculine attributes, the more she realized she very much wanted to know this man in a variety of ways, most definitely, in a singular, particular, very precise and impassioned way. Though Lark, still untouched, even unkissed at the ripening age of nineteen, wasn't sure exactly how she knew what she was wanting, there was no doubt about it in her mind . . . or nerve endings . . . or corporeal senses, in fact not anywhere in her whole yearning body—except her heart. *That*, the matter of love, was something else altogether.

Love, she told herself with a cerebral detachment bordering on smugness, had nothing to do with the shameless ideas she got every time she touched Logan Walker. *That*, she insisted, mistakenly as it would turn out to her regret, was just pure, unadulterated, youthful, lustful desire.

Yawning so broadly her jaws ached, Lark now looked over at Logan, lying some feet from her. He appeared to be snug and quite cozy, far more comfortable than she anyway, protected as he was by the oilskin and wrapped in the only blanket, his head pillowed on the saddle.

So, she crept closer to him, just to be within hailing distance, of course. That problem solved, she quite soon started in on another one, worrying about the likelihood of her coming down with grippe or catarrh and chilblains. Still, she hesitated, leaning against another tree, its knobby trunk digging into her back, the thinning leaves offering little shelter.

Eventually, after no more than about five minutes, she came to the unavoidable deduction that she'd be no good to Logan or herself if she fell ill—which, of course, was more than likely to happen if she went on shivering in the rain and cold.

So, for his sake at least as much as her own, Lark stripped off her clinging wet under clothes, lifted the blanket and slid beneath it. Relieved by the prospect of a little warmth and sleep, the tension that had been holding her together for the long days and nights broke like a shattering glass, and she began to tremble violently. She had tried, really she had, she would later insist, to keep some distance between their naked bodies, hers aching and icy, his so toasty and strong; but she had desperately needed something to hold on to, and Logan was all there was, just then.

Shuddering with loneliness, with fatigue and chills— and more, an odd, new, nearly indescribable hungry yearning—she pressed to him, cleaving gratefully to his strength, absorbing his animal radiance, taking sustenance from the slow, steady beating of his heart.

It was then she realized he had no fever. He was no longer hot, just wonderfully warm, and his breathing was slow and even. Relief washed over Lark and . . . well, she just drifted off into warm, deep, delicious sleep.

The next thing she was aware of was the sound of Logan's breath in her ear, then his voice, soft and rough and low, murmuring the most outrageous and tantalizing things, all mixed with love words and sighs and kisses on the most inaccessible, reactive parts of her. There was also the unique and interesting sensation of his hand completely enclosing her breast which was small and round and firm and growing firmer at the tip where his fingers worked to amazing effect, causing arrow darts of intense delight to shoot low in her belly.

As if he knew what he'd done to her, his hand went gliding down across the silky flat of her stomach to probe and explore between her thighs. And *that* gave her yet another startling and exceptional feeling, one she hoped would not end too soon, if ever.

Through fluttering lashes, Lark's dazzled eyes, still dewy with sleep, were imbued by the amber and gold gleam of Logan's primal, gorgeous animal gaze. When she glanced past his shoulder with a feeling not far from fear, she vaguely perceived sunrise — slants of light glimmering through trees and dancing among immense and voluptuous drops of clear rain water, hanging pendulous from every bough and branch. Each spangled droplet, it seemed, elongated endlessly and forever before falling with dreamlike slowness. The merging, the soft fusion of translucent water beads with rain-soaked dark soil and fragrant, wet, moldering leaves, became a syncopated and enchanted background melody for lovers.

Letting her eyes drift shut once more, Lark felt Logan's weight and warmth atop her. She allowed her lips to be parted by his gently thrusting tongue. Her thighs willingly divided to receive the span of his hips, and almost at once, her pliant, shapely anatomy yielded to another sort of thrust, this one rigid and strong as he delved to lodge himself completely in the velvet interlining of her pleasured body, as humid and warm and moist as the glade in which they lay.

Logan's first deep penetrating lunge drew from Lark a piercing half-note trill that was, briefly, a cry of pain before it soared in an aerial sweet sound of pleasure and exhilaration.

"Skylark!" Logan whispered. "Now you belong to me! You always will."

Lark had intended to protest then and there, tell him she would never *belong* to any man, least of all a fugitive like him. And if she ever did permit herself to love some man some day, that would be at some other, distant time, in a different setting, with a very different *inamorato*. She tried to say "no, no, not you, Logan Walker, not now, not ever, I've places to go . . . things to do." But he kissed her, and Lark said not a word until a long, long time later.

"What *do* you remember about Fort Smith and all?" Lark asked Logan. It was dark again by then. The fire she had built was leaping at the night sky, and they were enwrapped together in the blanket once more as they had been most of the long and lovely Indian summer day.

"I don't recall much. Some. Mostly what I remember is you." Logan smiled, leaning on an elbow, looking down at Lark. "Tell me about it."

They had ridden out of town, Lark began narrating, with no one but the spotted Catahoula cow dog trailing them. Soon after, the wind had picked up. Toward evening, an awesome show of prairie fireworks began as she urged the peevish black gelding along a high, pine-covered ridge. Far below, cottonwoods on the banks and steep ravine of a winding river obscured her view of the rushing water. Looming above in the distance were the Sugarloaf Mountains toward which she was heading. The cave-dotted hills, beginning to merge with the lowering sky, leapt into clear silhouette with each blinding, blue-white flash of lightning, then faded again in a roar and roll of thunder. The ominous sound got through to the wounded Logan and made him uneasy.

"You said to me, Logan, 'I've got to . . . get west, farther west . . . can't stop, not yet. Maybe never . . . stop. Demons . . . still on my trail. Haven't lost them. . . .' Those were the very first words you had uttered since we made our escape from Fort Smith." Despite the inauspicious implications of those words, Lark had taken heart.

"You sounded almost rational, even with your bloody head wound which was already staining through the bandage by then," she paused to comment.

"Bandage?" Logan lifted a questioning brow.

"I used my dress sash," she answered. "And let me tell you, it wasn't easy affixin' it to your brow at full gallop," she drolly complained. "Anyway, we were seven or eight miles out of town, still mounted up together on that there feisty, belligerent black horse, and I was pushing him to the limits of his endurance."

What Lark did not tell Logan just then, was that she had also been testing her own limits at the same time by keeping him more or less upright in the saddle in front of her. Her poke bonnet had blown off and bounced, dangling down her back, held by its big chiffon bow loops, and her dress had ridden up her thighs, the skirt draping the gelding's hard-working haunches.

"When you said that, about having to go far west?" Lark continued. "Well, that's when I told you that was where we were going exactly, west into the Oklahoma Indian Territory. 'But Mr. Walker,' I informed you. 'We can't ride west without crossing the Poteau River,' I said. 'And to do that, we got to go south a little ways first in order to find the ford.' I myself have never negotiated the Poteau, but Mama told me where she used to cross over as a girl. Though she ain't been back here since I was born, she was always so homesick, she recalled everything perfectly and told me all about it, instead of telling me children's fables and tales."

Logan nodded. "Your mother? The real pretty woman standing beside you at Fort Smith, right?" he said. "Go on."

" 'I'll find the way over the river now,' I said to you, 'so you slacken up worrying about that *and* about the law coming after you. We got a good start on 'em. I don't think a posse's left town even yet, what with all the uproar and so many of the criminal element on the loose and racing off in every direction, the ones still vertical leastways. So you just forget those so-called demons for now.' That's what I told you to do. You know what you told me?"

Logan's eyes squinted a little, and he shook his head. "What?" he asked. His hand, which had been tracing and retracing Lark's diminutive, shapely dimensions from thigh to breast to shoulder and back again, was still then, resting possessively at the curve of her waist.

" 'They—the Fort Smith law—aren't the demons I mean.' You coughed. Then you hunched forward with your head kind of dangling, and you hung on to the pommel of the saddle, lucky for you. I was afraid you might pitch off into the dirt. I took a grip on your shirt and readjusted your alignment so you leaned back against me again. I was scared for you, so I just kept talking at you. I said,

" 'In just a little bit, once we ford the Poteau, we'll rest, else you'll bleed to death. I'd stop over to nurse you now except I'm afraid I'd never get you mounted up again, once you got on the ground. Besides, there's a storm comin' on, hear?' I asked you that question, but you didn't hear. You were passed out again." And getting heavier by the minute, Lark recalled.

With her arms aching and her back stiff, silently cursing the moment she'd exchanged her good leather boots for satin dress-up slippers, Lark had summoned all the force she could muster to kick against the intransigent gelding's tough sides. "Get on, you devil, you damn Satan. You are goin' take us 'crost this River Styx 'fore the storm hits or drown fightin' me," she had promised the animal, throwing a new name for him — one that would stick — into the bargain.

They had ridden on in a hostile tussle, Lark keeping the bit hard against Satan's tongue, the animal flinging his head if she let up on him, even a little.

When the rain met up with the trio, Lark had greeted it, at first, like an old friend. It had been gentle, falling light and fine, straight down, enwrapping them in a veil of mist while abetting not hindering their flight. Later, she had reasoned, it might muddy their prints and make them harder to track and follow.

But even so, Lark hadn't been about to let down her guard against man or the elements. Behind the deceptively soft rain, she knew, wild late-summer winds were blowing. Unchecked and unhindered, those winds were advancing, churning over hundreds of miles of prairie, herding ragged clouds across torn skies above it, rolling tumbleweed below. It was raising sand storms in the high country and flattening the little bluestem grass and the clumps of switch grass already turned autumn gold. The gusts were roaring on, gaining strength, disbanding crowds of migrating butterflies, extracting tribute from the throngs of sunflowers in their path which bowed down their yellow heads in homage.

And it was just possible, too, that the prairie storm was towing a tornado in its wake, a whirling fury fraught with all the power and grandeur of the cosmos. The wind could well have been carrying hail stones as big as a man's fist that would come pelting down with force enough to split fence palings and break roof shingles, to kill wild birds and young animals—anyone weak or luckless enough to be caught in its path. At the least, the north-west wind, a portent of the cruel plains winter, would turn the rain to a cold, drenching deluge. Lark had known she had to get Logan sheltered before they encountered the brunt of the weather, but there hadn't been time enough to reach the hidden hill cave she was heading for, the one Charlotte had told her about.

Chapter Six

"You see, Logan, by then, the wind was agitating the trees something wicked. It was mostly cedar and pine like where we are now. The woods had thickened some as we neared the river, and the leaves muffled the splatter sound of the rain. There wasn't anything else to hear anyway, except the squeaking of saddle leather and my muttered oaths at Satan. He balked, seeing the Poteau ahead of us, near a minute before I saw it.

"My first glimpse of the river through the timber was . . . unnerving, my second and unobstructed view positively alarming! That white-water river was going to be a more formidable obstacle than I had formerly anticipated. 'This storm of rain must already have hit up stream,' I told Satan, having no one else to converse with, and him and me both studying the turns and surges of wild water moving, it seemed to us, in every direction at once and overflowing its banks. 'Here I am, mounted up on a nearly spent, ornery devil of horse like you, with my arms aching so bad I doubt I could swim if I had to, no less hang on to this unconscious gentleman. But anyway, Satan, we are going to try this crossing. If we stay here, they'll likely find us before daylight.' "

"So, I was a gentleman, was I?" Logan asked. Now he was stretched out, hands behind his head, and Lark, leaning, was tracing a small hand across his lightly furred chest and down along his rib cage.

"That was *before* I got to know you." She giggled. "Charlie—that's my mama—she thought there was something gentlemanly in your demeanor when you were up on the gallows. Now, I agree you are manly, and gentle enough, in certain delicate situations, but whether those two words should be made one word to describe a fugitive outlaw like you, who busies himself seducing innocent girls and murdering school teachers, I strongly doubt and, oh, Logan! What—?" Lark cheeped like a startled bird. He had risen, pressed her down and held her in place with a strategically located knee.

"I did not harm Rachel Blue. Don't ever say I did, understand?" His face had gone cold, his deep-set eyes hard and flat as glass. Shocked and a little scared of him, Lark just nodded. Her own large, elliptical eyes were round then as a child's. When Logan saw the fear they couldn't conceal, the menace in him was quickly gone. But she couldn't forget it, not even after he grinned and nuzzled her neck. "Get this long story told quick. I've other things in mind for you than talking all night," he murmured, then winced when his injured thigh brushed against her.

"I think, mister, you are taking on too much and . . . and you are movin' way too fast, for your own good, of course. You . . . well, you best have a care not to open that wound, now. We're clean out of bandages," Lark answered in a low purr, her voice divulging her desires. They were not unlike his own, Logan was quick to appreciate. Her petite and perfect body responded extravagantly to his voice alone, his mere suggestion of lovemaking enough to bring her to readiness. It was a realization that delighted him.

"Just go on and get finished telling, please," he asked in a tone that was somewhere between a command and an entreaty.

***

She had had to urge the reluctant horse forward into the river. For a few minutes Satan had waded, high-stepping suspiciously in water barely inches deep until, with no warning at all, he abruptly stepped off an underwater cliff and plunged, thrashing, headfirst, submerging his riders in the roiling current. Lark had shrieked and coughed and held harder still to Logan, sure they were all lost until she felt Satan strike out with his sturdy forelegs, swimming, his head raised just enough to keep his flaring nostrils above water.

"The cold dousing roused you again, Logan. 'Not south. South isn't . . . suitable for me. I'm headed west, damn it!' you insisted, unaware of our peril and taking up the conversation exactly where it had left off nearly an hour before.

" 'So that's where you're a wanted man, in the South? Any particular state or just . . . all over?' I asked you not without a hint of irony. I had to shout to be heard above the roar of rushing water."

Though she hadn't stopped to figure out the reason just then, she had been pained and disappointed that Logan Walker was apparently on the run from someplace besides Fort Smith. Deep down, even then, she'd been hoping . . . what?

" 'Chill in the air,' you mumbled at me just when the striving horse came up hard against a chest-high wall of sand and began struggling mightily for a foothold which he succeeded in securing after several failed attempts. Satan hauled himself onto a sandbar and stood, his sides heaving, only midway in our odyssey across the Poteau. See, I let him rest, and I listened in silence to your increasingly fevered rantings. You said, 'Got to keep going. . . . If I don't, he'll get me, pull me down. I'll have to wrestle Lucifer for my life . . . for my soul. I can't stop, can't ever. I'll go west to California . . . Sandwich Islands . . . Tasmania . . .'

" 'Logan, I've been calling this animal Satan not Lucifer, but it doesn't seem to matter much,' I explained, giving the horse an encouraging slap on the hind quarters. 'I myself have always wanted to go to New York. But where's that at, Tasmania? Is it as exciting as New York City?' I asked, only to find I was talking to myself yet again. 'Think nothing of it, a lady midstream and in distress in the wilderness, a lady who saved you from the hangman at that. But never you mind,' I chattered on nervously. I do that, chatter when I'm nervous. I was also prodding Satan into action once more, feeling water swirl about my um, thighs as he stepped off the sandbar already swimming. 'I'll just hang around you awhile, Mr. Walker, at least until I get a few answers about what you did and didn't do, to whom.' You owe me that much at least, I'm sure you'll agree."

But Logan didn't agree. As soon as he'd regained consciousness again, he had shut up as tight as a bear trap, about himself anyway, though he had been full of questions about Lark.

" 'Where'd you learn to handle a horse?' was the first of many you asked, just lying there, propped against a tree under an almost water-tight roof." Lark shook her head, remembering.

Using four bent saplings and the india-rubber cape, she had improvised a shelter over Logan to protect him from the rain. Tiptoeing so as not to wake him, though there had been no need to, she had collected a sizeable supply of windblown timber, dead wood and twigs, enough to get them through to dawn and still have some in reserve for the next night. She built a good fire.

"Next you said, 'And where'd you get that smile that lights up like a sparkler on the Fourth of July?' That was question number two from you, Logan." Firelight was reflecting in his wonderful, gold-flecked amber eyes that were, for the moment, lucid—and amazed.

" 'You must be surprised to be waking up alive,' I conjectured. 'Not really' was your cool reply. 'I supposed Clarence Cumplin might try to rescue his boys. I hoped they'd include me, as long as I was just hanging about, pardon the pun, with nothing better to do. It began to look as if the gang wasn't going to make a move in time. I seem to recall telling old George Maledon if I was going to leave this world, it'd be looking straight at you. Now, I'm still looking straight at you, but I haven't left the world, far as I know. So you see'—you grinned—'what I'm surprised about is you here, now, with me . . . looking the way you do so . . . implausibly beautiful in firelight.' I do recall," Logan added. "I also said, 'You're a dream come true out here in the wild Indian Nation. How do you explain that? How'd we get here?' Those were questions number three and four, right?"

Lark nodded. "After that, I lost count of your prying queries which followed in quick succession. 'Who are you? What's your name?' you wanted to know and, 'What chewed on your gown?' "

The chiffon dress, shredded into long neat strips, was hanging from one of the tree-limb tent poles. "What's a nice girl like you doing here with a man like me, a total stranger . . . wearing only your bustier and petticoats . . . and letting all that flaxen hair flow over your *fine* shoulders like liquid China silk?"

"We are not exactly strangers," Lark explained. "We have been together some number of hours and . . ."

"Glad to hear it," Logan winked. "Was I good company?"

". . . and we got to this place," Lark persisted, trying to ignore the interruption, "because I brought you safe here, me and that old misbegotten miserable black gelding who has won my heart with his bravery, ornery and ugly as he may be. He your horse?" She took a cautious step closer to Logan.

"No way, ma'am, though I've got to admit, this disreputable-looking canine does belong to me," Logan said. In response to his master's voice, the cow dog, wet and matted from swimming the river after them, startled Lark by crawling out of the underbrush into the fire circle, crouched on his belly, tail awag. "Meet Max. Sundance, my Tennessee stud, will find us, too, before long, but that hoofed animal right there is no relation of mine. I've been a horse trader, and he looks like US Army to me. The cavalry likes its mounts ugly and tough."

"Horse trader or horse thief," Lark responded, "either way, I'm glad he ain't yours, 'cause now the homely plug is mine. I've known a whole lot of horses in my life, rogues and Thoroughbreds and everything between. I've never met one I didn't like. I thought this mean Morgan gelding, Satan, was going to be the first, until he showed me what he was made of. He saved both our lives crossing the Poteau, and now I think I love the lout. Even so, if he was yours, you'd have to shoot the 'cussed creature for running off wild on you like he did. Oh, Mr. Walker?" Lark hesitated, "if you keep doing your head like that, shaking it with surprise, it's going to hurt bad. You got scraped over your left eye by a bullet. You remember?"

"That's what I asked you, Logan. Remember when I

54

asked you, 'Do you remember?' " Lark queried. She added a log to the fire.

"I remember." Logan laughed, and Lark giggled prettily. "Go on and finish telling, if you know what's good for you."

"I do know what's good for me, so maybe I won't go on telling," she teased. "That is, if I don't go on . . . will you . . . ?" He scowled with what was intended to be false ferocity, but the look made Lark a touch nervous.

"Hm, where was I? 'Oh, yes.' That's what you said, that first night when I asked if you remembered much."

"Oh . . . yes," Logan answered, his eyes fixed in an inward stare. "I recall . . . some. Look, miss, how can I repay you for what you've done for me? I've got to get on my way now."

"You don't owe me a single thing but a 'thank you, kindly.' You're free to go. Just . . . go right on," Lark answered. She stood with her arms folded below her bosom, creating a pretty cleavage above her bustier, her lips pursed. She tried to keep any shade of concern or even interest out of her voice, but her gray eyes gave her away. They were touching Logan all over just as, to cool his fever, her ministering hands had already done by that time, once or twice at least, after they'd come across the Poteau.

Her fingers had lingered before, when he'd been unconscious, lost to the world, as her eyes did now, on his bare wet shoulders and lean chest, on his arms with their pronounced muscles gleaming dark in reflected firelight.

Logan, who would have been very pleased to feel the touch of her cool hands all over him, was not exactly displeased by the caress of her eyes. He had often before discovered the same hungry, longing look in a woman's eyes, though he'd never before responded so unequivocally. It wasn't that he had been afraid of his love going unrequited, far from it. It was, he finally understood, smiling at Lark, that he had never been in it before — love. He had never ever wanted any woman so much and so powerfully hard as he did this flaxen-haired sprite hovering near him like a hummingbird.

She was a delicate little pearl with her fine, clear features and big, lavender-gray eyes and a low, husky-sweet voice that could drive a man wild. When Logan tried to struggle to his feet that first night, not because he was in a hurry to run from the law as Lark supposed, but to make the most of an exceptional moment, he was appalled to find he couldn't get up.

"My apologies," he said sheepishly. "I guess I'm not the able company I'd like to be, the sort of escort a beautiful lady like you deserves. Hell, I'm sure not blind, but in every other way I *am* feeble as a two-day-old kitten," Logan added with a chagrined, crooked smile. "But I'll make it up to you for lost time when I get my strength back," he promised with a wink. "Will you tell me your name at least? Please?"

"I'm Lark McKay," she said. "And I already *know* who you are. Be easy in your mind and sleep, Mr. Walker, that is, if you're serious about getting your strength back." Then it was her turn to wink. "We're well hid, and I'll tend to what needs tending."

"Why?" he managed to inquire in a fading voice. He was shirtless and bootless and his left pant leg, he noticed, had been ripped from ankle to thigh. A band of chiffon, used as a tourniquet, was holding some frill of feminine under garment against a wound several inches above the knee.

"Why, what? Why did I save your life? Because *I* don't think Judge *Parker* thinks you done it—killed that school teacher, that's why." Lark obstinately placed her fists on her hips.

"I didn't, but . . ." His eyes glazed, and he winced with a pain.

"You said some things when you didn't know it. Were you running from somewheres else when you got in trouble with the law in Fort Smith, Mr. Walker?" Lark's voice had gone grim. Logan was slow to reply.

"You shouldn't be asking any such questions of a man out here in the territory, but . . . well, yeah, in a manner of speaking, I was on the run," he eventually said. "Tell me, did we ride into a heat wave or is it looking at you makes me feel this way? I'm burning."

"Mr. Walker!" Lark exclaimed with true consternation. "You're starting in to shiver anew, I see. Your temperature must be spiking. I'll go get more cool water from the river and bathe you again so—"

"Again?" Logan grinned devilishly through a fast-enveloping fog of fever. "Well, sometime . . . perhaps I can . . . return the service, ma'am, or try to, and if not now, well . . . soon . . . then. That's . . . a promise."

Those were his last words before he slipped into agitated slumber once more. Soon after, when Lark knelt at his side, her leaky poke bonnet filled to overflowing with clear river water, he was burning hot to the touch and shouting, fighting those demons of his so hard, she was fearful he might not last the night.

Chapter Seven

Logan of course *did* last the night, and for that he could perhaps credit his strong constitution or possibly a whim of the gods. Most probably he owed his life to Lark once more, for two reasons this time—his fierce desire to see her again, and her dedicated ministrations to assure that he did.

To lower his temperature, she knew she had to cool his body again and again, all over, even in—especially in—certain less accessible nooks and crannies where fever heat was persistent—under the arms, behind the knees, between the muscled thighs. Well, she was no giddy, fainthearted, blushing female, she told herself, hesitating nonetheless to relieve Logan of the one item of clothing still left him, his faded, torn old indigo britches. But no false modesty on *her* part was going to cost Logan Walker his very life, Lark argued silently. Really, even if she had no brothers and never had been with an all-the-way undressed man, hadn't even seen for herself one of those naked museum statues Charlie had told her about, she *had* spent all her life around breeding stock. She knew the power of a randy, bellowing bull, and she had seen stallions covering mares more times than she could

58

count. It was the natural thing, that's all, male and female, so what could be the danger—or the shame—in her seeing this man from stem to stern, in all his parts?

"Nothing!" Lark said right out loud, startling Satan, who was browsing a few feet from them. He snorted and rolled his eyes at her. "Oh, you just mind your own damn business or you'll end up sidelined!" she snapped at the horse, a threat to tie him front leg to back on one side, a practice routinely followed by plainsmen to keep a spooked horse from running off or being stolen by rustlers or Indians. But it also hurt an animal's gait and made grazing painful. It was something Lark would do only in the most extreme situations, and this wasn't one of them, except for Logan.

She started by pulling off his tall-shaft boots which were unadorned, very soft and flawless, made of brown calfskin and lined, shaft and vamp, with buttery kid leather. "Bet they set you back three months' wages, cowboy," she muttered, setting the boots aside where they wouldn't collect rain water. Then she resolutely grasped Logan's belt buckle.

At the time, preoccupied with his stamina and survival and her own fortitude in a trying, awkward situation, Lark wasn't particularly aware of memorizing the details and fine points of his *fine* body and its adornments. Later, however, Lark would especially remember that belt buckle—and a whole lot more—in perfect detail. Like his boots, it was too costly an adornment for a catchpenny drifter to be sporting, or even for a hardworking broncobuster to flaunt. The object was masterfully crafted of bronze-edged silver, its scrollwork pattern nearly obscuring some initials, not his own, indelibly etched there just as her love for Logan Walker would inevitably and forever be etched on Lark's heart.

That first night, in the rain and cold, her still-intact heart thundered, and her hands were unsteady as, admonishing herself not to behave like an asinine ninny, she started on his pants buttons and got her first glimpse of the alarming and fascinating mound beneath. Though as good as alone, she blushed, reluctantly directed her eyes elsewhere and got about her night's work. Before sponging him down again, Lark's finger tips touched and traced over Logan, everywhere, as though she were trying to repair him, as if she could put him back together with just her hands.

Hours later, after she had lowered Logan's fever, cooling him from his brow to the soles of his feet with river water, she loosely rolled him in Satan's saddle blanket and then went through his pockets.

The faded denims yielded a yellow bandanna, a patterned silver bolo that matched his belt buckle and a porcelain, cork-stoppered pocket flask capably painted with a likeness of a peregrine falcon at the apex of a dive. Unaware of the initials hidden in the peregrine's wing feathers, NWC, the same as those on the bolo and buckle, Lark opened the flask, took a warming sip of the rye whiskey it held, then set it for safekeeping in the hollow of a tree. As she was about to drape Logan's denims over a branch of the same tree, something fell glinting at her feet, an oval gold locket trimmed with delicate and small freshwater pearls. It lacked a chain but within held one baby-soft curl of amber hair. Had it belonged to his mother? A sister or . . . a lover? Lark wondered, deciding she would ask about it when he was all better and much stronger.

But by the time, weeks later, those words could be used to describe Logan, Lark had other, more pressing interests, and so did he. Neither patient nor nurse were inclined to give much thought to anything but each other and heading west.

"You know, Logan," Lark began in a sweet and whispery voice, "I can't hardly see it any more."

He responded with a low noise deep in his throat. Lark was fairly sure she had heard the word "what" with a question mark tacked on the end of it, though there was a possibility he'd only grunted in his sleep. Either way, he'd been napping long enough, she decided. She was craving his company.

"I'm talking about the nasty white patch the hangman put on you when he shaved your neck. Now, your neck, Logan Walker, in case no one ever before told you, is kind of like . . . mm, a strong pilar, I'd say, and your shoulders . . . oh, your shoulders . . . !" She took a deep breath. "Well, it seems to me as if you've been hewn out of some fine . . . hard . . . smooth . . . sun-warmed rock — marble or granite, maybe."

All Logan actually heard of her little speech was a long, drawled-out *fahn* and *hahd* and *smooooth*. Lark had uttered her first baby words — Bah ba, y'all — in Texas when she left the circus ring with Charlotte, who had been working with the Aunt Mollie Show. Later, when they had joined Professor Gentry, they had frequented the towns and cities along the banks of the Mississippi River, and she had often allowed a touch of the deep south to slip into her speech. The *smooooth*, said in a husky murmur, was nearly lost in the burble of her low and lazy laugh as she pressed her lips to Logan's nape. He was stretched out to his full six-foot-two-inch length with his back to the sun, his bandaged brow resting on his crossed arms. "And you know what else, Logan?" Lark sighed. "Your hair's grown real thick and long and . . . silky. It's real soft, too, and *so* good smellin', full of sun and clear river water."

"My hair has had ample time to grow long and silky, sweets. What's it been, four or five weeks since you abducted me?" Logan answered, shaking off sleep in response to Lark's fondling and the special rasp in her voice that he'd learned early on, by day three of their friendship, to recognize and take good advantage of. "You'd best have a care, McKay, or your great uncle, the Hanging Judge, might get the sheriff after you for kidnapping." Logan laughed softly, not yet lifting his face to hers, not quite ready to meet Lark's gorgeous, tempting silvery-eyed stare. He was harboring anticipation, savoring the delectable ache of desire for what he knew, once he looked up and they smiled at each other, would follow, just the way day came after night.

Lark was lying beside Logan on the saddle blanket under a cloudless, blue prairie sky. Her head propped on one elbow, she studied his superb body which she'd come to know better and better over the past weeks and to appreciate in an astonishing variety of ways. Now, she used her free hand to repeatedly trace the ladder rungs of his rib cage and the broad spread of his shoulders. She lovingly massaged the prominent muscles that ran flexing and knotting in response down his spine. Her hand travelled the length of his bare back and caressed the rise of hard flank below. To more quickly rouse him from sleep, she leaned, every so often, to place her lips on some particularly irresistible hillock or declivity of his sun-warmed flesh and sinewy ripples, each time skimming the velvet-soft tips of her bare breasts purposefully over his tanned skin, stoking him, and herself, into a languorous, slow-seething heat.

"Kidnapping?" Her throaty voice rasped in his ear where her tongue had darted seconds before. "Aiding and abetting the escape of a vicious killer is more like it. My, but you are the ingrate, Walker. I wrenched you from the very jaws of death . . ." Her teeth tugged at his lobe. "I stanched your wounds . . ." Her lips did something lovely along his shoulder blade. "I stopped your life's blood from flowing away . . . soothed your fevered brow, warmed you the most natural way—the only way—I could, us hiding up in those chilly Sugarloaf Mountain caves Mama told me about, with just this one blanket and no supplies, 'cept some good rye whiskey and the old india-rubber slicker I found in Satan's saddlebags. And now you accuse me of kidnapping when you should be showing your appreciation." She shifted her slim, naked body, tanned to a creamy caramel shade, over his darker-hued longer, more rugged form, paralleling its configurations, folding to the muscled angular contours, her small, high firm breasts pressing to his back. Her fingers raked through his fire-sparked mane, and her thigh slid between his. Logan moaned happily.

"You know I've been your prisoner, right from the first. Even so, I didn't once try to escape. I warmed you, too," he said, "just as soon as I was able, didn't I? As soon as I came to my senses and realized what exactly was going on."

"Mm, did you ever make things steamy right quick," she answered. The sensual throaty purr of such a womanly voice issuing from so petite a female pleased Logan, and he laughed lecherously.

"Now, haven't you got this all topsy-turvy and arse-backwards? It's contradictory to nature," he said huskily. "It's the stud stallion who mounts the mare."

"I've never known a good stud horse to go dozing in the

sun when there was a ready, willing filly within a mile of him — except maybe some wore-out, broke-down broomtail old plug. Besides, I am no mare. I am a resourceful wily human woman, and I want what I want; and one way or another, you'll give it to me, unless you're too debilitated. . . ."

"There's no female can wear out *this* buckjumper. We'll just see who's first to cry quits!" Logan roared with feigned ferocity, rising up on all fours with Lark clinging to his back and laughing, too. Her legs enfolded his hips, and with one hand on his shoulder, the other held aloft in perfect, prize-winning bronc buster style, she kept her seat long enough to have won a rodeo ribbon before he got serious and bucked her off.

Landing lightly on her toes, Lark hit the ground running, but not her fastest. She wanted him to catch her without too much exertion. Though his leg injury was almost healed, Logan still sported the one bandage, a last remnant of her chiffon dress, tied round his brow. Mainly, she insisted he wear it to keep dust off the newly knit gash where the bullet had grazed, but also because it pained her to look at the raw scar of the wound. Every time Lark saw that streak of newly mended tender skin, she couldn't help thinking how fragile even a strong, well-made man really was and how close to death *this* man, Logan Walker, had come recently, not once, but twice — from hanging *and* shooting. It was a thought that made her heart lurch in the most terrifying and glorious way. When that happened, she couldn't help but conjecture that she might be even more like her mother than she'd realized — too ardent and warm blooded and, worse, weak enough to tumble for the wrong man. It fretted Lark to think she might have gone and done just what Charlotte had, what she swore she herself never would do — fall in love with an outlaw.

The thought was so arresting, she forgot to run, and Logan caught her, as usual. And she didn't mind a bit, even if he was a fugitive desperado outlaw bandit.

Because for all his courtly manners and his cultivated way with words, that was exactly what Logan seemed to be. It might, of course, just be true, as he said, that he didn't kill the Fort Smith school marm, but that didn't change anything. He had already been on the run before that ever happened. He was still looking over his shoulder for those demons of his, the ones he'd told her about on the first night of their flight when, nearly insensible with fever, he'd let down his guard — fleetingly.

"Walker," Lark had informed Logan after their first few days together. "I will never love an outlaw, but, seeing as you and me are already . . . close, we can just go on being that way — close — until the time comes for a parting of the ways. Then you'll head farther on west, I'll go in the opposite direction and there'll be no looking back."

"Are you trying to say you don't love me?" Logan asked conversationally as if only mildly interested.

"Exactly," Lark answered, relieved but also a little disheartened that he was swallowing the falsehood without fuss.

"What you mean to say is, you don't love me — yet." He grinned fast. She couldn't help laughing.

"I'm to meet Mama and Mr. Ringling in Fort Smith in about two weeks from now. Even in the unlikely happenstance that I am in love with you by then, which I strongly doubt will be the case, I am leaving you anyway," Lark explained, trying to sound matter-of-fact and flippant. "I'll go my way, and you'll go yours just like . . . like nothing ever transpired. Understood, Walker?"

For the longest time, Logan just looked at her straight and steady from under his brows in that hard way he could, not showing anger exactly, but not smiling, either. His long fingers worked a lariat of buffalo grass into a slip noose.

"Well, sure enough I understand, sweet girl," he said at last. "This is nothing but a brief interlude for me, too, just a little lark." He winked.

"Ha ha. Cute pun," she said testily.

"I never had anything else in mind for you and me than an early fare-thee-well. I never thought of marrying, or settling down on a big spread; I never planned on giving you a big brick house to live in, painted all white on the trim, even the shutters. I never thought about you keeping coffee always going on the stove for me and the hands, or about your hens scratching in the kitchen yard, our tykes playing in the nursery, us raising long-horned Texas beef cows, too, and Thoroughbred Tennessee race horses . . . and a line of Catahoula cow dogs like old Max." At the sound of his name, the dog, who had been digging for gophers, paused briefly and looked in their direction, one ear cocked.

"You never considered anything of the kind?" Lark asked. Her tone was dubious.

"Nope. As soon as you told me of all your big schemes and goals, Larkspur . . . about becoming famous in the great cities of the world, well, I knew you weren't the one for me even if I were the marrying, settling kind. Which I'm not. Right now. I'm a man who loves lonesome places. You're a woman who doesn't. Any time now, I might be gone, like the morning dew."

"You really mean to say I would *not* be the one for you even if I didn't have plans and ambitions?" Lark unintentionally burst out, taken off guard. Expecting blandishments, she had let her indignation — and disappointment — show in her eyes and voice.

"I'm afraid not." Logan shrugged, squelching a triumphant laugh. Bedding and deflowering his inviolate, lovely meadow Lark had been so fine and easy, and every lustful night . . . and morning . . . and afternoon . . . since was nothing short of spectacular. Even so, he was aware that winning Miss McKay — not just body but heart and soul, too — might be the greatest challenge he'd ever confronted. But from his first look at her, even if he was on the gallows at the time, that was just what he'd resolved to do. If he'd given her the slightest inkling of that, she'd have been long gone by now, Logan reasoned, so his best dodge was to keep playing it cool while he kept her hot and bothered — and amorous.

"Apparently, we aren't meant for each other, Larkspur," Logan said, nothing if not nonchalant. He half smiled, lying through his teeth, saying the exact opposite of what he felt, but for a good cause. "No sir, providence has not brought us together for the long run, though over the short haul what we were lucky enough to stumble into can only be described as uh, well quite . . . interesting, even incredible," he added, standing and moving away from their evening fire, shaking his head, his arms folded over his chest. He vanished into the prairie dark, and soon Lark heard him mount up and ride off as he'd done before under duress, on his green-eyed Tennessee stud.

Sundance, his aptly named stallion, was as long and lean as his master, with good lines and an intellect to match the shine of his sleek hide. Just as Logan had predicted, Sundance had found him. The animal had come trotting into their mountain camp one afternoon, his saddlebags filled nearly to bursting with provisions and sturdy clothes, a rifle and buffalo robe tied across his flanks.

"So! You *were* planning your escape all along!" Lark had exclaimed. "He's carrying enough supplies to get a fellow through winter and right into spring."

"I'd given Sundance as a parting gift on my way to the gallows, to my friend, Dario Heyward. Dario must have set this gift horse loose when word of the great escape got abroad in the territories. Before too long, before you and I go our separate ways, we'll go together to thank Dario. You'll like him," Logan had explained.

Chapter Eight

Since Sundance, carrying supplies, had found Logan, the runaways, in no hurry for company, had been well fed and comfortably dressed, on those rare occasions anyway when they chose to slip on fringed buckskin trousers and shirts which Lark had to wear rolled at ankle and wrist and cinched in at the waist with a length of leather harness.

Through those Indian summer days, the weather, like a heavenly gift, had been more than kind to the playful lovers. On a particularly golden October afternoon when both were unclad, an au naturel, high-spirited Adam and Eve, alone in their high plains Eden, they were playing rodeo tag again. Logan ran Lark down and lassoed her with his arms which enfolded her waist. He pulled her back against him, and she turned, eager to be molested by his amber-eyed stare. They sank down where they stood, lost to the world in tall prairie grass, and as Logan pressed into her, Lark's dancer's legs enfolded his narrow hips. This time it was her turn to be the one surmounted and for Logan to be the easy rider not about to be unseated by the increasingly vigorous maneuvers of his flaxen-maned mustang. Like Lark, Logan, too, was going for a prize, not a trophy or a ribbon, but a gold ring. As exquisite as a carousel pony and warm blooded as a wild pinto, Lark surrendered to his virility. Her head thrown back and her spine arched, she was a more than willing accomplice to her own taming, a fervid accessory before, during and after the fact, to her thoroughly gratifying ravishment.

When the lovers awoke, it was almost sunset. The nearby hills were blazing golden. Long streams of light, alive with motes and granules, turned the color of bubbling champagne as they filtered through a vast sea of tawny grass. Logan and Lark lay in each other's arms oblivious, for a time, to everything but each other, even to the pricks and scratches of the pokeweed crushed beneath them.

"Logan?" Lark said, nuzzling against his cheek. "Will you tell me now what you were doing and who with when Miss Blue was killed?" She felt him stiffen. Then he laughed.

"This, what you and I have been doing, what I'm ready to do again," he said, shifting his leg over her and drawing her to him. "I won't say who with except it wasn't Miss Blue. Hold on now, sweets! Stop!" he guffawed, catching hold of her wrists to prevent her flailing at him. "Don't be jealous of the past, mine or anyone's. The past's gone. The future counts now."

"If that's what you really think, then you can tell me who you were with, can't you?" she coaxed. Her intense eyes had gone almost lavender. Her lower lip puckered in a pleading pout.

"Son of a gun . . . !" Logan suddenly exploded, sitting straight up and slapping hard at his knee. "Devil take these infernal black ants — well, God . . . damn!" he said, his voice changed to a hoarse whisper as he uncoiled back into the tall grass beside Lark and lay as flat and still as a hunted animal. "There's mounted men strung out along the horizon."

"Is it a posse, Logan?" she asked, also in a whisper; lavender turned steely gray in her eyes which were now big with worry. She sat up and clasped her knees, peeking over them. "I told you Uncle Ike would send them after me, Logan, even if he gave up on hanging you, which I doubt. I told you we had best not stop to play until we were well into the Badlands. Now they'll accuse *you*, not me, of kidnapping unless I tell all and then—" He put a hand over her lips to silence her.

"I might's well be hanged for sheep as a lamb." He shrugged, grinning roguishly. "If ever again you see me standing on the Fort Smith gallows, sweet thing, remember, I'll die happy. It'll all have been worth it to me, knowing you. . . ."

"Logan, don't you dare be funnin' with me now. It ain't right to hang for something you didn't do instead of for something you did. You should tell Isaac Parker . . . tell *me* your alibi, say where you were and who it was you—"

"I was two rooms down the hall at Ella's Hotel having an illicit tryst with a lady, okay? No gentleman kisses and tells, especially if the one he'd be telling on is another man's wife. He does not divulge her name even if his life depends on it. Understand now?" Logan asked, peering in the direction of the approaching riders, his eyes narrowed to slits.

"So, it's tolerable, according to your high principles, Walker, to sleep with another man's wife, long as he doesn't even breathe her name aloud. But why, when he gets himself in a real quandary, and the cheater he was trysting with doesn't even have the spine and scruples to come forward to clear his name and save his neck, does he *still* have to act like a so-called gentleman, according to your high principles, I mean?" Lark was incensed.

"He just does" was Logan's succinct reply.

"He just gives up without a whimper or he turns tail and spends the rest of his worthless life on the run from the law, all for the sake of a no-good, faithless, sly and cowardly damn female who doesn't care enough for *him* to save him from the hangman?"

"Whoa! Slow down there. Be more forbearing, sugar. Have some sympathy. Self-assured and determined as you are, until you stand in another's shoes, you don't really know what you might do or how you might behave, faced with the same choices. The lady we're speaking of isn't as wicked as you're making her out to be. She's only . . . lonely and not strong, just human, Larkspur, like you and me."

"You still care for her!" Lark whispered. "You love her, that it?"

"No. Yes. Not exactly. What I mean to say is no, I don't love her and never did. She's a very, well lonely, very available woman and . . . warm and generous, in certain ways. She took to telling me her troubles, and I felt sympathy for her. She flattered me by asking my advice about one thing and another, and one thing led to another and — I got asked to a necktie party. It was an invitation I had no choice about accepting, thanks to her. Even so, I care for her still, in a way, just as I do for all the girls who ever graced me with their tender affection."

"The way you're going to care for me . . . tomorrow?" Lark's voice broke, and she reached for her hand; but she moved away beyond his grasp. "Will I be another notch on your bedpost, too, like the others . . . another scalp in your belt? Got a blond trophy yet, Logan? When you leave me, I'll be real proud to give you a hank of my hair to go with the others and then—"

"Now, Larkspur, listen fast and listen good. I don't have much time now. I never felt before the way I feel for you. It's different with you and me. I need you to understand that."

"You need a lawyer, is what you need, or maybe a bottle to give you a shot of whiskey courage. You are innocent, Logan Walker. Be a man, damn you, and prove it to everyone—especially me. What if I could convince that forlorn and lonely woman friend of yours to come forward?"

"I would never ask her to, but if she offered, I might consider. . . ."

"Oh, you might consider letting her save your life?" Lark clenched her fists and rolled her eyes heavenward in disbelief. Well, I won't let you give over without a fight."

"I know what I'm doing. Just trust me, can't you?" Logan's expression was one of miffed helplessness.

"If you don't even try to save your own neck, you're a damn coward! You'll be running all your life long!"

"I'd rather be a live coward for a while longer, than a dead fool forever. Miss Blue was a well-loved lady, and what with that and then a posse finding you out here . . . like this? They'll string me up in a flash if I stay around and try to explain. Now, don't you talk at me any more," he said, his tone curt and commanding. "Just let me think here a minute what's to be done about you now, and don't move," he added. "They'll see the grass stir."

"But Logan!" Lark hissed. "I am buck naked in the middle of the high plains with a buck naked man, a wanted criminal at that; and now there's a posse 'tween me and my clothes, and you tell me don't move?"

"I'm also telling you for the last time to shut your lovely mouth," he growled, slithering closer to her. "Now, lie down and roll over on your tummy. Put your hands behind you. Don't argue. Do as I say . . . or else," he ordered. Looking quizzically at him, Lark opened her mouth, about to refuse, when Logan simply flipped her over. With a double strand of broom sage, he tightly bound her, first at the wrists, then the ankles, careful to keep low as he worked and she whispered furious protests under her breath.

"When they get here, Miss McKay, in . . . I'd say thirty . . . forty minutes—they're moving slowly, tracking us—it'll be to your advantage to be found trussed up this way. It might save your good name."

"I don't give a hoot in hell about my good name, Logan Walker! If I had my druthers, I'd have my daddy's bad name, an outlaw's name. You stay by me. Don't run. I'll tell it like it happened, the whole truth about . . . you and me and you not being guilty, that's if you'll tell who you were with that night. I won't give her away, I promise. But I will try to convince her to do what she's required to—tell the truth."

Logan's eyes narrowed, and he hesitated, Lark thought hopefully, before he shook his head. "If the real killer turns up, as I expect he will, in time, I won't be needing any alibi. Stay out of this."

Furious, hurt and, not least of all, jealous, Lark swallowed a little shriek that was part sob, part rage. "If you are all that dumb, Walker, I don't want nothin' more to do with you. You'd best just go on and run, damn you!"

"Well, I know where I'm not wanted, a brick wall doesn't have to fall on me," he teased, his breezy tone further fueling Lark's outrage. "I'm going, and when I'm gone, *you* had best inform that posse that I carried you off from Fort Smith at gunpoint, that you mercifully nursed me to sound health, and then, when I was strong and had no more need of your various talents and ministrations, I turned on you and left you for the buzzards to find. Tell them I said you were slowing me down, anyway. Say how fortuitous it is they happened along when they did. Tell them I went south."

"L-logan," Lark stuttered, her voice faltering as she strained to look up at him. "Is all that . . . true? Is any of it?" she demanded.

"Well now, what do you think?" was his sharp response. She felt his hand on the crown of her sun-warmed head, almost caressing, before he forced her to lie flat again, her nose to the ground. "Just keep in mind, Larkspur, what you told me first thing. You have big plans that don't include any outlaw renegade like me. If I understood you correctly, you were not about to do as your mama did. *You* weren't going to repeat *her* mistakes, no *sir!* You're going to be famous . . . make your own fortune . . . have a suave, well-bred, handsome man for your husband whether you love him or you don't, long as he's made a mark in the world . . . all that." Logan was moving about carefully, crouching low as he spoke, his voice a wounding, harsh rasp. "See, I took your words to heart, sweet thing; but now that we're about to part, I wonder, was all that *you* said true? Do you still feel the same as you did before we met?"

Logan had undone the band of chiffon circling his brow. Now he draped the flimsy material across Lark's back and hips. "That's a little better," he decided. "At least you aren't altogether in the altogether. This way, Sheriff Morahan won't take a fit when he finds you. Well, McKay? Was it all true, what you said? Do you still . . . mean it?" Logan's question was more a supplication than an inquiry, but wrought up as she was, Lark didn't hear the quaver in his voice, or the plea.

"Well, now, what do you think?" she echoed his answer to her question. She turned her head, letting a tuft of prairie grass scratch her cheek, and caught a glimpse of him out of the corner of her eye. He looked as he had the first moment she had seen him, facing death on the gallows, his face unreadable and hard, his lips drawn into a thin line, eyes flat as stones.

"I think we're both deceivers," he answered. "Question is who's the bigger one? Are we telling each other whoppers or little white lies? We were both having ourselves a *good* time. Too bad it can't go on awhile yet, at least until we'd had enough of one another. How long do you suppose that might have taken, Larkspur? Another night . . . a week . . . a lifetime? One of these days, I may be back to kidnap you for real and take up where we left off. Then we'll see if what . . . if what we shared out here in these hills and prairies was . . . special or just a little recreational diversion to help pass the time of day. You ponder on that. I'm going now, McKay."

"Recreational die-version," Lark mused. "Isn't that a short pithy phrase with a nice bookish sound to it. It sure rings true, for me, leastways." She was trying very hard to sound as if she meant it.

"Larkspur, wish me godspeed now." Logan's hand was on her shoulder. She didn't answer. "Well, if you don't care to do that, at least say you won't put them on my trail right off. If I'm caught, that posse will turn into a lynch mob sure as shootin'."

"Logan Walker, I'll ask you one more time. Come back to Fort Smith and defend yourself." Now it was his turn not to answer. "Logan, if you ever had any little bit of true feeling for me, prove it now by trusting me. Tell me the name of that woman who's your alibi so I at least can try to clear your name. I said I won't give her away. I don't ever go back on my word, honest. From what I heard tell, I'm like my grandad that way," she added.

"I'm going, Lark. I'll come looking for you one day, to see if you missed me, and I'll find you wherever in the world you may be. I don't go back on my word either, ever. But that'll be after I settle things — my own way. Just give me the chance, will you, please?"

"Sure I will give you a chance to run again, Walker — for old-times' sake. But if you do, don't bother to come back looking for me, understand? I'm sure to be in New York City or Paris, France, maybe, by the time you clear up your troubles, if you ever do, or you get around to missing me, if that should happen. By then, even supposing there might just be a prayer in hell of something resembling love blooming 'tween you and me, it'll be withered on the vine. It'll start to shrivel soon's you turn tail so go on. Git!" she choked, unable to hold back a sob.

And then he was gone, moving low through the tall grass, setting it wavering as if a gentle wind was passing, that's all.

Lark twisted about, got to a sitting position and struggled to her knees. To the west, she could see the grass wavering, to the east, armed riders coming. She looked in one direction, then in the other, looked again, gritted her teeth, pursed her lips and emitted a shrill, high-pitched whistle, the one she used to control her show horses.

"Help! Help! Here I am," she sang out. "Come get me! Catch that no-account coward, Logan Walker! He's getting clean away." She called so loudly her throat hurt. Lark saw the lead riders pause, stare in her direction and point. She also saw Logan in the distance out of the corner of her eye. He was fully clothed by then, standing up straight and tall, his rifle cradled in his arms.

"Am I glad to see you!" Lark proclaimed when the first riders reached her. Bemused by her half-clothed state, some stared while some got red-faced and looked away. Logan had secured the chiffon scrap at her waist. Partially, at least, it concealed the curves of her hips and thighs to which it clung. Above though, Lark's slender body and her high, pink-tipped piquant breasts were bare. No one moved.

"Well, will one of you restore my modesty by giving me the loan of some clothing, please, before you go after that yellowbelly, Walker? Um, I don't see any gold star. Which one of you all is Sheriff Morahan?"

"Sheriff?" the lead rider's jaw dropped. "Hey, boss!" he squealed in high-pitched excitement. "This here little lady thinks we're the law! She was steering us after Logan Walker!"

The man addressed as "boss," his face almost completely hidden by the shadow of a Stetson with a high crown and deep five-inch brim, maneuvered himself to a place in the front rank of mounted men. He sat his tall roan horse looking down at the half-naked girl. He spat in the dirt and snickered, a mean sound that soon turned into a very nasty laugh. Most of the others, about twenty in all, joined in, though a few of the outlaws, their sense of chivalry aroused by Lark's vulnerability, scowled, clearly uncomfortable.

Her hands were still tied behind her, but she had snapped the cords at her ankles, scrambled to her feet and turned away, her back to the semi-circle of men. Looking closely at the "posse" over her shoulder, she discovered a few familiar faces she had seen in Fort Smith. But this was *not* the sheriff and his posse, nor the soldiers and deputies she'd been expecting. They were the dusty trail riders who had drifted into town for the hangings. Among them, were the three surviving men of the eight who had shared the gallows, and been saved from hanging, along with Logan Walker. By the time Lark realized who they were — the notorious Clarence Cumplin Gang — it was too late for her to do one thing about it. She had made a dreadful, perhaps fatal blunder: put herself into the hands of villains. Worse, she had, it appeared, been eager to betray Logan. They knew it, and by now, he knew it, too.

With a great whoop and shout and slapping of leather, Logan, on Sundance, was racing straight toward the outlaws — and Lark. The thought of facing him after what she'd done made her weak in the knees, though looking at her, no one would have guessed. For what seemed an infinity, she just stood proud, frozen as a statue, under the lustful eyes of the gang and kept her own eyes on clouds that were piled high, gilded by the last of the sunset, a fanciful golden stairway to escape. The heavy thud of her heart kept pace with the sound of racing hoofbeats that grew louder and louder until Lark thought Logan, in anger, might ride her down.

"Sundance! Whoa!" she commanded, her brave steel-gray eyes wide as she braced herself for the collision, imagining the blows of iron-shod hooves against her delicate body. What she actually felt was Logan's arm enfolding her waist as he hauled her up to sit astride the horse in the saddle in front him. He drew her back against his chest and enveloped her in the buckskin jacket he wore, hiding her bare breasts as he carried her out of that circle of scoundrels, beyond the reach of their ravaging stares.

* * *

Her whole life long Lark would never forget the way Logan looked when he set her down and then dismounted himself. At first, she kept her eyes averted, afraid to look straight at him as, with a furious oath, he draped her in a long drover's coat he grabbed out of his saddlebags. Then, his hand beneath her chin, he forced her to look up into his eyes. They were afire with anger, the heat of it sparking all over his face like lightning before a prairie storm.

"Double-dealer!" he hissed.

"Liar," she whispered with false bluster. "You *are* one of this gang."

"Traitor!" he lashed back. "When it comes to betrayal, my last lover has nothing on you, sweet thing. *She* was going to watch me hang. *You* were going to see me lynched. Well, you both got gypped, and I've learned one thing for certain: I've got to take up with a more trustworthy type of female. Hell, the fallen women who work Ella's Hotel have more real class than you and —" he broke off before uttering the name on the tip of his tongue.

"I'm sorry . . . Logan, I'm sorry!" Lark insisted. "I only wanted you to . . . to do what was right, make you face . . . those demons, oblige you to prove that you really are innocent. I wouldn't have let a posse — or anyone — harm you . . . because, oh, Logan! I didn't want to lose you because you're right, we had something and I —"

Lark was trying to get her tongue around the word "love" when Logan, avoiding her eyes, pivoted on his boot heel and put some distance between them.

He knew exactly what she was about to say. He didn't want to hear it. He was afraid that if he did actually listen to "Logan, I love you," spoken right out loud in that husky, hurting voice of hers, he would melt, go soft, relent. His anger would abandon him, and he would give way to his heart's immeasurable yearning, fall victim to a wonderful and terrible, powerful urge. If he let her speak, he knew what he'd have to answer. "Beautiful little fool!" he'd say. "In spite of what you've done, I love you, too! I have from the first . . . and I will . . . to the end."

And then, he'd have to gather her in his arms, there would be no choice, mount up on Sundance—and run. And keep on running—with her. Impossible, Logan told himself as he turned to look at her again, straight and hard. And silent. He saw her heart breaking. He let it happen and felt his own heart shatter at the same instant.

"Someone put this bit of baggage up on the wild-eyed black gelding, Satan," he said in a hard-graveled voice. "Satan and Jezebel, they belong together. Tie her on, hand and foot. She's as two-faced as Janus, and she knows more tricks than a thimblerigger, especially when she's in the saddle." He strode away, again leaving her the focus of some very evil eyes, though this time all they could see was the duster that covered her from throat to ankles. "Oh, you men remember one thing," Logan called over his shoulder almost as an afterthought. "She's *mine*. No one touches Lark McKay except me. That goes for every blasted man here, even you—especially you, Clarence—until I'm done with her for good and all, that is."

"You'd best be getting your fill right quick. My appetite's roused up for more of what I just got a peek at." When Clarence Cumplin, the man in the Stetson, swept off his hat and tipped it to Lark, a chill prickle of fear raised the downy golden hairs along her arms and slid down her spine. The devil himself, it seemed, was looking at her from behind the man's lunatic blue eyes. Adding to their bizarre effect was the long snow-white hair that framed the outlaw's smooth baby face with an upturned nose and a narrow puffy pout of a red mouth. When his tongue, like a rattler's, flickered, Lark looked away following Logan's disappearing back.

Chapter Nine

"Clarence Cumplin's a man who'd do most anything for money and some worse things just for nothing but fun. Why is it you don't want me going out after Lark again?" Jake asked Charlotte while miles away, Lark was making her first acquaintance with Cumplin. Her mother and Jake were sitting, leaning shoulder to shoulder, on a love bench—a cushioned, spindled oak rocker big enough to accommodate a couple. It sat on the porch of what Jake called his little cabin, actually a big, rambling, well-appointed log house. Charlotte had been staying at his JAK Bar Ranch since Lark had disappeared, and Jake had been agitating the whole time to step up the search for the missing girl begun on the day of the interrupted hangings.

"Now, Mr. Chamberlain, really! You aren't even ready to get up on your feet, no less your horse. And how could you be sure we'd be tracking the right riders what with all the mess of prints and general confusion?" Charlotte had asked on the day of the great escape. By then, the bullets had stopped flying, and dead and wounded men lay everywhere. Five dangled on the gallows, nooses around their necks, shot where they stood before they could be hanged. Charlotte was cradling Jake's head in her lap in the middle of the street where he'd fallen, waiting for help. Unlike him, she had been in no hurry to overtake her daughter and the wounded boy, not after the way she'd seen Logan Walker and Lark gazing at each other, as though they'd been struck by lightning or Cupid's arrows, or both.

"I only got a glimpse of her little slipper and his boots together, but I saw those horseshoe marks very clear after they galloped past me. I got a picture in my mind, so we can pick up the trial at the edge of town where the prints will be more distinct."

"The only reason you got such a closeup view of those hoof prints was because you were sprawled in the dirt, shot. Right now, you should be lying in your big iron bedstead at the hotel letting . . . someone fuss over you. You are not in a condition for a rough ride," Charlotte admonished.

"I feel responsible for Lark, Miz McKay. I was supposed to be looking after her, and you. That was the whole point of me escorting you today," Jake answered, his brow furrowing in a frown. "If Lark should get lost out in Indian Territory, with a convicted killer no less, heaven knows what might happen. I'd never forgive myself. . . ."

"Convicted or not, that boy is no killer. Besides, I'm the one knows Lark, and you don't. She has good travelling instincts. That girl never gets lost. She'll do all right and find her own way home—when she's of a mind to."

"What if she's of a mind to when her kidnapper ain't ready to let her go? And travelling instincts aside, I have known experienced men to get "turned around" out on the flatlands. Even old plainsmen who know how to follow the rivers and divides, who can stay unerring and level-headed passing through wooded canyons and twisting ravines, men who can find their way by the slant of plains grass in early spring, knowing the winds of the long winter are from north to south — even such as they *do* get turned around out there. A man can get so unstrung he's as certain the sun is rising in the west as he is of his own name, though he knows that just cannot be."

"It happens in cities, too." Charlotte nodded. "You step out onto a busy street and go the *wrong* way, sure you're right and everyone else is backwards, deluded. Even when street signs say you should be going one way, something sends you another."

"But at least in Chicago . . . New Orleans, there's people, buildings, landmarks. On the plains or in the thick woods, a kind of madness comes over a person, a wilderness panic. So, I am going after your daughter while the trail's still warm, ma'am. I hope you'll come with me — soon as the doc's done his job."

" 'Course I will." Charlotte sighed as two of his ranch hands hurried to his side. "Let's get this stubborn critter to the infirmary," she told his men, "so's he can get back in the saddle quick as a cat can wink an eye." Charlotte knew only too well there was no point in arguing with a man like Jake Chamberlain.

The Fort Smith post surgeon, Dorsey Middleton, working as considerately as he could, prodded a piece of lead out of Jake's left shoulder. The bullet had made a clean entry wound and had passed almost, but not quite, through the fleshy part of the upper arm.

Rather than dig, the doctor pushed. It was a painful treatment, but it was also quick, which was what Jake wanted. Despite his agony, the patient made not a sound or twitch during the procedure, though he did go chalky pale under his mahogany tan and grip Charlotte's hand forcefully. His nails, she saw, as she felt the calloused hardness of the palm, were neatly manicured and buffed.

Soon after — too soon, both Charlotte and the doctor complained — Jake, bandaged, his left arm strapped tightly to his big chest, was mounted and anxious to get started. Though he claimed to be feeling fit and fine, Charlotte saw real pain in his expressive brown eyes.

A couple of hours after the Fort Smith fracas and Lark's disappearance, Jake and Charlotte rode out of town with a few of his men, easily tracking a horse with a distinctively chipped shoe.

"What do you mean, the animal's being rid double?" Charlotte asked at one point. "Those two together, my girl and Logan Walker, don't weigh as much as one husky man.

"They were both *still* mounted up together when they got as far as this, and they hadn't stopped yet. I know by the way the animal's placing his feet. Walker is heading for the ford on the Poteau so's he can run west."

Charlotte knew that, too, without hoof prints to tell her so. But she also knew the escape route wasn't Logan's plan. Lark was taking the boy up to the Sugarloaf Mountain caves which had played so important a part in the bedtime stories of her childhood. Charlotte had told those fantastical tales over and over, of clever and magical, wild creatures and their yellow-haired, little human friend, a girl named Lark. The characters had been make-believe, but the settings were real; and Lark, who had never set foot in the Sugarloafs, knew every one of their nooks and secret crannies as well as her mother did. Charlotte didn't offer that bit of information to Jake, but she didn't purposely mislead him in the wrong direction, either. A woman who believed in letting providence take its course, she didn't try even once to dissuade Jake from carrying out his self-assigned task. There would have been no point in even trying, not with a man like him.

Relentless in this as in everything he undertook, despite the pain he was suffering, Jake would have kept going until he dropped or accomplished what he'd set out to do—find Lark McKay. And he would have if the heavens, in Charlotte's opinion acting in collusion with destiny, hadn't opened just as the search party neared the Poteau, and made the river impassable. Lark and Logan were camped just on the other side. "Jonah's luck is what circus people call a downpour like this," Charlotte told Jake later, back at Ella's Hotel, where he had booked two rooms, insisting she avoid her tent on such a wet night and avail herself of indoor amenities.

When he had come in from the stable, stamping his feet and shucking off of his oilskin, he went to warm his hands at the fire before joining her for a hot milk and Scotch whiskey in the bar. He tipped his head, and water poured from the brim of his hat, hissing and splattering on the hot coal stove. A man drowsing at a back table awoke with a start, looked furtively about and pulled his hat low, signalling for another drink.

"Jonah's luck," Charlotte repeated. "Three years ago, during the 1888 season, there was so much rain it almost put us out of business. The wagons got mired in the mud, then broke apart when the razorback horses tried to free them. Tents couldn't be put up in the wind, and we missed show dates. Professor Gentry was down to his last hundred dollars; but we held on, and you know, one day, the sun took to shining on us again. We outlasted the stormy weather and made it through. There's a moral to my story: Rain or sun, stick to your guns and you might could be fine, might not, it's the way life is—chancy. I needn't be telling about all that to a man who started out dirt poor and now has the finest spread in the Oklahoma Territory. I hear you built your house with your own two hands and you still brand your own cattle."

"Now, who's been talkin' at you?" Jake asked, sliding into a chair across the checkered table cloth from Charlotte, the sun wrinkles at the corners of his eyes deepening with the slow, almost shy smile spreading on his weary face.

"Miss Ella. Since you wouldn't let me see to the horses, I was just waiting in here for you, and she and I struck up an acquaintance. Ella said you are not a prideful man, that you do not like divulging much about yourself," she said, "so I won't ask questions. I'll only thank you for going after Lark and say good night."

"I haven't got anything to divulge, is all. I'm a dull man living a simple and solitary life. And don't be thanking me for anything. I didn't find Lark. Yet. I'll take up the pursuit again at first light. Will you come with me?" He rose to his feet in gentlemanly fashion when she stood. "Good night, Miz McKay." He smiled.

"Call me Charlotte, please," she answered. "See you in the morning, then, Jake."

They had seen each other the next morning and every morning since. And each and every afternoon and evening as well. They hadn't found Lark and Logan. Satan's tracks, bleared by rain, had eventually filled with the downpour to become little pools, then bigger ones, finally disappearing altogether, overflowing in rivulets of mud and silt that poured down the banks of the ravine to join the surge of wild, white river water that held Jake Chamberlain at bay. Next day, when he tried to pick up the trail on the near bank of the Poteau, it had been washed away without a trace. Leaving word in town of their probable whereabouts, in the event of Lark's return, Jake and Charlotte collected the McKay's horses and dogs from Professor Gentry and headed west, looking for fresh prints, until they reached the JAK Bar Ranch, where they had remained since.

Charlotte's Russian wolfhounds, Ivan and Alex, were as motionless as bookends poised back to back at the edge of the porch, surveying the country for prey, preferably wolves, though an antelope or deer would do. The terrier, Ralph, like others of his compact aggressive ilk, was more interested in smaller game closer to hand and tooth — gophers, prairie dogs, rats and the like — and he snuffled noisily under the veranda, his protruding tail wagging furiously.

"That outlaw bandit boy Lark rode off with?" Charlotte said, then quickly amended, "I mean, the one rode off with her? He was no member of that Cumplin Gang. My Uncle Ike said so. You said yourself, Jake, this Logan Walker was no ordinary, ornery criminal, if he's a criminal at all. I don't comprehend why you are worrying so. Lark's *my* little girl, not yours. Honestly, the way you're takin' on, you remind me of my daddy. Rufus McKay was always brooding and fussing at me when I was a girl like Lark."

Tapping his boot toe and rocking the bench a little faster, Jake didn't answer. He was disconcerted, though not displeased, by the notion that he, a childless widower, was fretting like a possessive father over a girl he hardly knew. It was a role he'd never actually played. It appealed to him but also made him edgy, even tongue-tied for the moment. Though shrewd and sharp when negotiating a deal, tough and blunt handling his crew of chronically uproarious trail hands, Jake was not in the habit of putting his deeper feelings into words. For a time, he sat in restrained silence beside Charlotte, gathering his thoughts.

She understood perfectly. She didn't mind his stillness. She had known men like Jake Chamberlain all her life, trailblazers, woodsmen, natural pioneers. Whether as soldiers, ranchers or farmers, or the politicians, lawyers and the like who soon followed them west, most were gallant men unwavering in their ambition to take and tame the continent, and if, in the process, they happened to get rich, so much the better.

A certain number of such driven men had been Charlotte's darlings, her chivalrous, if laconic, lovers. Whether it was her own fault or just coincidence, all the men to whom she was drawn, the ones who fulfilled her ideal of heroism, happened to be men who could face anything — but themselves. And do anything — but settle down. Jake was like them, the brave, strong silent type, but he was different, too. He had settled. He had put down roots, and he loved his ranch, she could see. To have survived the loneliness and back-breaking work it took to carve a home place out of untamed grassland and prairie, he must have, Charlotte reasoned, the same blind streak of recklessness, a reserve of stubborn stamina and the fortitude she admired in a man. Lacking that singular strength, no man would ever have left the surety of settled places, no matter how oppressive or repetitious his days, to gamble on wresting wealth — and freedom — from wilderness. Charlotte's own father, and her daughter's, were of that remarkable breed, and their adventurer's blood ran in her veins, and in Lark's, too. She and Lark shared with such men and the women who helped them realize their hopes the strong pioneer spirit. The best of the self-made men were tough and gentle both, fair-handed and generous, but rock-hard when they had to be. Instinctive survivors, like she and Lark were, they came to know their own worth, not only in land and cattle and currency, but as men and women who walked the world in seven-league boots and sometimes made daunting dreams come true.

Charlotte glanced up at Jake beside her, square-jawed, barrel-chested and handsome with his weathered face and silver-tipped dark hair. He was looking out over land that belonged to him as far as the eye could see, and farther.

The JAK Bar was fifty thousand prime acres of hill and prairie, its brook-watered pastures and stands of cottonwoods supporting thousands of head of long-horn beef cows. With its outbuildings — stables, bunk houses, corrals, calving sheds, cook houses — the JAK Bar was one of the biggest spreads in the Twin Territories. It ran for miles along the Deep Fork River west of the town of Welty and not too far east of Sparks, where the Topeka and Santa Fe Railroad stopped.

"I think Logan Walker is really a good boy," Charlotte said. "He has the kind, considerate face of a man who's dealt with . . . oh, some deep sorrow perhaps, or loss, and overcome it."

"I've seen more than one kind-appearing gentleman turn cold-hearted and go mean when the mood came on him." Jake shrugged. "Logan Walker? No one here knows about his past. No one knows the lad hardly at all. Now, Cumplin and his gang control what land to the west of here my men don't. 'Tween here and the Indians there's a lot of square miles, but we've covered most of it. If my best trail-tracking boys haven't found them yet, you can bet Clarence Cumplin has. No pun intended, but there *were* rumors that this Walker was thick as thieves with Clarence. But it was just hearsay so—"

"Even if it's true that Logan is a member of that gang, Lark can take care of herself. She's always been a real clever, brave girl. Why, from the time she could first talk and walk — she'll say so herself if you ask her — it was her who took care of me instead of the other way 'round. There's some truth to that. I had my wretched days, truth to tell, and if Lark hadn't been there — well, we've always been more than mother and daughter. She's my best friend in the world. She has seen me through some bad, bad times."

"I still don't understand how it is you aren't more concerned about her getting kidnapped," Jake complained.

"Jake darlin', the truth of it is, I liked the look of that boy, Walker. I don't believe he'd do my child harm. He was shot up badly when they rode out of Fort Smith on a real tumbledown-looking specimen of a horse." Charlotte frowned. "I could be wrong, but I'm supposing that Lark's played Clara Barton to the boy. Lark's a fine nurse and has probably got him through the worst of it by now. Know when I'll start in to worry, Jake? If she doesn't show up in Fort Smith for opening day of Mr. Ringling's circus. Lark wants nothing so much as to be a star with a big top, three-ring show."

"So I gathered, but did she, or you, Charlie, ever think about a wild west show like Buffalo Bill Cody's?" Jake answered pensively.

"Gosh, what Bill does — fake stagecoach holdups . . . a little horseback square dancing — Lark could do with one eye closed and one arm in a sling. She's got circus in her bones, starting as young as she did. Listen, nothing but trouble could make her miss the Ringlings' big day. Now, you stop distressing yourself—and me—Jake Chamberlain. I'll be the first to say when it's time to go after my own daughter."

"I never meant to upset *you*, Charlotte," Jake said, sweet and contrite, almost shy. "I want you to know . . . I'm pleased you're here with me to share my pleasure in the bright horizon, in this big sky. Since Maddy, my wife, passed on, I've been alone, mostly." Something jagged in his throat stopped him from talking for a time. Charlotte simply waited, hardly breathing, watching a little sparrow hawk hovering into the wind before it plunged for a mouse or a grasshopper. She started when Jake cleared his throat. When he began to speak again, it was as if the floodgates of a dam had opened.

"Tomorrow, would you ride up on the ridge with me, Charlotte, to see how the fall harvest is going?" he asked, and she nodded.

"Sure I would. And you can look around for Lark and Logan on the way, right?"

"I sure won't be riding with blinders on." He grinned fast, aware she'd seen through his ploy. "My men are just rounding up the few strays they passed over in the spring, nothing important, but it's an excuse to kind of survey the countryside, pick up a bit of gossip. I needn't be there at all for this little roundup, but I want to be. A cattle camp's the one place I feel truly at home since Maddy passed. This house just has gotten too big for a man alone, too quiet. If there were children, they'd be half grown now, and it might be different; but as it is, much as I love the ranch, the house just gets me down sometimes, 'specially on fall evenings when the light's just going and you can't deny winter's coming on. There's no better cure for gloom than the congeniality a man finds in a well set up cattle camp. Even as a boy I always was most contented riding night herd, watching the Big Dipper rotate round the North Star as the dark hours went by. There's nothing like that first hot cup of coffee in the morning or a friendly crap game after a supper of sowbelly and beans. There's some range cooks give a man a better shave and haircut than a big-city barber, and I'm needing one now so—"

"Now, you know, Jake Chamberlain, no range cook's going to buff your fingernails the way you like." Charlotte laughed. "*I* can do that, and I can do some skilled barbering also. And speakin' of supper, I bake a real *fine* pie and—"

"You'd best not set even one dainty little foot in the cookhouse. That's Aida's territory. She's been keeping my house and feeding me for more years than I care to count and—say, Miz McKay, if you'd be willing to act as my hostess, I'll invite callers. It's been too long since a lady filled that place at my table. As you're planning to stay on in this part of the world, you could meet your far-flung neighbors. It would give me no end of pleasure to receive them and introduce you." In the last of the light, Jake's warm dark eyes lingered on Charlotte's lovely face.

"I'd be pleased." She smiled, grossly understating her true feelings. Her eyes met his, and her heart leapt and fluttered in a very, very strange way. "Speaking of guests, is anyone expected here today? Is that trail dust I see rising off there, or only night mists settling in?"

Jake narrowed his eyes and squinted in the direction she pointed. "It's a caller. From the way he sits his horse and holds his head, I'd venture a guess as to who it is. I think Rufus McKay has quelled his pride and come calling on his only daughter."

"I think you might be right. And wrong. Right, it *is* Rufus approaching, I can see that now. And wrong. He is not a man to even contemplate humility. With him, pride is all. If Rufus McKay has come to call, it's on you, Jake. He won't even acknowledge my presence."

"Want to bet?" Jake asked. "How's dollars to donuts?"

"A baker's dozen sound okay to you—donuts or dollars?"

"Well, ma'am, thirteen donuts won't be half enough to satisfy me. I am a man of prodigious appetite, so let's just say . . . fifty, dollars or donuts."

"Sir, you are on!" Charlotte sighed, nervously watching the tall, erect, white-haired figure on a pure-white horse, both the aging man and mount moving together in smart military manner.

Chapter Ten

"Logan! You are causing me to miss my appointment with Mr. Ringling at Fort Smith! Let me *go*. My whole future depends on my being there." The very instant he had removed the gag from her mouth, Lark began speaking like a wind-up toy, as if she hadn't been muffled by his yellow bandanna for the past eight or ten hours.

The Cumplin Gang had been moving from one hiding place to another, most often in a westerly direction, keeping to their haunts in Oklahoma, although they had many throughout the territories. After days of travelling, kidnapped in actuality now, Lark was still fuming at Logan, and herself.

She'd been compelled by her sympathetic disposition to come to the aid of a wounded, innocent man, or so she thought, only to realize she'd been tricked and used by a common, if clever, criminal. He'd been crafty enough to discover her greatest weakness right off, one she'd not even known about herself—her passionate nature. Ardor was the cause of her downfall, that and a fault of which she had been well aware and secretly proud; the daring, even reckless impetuosity that made her a great equestrian also made her an April fool for Logan Walker.

She was a real greenhorn at romance, and he had taken advantage of that, too. Logan had gone and made her fall in love with him, rogue that he was, and now, damn it, she was raging at herself and jealous of the Other Woman—the one he was protecting so doggedly that he was even ready to give his life for her.

So Lark was furious, and because she couldn't say what was really on her mind, she badgered Logan incessantly about everything else, especially the company he kept and them keeping her from getting on with her life as she'd planned.

"Your bit of calico—that yellow-haired girl—the way she keeps scolding at you puts me in mind of an unruly pup nipping at the heels of a cart horse. Dangerous thing for a pup, or a woman, to do," Clarence had irritably complained to Logan after four or five days. The lid of Cumplin's right eye was flickering when he added, "She is really putting my nerves on edge, brother. Grasp what I'm saying?"

Logan had, and he knew he had to shut her up in the quickest, most effective way possible.

"It's for your own good," he had whispered to Lark, his amber eyes half apologetic, half furious. "You haven't got the sense of a suckling foal, darn you, ruffling Clarence. Clarence spills blood like it was water. Can't you tell that just by looking at him? No passable-sane man has a face hard as that, or such eyes."

"Looks are misinforming. You're walking, talking proof of that, Logan." She'd laughed icily.

"I could say the same of you. You don't appear ready for a six-foot bungalow—a five-foot coffin would do in your case—but that's what you'll be laid out in if you don't have a care and curb your tart tongue."

He stood back from Lark a little, undoing the yellow

bandanna from inside the neck of his red shirt, and in her eyes, he glowed like the sun, handsomer than any dime novel frontier hero. His deep-set eyes sparked. His brown, gold-tipped hair, which had grown long, almost to his broad shoulders, glinted. He'd lost any trace of his prison pallor and life-threatening wounds except for the scar on his brow that was fading but would never disappear. The expression on his handsome, narrow face was resigned, but determined.

"I have seen Clarence Cumplin put six bullets in a man—bang, bang, bang, bang, bang, bang—just for sneezing twice. One sneeze puts Clarence on edge, two pushes him over."

"I am not sneezing, Logan, I am talking. And I am not a man. He wouldn't dare—"

That was the last word Lark had been permitted to say since breakfast that morning. The gang had done a hard day's ride, and now that she'd been allowed to dismount and watch the so-called cook make supper, she was stiff, tired, indignant and ravenously hungry. Enveloped in Logan's fringed buckskins which were far too big for her slender figure, the britches held up with a braid laniard used as a belt, she leaned against a straggly tree. They had stopped to make camp up near the timberline of a rise in the middle of nowhere, and Lark complained to Logan that life was passing her by.

"Sweet thing, you're damn lucky you still have a life to go on and pass you by. You can thank me for that." Logan grinned, relieved to see all of her gorgeous face, however irate the expression, not just steely-gray eyes glowering at him over a yellow bandanna and from under a hat brim. "To pick up where you were so rudely interrupted this morning, talking of futures as I recall, mine depends on staying here in bandit territory with Clarence and the boys and out of Fort Smith with George Maledon."

Logan offered her a crooked little smile and set two tin plates, piled with hardtack and pinto beans, on the ground near her. "You had the misfortune to be in my vicinity when I met up with my buddy, Clarence, and these other gents you so admire. I was trying to arrange it otherwise. If you hadn't opened your luscious mouth at the wrong time, you might have gotten clean away. If you'd felt the slightest tinge of tenderness for me or had at least the good sense to look before you leapt, to see who was there to catch you, either one, you could be prancing around under Ringling's tent now with your dogs and ponies and all. But as it is, your future prospects, to say nothing of your life, depend entirely on me. You're in my power now, McKay, and I've got the whip hand. You'd best not forget that."

"I've heard it said that no good deed goes unpunished, so don't go putting yourself out on my account. I'm sorry I ever did on yours. Why I took up with such an egotist as you in the first place, Walker, I can't understand. An *egotist* and a fool to boot. Logan! Come *on!*" she called as he started back toward the chuck wagon. "Untie my hands, please! The smell of even these inferior victuals is driving me wild. I am perishing of hunger! You know I ain't had one bite of food since sun up, just little drinks of water. LO-GAN!"

"Brother, you are running with one fractious little female," Clarence said, glowering in Lark's direction with his maniacal eyes that were more jittery than ever. "Any time you can't handle the spitfire, you call on me to give you a helping hand. It will be my pleasure."

"Not necessary, son. I'll tend to her myself." Logan winked. "I'll just take her off a little distance so her entreaties for mercy won't bother you all. I'll show her who's boss, so if you *do* hear any . . . unaccountable sounds in the night, why, just ignore them." He spoke in a low voice, and Lark couldn't decipher his words. She had no difficulty, though, making sense of the rumble of sniggering laughter from the men gathered around the cook fire. It accompanied Logan as he returned to her, this time carrying two battered tin mugs filled with steaming coffee. He hunkered down on his heels in front of her, his back to the others. He removed her hat, a white Stetson sitting low on her brow, and let a mass of flaxen hair spill down about her shoulders. He said nothing as he redid the folds, giving the hat one-dent on top and a crease on each side, the pattern known as the rancher pinch. Then he looked her square in the eye.

"You'd best comport yourself in a more genteel and less showy manner," he said very softly, "because you've got a serious problem, ma'am, just being. Sitting still, or sitting a horse, walking from here to that hill, say" — he glanced up — "and walking back again, you stir up more covetous consideration than any mere mortal woman ought. There's always at least one pair of eyes on you, mine, usually a lot more than one. No matter what you do, honey, you're center ring stuff with this crowd. You are in no way an inconspicuous woman, so in the vicinity of a savage like Cumplin, you definitely shouldn't be drawing any extra attention to yourself. It'll cause nothing but trouble — for you *and* me. Understand?"

Lark, who had been calculating her chances of escape from that night's campsite, was somewhat unnerved by what Logan had said, but more so by the way he said it. If he, or someone, was always spying on her, the odds of her getting away dropped. Not wanting him to get any inkling of her disappointment, she avoided his eyes and scowled over at the outlaws.

"Nice company you keep, Walker. Even at supper they bristle with weapons like hedgehogs with quills," she commented in a clear and carrying voice, about to launch a more stinging verbal attack. Instead, she yelped as Logan's strong arms went round her, drawing her to her feet, crushing her against him, and then, his hard, bruising mouth, covering hers, stole away her breath and her voice and her inclination to run. He was, it took her a moment to realize, really kissing her like he meant it, and the last thing in the world she wanted just then was for him stop. He didn't.

He kept on kissing her, feeling her lips soften and part and her small and perfect body bend, then melt to his. He didn't stop kissing her as he fumbled to untie her hands.

"Put your arms round me—now," he whispered hoarsely, and brought to her senses by his imperious directive, she stiffened and tried to back away. She forgot that her ankles were still shackled. Only Logan's quick action kept her on her feet, and there was a loud hoot of laughter and shouts of encouragement from some of the men.

"Show the little scold who's master, Logan!"

"Bring her to her knees, man!"

"Discipline the filly . . ."

"I said, put your arms around me. That's not a sentimental lover's request, sugar, it's an order, but don't get the wrong idea," he grumbled darkly. "This isn't kiss-and-make-it-up time for you and me and all past treachery forgotten. We're putting on a show for the boys. It might keep them away from you for a while or . . . it might not. Now, kiss me."

"If there's one thing I know how to do, Logan, it's put on a really good show." Lark's smile was kittenish and sly and excessively honeyed before she did as he asked, kissed him slow and deep and long, sinuously twining, taking pleasure—and strength—from him, from the physical immediacy of his lean body and the taste of his lips but mostly from the hard rising swell of his manhood that told her more than words.

"Putting on a good show isn't all you know how to do rather well," Logan said in a rough, raspy voice. "Now, stop kissing and start listening. Clarence is the one to be real careful of," he whispered, tonguing her ear, his two hands encircling her waist.

"Even William Clarke Quantrill, the meanest, most ferocious lunatic outlaw there ever was, spared women." Lark sighed, her whispering lips against Logan's throat, her hands, which had been ranging up and down his back, sliding down past his belt, pressing him to her. He imprisoned her wrists behind her.

"What do you think you're doing?" he asked in a gruff, hungry, almost dazed moan. "You are being . . . downright immodest in view of . . . them." Logan was now the indignant one.

"Well, there's just no pleasing *some* people, is there? I am putting on the show you asked for. What are *you* doing?" Lark laughed, seductive and teasing. Not overly gentle, he set her down against the tree, loosed her ankles and shoved a plate and knife into her hands.

"Eat," he ordered, and she obeyed that order, too, using the knife *and* her fingers to shovel up the beans because there was no fork and she wasn't going to ask for one. The food gone, she licked the plate clean of even the last drops of fat and red gravy. If she did manage to get away in the night, it might be a while before she ate again, and she'd need all her strength. Her eyes met Logan's as he hunkered down next to her eating steadily, chewing slowly and contemplating her unwaveringly. She looked away at once, feeling as though he could read her escapist thoughts. He couldn't, of course. It was her evasiveness that gave her away. The corner of his sensuous mouth curled in a reluctant smile.

Lark wasn't one to just do as she was told, Logan realized, not a girl to give over without a struggle. Besides loving her, he had to admire her for that, even if he couldn't let her know, not about either one, the love or admiration. If he didn't keep her at least a little afraid of him and uncertain, always on her guard, she might fall into Cumplin's clutches. Then she could—likely would—give him away again. But this time it would be fatal. Much as he yearned to, Logan knew he couldn't take Lark into his confidence and tell her his plans, not yet, anyway, not until she saw for herself how much he loved her, and how dangerous Clarence Cumplin really was.

"I want more, sir." She giggled, holding her dish forward in both hands.

"Stand!" Logan barked, taking and hurling away the empty plate. When she scrambled to her feet and saluted, the men laughed again. Thinking she had been set free, hand and foot, to stretch and exercise and go on with their performance, Lark was incensed when, before she could budge, Logan tied her left wrist to her right ankle leaving just enough slack for her to stand up straight, but surely not to sprint.

"You're doing worse than sidelining me, you cad!" she exploded in obvious frustration. "I wouldn't even do such a thing to a killer wild mustang."

"This isn't horseplay, sugar." He grinned, sitting her down again and going down on one knee beside her. "Clarence belongs to the devil, and the devil takes care of his own. You belong to me—they think"—he rolled a shoulder toward the others—"so I'm taking care of you whether you like it or not. I'm a man who pays his debts. I owe you that much at least, for saving my life, even if you did try to do me out of it first chance you got."

"Logan, I told you why I did what I did," Lark said, her voice as soft as rain, her gray eyes pearly and misted. "To save you . . . to keep you with me so we could prove you didn't kill Miss Blue and . . . because. . . ." No matter what, she just wasn't about to say she loved him, not first anyway, not before he told her his feelings. He'd probably never say he loved her, because it was becoming more and more apparent he didn't. He'd used her, and now he was stuck with her, that was all. And even if it had become something more for a little while and might again, if he kept up this kissing game, she wasn't having any outlaw father *her* babies, and that was that. Lark's hair was half in her eyes, along with tears, when she took a deep breath and swallowed hard, hoping he hadn't noticed. He had.

"Don't . . . don't you take to thinking that a little defenseless female weeping is going to sway me," Logan lied, standing, cracking his knuckles, then clenching his fists, finding it all he could do to say anything at all just then. He took off his own hat this time, a sueded pigskin with a four-corner crease and a darker leather band. He crimped, recrimped and pinched it a few times, a habit that was the only evidence of inner agitation he ever allowed to show. He wiped his brow with the back of his hand and jammed the hat back on again.

"Hold your head high, ma'am, and swallow those tears," he continued. "I want you to know . . . to know that first chance I get, when it'll be safe and we're near a town maybe, or a ranch, I'm setting you free. When I do, you better run. Do not look back even once or that crowd will be on you like hungry wolves on a rabbit. Clarence will take his pleasure—first. He's already panting after you, and the way he is, I can't let you out of my reach, no less my sight. So—until I tell you to git, like you told me, you might recall, we are going to have to stay close as peas in a pod, you and me, day and night. I'll have to make them all think I'm the insanely jealous type, that I might just kill anyone who so much as looks too hard at you, no less touches. . . ." He shuddered. "I know it's going to be a real chore, not a pleasure, for us both, but you'd best resolve to be businesslike about it. There's not much choice so . . . now, you put your arms round me, damn it, and kiss me like your life depended on it. It does."

Chapter Eleven

The Cumplin Gang had a string of hideouts, caves and other natural refuges, running from Texas north to Missouri and Kansas and east into Tennessee. During the few fall weeks of 1891 that Lark McKay found herself travelling with the outlaw band, they mainly kept to remote areas of the Oklahoma Territory.

Until a year before, there had been no Oklahoma Territory, just the Indian Territory, a region given by treaty in the 1830's to tribes of the south-east United States: Seminoles of Florida and Creeks of Alabama; Cherokees, Choctaws and Chickasaws from Georgia, Tennessee and the Carolinas. Moved from their own then more valuable acreage, they were granted that part of the world destined to become the state of Oklahoma. The Five Civilized Tribes, distinct in language and custom from the fighting Plains Indians, settled in the hills and valleys in the eastern portion of the Territory and thrived there, until the outbreak of the War Between the States. Southerners themselves, many of them cotton farmers and slave holders, the resettled Indians sided with the Confederacy and after the war suffered retribution in the loss of some of their land. After the war, part of the Indian

Territory was handed over to other eastern tribes — landless Delawares and Shawnees — and some was granted even to "wild" fighting Indians — Sioux and Apache and others.

Right after the Civil War, too, the legendary cattle drives began, and the great trails — the Shawnee and Chisholm — ran through the Indian Territory. The herds, which had already traversed the vastness of Texas by the time they forded the Red River, were rested on the high plains virgin grassland of the territory. Fattened and ready for market, the cattle were moved on to rail depots in Dodge City, Kansas City or St. Louis by men who didn't forget the vast, vacant, lush grazing land of the Indian Territory.

By the 1870's, the railroads sent a spur south from Kansas to carry beef cows to market, and where the rails went, white men in numbers followed. Those cowboys and ranchers who had crossed the plains returned to claim it, settle it, and raise their herds on what was still Indian property, but only nominally — deals were made between tribes and ranchers.

In the 1880's, Indians lost more of their domain when the Cherokee Strip in the Oklahoma panhandle was opened by the federal government to settlers. At high noon on April 22, 1889, the land rush began, a mad race across a designated line by would-be homesteaders who for weeks had lined up on the border ready to stake their claims. A few impatient settlers, who crossed over early and were therefore dubbed "sooners," gave Oklahoma its lasting nickname — the Sooner State — a status the territory achieved in 1907 when it became the forty-sixth of the United States.

In the fall of 1891, the Clarence Cumplin Gang and other hunted outlaw bands were still roaming the Oklahoma Territory, Lark McKay and Logan Walker with them.

On a night in November when north winds were rising and the weather turning chill, the two were stretched out side by side, as they had been for many nights past, under Logan's big bearskin blanket. At each new campsite, the space they put between themselves and the others increased, though only little by little to avoid Cumplin's notice and further their escape plan: Lark would disappear at the right time, in the right place, and Logan would report she'd slipped away under cover of darkness. And so, though distanced from the others on that blustery night, they were still near enough to the gang to see the glint of the main campfire and hear boisterous voices getting louder and angrier by the minute. A card game, started soon after supper, was continuing into the small hours.

In most of his hideouts, Clarence had left hidden caches of guns, bullets, money and moonshine, and when the mood came on him, he unearthed a jug or two and spent the night gambling and drinking with his boys, sometimes shooting at the moon and, as the night wore on, at those of his men who were winning too much of his cash. This was the first time since Lark had been with the gang that matters had progressed so far, and she sat bolt upright when the gunplay began.

"Clarence is letting off steam. The man can't handle liquor, or losing at cards. But if the worst he does is waste some iron rations shooting at the sky, we'll all be lucky." Logan yawned. "Get some sleep. You'll need it. We'll be doing some hard riding, starting tomorrow. Your big day could come pretty soon now."

"Oh?" Lark asked reluctantly, the first word she'd said to him in hours, since "pass the salt" at supper time. She'd made up her mind not to speak to Logan, unless she had to.

They had been hand-in-glove close for many days and nights now, and he hadn't kissed her again since they'd put on their display for Clarence and the outlaws. When they'd been alone, he hadn't even so much as touched her with anything but his eyes and then only when he couldn't avoid looking at her, it seemed. She was hurting to hold him, have him enfold her in his strong, protective arms. She was hankering to see his sparkling flash of a smile and hear his low voice intoning the candied nicknames he favored for her — sugar and sweets and sweet thing and honey — syllables rolling on his tongue as if he were savoring bon bons. If she had gotten her way, his tongue would be savoring her each night, his lips agitating and his hands touching her, and the two of them would be coming together, close as a man and woman could and . . . Lark was getting none of it. She was perturbed.

"I'd grown sort of . . . accustomed to . . . cuddling and the like, on chill nights 'specially, and since we already have been so close, after all, what could be the harm in carrying on our affiliation, just for as long as we have to be together like this, anyway?" she had asked him, truly baffled, after their second cool night together.

"We both know that's not going to be forever, or even very much longer, so where's the sense in starting things up again? There never was the chance we could have a future together, right?"

"Right." Lark had nodded. "But—"

"No buts. The hardest part of giving up an addiction is the first few days of doing without whatever it is you're craving. We're past that now. It's over between us," Logan had answered brusquely.

It hadn't been at all an easy thing for him to do, not with Lark standing there so close, her big, puzzled, pained gray eyes going all over him. He had tried not to look at *her* at all, knowing that if he did let his eyes taste, even a little, no less drink in all that loveliness, next thing, he'd be wanting more — and taking it. He wasn't about to, for a number of reasons.

"Well, if that's the way you feel about it, fine with me." She had pouted, and he'd replied, "It is the way I feel," stating a bald-faced lie. "That's my last word on the subject, and there's an end to it, understand?"

Though Lark had nodded, the exchange hadn't put an end to anything. Spurned, she went after him hammer and tongs. Wanting what was being withheld, but too proud to come out and say so or take the first yielding step toward him, Lark tried to compel Logan to abandon restraint. He'd want her so fiercely before she was done, he *would* play the role of supplicant, she swore. And then, of course, she would be . . . well, more than just lenient. She would be positively magnanimous.

It had been tougher than she'd expected. After many days of unbroken proximity, during which she had either chattered incessantly or kept long silences, dressed and undressed, eaten and slept with the man, she had gotten nowhere. He was always polite and protective — helping her mount and dismount, seeing to it she was well fed and warm and that none of the men overstepped the bounds of propriety in her presence. But he remained impervious to her stratagems, and that only made her all the more determined.

Just that afternoon when they'd come to Cold Water Creek, Lark had beseeched him to let her have a bath, and when Logan, suspecting some prank, finally agreed, she insisted he stand guard. He warned off the others and watched over her, stolid and impassive, no expression at all on his lean handsome face, though his innards were twisting and his heart going like a steam hammer.

As she shed her trousers, exposing shapely dancer's legs, and then pulled the shirt over her head to stand naked as riverine sprite, a gorgeous mirage sweetly smiling up at him, he had a very difficult time not taking her then and there. He grappled to hold himself back as she did her utmost, turning this way and that, testing the water with a toe, to meddle with his aloofness.

Though there was still some warmth in the sun, the water which ran down from distant mountains was icy, and she gasped when she pranced in, high-stepping like a fledgling heron, emitting little shivery chirps before completely submerging herself. When she had remained totally under water as long as she could stand the cold of it, long enough to worry the most disinterested observer, even Logan, Lark came bursting up in a spray of crystal droplets, letting the stream flow in intimate little eddies about her thighs as she stood, beckoning.

"It's mighty stimulating, Walker. Join me!" she called, her voice quavering with shivers. When she smiled at Logan, her misty carnal eyes were soft gray velvet. His eyes were unanswering, and she arched and stretched like a preening water bird sending rainbow splashes toward the sun, and toward him.

"I'll swim when you're done," he'd answered, resolutely reminding himself that before he'd touch her again, no matter how much he lusted for her elegant jewel of a body, there was something he craved even more — her full and unconditional surrender, not just body, but heart and soul, too. Before he was done with Lark McKay, he would hear her say to him, "I love you," and "I'll follow you anywhere, now and forever," even, "Yes, I'll marry you," or something to that effect, or he'd lay himself out trying.

On the night Clarence started acting up, the contest between Logan and Lark had been going on long enough to have stretched their nerves taut. A talented poker player, Logan could conceal his emotions, but Lark was in a state of evident and permanent agitation. Being *so* close to him day and night, yet distanced by his impeccable formality, was making her wakeful, and unable to sleep, she quite naturally became even more conscious of his long body stretched out beside her in the dark. He was so desirable but so inaccessible he might as well have been on the full moon Clarence was wasting his bullets shooting for. Lark was on the brink of abject surrender when Logan spoke, and everything changed.

"Lord, it's so big and close you can almost smell it, can't you, that moon?" he said, taking her by surprise, his tone soft and sensual.

"Is that a strong, silent, shy-type cowboy I hear, talkin' sentimental about the moon?" Lark laughed provocatively, not even trying to hide her true feelings, relief and love and longing bubbling out of her. "Well, mah, my!"

Logan grinned in the dark, drawing a deep breath and inhaling the fragrance of the sweet river water she had bathed in and the verbena with which she had scrubbed her silken skin, first crushing the leaves of the late-growing blue vervain, a pretty weed she'd found in a sheltered rock cleft near the river.

Now, enwrapped in a cloak of fur and lost in moonlight with her right there at arm's reach, Logan couldn't stop himself thinking how lovely she'd been in sunlight, dripping and shivering delicately as she stepped onto the stream bank, her ivory skin tinted soft pink by cold mountain water, the rose tips of her breasts a shade darker, puckered with cold — and the heat of desire. Logan was about to reach out and touch her where she waited, he knew, so needy, as needy as he, in the dark. Then Clarence started shooting, and Logan sighed and turned his back to Lark. "You'll be glad tomorrow for whatever little shut-eye you get tonight," he mumbled. "Tomorrow, we're starting east, and we've quite a way to go. Day after tomorrow, maybe the one after that, we're going to rob the bank at Caldwell, Kansas."

"NO! You are not really?" Lark burst out, appalled. "You might get caught again and hanged, or killed in the act. And what am I supposed to do while you and your rowdy friends are committing this felony, lollop about whistling Dixie?"

"The plan is for you to go right in with us," Logan answered.

"You really *are* bad, Logan Walker, just as Judge Parker suspected. If only I'd believed my ears instead of my eyes, you'd now be where you belong — six feet under."

"I just said that was the plan, not that it would actually happen. I've no intention of letting you get involved in a holdup. But, sugar, now that my life might be on the line again, tell me true, wouldn't you be just the least bit sad if I really was six feet under?"

She only shrugged.

"Regardless of whether your answer is yes or no, that's not a nice thing to say to man who's saving you from a fate worse than death." Logan shifted to his other side again so that he could see Lark's face in the moonlight. "It's pure sin . . . anything so lovely. Uh, it's that moon I'm talking about," he added when her gaze came down from the heavens to shine into his.

Logan's eyes were lit, she could see, with a gold fire of passion every bit as seductive and sinful as the moon. Lark folded her arms around her knees and moved away a little, though she didn't release Logan from her lavender gaze.

"Indians call the one after the Harvest Moon, 'The Moon When Water Freezes.' Did you know that, sugar?"

"I don't want to talk about the moon. What's this fate worse than death? You mean Clarence? He isn't exactly a bad-looking young man. In fact, with his untimely white hair and boyish face and his eerie blue, *blue* eyes . . . well, there's *some* women could get real infatuated with him." Lark sensed something begin to simmer in Logan, jealousy she supposed, and decided to make the most of it, provoke him into doing something—anything—even just get up and walk away. "Even crazy as Clarence may be, he *is* the boss of this gang," Lark chattered on, sure she was finally getting to Logan, "and you know what they say?"

"No. What do they say?" he asked. Beneath his apparent calm he was seething, thinking of Clarence as a rival for Lark. Logan had never before in his life felt what he was feeling just then, possessive jealousy. He didn't like it. When he half sat, propping his head on the heel of a hand, the bearskin cover slipped. He'd kept his trousers on but wore no shirt, and Lark, too, was suddenly jealous, she of the moonlight caressing his lean, hickory-hard body.

"They say . . ." she whispered in her throaty low voice, the one that told him without exact words what she wanted, the give-away bedroom voice that always drove him a little crazy, "they say that if you aren't the lead dog, the view never changes. Now . . . there's some women who find leaders of the pack more interesting than followers. I'm not saying I'm one of them, mind, but if a girl's going to throw in her lot with an outlaw, it might as well be the top sawyer, the head of the gang, mightn't it? He's the one with most of the money, the real say-so and, in the case of Clarence, good looks of a *mean* sort so—why, what *are* you doing, Logan?" He had risen to his knees in a fast glide, pushed her down hard and, in a continuing fluid motion, stood and spun about, a pistol in one hand, a knife in the other.

"Easy, brother, easy!" Clarence cautioned. Also armed, he'd materialized a few feet from them, rising like a white snake from tall grass. "Hey, it isn't my fault your woman finds me fascinating and comely. I like her looks, too." His eyes, with the moon full in them, reflected flat, nearly colorless and empty as mirrors from the void of alcohol and lunacy in which he existed. "I had an inkling you fancied me, Miss McKay. Ladies can't seem to help that. Now that I know for certain you do, why, Logan and me, we can have us a little competition, say a boxing match or a tournament, like knights of old, you know? Only ours'll be a 'ro-day-oh'—roping and riding—to see which one, me or brother Logan, wins the fair damsel—her ripe little body anyways. I've not had any traffic with hearts or souls in a long while." Clarence emitted a high shrill, silly sound, probably a laugh, Lark reasoned, watching him stumble forward out of the brush.

"You'd not be on your feet after one clout, Clarence. Neither fisticuffs nor rodeo is your style. What is it you want here?" Logan's voice and gun hand were steady. So were his eyes. They were also narrow and lethal.

"I just come by to be so . . . so-ciable, and now you don't want me around it seems," the outlaw simpered, excessive drink slurring his words and bringing a sentimental throb to his voice. "I am tired of those other fools I ride with. Big as boulders and thick as weeds in summer, the lot of them. There's not a wit or a thought among 'em. A man needs to converse with a bookish person now and again. That's why I always have liked you, Logan." Clarence swayed on his feet, his white hair gilded by the moon, then sat abruptly, Indian style, with crossed legs. As he did, his gun went off, but he seemed not even to notice.

"That's right, dear," he went on talking to Lark, "Logan's got book learning. He writes a clear, legible hand, too. Is that what the poor murdered school marm was teaching you all those nights, Logan?" Cumplin's mindless, mirthless laugh broke from his throat again like a trapped bird freed from a cage, then halted abruptly in mid-flight. Bowled over by a slam to his jaw, Cumplin's guns went flying, and he found himself flat on his back, Logan's knee digging into his chest and the knife pressed against his gullet.

"You almost winged me, Clarence. I know you're not worth a fleabite as a marksman when you've been into the mash. It's a good thing, too, because I also know you were aiming for my heart. You want this girl *that* bad?"

Feeling the honed edge of the steel blade nick his skin, Clarence didn't speak or swallow or even breathe for fear of doing himself injury. He just glared up. Logan stared right back, hardly appearing to move at all, and drew a fine, thin line from ear to ear on Cumplin's throat. The streak turned red, blood seeping up along its length like ground water rising in a dry culvert after a spring rain. Logan stood and helped the outlaw to his feet.

"Cut me, did you, brother?" Clarence asked affably, fingering his wound.

"Not so as to leave a scar — this time. That's a pointed

warning to stay away from my girl." Logan wasn't affable at all.

Lark was completely motionless during the confrontation, except for her eyes as she looked about for a weapon. Her glance had just fallen on a well-formed heavy rock when Logan said, "Reach into my left boot, sweetness, and take out the little Derringer." As she jumped to do as he asked, he told her, "You keep that by you always, Lark, never put it aside. If I'm not right close by you . . . if anything should happen to me, it'll help some if you find yourself in a predicament. Shoot fast and ask questions after." Logan's sham grin at Clarence sparked hard, white and very cold. "She'll do as I tell her, Cumplin. Try any tricks on this lady, and someone'll be putting you to bed with a shovel."

"There's many a man who'd think you'd gone loco, brother, cutting me, Clarence Cumplin himself, and over a treacherous female ready to turn you in to the law the first chance she gets."

"Just a lover's spat." Logan shrugged. "She was jealous."

"Logan Walker, how dare you—" Lark began all in a huff until she glanced at Clarence and decided to play along with Logan's act. "How did you know, darlin', that's what it was upset me?" Her smile at Logan was sugary, but her voice was poisonous.

"Now, don't neither one of you underestimate old Clarence, putting on your trumped-up lovey-dovey show. I'm not so inebriated or dumb, neither, I don't see how you two really are together, even if you don't see it your own selves. Love just kinda oozes out of the both of you, even if you're trying to bottle it up inside, and oh, it does makes you shine! I had that love luster one time, over a woman and she over me, as you know, Logan."

Almost shyly and very fast, Logan and Lark glanced at each other and verified the truth of Cumplin's observation.

The violent, dangerous outlaw, slithering so close without being discovered, taking them both off guard, had unnerved them. They could, one or the other or both, have been killed — or worse. The dread each had felt of losing the other opened a chink in the wall of defenses they'd set up between them. Even if it had taken a madman to speak the truth aloud, stark blatant love, lusty and ethereal both, and undeniably magical, drew them together. The gun in one hand, Lark extended the other to Logan, who took it and pressed to his heart. Neither was looking at the other. They were both watching Cumplin, who had, briefly, appeared quite sane before he put a warped smile back on his face and dabbed at his bleeding throat with his shirttail.

"Brother, I must warn you, you are corrupting an innocent young girl, putting a gun in her hand. She'll either turn it on you, or someone else. You are setting her on the path of unrighteousness, yeah you are! And you are starting her down the road to perdition, along the thoroughfare of criminality and on the highway to heartbreak! You know about Belle Starr? No? I'll tell you. Hold on just a moment."

Logan tensed when Clarence went flailing about in the scrub, supposing the outlaw was looking for his guns, but he returned instead with a jug of whiskey. Again Clarence sat Indian fashion, pulled the cork, drank and passed the bottle to his companions.

"I was there when they buried Belle with all her jewelry right with her and a fine revolver in *her* hand, the same one Cole Younger give her years ago, before he got all crippled up at the Northfield robbery and sent to prison.

It was Cole's gun, her first, turned Belle wild. After he was jailed, she made her livin' horse and cattle rustling, selling moonshine. Cole Younger was Belle's first man. He give her her first baby and her first gun. Gossip is she never stopped loving him even if she had quite a number of gallants to bed later. I personally know of several, most all of them dead now, except me and maybe Jim French. Knowing Belle brought a man nothing but trouble. All of her men come to violent ends, sooner or later, from shooting or hanging—including Sam Starr. She married the big Cherokee by 'blanket custom,' crawling under his, and she become a full member of the Cherokee nation then. Her daughter, Pearl Younger, is madam of a bawdyhouse in Fort Smith, you know." Clarence took a deep swallow from the jug and shook all over like a wet dog. Belle Starr got herself killed, shot in the back, over two years ago now, and it hasn't yet been settled who did it.

"Nice women like you, Miss McKay, have been known to take up with outlaws, even to chase after them, so there's a chance for us, you and me. Oh, don't go giving me an uppity look. Kate King ran off with my personal he-ro, William Clarke Quantrill. Your own mama, a rancher's daughter like Kate, married up with Mark Larken so—"

"They never were wed," Lark said.

"That right? Isn't what I heard. I heard the knot was tied by Hanging Ike himself, pardon the pun, but Mark didn't want you and your mama carrying his name like a Cain's mark all the rest of your lives, the way Pearl Younger carries her father's, the way your young 'uns will, too, if you prove true to your past and—"

"If Lark ever carries an outlaw's child, it won't be yours, Cumplin, not while I draw breath!" Logan's voice was cold—colder than ice, and lethal. Clarence let his head fall back. His eyes rolled up in their sockets, his jaw dropped open and he laughed his mad laugh.

"Logan, I'm afraid you ain't going to be drawing breath much longer. She may love you because she can't help herself, but she sure doesn't want to. If she don't get you killed, I just might. When you said fist fighting and steer roping wasn't my style, you were right. Dead right is the way you are going to be one of these days. My style is back shooting, same as the man killed Belle Starr. *Her* style"—Cumplin looked at Lark, his strange eyes glowing—"is treachery. You are warned, brother," he said, not laughing. "Oh, you can sleep easy a little while yet. It won't be today or tomorrow your moment will come. She needs you to protect her from me. I need you for a job or two, a bank stickup here . . . a train robbery there, and you need money to go on running. See, I ain't champing at the bit to kill you or have my way with her. I am a patient man. I can cool my heels, wait and see which way the cat jumps. Maybe I won't have to kill you, if the little yellow-haired kitten springs my way. If not? Well . . . some day, I'll be there behind you, Walker, with a gun in my hand."

"Join the crowd." Logan grinned. He didn't see Lark go pale as she stepped in back of him, perhaps for shelter, perhaps to shield him. At that moment, watching Clarence stumble away, pausing to suck at his whiskey jug every few steps, she wasn't even sure herself.

"Oh, I almost forgot why I come lookin' for you two in the first place. I caught Mose and Apache Joe cheating at cards. I thought the lady might be curious to know how I treat double-crossers. Even if you ain't curious, little yellow-haired girl, you'd best come on now and see how swift justice can be done, when I'm the one doing it."

Chapter Twelve

Meanwhile, back at the JAK Bar Ranch, Charlotte and Jake were still sharing the sunsets. As dusk came down one November evening, they watched and then just listened to a wagon that proceeded up the long rutted trail toward them.

"I do so hope it's Lark come looking for me—at last," Charlotte said, peering into the twilight. "And I do so regret I didn't let you mount a search party right off, Jacob. Now the Ringlings have done performing in Fort Smith, and still she isn't here. I just *know* something terrible must have happened."

"Now, Charlie, remember all the calming things you told me about Lark when I was alarmed about her— how brave and clever and resourceful she is. That she brings out a . . . a sense of valor, you said, even in the roughest roustabout, what with her glow of innocence and her face like an angel's."

"That was before I saw that drawing of Clarence Cumplin on a wanted poster. I don't believe I ever have looked into such mean, cold, just plain *crazy* eyes."

Jake couldn't disagree and cast about in his thoughts for an encouraging word. He rested a hand on her shoulder. "Come on, Charlotte, they probably haven't even run into old Clarence, and supposing they did? You said Lark has an imagination lively as Sheherazade's and knows enough circus lore and travelling tales to talk on longer than a thousand and one nights, which was how many the Persian princess talked, long enough to save *her* life. Why, according to what you said, Lark could charm the rattles right off a snake. And if she can do that, there's not a man anywhere, not saint or outlaw, not even Crazy Clarence Cumplin, she won't have bewitched and eating out of her little hand."

"I might have . . . exaggerated a little, Jake. You know how mothers can be, bragging on their babies." Charlotte went to the edge of the porch and leaned against a post, peering into the dark anxiously. When the slow, noisy vehicle finally pulled into the circle of light cast by the oil lamps of the house, she and Jake saw silhouetted against the early risen moon an overloaded, old box wagon spouting mops and brooms like sparse hairs on a balding head, and hung with tin ware—pails, pots and pans—that had set the night ajangle. Between the shafts, in ragged harness, was an incongruously regal, glossy, well-fed dappled mare who appeared to think very well of herself, tossing her head and pawing the ground as though she'd just arrived pulling a royal chariot instead of a jouncing carryall. Behind her, on the wagon's leather bench, which was cracked and sprouting tufts of cotton batting and horsehair, sat a tall, moon-faced, balding man, notable at that moment for his unique sartorial style.

His galluses held up pin-striped trousers which had seen better days, perhaps behind the counter of a bank or dry goods emporium, Charlotte speculated. The driver, who wore nothing else except a pair of beaded, fringed and sueded leather moccasins on conspicuously large feet, managed even so to project a combination of dignity and jollity as his conveyance came to a clinking, clanking, glittering halt, plates of glass strapped to its sides reflecting moon and lamp light.

"I would tip me hat to you, madam, if I had one and the same, but as you can see, I have not," the man said in a sonorous deep voice and simulated Irish brogue. "I traded me derby hat, shirt, collar, boots and all, even a dear little Tamworth suckling piglet I was bringing as Mr. Chamberlain here as a gift, to an Indian maiden — for this." The man looped the reins around the brake handle and climbed down from the wagon, unfolding the long fingers of one bony hand to display a ring resting on a calloused palm, a wide silver hoop worked with scrolling and inset with turquoise and onyx. "For me bride!" he reported. "Evening, ah . . . Miz McKay, I presume . . . and top o' the twilight to you, Jake. I've come looking for Logan Walker."

"You and every lawman and bounty hunter in the territories, Dario," Jake explained, formally presenting Dario Heyward to Charlotte McKay.

"Yeah, but I'm the man's friend. You can tell me where he is," Dario said when the formalities were done with.

"Can't. Wouldn't if I could, what with the size of the bounty on him, dead or alive, enough money to tempt an archangel. We were hoping you might be bringing *us* news of his whereabouts. Miz McKay's girl left Fort Smith with the boy and—"

"I know." Dario nodded. "I heard. I was on my way to look for them, Logan and your daughter, but I thought

123

I'd best see if they had already come in from the range, if they were hiding . . . uh, residing here at the JAK Bar. I sent Sundance out to Logan day after the hangings that wasn't. That horse is better'n a bloodhound when it comes to tracking Logan. The stallion was carrying plenty of blankets and provisions, and the fall's been kind; but now the wind is starting to blow cold on the trail of the buffalo. I expected them to have shown up at my cabin before this but—oh, say now, Miz McKay, don't go looking so sad and worried. Ma'am, he'll take as good care of Lark as you would. I'd trust Logan Walker with my own life."

"Ah, but would you trust him with your daughter?" Charlotte asked, trying to make light of the matter.

"No harm will ever come to her through Logan Walker. I guarantee it won't. Logan is a fine horseman with an eye for terrain, a good shot and—"

"And Clarence Cumplin is cross-grained and mean and a homicidal maniac when intoxicated. I know all about it."

"Have a donut, Dario? Charlotte's been baking up a storm because she lost a bet. Her old dad stopped by and spoke to her—in a manner of speaking."

"Jake, really!" Charlotte wailed, clenching her fists. "Sometimes I think you were right. On occasion you *are* about as smart as a box of rocks, telling every stray that wanders in here about the bounty besides embarrassing me so in front of strangers, bringing up my father.

"Please understand, Mr. Heyward, I lost the bet on a technicality. My father didn't greet me so much as issue a proclamation. He wanted his granddaughter. *He* put the price on Logan Walker's head, and it'll get the boy killed yet." Charlotte bit her lower lip.

Jake, looking chagrined, belatedly tried to change the subject. "Say, Dario, I didn't know you were getting yoked any time soon. When's the wedding? More important, who's the lucky lady?" The rancher took the marriage band and held it to the light.

"I have the ring, but I've not found *her* yet—my bride. I told the pretty Cherokee lady I'd be back to ask for her hand, in about six moons, give or take a few, when I come by this way again, if I didn't have me a wife by then, nor she a buck. That might be soon as March under the Crow Moon, or not until June under the Strawberry Moon or never if—How about you, Aida?" Dario asked Jake's housekeeper, who had come gliding soundlessly out onto the porch, appearing rather than making an entrance. "Want to marry me right now under this Frosty Moon?"

The big-boned and tall, cozy-bodied woman put some men, Dario among them, in mind of an agreeable she-bear. Her skin was the pleasing tawny color of nutmeg and honey. Her square face was framed by a bowl of short, straight, thick black hair. Aida was mostly Indian. She was also some part oriental, some white, some black, and a touch Mexican, too, called in that part of the world, "a breed." Her soft-spoken and brief declarations might have made her seem either dull or dreadfully shy on first acquaintance if her reserve had not been offset by flickering black eyes that showed both curiosity and intelligence. Aida had come out onto the ranch house porch with a small bashful child clinging to her leg, hiding in her voluminous skirts.

"Oh," she said on seeing Heyward. "Joachim and me thought it was the peddler. We know it is too soon for his visit, but still, we had a hope. We like to hear his wagon rattle. He brings news and objects. We like to see the peddler in his dusty, old, black stovepipe hat and coat. We even like his pinched, pointed face, like a vole. It is only just you we see this time, Dario Hayward, and your grin like a Hopi kachina mask and your teeth like a mule," she said, not without a suggestion of humor that would have escaped the notice of a stranger. It wasn't lost on Dario, who slapped his thigh.

"Ain't she the zany one tonight, though?" He guffawed, teasing. "Keeps a feller in stitches, she does!"

"Thank you for your marriage offer," Aida added. "But I would not have a man from the city where Hell's Kitchen is. I have got my own kitchen."

"The devil does not dine in New York, contrary to what you may have been told. I am *not* sent by him to ask you to sup at his table and do his deals. I no longer call that city home myself, not any more, so the woman I take to wife will not be taken there. Aida! Don't rush off. Wait, please! Just look at what I have here. I really *am* a peddler now, since I took this rig in trade for my big view camera and all its lenses. All I kept was Mr. Eastman's new invention, the little box camera he calls a Kodak. It uses special coated paper, so I got rid of most of my glass plates; but I kept back a few for you, Aida, to put where you've got the oilskin stretched over your windows. I've other things, too."

Dario strode to his wagon and began to pluck out his wares: bolts of fabric that shimmered when he brought them into lantern light, cards of pins and needles, spools of thread and rolls of ribbon, sterling button hooks, and gilt posy holders. There were even books, though only two, both copies of *Bracebridge Hall*, by Washington Irving, but it was the worn volumes that drew Aida toward Dario's wagon. An automaton toy brought the child out into the open, a beautiful boy of three or so with sleek hair not as dark as his mother's and eyes as bright a baby possum's.

"Watch, Joachim, watch!" Dario said, beaming, showing big tobacco-stained teeth in a full-lipped cavernous mouth. He whispered the last word—watch!— investing it with a wonderful enchantment as he wound up the mechanical toy. A small figure in high boots, buckskins, wide-brimmed hat and red cravat, it blinked its eyes each time it brought its hand to lips which parted to puff on a big cigar. "This Buffalo Bill mannequin *was* made in France." Dario sighed with pleasure, offering the best explanation he could think of for the existence of such a marvel. He, like the child, was in total bliss when the Wild West hero became wreathed in a ring of smoke.

"That toy's a fine, ingenious piece of work, and so is *this*. What will you take for them both?" Jake asked, holding up the ring.

"Neither is for sale. I'm gifting Joachim with Buffalo Bill. The ring . . . well, I must keep it—just in case." Dario extended his spider-fingered hand, palm up.

"You'll never make a fortune or even much of a success as a merchant, friend, if you won't cut a deal and sell your wares." The rancher laughed agreeably, though he did not hand back the silver band. "Tell me, Dario, when was it exactly you became a peddler? I hadn't noticed you'd taken up a new line of work."

"I've changed my face and my trade so often no one knows who I am now, least of all me. I have been a farrier, a saddler, a wagoner, a horse trader, a bell maker, a school teacher and a blacksmith, to mention just a few of my pursuits. That's for Miz McKay's information."

"You're a variously talented man, Mr. Heyward. What are you, really? Answer quick now, don't stop to think. That way I know you'll speak the truth," Charlotte pleasantly challenged.

"I'm a bell founder really, because I love bells, ma'am. Bells are nature's gift to us all — seeds rattling within gourds inspired the first man-made bells! Bells touch gods and advise mere mortals. They bring harmony to the world, turn foes to friends, inform all, near and far, of births and deaths and nuptials as they measure away moments and days, and centuries." Tipping his long head to one side, Heyward squinted at Charlotte through the dusky dark. "I've taken to peddling and taxidermy to support my addiction to those divine devices which peal and ring and toll and reverberate."

"And scream and jangle and knell. You've passed some time in the company of poets. Have you been reading Mr. Poe on the subject of bells?" Charlotte asked with surprise. Dario nodded. "So, you are a musician and a craftsman. Now, why have you turned your hand and heart to . . . things inert and dead, Mr. Heyward? I don't understand, nor do I understand what lured you from New York all the way to Fort Smith and beyond where there isn't much use for your product, except perhaps for dinner bells at the isolated ranch or two," she said. Puzzled by the man and intrigued by his exuberance, Charlotte hadn't lost sight of the fact that Jake still held the silver wedding ring.

"I left the city with the intention of strolling clear across this land. On my way, I planned to strew America with bells, like Johnny Appleseed is supposed to have done with seeds and fruit trees. I started out with a pack on my back filled to bursting with the little bells I had taken months and used all of my minuscule savings to make. I intended, and do still, to teach my euphonious art and craft to others wherever I go. Now, as I walked across this country of ours, my best company was often — birds.

"First, I decided to photograph as many varieties as I saw. I purchased a large camera, and while photographing, I couldn't help but listen to my subjects singing in bell-like tones, Miz McKay. One thing led to another and I began transcribing birdsongs, heaven's music. I hope to get down on paper in written notes the trills of all the birds I hear. Instrumentalists and vocalists will be able to recreate truly heavenly harmonies when I've done my work.

"In the process, I began to wonder if, one day perhaps, we would learn not only why but how birds sing. In that regard, I wrote to the Museum of Comparative Zoology at Harvard. Biologists have a good idea of why *and* how birds sing but not of where and by which birds it is done when. I was asked, as long as I was making this cross-country jaunt and writing music, to preserve as many actual bird specimens as I could of lesser known varieties of our feathered friends, making note of the exact location of their capture. Thus, my latest expertise, taxidermy, which enables me to pick up the occasional dollar and give a sort of temporary immortality — an oxymoron, that — to the Creator's beauty and wit by mounting and stuffing trophies for sportsmen, as long as I've the skill and tools anyway."

"Oh, I see," Charlotte managed to say, feeling breathless just listening to the man, before Heyward was off and running at the mouth again.

"Shooting these days has more to do with sport than food, and I suppose if a man's come from the other side of the country, or the globe, to shoot our game, he must have something to show for himself back home. I'll stuff anything anyone's of a mind to take home to anywhere with him."

"So, you've given up strolling and acquired a horse and wagon for all your gear, is that it, Mr. Heyward?" Charlotte asked as she pulled a fringed cashmere wrap closer about her shoulders.

Earlier, Jake had handed it to her, wrapped in yellowed, crinkly tissue paper, saying softly, "You might's well get the comfort of it, with the chill season almost on us." When she'd undone the parcel and gasped with delight, ready to fervently thank him for the gift, she was silenced by the reverence of his expression. Jake's hard hands caressed the cashmere lovingly before he draped it over her shoulders.

"It's Mrs. Chamberlain's," Charlotte hastily explained to Dario, aware of his questioning look. All the while she felt Aida's black eyes fixed on her.

"I guessed that," he answered thoughtfully, glancing from one woman to the other and then at Jake. "Few other women out here could have afforded such a costly luxury."

"I'm borrowing it," Charlotte said, letting the wrap slip to the chair at her side. In flickering lamp light her blond hair, coiled demurely at her nape, highlighted the elegance of her profile. Her fine, pale hands, Dario noticed, set now at her tiny waist were the finest hands at the tiniest waist he could ever recall seeing.

It was just then, struck by Charlotte's understated,

refined beauty, that Dario understood what Jake was up to. The rancher had found a woman, after all his years alone, who belonged exactly where she was at that moment, on the threshold of the finest, most hospitable ranch house in the territories. Dario realized, too, why his friend was so determined to buy the silver ring. He intended to place it on the hand of this lovely and romantic woman, still young enough to fall in love but no so young she didn't know what love was really all about.

"Do go on, Mr. Heyward," she said gently. "You were saying?"

"Yes, walking became impossible. So you see me with this wretched rig, the latest of many, and a sorry outfit it is, if ever there was one, with the exception of that self-important mare. *She* thinks she belongs on Broadway performing with the Floradora Girls at the Casino Theatre, don't you, Divine?"

"*Really,* Mr. Heyward! Divine?" Charlotte laughed, moving toward the horse for a closer look.

"Yes, really. She's named after the Divine One, Sarah Bernhardt, the lady with a voice like 'a golden bell.' It was Logan who acquired Divine for me and at a good price for such a sassy mare with *fine* strong haunches and sweet flirting ways."

"She is quite the lovely thing, Mr. Heyward. Good bright eyes," Charlotte said. She was at the mare's head, petting the velvet nose.

"Divine can be a mite snappish, so you'd best move away from her, and the wagon, with all its odds and ends," Dario cautioned. "Brrr. Getting too chill out here for me and the ladies, Jake. Listen, get Miz McKay away from that cart and let's all go inside. Have you some clothes I might make loan of?"

"The shirt off my back and a hundred dollars are yours—in exchange for the ring," Jake persisted, reaching up to pass an arm about the taller man's bony shoulders, guiding him to the door as Dario looked back toward Charlotte, Divine and the wagon.

Inside the house, a fire was roaring in a stone fireplace big enough to barbecue a steer.

"Forget the ring and listen. I must talk to you, Jake," Dario insisted, but Jake didn't listen.

"Warm up. Think over the offer while I go get us a bottle," he said genially, following Aida and the child in the direction of the kitchen.

It was then that Charlotte's scream tore the stillness of the moonlit prairie night.

"Damn you, Jake Chamberlain!" Dario roared. "I asked you to listen to me. I *told* you to get her away from the wagon and indoors before she saw."

"Damn you, too! Why the hell didn't you speak straight? Before she saw . . . *what*, you gabby bastard?" Jake hollered as they both bolted toward the door.

"Saw what I got in the back of that wagon! Two dead bodies, and they sure ain't birds. It's humans I found, swinging in the breeze. It was a convention of buzzards over 'em that drew my notice to the deceased. When I cut 'em down out of the tree they were hanging in, I saw they were each holding a pretty little bunch of wild flowers stuck in their bound hands behind them. The real odd thing is, those flowers are tied with strips of pretty, pure-white chiffon."

Chapter Thirteen

Two men swinging from the limb of the only tree for miles was not a pretty sight. One was not yet quite dead when Lark and Logan followed Clarence into the firelit circle of outlaws gathered around them.

"Is that Mose Blakely up there, still kickin'? He wouldn't be if we'd a done this thing right, like George Maledon. Cut Mose down, one of you inebriates." Clarence giggled, but Logan was already sprinting over to do so. "A man who clings that hard to life deserves another chance. But you gotta give back my money, Mose, you hear me?" Clarence asked as two outlaw brothers, Bobby and Billy Midgette, moved quickly to the aid of Logan and the dangling man.

Moses Blakely, half hanged, his head lolling to one side, his face blue on its way to turning black and his tongue protruding, responded to Cumplin's question with a small gurgling sound as Logan grasped him about the knees and lifted, to take the weight off his throat. Bobby Midgette had jumped on a horse and ridden fast forward, the knife in his hand severing several strands of rope at his first pass, the job completed on a second ride-by. Mose plummeted. Caught by Logan and Billy, he was stretched out on the ground, where he lay gasping, more dead than alive, as the noose was removed from around his neck.

"Save it. Don't try to thank me — now," Logan whispered, leaning over Mose.

"Where's my money? I want it," Clarence whined, stamping his foot. "And I want someone else decorating that tree. It ain't symmetrical, just one feller strung up like that." He took a long swallow from his jug, then tossed it away. In the tense silence, everyone listened to crockery shatter against a rock out of sight in the dark. In the distance a coyote howled as Clarence, a pistol now in each unsteady hand, looked from one face to the next. "What? Ain't none of you volunteering to swing with Apache Joe and balance things up? Bobby Boy . . ." he said, grinning at the younger Midgette as the older brother, Billy, made a move for his gun. Logan outdrew him, took aim, but didn't fire. He winked.

"That's something else I like about you, Logan Walker," Clarence said, shaking his head as if with wondrous admiration. "You ain't just plenty smart with book learning, you are *shrewd*. You know I am not about to dispense with a man fast on the draw as you, not *before* the two big jobs I got planned. Outdrawing Billy Midgette, you reminded me, in case I might of forgot, just how good your reflexes are. And you saved me from killing Big Bill and Bobby Boy, who ain't no slouches neither, when it comes to guns and explosives, generally raisin' hell and such. They're good men to have on a business trip, both of them. Billy, you relax now, hear? I was only going to ask your little brother, Bobby Boy, to get us more booze, bottled dynamite, was all I was going to ask him." Clarence grinned, and his gun went off. Firing with his left hand, he shot a man, known only by his surname, Ruffin, right through the heart.

"Cumplin, you jug-bit jackass! Now look what you gone and done!" Lark shouted spontaneously when Ruffin pitched forward and fell at her feet. Then a frost of fear settled over her as Logan and Clarence, both with cocked guns in their hands, slowly swivelled to face each other.

Finding the tension more than she could stand, Lark hurled herself forward, deftly drawing her own little gun. She stood in front of Logan and spread her arms wide. "If you try and shoot him, you'll have to shoot me first, Clarence Cumplin," she said, clenching her eyes shut. Clarence's wild laugh filled the night.

"Will you say you're sorry?" he asked her. Peeking at him with one eye, Lark nodded vehemently. "I *am* going to take the girl away from you, Logan, if it's the last thing I do. That doll is pretty as a picture . . . fresh as a daisy, and she's going be *my* plaything, you wait and see. Now, Lark, did you call me a jug-bit jackass 'cause my gun went off and accidentally killed my man Ruffin?"

She nodded again, eyes wide. All atremble, she curved back against Logan like a wilting flower. He holstered one gun, kept the other pointed at Cumplin and brought an arm about her waist.

"Well, you had no call to call me any such thing," Clarence went on. "I *meant* to shoot him. Now Logan can't say I ain't worth a fleabite as a shooter just because I'm a mite pie-eyed and raddled. Logan, you take her on back to your own little camp and patch up your spat you was telling me of and smooth her ruffled feathers some, while the boys hang up Ruffin opposite Apache Joe. Hey, Logan, weren't they right up on the Fort Smith gallows next to you—Ruffin and Joe? I'm doing George Maledon's job for him, it seems, and if you were to be found dancing on air along with those two, I might just collect a reward, if there is one, or at least the two dollars a piece a deputy marshall gets from the U.S. government for each of us rapscallions he brings in. 'Course, the deputy, he also gets six cents a mile travel expense and . . ." Clarence, abruptly sitting, crossed his legs and smiled. "Why do you suppose those deputies bother? It just ain't worth it to me to try and collect right now, so that makes you the last survivor of the Fort Smith Nine. All the others supposed to die that day have, one way or another. I think you are living on borrowed time, brother Logan, I really do! Make the most of it.

"Now, one of you gents get me a full jug and then leave me in peace, hear? Oh, uh, Lark? If you want to uh, say a few words over . . . well, *under* these departed sinners, maybe decorate 'em with a flower or two, that'll be okay, hear? Night, night you all."

"Don't be scared. It's done with now. It's all right," Logan said softly as he followed Lark along the narrow track to their own campsite. In silence, he had helped her gather wild flowers which she tied with the last two strips of her chiffon dress.

"I am not scared," she whispered back.

"But . . . you're shaking. I can feel it."

"I am trembling with fury," Lark hissed. "Why didn't you just kill that terrible man Cumplin when you had the chance? You had the drop on him. Let me tell you, first chance *I* get, I'll kill him, sure as shootin'."

136

"No. Don't," Logan said as his hand on her shoulder turned her to face him. "Don't take his life if you value mine. You seem to."

"I do," she answered, and the look she offered him was so beautiful, his heart stumbled. She stepped into his open arms. He kissed her, softly, slowly drawing her body against his. "I missed you so," she said, rediscovering the expanse of his wide shoulders and the long muscles of his arms. She could reach just far enough to enfold her own arms about the strength and substance of him; he fit perfectly within the circle of her embrace. Her hands traced the channel of his spine as she arched to press her supple breasts to his chest, muscle-ridged, hard, the heart within it beating as hers did, wildly.

"I'm completely in love with you," Logan said.

"You've been fighting it," she answered, after a time, when they'd stopped kissing just long enough to look at each other. "I won't marry you, you know."

"You might. Do you love me? Can you say it?"

"Yes," she said, her eyes moonstruck, her heart in them.

"Say it. I want to hear you."

"Logan Walker, I do love you."

"All right, then." He smiled. It was like sunrise. His eyes danced with golden light. "I *know* you want me. I don't have to ask."

"But I'd like to say so. I am paining for you something fierce." They moved apart a little, delaying fulfillment, deferring relief, wanting to need each other a little longer, to extend the ache of shared yearning so well-honed and sharp now it had become an opulent pleasure in itself—once the promise had been given that soon, here and now, tonight they would give each other all—whatever the future held.

When, half undressed, they eventually got to their campfire, it was down to embers, miniature caves of glowing heat and light in the vastness of the high plains night. Logan soon had flames leaping at the sky, turning tangible twigs, branches, and logs to incorporeal warmth and luster that touched Lark's skin as his hands soon did, and his devouring mouth. And, at the same time, her finger tips and lips and tongue were on his body, in it, everywhere, neither of them still, not one or the other lying back to accept offerings, to passively savor received ecstasy. Both gave and demanded. There was no delaying any more. The bearskin was a dark and wooly soft bed beneath them, stars all the blanket they needed. On his knees, straddling the slenderness of Lark's pale, golden-fleeced open body, Logan invaded it in a moment that brought low, primal love cries from both. His muscles tinted, lit and shadowed by firelight, worked and contracted, swelled and surged with such power and beauty Lark never closed her eyes, or even blinked. Not the first time—or the second. Somewhere in the space and time before dawn, Lark did let herself just feel, not see, but Logan never could do that. He never did during those hours, and never would, willingly stop looking at Lark.

It was a long and lovely night. When dawn paled their still-leaping fire, they were in each other's arms, warm beneath the bearskin, ready to greet the day and face the world, together.

"This is the thing. I'm almost a hundred percent sure Clarence killed Rachel. I want him to confess. I have to hear him say it." Logan had pulled on his boots and, doing up his belt buckle, scanned the horizon. When he put his handsome face into a north wind that flattened back his hair, he reminded Lark, who couldn't stop watching him, of a brindle wolf she'd seen once, a wild beautiful thing with amber eyes and a trace of shepherd or border collie in him, a creature tame enough to touch—but not to keep. Logan took a gulp of arctic air, and his smile gleamed, his teeth blue-white as ice, amber-flecked eyes aflame with anticipation. "The first snow's on the way. Bundle up, sugar. I've got a sheepskin duster for you. It's kept me safe at fifty below, out on the range moving cows dumb enough to stand still, looking winter in the eye, while they froze to death." He rolled back the bearskin, extended his hand to Lark, pulled her to her feet and enfolded her rosy-warm, naked, arrow-slim body in his arms.

"Maybe I can . . . well, tempt Cumplin's confession out of him. What will you do then, kill him?" she asked.

"I want to do more to avenge Miss Blue than shoot her murderer and throw a few spadesful of dirt over his miserable bones. Rachel . . . she was a fragile, gentle soul who was trying to bring a taste of kindness and poetry to this half-civilized place. In a way, she was trying to do the same as Hanging Ike, only her methods were different. She used a book, not a rope. What I want to do for her memory is take Cumplin in to face the town and a jury of its citizens . . . the hangman . . . and himself. You stay out of it. I am not going to use you as bait and lure for a madman. As he likes to say himself, he's not as dumb as he looks."

"Let me help you." Now mostly dressed, Lark was brushing her shining yellow hair with a curry comb she'd appropriated from Sundance. "If you don't let me help, I won't . . ."

"You won't . . . what?" Logan asked, turning up his fleece collar and pulling his hat low. There was a threat in his look, until he grinned. "Honey, after last night, I *know* there's nothing I want you won't give me. Right?" he asked with his confidential wink and little shrug that made him adorable, like a big puppy or a yearling colt. Lark laughed with delight.

"You think you're pretty cute, don't you, Walker? Well—y'are. What the devil is your plan?"

He turned up her collar, kissed her nose, took her one ungloved hand—they were sharing a single pair—and thrust it into his pocket. He started walking but not talking.

"If you won't tell me *how* we're going to get out of this, I might get to thinkin' you still don't really trust me, Logan Walker. Would I be right? Well?"

He looked at her face and swallowed hard, and she saw a fleeting instant of doubt in his eyes.

"Oh, Logan, it's asking a lot, I know, after what I did. Won't you ever let me live that down? Must I regret one moment of rash, jealous anger all the rest of my life? I was only hoping to make you do what you want Clarence to—face the truth, and the law. The difference is, you are an innocent man and I *knew* that. Right now, you need me, and I sure need you. If you don't trust me, we might neither of us have much of a life left." Her eyes were big and round and limpid, pearly gray. Logan could see right into her heart.

"I've been alone for so long, it's hard for me to share my secrets and bare my soul, but . . . I'm going to take another chance on you, sweetness, because . . . someday, I expect you'll take a bigger one on me."

Lark's happy laugh then was like the music of little silver bells.

Logan couldn't help but kiss her before he said, "This is what I have in mind. Some of the men are with Clarence now because they hope for better things in days to come — spreads of their own, farms, livery stables, wives, children. Money can help a man get those things, and Clarence is making some of them rich. He pulls off successful robberies, finds full safes, makes big hauls, and it's rare anyone ever gets caught or hurt. For doing trains, he follows the Jesse James plan. It's nearly perfect. When a California-bound train pulls into a little border town, a couple of his men mount the cabin and keep the engineer and fireman under the gun. Two others work back through the passenger cars collecting valuables until they come to the express car, where the real money is. They tumble the safe out onto the ground, blow it and run with their loot.

"Sometimes Clarence shoots the telegraph operator, just to give the gang breathing room getting away, or so *he* says. Some of the men who never were killers, just robbers, don't like that much, because when it comes to Ike Parker, they know he'll hang them all, no matter who it was pulled the trigger.

"Besides that, a lot of the boys are resentful of Cumplin's bragging or afraid of his temper and his gun. Mose Blakely and the Midgette brothers are already on our side, ready to break with Clarence — or kill him. My plan is to create a gang of our own within the Cumplin gang, whittle away at Clarence's true devotees, kill the real bad operators if we must, and win all the others to our side, get them to cooperate in taking him in to clear my name. There might even be one or two willing to take the witness stand if a deal can be cut with Judge Parker. Lark honey, will you help me?"

"Fool! Must you ask?" She pulled him to a stop in the middle of the track they'd worn between their hideaway and the main camp, where they were headed for a breakfast of coffee and grits, all the gang had left in the way of sustenance, besides whiskey. She stretched up on her toes and kissed him on the chin, already thinking how she could help manipulate Logan's plot, clear him and hasten the downfall of Clarence so that she could get on with her own business — becoming a center ring star with the best circus in the world. Her plans hadn't changed, though now there was the thought of including Logan in them — *if* he'd go along.

"Morning, and thank you, Mr. Midgette." Lark smiled over the rim of the tin mug of coffee the man handed her. "You the one Clarence calls 'Big Bill'?"

"Shucks, yeah, that's me, ma'am," he responded, kicking up some dust with his boot toe. "I don't rightly know why. Me and my brother Bobby are about the same size, and neither one of us is real tall."

"You are not tiny, either, like General Tom Thumb. His real name was Charlie Stratton. It was Phineas Taylor Barnum called him Tom and said he was a dwarf, but he was really a true midget."

"What's that mean?" Mose croaked, noisily slurping up grits. "Sorry, still can't talk good . . . after last night."

"No loss there," Clarence snarled, looking grayfaced. His head hurt from drinking so much the night before, and the whites of his eyes were red-streaked.

"They say fine-powdered charcoal in a glass of water is good for headache, Clarence."

Clarence didn't answer Lark. He just got grayer.

"Well, anyway, a dwarf has got a regular-size upper body with very little legs. A midget is of a piece, a miniature man, all in scale," she continued.

"Did you ever see him, this little man?" Eldon Link, one of the less pleasant desperados, asked.

"I never saw Tom Thumb. Mama did, in New York at Barnum's Museum. When he was five years old, he only weighed fifteen pounds and was twenty five inches tall. His teeny feet were just three inches long! Little Charlie was one of Barnum's real wonders, like the Siamese Twins and Anna Swan, the Nova Scotia Giantess, who was seven feet and eleven inches tall and weighed four hundred and thirteen pounds. Some of Barnum's other attractions were pure hokum, the Feejee Mermaid and such. Is there more coffee?"

"If you can call it that. Looks like sludge more'n coffee," Link muttered. "Uh, tell us more about Tom Thumb."

"Barnum named Stratton for one of King Arthur's knights, little Sir Tom Thumb. Legend has it he lived in a tiny golden palace and rode in a coach pulled by six white mice. Barnum's Tom had matched ponies for his little coach, and small boys in blue livery up top. He toured the world with Phineas T. and became rich and famous, as I hope to do when I join Mr. Ringling's circus. But I won't do what Tom Thumb did. He squandered his money. When he died at forty-three, he was broke as he started out. But he had lived grand! He had yachts and race horses, and a wife just his size, Mercy

Lavinia Warren Bump. He bought tons of jewels for her. They were married at Grace Church in New York City and got a gift of a set of fire screens from President Lincoln."

"What was *she* like, this Mrs. Thumb?" Some of the men were enthralled by the possibilities, some made ill at ease.

"She was the same height as her husband, with a really pretty round face and a nice smile. Another circus midget, Captain Nutt, fell in love with her, too, but she chose Tom Thumb," Lark explained. "Barnum put it about that the little couple had had a baby who didn't live long."

"I think I've seen a picture of Mrs. Thumb and the baby," Logan mused. "Midgets have normal-size children, I understand."

"They do, it's so, but the baby in the picture you saw was borrowed, taken from out of the audience for the photo. Barnum sold a lot of copies of that picture for twenty-five cents each. He didn't miss a trick," Lark said, slowly ingratiating herself within the gang.

Chapter Fourteen

The gray November day had darkened early. By three o'clock, the driven rain which had been lashing the countryside since morning turned to swirling snow. It muffled the saddle creakings, jingles, hoofbeats and the occasional sneezes of a large band of riders, the Clarence Cumplin Gang, on its way to work. They were hunched in their saddles to conserve body heat in the brutal cold. It didn't help much. They were facing a knifing north wind, heading across the Oklahoma border toward the Kansas town of Caldwell, a small, prosperous homesteading community snuggled close against the now-fallow earth under a big prairie winter sky.

"They'll be able to follow us out of there too easy, Clarence. We'll be leaving hoofprints in the snow," Bobby Midgette complained, not for the first time. There was a general grumble of agreement from other riders close enough to hear.

"Midgette, this bit of weather is blowing itself up into a blizzard. It's going to keep on snowing long after we are *gone* from this burg. Our tracks will fill in before the first farmer gets his nightcap off. By then, the surface of the terrain behind us will be perfect as a new-risen loaf of bread, you know, before it's even baked and crusty, just when it's all puffed up and white. If the wind keeps on, the snow'll drift, and then the land will look like a new bread, baked in a tilted oven, kind of higher to one end of the pan than the other, but still smooth on the surface and crusty, like ice will shell the snow. You all know what I'm talkin' about?" There was another grumble and a couple of sneezes.

"How we going to take these farmers and bankers by surprise if you keep sneezing, Billy?" Clarence asked. "Your brother never sneezes once, always two . . . three times running, Bobby Boy. I can't take it, sneezing."

The brothers were both wiry, medium tall, dark-haired and dark-eyed. One was handsome, the other wasn't. Though their features were much alike, they were differently arranged. It was the good-looking one, Billy, who always got the grippe at the start of winter.

"He might of got the good looks, but I got the strong constitution, Ma and Pa always said," Bobby answered. "He can't help it, Clarence, sniffling and sneezing."

"What about sniffling, Clarence?" Lark asked with deadpan seriousness. "Or coughing? Find sniffling and coughing easier on the nerves than sneezing?"

Clarence looked over at her and scowled with uncertainty. He suspected she might be teasing, but no one was ever so foolhardy as to make fun of *him*, Crazy Clarence Cumplin the killer.

"I find sniffling more nerve-wracking than coughing but not as bothersome as sneezing," he answered Lark with utmost solemnity, giving her the benefit of his doubt. Besides, it was too damn cold to go taking off a glove and waving a pistol about, and he really didn't want to shoot her, not yet, anyway.

Lark was mounted on Satan, riding between Clarence

and Logan. Three abreast, they were leading the gang. The dog, Max, lounged across Logan's saddle, something Sundance was used to. Lark, in particular, was so well bundled her face could not be seen at all except for her eyes, and even they, when the time came, would be further hidden, if Logan had his way, behind a black outlaw face mask narrowly slit just enough so that she'd be able to see without stumbling.

There had been a meeting. Logan had insisted on the mask. If she was going in with the gang, she had to be unrecognizable. They were all already wanted by the law. She wasn't.

"If she leads us into the bank, that will prove she's loyal to us, or to you, leastways," Cumplin had asserted. "She'll get her share of the money, don't worry."

"She is not going in, Clarence," Logan said. He had rolled a cigarette. It dangled unlit between his lips as he passed an arm about Lark's shoulders. "Not unarmed she isn't, no way, son."

"You already gave her a Derringer. Now are you asking me to put a repeating rifle into *her* hands? I won't."

"Then, she's not going in at all, Clarence," Logan repeated with a shrug.

"How about I put an unloaded rifle in her hands? Otherwise, she might could turn on us all like she did on you, brother, and holler for the law." Clarence was shaking his head and pinching up his mouth as the rest of the gang, gathered round the campfire, listened with interest. "I ain't got no one to baby-sit her, and she can't be left alone. What if she runs? She knows where all my fastnesses and hideouts are. She has got to come along with us, Logan. That's it." Clarence was picking at his teeth with a whittled stick.

"Carrying an unloaded gun is worse than having no gun. A trick like that can get a person killed. I won't have it." Logan reshaped his cigarette and jammed it back in his mouth.

"Let's take a vote," Cumplin's second in command said. Eldon Link was the gang member who most enjoyed their leader's depraved performances. Called "Skeets" because he was small and very skinny and as whiny-mean as a swamp mosquito, he did his best to replicate Clarence, who himself revered and imitated the infamous Quantrill by wearing a collection of scalps on his belt taken from the men — and women — he'd killed in the course of holdups or just for thrills.

"Take a . . . *what?*" Clarence asked. "This isn't a town meeting. No one has a vote but me. What I say is, is."

"She ain't going to help us at bank robbing, gun or no gun. She is bound to be a hindrance." Skeets spat tobacco juice into the fire. "I don't trust a woman. I don't like a woman. I never give 'em my money 'cept for one thing, lying on their back, and here this Walker is keeping this woman to himself and asking us to give her a portion of our loot. That ain't fair. I think most of you boys agree with me."

Apparently no one, with the possible exception of Clarence himself, did agree, and even Cumplin looked askance at the insult to Lark. A mutter of anger ran through the men before they went stony silent.

Logan got to his feet. His face was still; not a nerve twitched. They all knew that look, what it meant, even Skeets, but thinking Clarence would defend him, he pressed his position. "Now, if it was share and share alike, Walker. . . ." Skeets held a burning brand up to Logan's cigarette, then leaned over the fire to light his own.

The hollow thud of a log striking the back of Skeets' head surprised no one, with the exception of Link. The blow sent the outlaw pitching forward into the fire, and he screamed when his face hit the hot coals. Half dazed, half blinded, his eyelashes and brows on fire, and shrieking with pain, Skeets crawled around on his hands and knees until he found the water bucket and emptied it over his head. Then, a shovel gripped in his hands, he struggled to his feet to face Logan Walker's fury.

Logan just stood, coiled with anger, waiting for Link's head, and eyes, to clear. His own eyes were hard, flashing, the rest of his face dark.

"You didn't give your buddies here, not even Clarence, a chance with that pretty Cherokee lady, did you, Link? The one we passed a couple days ago, that you went back for?"

"Huh? what the hell you talkin' about, Walker? I . . ."

"You must recall the girl. You killed her . . . when you were done with her. I had done some trading with her myself. I bartered my silver bolo for . . . a silver finger ring." Logan's hand on Lark's shoulder tightened. She understood.

"No, Logan," she said softly so that only he could hear. "I won't wear it now, maybe never."

He ignored her words and pulled her closer before continuing his tête-à-tête with Skeets, who was rubbing his singed face with lard.

"The next day after I traded with that pretty girl, you come riding into camp with a new silver bolo round your neck. I recognized the craft of it, the artist's hand, right off. Besides the bolo, you also had a bloody new scalp on your belt. I recognized that, too. You kept her all to yourself, to play with — and to kill, before you stole her goods. I'd wager, if I shook you upside down over that fire, my pocket flask would come tumbling off you."

"Maybe I do have your flask, Walker, but one thing I ain't got no more is eye lashes 'cause of you, college boy!" Skeets shrieked and lunged forward, the shovel raised.

"Logan!!" Lark called out, going for her gun. Before she could take aim, the fight began. And ended, too. It lasted about a minute and a half from start to finish, and it left Skeets Link dead, his throat cut, ear to ear.

"You were right about Skeets, Logan," Clarence said. "A selfish man. And he'd have got pneumonia anyway, all soaked like that and in this weather. He'd have started in sneezing, and I'd of killed him anyway. You saved me the trouble.

"Tell you what, brother Logan. You and me have got to come to a compromise here about this bank robbing. What say Lark goes right with us into the bank armed while I'm using you as a shield, you standing between her and me, me with my gun sort of at your head. She does anything odd, I shoot you. How's that?"

"I say that's a deal." Logan nodded, tossing his cigarette into the fire.

At the same instant Lark said, "No! Cumplin, once a self-described back-shooter like you gets the drop on Logan, I know you'll pull your trigger. The only way to handle the situation is this; we all three go in, side by side — and come out the same way, all three of us, side by side. We take Mose, Bobby and Billy in with us as backup while the rest of the men keep things covered over to the telegraph office, the sheriff's jail, rail station and the like."

"Now you're sounding like Mark Larken's daughter!" Cumplin nodded. "And what a hell raiser he was. He never went slinking into a town quiet, like Logan wants us to. Larken used to let 'em know he was coming. He'd do a lot of whooping and corn shelling—that's shooting at the bunches of corn the feed shops hang out front, sort of as an advertisement, you know. Every vagrant hog and hen for miles'd be waiting for the easy eats your daddy provided 'em—all that free corn on the ground. He'd scare the wits out of the bankers so bad, they'd have their safes open and ready to be cleaned out. Well, those good old days are gone forever, I suppose." Cumplin's wild eyes were almost sad, his tone nostalgic, just thinking about bygone better times.

"It's a two-day ride to Caldwell." Cumplin returned to the present. "We're starting first thing, so you all turn in now. Oh, and uh, Logan? I'm taking Fred, Jim and Harry into the bank with us, too, just for some extra insurance, like. I'd take Skeets if he wasn't deceased. He was the one man I liked to have watching my back."

Logan and Lark exchanged bemused glances. The participation of Fred, Jim and Harry inside the bank would prevent them from overpowering Clarence as they'd planned. But without giving themselves away or at the very least raising suspicions, there was nothing they could say or do about it now, but play along.

Two days later, with her most remarkable features hidden—yellow hair caught up under her hat, her small curvaceous figure enveloped in the sheepskin duster—Lark was disguised enough to pass for a stripling boy, she hoped. She'd have to keep her mouth shut, though, Logan had warned, because there never had been any boy with a voice like hers, throaty and low and as sweet as maple syrup.

The Cumplin Gang rode into Caldwell at two-thirty on that snowy afternoon. Lamps were already burning in the dry goods store and the saloon, which was empty, the riders could see, except for the bartender.

"This little blizzard is keeping folks to home. Why not stop for a drink, Clarence, to warm us up a mite?" Freddy Madden asked, looking longingly at the tavern. His face, his nose in particular, was raw red with cold, and his eyes, like those of the other men, were tearing in the wind. Their lashes were frozen.

"We'll head to our favorite joy spot *after* the job's done. They'll be waiting for us with open arms in Ingalls, all the women and liquor you can stand," Clarence snapped, unholstering a pistol. The others followed suite as the outlaws, according to strategy, dropped out of the entourage two by two, at the livery, the train depot, even at the saloon. When the actual perpetrators reined up in front of the bank, their number had been reduced to nine. Lark carried a rifle and was flanked by Logan and Clarence, both with pistols at the ready, as they sauntered inside and looked about.

"Hello! Anyone here?" Clarence called to the seemingly empty room. There was a scuffling sound, as if mice were scampering in the walls. It was followed by a great flurry of papers sailing up in all directions from behind the counter of the teller's cage. Someone began cursing, after a fashion, in a squeaky tenor voice.

"Dag nab it and gall darn it all! Fiddlesticks and blast it! In your hat, Jesse, in your hat! You've gone and done it again!" The smooth, shiny curve of a bald pate appeared on a level with the counter top as the voice rose to a higher pitch. "I can't add, I can't and I never could! Blast! It won't come out right!" A green eyeshade surfaced, followed by a metal-rimmed *pince-nez* perched on a wide, short nose. "I am sorry, boy, to keep you waiting," the voice said, its eyes seeing only Lark's hat. "Be with you soon's I can." The bald head disappeared again. "Don't suppose you'd rather come back tomorrow, when the head teller's in, nine sharp?" the voice asked hopefully.

"Stop dithering about back there and stand up. Now!" Clarence commanded with extreme annoyance.

"Is that any way to address your elders, son?" the bank clerk asked Lark. He surfaced, though not in his entirety. A soft, short, middle-aged fellow, with a round red face, he could be seen in his stall only from the chest up. He wore, besides the eye shade and eye glasses, a white shirt with banded sleeves and a black bow tie at a starched, high collar that was too tight. The man's fleshy neck extruded over the top of it. His pink mouth dropped open at the sight he beheld, eight armed men and a masked boy holding a rifle. "You're robbing the bank, I take it?" he asked. He did not edge toward the alarm button or reach for a weapon. He stood patiently.

"Yup. Who's back there with you?" Logan asked. "Where's this Jesse you were talking to?"

"That's me. It's only me here, Jesse Jaynes. I always talk to myself 'round this time of day, trying to justify the numbers and close up. I never can reckon the sums right, not the first time I try. Or the second. A quill driver is supposed to be able to add, subtract and multiply, and I cain't, I cain't! I'm into the wrong line of work. I may look like a bank assistant teller; but inside, I ain't one, and I'm no hero either so don't go getting edgy. I think I may be a hog farmer at heart, honest. I'm planning on saving up enough to buy a big bellied sow and—"

"I don't want to hear your troubled life story, mister. I got one of my own. Shut up and open the damn safe." Clarence was growing more jittery by the second.

"It's open, it's open! I didn't expect any crooks would be out on such a blizzardy sort of day. Oh, Lord! Now I am really going to catch heck from my boss when he finds out."

"Who you callin' a crook?" Harry asked. "We are outlaws."

"I meant no insult, sir," the clerk answered. His eyes began to water. His fat hands shook as he carefully took off his eye shade, then his glasses, opened his mouth wide, threw back his head and made a loud yelp that was followed by a snort of the type a sounding whale might make on its way to the bottom of the sea. When Jaynes sneezed again, dabbed at his upturned pug nose and got himself set for a third paroxysm, Clarence growled low in his throat and started forward.

"Don't hurt him, Clarence, don't!" Lark pleaded as, somehow, one of her boots got tangled up with both of his. She and Cumplin sprawled on the floor, her mask askew, her hat knocked off, her flaxen hair falling about her shoulders.

"Who *is* that masked blond woman?" the bank clerk asked with awe.

"Goldilocks. Get your damn coat, Jesse. Now that you've seen her, you have to come with us," Logan said with a wink at Lark and a flash of the hard-sparkle smile, saying without words, *Good job, sugar, foiling Clarence. You can join my gang anytime.* "Didn't I say something like this would happen, that she'd be seen?" he asked Clarence as he helped Lark to her feet and brushed her off.

"So did Skeets say so," Clarence shrieked and pounded his fists on the floor in frustration.

"You—Jesse, come with us or die, your choice," Billy Midgette said, like Logan pleased with the turn of events. They'd just drafted a new recruit for the Goldilocks Group, as members of the gang within the gang had privately agreed to call themselves.

"I'm coming, I'm coming! I don't have to be asked but

twice," Jaynes assured the perplexed little crowd. "Uh, you fellers want this money or don't you?" he asked, pitching a bag over the counter at the outlaws. Harry had to swiftly holster his weapons to catch it.

"Living with a name like mine . . . ugh—" Jesse hurled another bag, this one to the equally quick-responding Bobby Midgette—"Jesse . . . ugh . . . *Jaynes* . . . ugh . . ."

It was Billy's turn to catch, then Logan's.

". . . has not been easy. My mother said, 'Son, perhaps if you work *in* the bank . . .' ugh—" Fred caught the next flying bag—" 'people won't always be funning you about robbing it.' But they never let up joshing me, so now, maybe with you *real* outlaws, I'll . . . ugh, find my true vocation." Ugh . . . Ugh . . . Ugh. The last three money bags came flying in quick succession, one each to Lark, Clarence and Jim. The last landed on the floor and broke open, spilling buffalo nickels all over the bank. Clarence banged his head against the wall.

"I sure as hell hope there's something besides five-cent pieces in those other bags, Jess. For your own sake, I sure hope it's gold," Clarence said in a doubting voice. "Lord, Logan, I don't know what this gang's turning into. Now we've got a damn girl who can't keep her hat on, a bank clerk can't add and nine bags of buffalo nickels, most likely. What the devil's next?"

"This," Mose Blakely croaked. He had pulled a wanted poster from the wall. In large yellow letters it read:

REWARD
$1000 for desperado and condemned killer,
Logan Walker, dead or alive.
BONUS!!!!! $500 for the safe return of
LARK MCKAY — Kidnapped

Last seen Fort Smith, being forcibly taken off. Generous remuneration for any information. Contact **Rufus McKay, Fort Smith** or your local sheriff, deputy or US Marshal

"Don't worry, Logan. That's a poor likeness of you." Clarence smiled, taking the poster from Mose and folding it up very small, so small it vanished into the palm of his hand. He looked from Lark to Logan. They were staring at each other, speechless.

Chapter Fifteen

With Ivan and Alex, her pair of wolf hounds, at her side, and the fox terrier, Ralph, rushing ahead, Charlotte hesitated in the double-wide doorway of the JAK Bar's fire-lit main room. She looked about with subdued happiness. Each time she entered the parlor, it became more pleasing to her. The panelled walls, richly polished, were decorated with the antlers of pronghorn antelope, deer and buffalo skulls. There was a moose head mounted above the fireplace, several black bear skins lying in front of it. The wide-planked floor was also strewn with Turkey carpets from Persia and rugs woven by Plains Indians, mostly of the Sioux tribe, showing an eight-pointed morning star, the sacred symbol of hope. The rug colors were earth tones, yellows and shades of red from cinnamon to cherry. The same were used in the Indian blankets draped over leather settees that were piled with butter-soft deer-hide pillows. Every time Charlotte stepped into the room, she looked back over her shoulder at the dented old steel and hickory wheel which hung above the door frame.

"It was saved from the wagon that brought Jake's first wife—I mean, first brought Jake's wife—home here, to the JAK Bar. In those days, all they had was a one-room cabin," Dario Heyward informed Charlotte.

"Yes, so I've already heard. That's all they needed. One room is all anyone needs, if there's love. That's all Mark Larken and I had, the short time we were together. One room. Love was plentiful. Nothing else was. I polished the floor with bacon grease, and it did *shine!* I didn't see you there, Dario," Charlotte smiled, starting toward him.

Ten days after he'd arrived, Dario Heyward was still at the JAK Bar and showing no signs of imminent departure. Jake, who became aware of his feelings for Charlotte only a minute or two before Dario did himself, was being nobly tolerant, even generous, to an increasingly irksome rival for her attention. Charlotte spent considerable time in Dario's company each day, and continually grew fonder of him, but she had loving eyes for Jake only. She was aware of the tension between the two men, but feeling as she did, it never occurred to her that she herself was the cause, and her even-handed graciousness in maintaining a civilized accord had led Dario to suppose there might be some hope for him.

This misconception was enhanced by the men's very different preferences and habits. They were not often in the same place at the same time except at meals, and the group became a threesome only at dinner and after. Jake, robust and energetic, loved the range. In heat or cold, in sun or snow, he liked nothing better than riding over his open land under a big sky. He gloried in his vast herds and enjoyed visiting the line camps and lollygagging, as he called it, with his cow hands when the day's work was done. So did Charlotte.

Dario, though of sturdy enough build, was more cerebrally inclined. Like a lean, city street cat on familiar terms with windy alleyways, once he finagled his way indoors, he staked out a soft spot near the fire and stayed there. That was exactly where Charlotte, who was as fond of the hearth as she was of the range, found him when she came in from one of her excursions with Jake.

On that particular afternoon, Dario was slouched in a corner of a sofa, his long feet, in moccasins, propped on an ottoman, his legs stretched toward the fire. Though he'd been fretting for hours, both looking forward to her arrival, and dreading it, he returned her smile with what she had come to call his jack-o'-lantern grin.

"Just a roof . . . as long there's love, you say?" he mused, repeating her remark and filing it away in his memory for later reference. Since coming to the JAK Bar and falling in love, Dario had gleaned considerable information from Charlotte about Charlotte, all flavored with her intriguing *bons mots*. As she crossed the room now, he gazed at her, delighting in the refinement of her features, the snow drops melting in her coiled golden hair and repeating in his mind what she had just said. He suspected this latest expression of her romantic nature would prove to be his favorite of her self-revelations and, perhaps, the most useful to him. It was on a plane with her assertion that "the true spirit of hospitality resides in a ruddy blaze and a nicely decorated mantel," and her statement that joy was a "beneficent passion" and prudery a "kind of avarice—the worst of all."

He had been most thrilled last evening when she read aloud her favorite verse from a book of poems:

I think true love is never blind,
  But rather brings an added light,

An inner vision quick to find
　The beauties hid from common sight.

Of course! Dario thought, sitting bolt upright. *She's chosen that verse for* me. *It's her way of saying she sees the inner man, the dashing, stouthearted,* real *me, beneath my less than heroic appearance — my big dumb grin, gangly body, receding hair and all.*

Charlotte, though, had been quoting for Jake's benefit. The rancher was leaning back drowsing in a bentwood rocker, his strong profile highlighted by an oil lamp's glow, his eyes half closed. He smiled.

"It hasn't felt so familial and peaceful here in a long while, Charlotte. How I love hearing your voice. Do you feel like reading some more?" he asked, and of course, she did. She went on reading until the mantel clock struck eleven, a late hour for bedtime at the JAK Bar, where the day began by five in the morning when the ranch hands invaded the big kitchen for breakfast and work orders. After counting the chimes, Jake stood, stretched, thanked Charlotte for a most pleasant evening, shook Dario's hand and said good night, leaving his guests alone together.

"Have you ever seen a bullfight, Charlotte?" Dario asked.

She nodded. "In Mexico some years back. Why?"

"Jake puts me in mind of a matador so damn confident of the kill, he turns his back on the bull. Sometimes the bull takes him by surprise."

"Oh? I don't understand, about Jake and the matador." Charlotte sighed, not really paying attention. She lapsed into musing silence.

"Hey, remember me? I'm still here," the bell maker reminded her. "Will you read some more?" he asked. She smiled and began again; but her voice soon gave out, and she followed Jake upstairs, looking a trifle tired, Dario decided, or perhaps downcast, he wasn't sure which.

Next day, scrutinizing her as she crossed the parlor, Dario was relieved to see no hint of dejection, in fact, just the opposite. She was glowing with cold and inner warmth and who knew what else? His heart lurched, and he couldn't stop himself thinking, *Love gives the keenest possible of all sensations*. It was an idea that leapt into his brain and drove him nearly wild each time he set eyes on Charlotte and wondered how things *really* stood between her Jake Chamberlain. Discomfited by Dario's grimace, she paused in her progress across the room.

"Dario, what's wrong?" she asked. "You look . . . pained. Is it a tooth ache or something?"

"No, not a tooth ache. I was recollecting something Stendahl wrote and feeling another kind of ache, but it can't be helped. So, to answer your question, nothing's wrong, nothing," he insisted, lying. Something was terribly amiss. He wasn't anxious to tell her what until he'd talked the matter over with Jake. Dario awkwardly scrambled to his feet, hoping his belated gesture of politeness would disguise his furtive attempt to slip something beneath a pile of pillows at his side.

"You'd never make a sideshow magician, Mr. Heyward!" Charlotte laughed. "Well, what are you trying to hide? Be a good sport, now that I've spotted your inept sleight of hand, and pass it over, whatever it is because —"

Silently cursing himself and adoring her smile, knowing it was about to disappear, Dario abruptly thrust out a long arm and handed Charlotte a ragged piece of a paper. In the failing afternoon light, she took it close to the fire to read.

"Why . . . Dario, where did you get this?" she asked in

a tremulous voice. Her smile went out like a snuffed candle, and the color drained from her cheeks. "It's a wanted poster for . . . the Goldilocks Gang and . . . oh, my God! This is my worst nightmare come true! It's got Lark's likeness on it! I've always worried she might go to the bad because, deep down, she might be a little like the daddy she never knew. Even if she isn't *like* Mark, if there's no such thing as a bad seed or bad bloodlines, I fretted she might copy him, sort of as a way to understanding and forgiving the man who abandoned her and me, both." Charlotte's gray eyes, filled with dread, locked on Heyward. He moaned and rested his brow against the mantel.

"And, Dario, you *knew* my fears for her. I spoke words to you about my child I'd uttered to no other soul on earth. Remember what you said to me? You said, 'Don't worry, there's no need to go after her and Logan.' Jake wanted to form a posse the first minute she went missing, but romantic fool that I am, I wouldn't let him. Then, when I got to worrying over her, Mr. Heyward, you came along and swore to me the man, Walker, would never bring my daughter to harm. And now . . . this." She flourished the poster. "What on earth does it mean?"

"It has to be a mistake, a lie, a trick, Charlotte. I stand by Logan." Dario brought his long fingers together beneath his chin, like a man praying. "I'll go find them for you. You know I was on my way to do that when I stopped by here. I'll leave before dawn. Charlotte! You trusted me with the deepest secrets of your heart!" Dario said desperately. "And it seems I let you down. But, you'll see, I was *right*."

They both thought back then, to their first real talk. During it, Charlotte had found a friend. Dario had lost his heart.

* * *

Charlotte had examined Dario's mare, Divine, moving around the sprucy horse, exclaiming over her feathery fetlocks, her withers and strong haunches. About to follow the others inside the house, she came upon the two dead outlaws, their boots and spurs protruding from under a blanket in the back of the wagon. Charlotte, anything but squeamish, looked under the blanket, screamed and promptly fainted.

When she came to, she was in the main room, lying on a settee with a pillow under her head. Jake was nowhere in sight. Distraught, Dario was pacing and loudly castigating himself, in several languages, for his idiocy. The patient laughed aloud — she just couldn't help it — at the sight of that bony, balding, shirtless man flapping his arms and raging up and down before her just-opened eyes.

"Where's Jake?" she inquired, the sound of her voice so surprising Heyward, he jumped, his limbs jerking like a puppet on a string.

"Jake's gone off to get some whiskey for the second time this evening. First it was for me. Now it's to help revive you. Are you okay? I am a dolt and a dimwit and a raging ignoramus, leaving those two felons for you to come upon unawares." Dario flapped his arms and reverted to the combination of languages in which he'd been rebuking himself until Charlotte had him calmed somewhat.

"I didn't mean to have so upset you," she said, daubing at his sweated brow with her pocket handkerchief. "It wasn't the sight of your passengers that unnerved me. It was what they were holding in their hands. Those wildflower bouquets were made with scraps of my daughter's dress, and I . . . panicked."

"She's with Logan Walker. *She's* all right," Dario answered, standing then dropping back into his chair. "But I don't know about myself, how fine I am. *You* gave me a fright."

"Sorry. I had heard you're a good friend of Logan Walker's. Except for Matt January and his wife, you know him better than anyone in the territory. Can you tell me about him? I've a real special interest."

"If you're asking did the boy, Logan, kill Rachel Blue, the answer is a resounding *no!*" Heyward proclaimed, not so much indignant as fiercely devoted. "I'm as good a judge of human kind as Logan is of horse flesh. You can trust my word, Miz McKay, and that's fact."

"This man Walker knows a lot about horses, does he? From before Lark could walk, she was ready to ride. She can handle anything as well as a man can, even broncs. Logan and Lark have that much in common. I hope, by the time this episode is over, that's all they'll have shared."

"You worrying about . . . well, love and such?" Dario mumbled self consciously.

"I don't ever worry about love, Mr, Heyward. It's lawlessness frightens me. Lark's father . . . he was led astray, and he went bad and — can I tell you something I've never before said to anyone in the world?"

Dario nodded vehemently.

"Lark is so . . . well, willful, that I've always had a deep-down secret worry there might be a bit of . . . wildness in her, too, just the smallest seed of it that would never flower unless . . . she took up with the wrong sort of folks, someone who'd nourish that dormant seed and start it to growing. Could your Mr. Walker be that someone?" Charlotte, feeling dizzy again, covered her face with her hands. "You won't repeat what I've said? I wouldn't want Lark to hear what I've just told you, not ever."

"Don't worry! Oh, please don't worry. I . . . I'm touched you could share your troubles with me. Your secret's safe for as long as I live and longer. And your daughter's safe with Logan, I promise. He is a true southern gentleman. He has got real integrity. That boy admires the Code of Chivalry, and he lives by the Code of the West."

"Chivalry? I understand about that—honor, valor, loyalty to God, king and the mistress of the heart, the lady who was a knight's sworn love. She had to be some other man's wife or a young virgin, one or the other, didn't she? In either case, it was a woman the knight was never ever supposed to lay a hand upon, not to touch or kiss or—" Charlotte blushed.

Dario was smitten. Not only by the charming self-betrayal of that rush of color to her smooth cheek, but by the gray eyes . . . the sweet voice . . . the pretty mouth that was the exact shade of rose petals.

"Well, but what is the Code of the West, exactly? I always have wondered," Charlotte asked.

"It's the Golden Rule, and then some. Do unto others, feed the stranger but ask him no questions, return your neighbor's strayed livestock. Like that," Dario explained, reclining and stretching to his full length on the settee.

"It was Charles Goodnight at the Home Ranch in West Texas started the code," Jake said, rushing into the room, Aida on his heels, a bottle and three glasses on a silver tray in his hands. Finding Dario stretched out now and Charlotte fussing over him, Jake had to laugh. "Well, what's this?" he asked, and Dario, as if guilty of something, shot upright looking befuddled, beguiled and totally captivated.

"The lady's better, Jake," he said, grinning sheepishly, showing his big teeth, but not trusting himself to speak her name, knowing he'd been hit hard. Cupid and Eros,

Aphrodite and Amor and every other love god or goddess there ever was had struck him one after the other, like chain lightning. "Go on about Mr. Goodnight."

"Any cowboy who signed on to work at the Home Ranch had to put his name or make his mark on a paper saying what he agreed to do. Also that paper said if one hired hand shot another, the shooter would be tried then and there by the outfit and hanged on the spot if found guilty. That was the beginning of the Code of the West. Bravery, independence and self-reliance got to be part of it too, over time. From what I know of Logan, Charlotte, I must agree with Mr. Heyward. The lad appears to live by it."

"Now, that doesn't mean he can't be a bit bull-headed maybe, but he is not wild," Dario said, reclaiming the limelight. He slipped into the shirt Aida had brought him, one of Jake's best, with a square bib front and pewter buttons. When he thanked her almost formally, Aida's black eyes moved from Dario, to Jake to Charlotte, the lines of a triangle apparent to her.

"Logan is brave but not reckless or foolhardy," Heyward continued. "He's a man of informed courage. So, you have my word, Miz McKay, your girl is in good hands. She couldn't be safer if she were upstairs right here at the JAK Bar, sleeping the sleep of an innocent baby."

"Supper's on," Aida said, her tone, as always, betraying no emotion. At that moment, Aida was riled, to say the least. She knew trouble when she saw it. She knew Jake and she knew Dario. She even knew that Walker boy some. But this woman? Aida didn't hardly know her, didn't know the daughter at all. Another thing she *did* know; there wasn't anything like pretty women for upsetting the order of things and disturbing the peace and quiet of a place. Pretty white women never left well enough alone. They didn't seem to know how to. This house was *her* place, Aida told herself. She'd kept it up these last ten years, polished every panel of its walls, scrubbed the wide planks of its floors, and shined its brass and silver, washed and cooked for the man — and more. She didn't want to leave the JAK Bar. But she wasn't going to watch any yellow-haired woman change everything. She and the child might have to accept the offer to go with the man from Hell's Kitchen — after the dust finally settled.

"Uh, say, Dario? What'd you decide about the silver ring?" Jake asked on the way to the dining room. He kept his voice low, almost conspiratorial.

"I already told you, my friend, that ring's for my future bride. It isn't for sale," Dario insisted. "I will never give it up to you, Jake Chamberlain. See, there's no way under the sun I, Dario Heyward, am going to make things one wit easier for my only rival, far as I know, for the hand of Charlotte McKay."

"I see." Jake nodded. "The gauntlet's thrown. The battle lines are drawn, and may the best man win. Now, maybe there's some women who might think that was you, who would choose an itinerant pauper, chasing after birds and rainbows, over a land-holding rancher with more acres and cows than he can count. But if there are such witless women, I am ready to wager Charlotte McKay ain't one of them. She's had a hard life, done all the roving she's of a mind to. She deserves something better. See, she *belongs* here at the JAK Bar. You really think you got a chance with her, Dario?"

"I'm ready to bet on it, just like you."

"What the hell have you got to bet, my friend? Nothing I'd want." When Jake's competitive juices were flowing, he could turn mean and as hard as oak.

"If you're trying to demoralize me, my friend, pointing out what I ain't got in wealth and possessions, it won't work. I don't care about such things. Charlotte doesn't either, I don't suppose. But I do have one thing you want. I'll bet the silver finger ring. Now, what might you have that'd interest me? Not cows . . . money . . . land . . . what?"

"Maybe only warm welcome if you ever pass this way again, to pay your respects to the new Mrs. Chamberlain?"

"I'll take the welcome if you'll agree to extend it to Mrs. Heyward, who's certain to be sitting right up at my side, whatever kind of conveyance I'm driving!"

In the days since that conversation, Dario had lived in hope, and Jake had remained absolutely sure of capturing her heart himself—until he came in from the stables to find Charlotte in his rival's arms.

Chapter Sixteen

"You've got your own poster now! Ain't that something, 'specially for a pretty little old girl like you?" Clarence remarked.

"It's going to worry my mama something terrible, seeing that. Anyway, it's not the first time I have had my picture on a poster, Clarence. When me and Mama worked for Mollie Bailey's Circus, Arkansas and half of Texas were plastered with pictures of us and the others. Now Professor Gentry features Mama and me on his, and Mr. Ringling promised I was going to have my own lithograph with only Pumpkin, my counting pinto pony, and our sweet old Clydesdale, Minnie, in the background. God, I do miss them all — Ivy and Ali and Ralph and Pumpkin and Minnie. Mostly I miss my mama." She sighed, adjusting her mask. "We have never been apart in nineteen years."

Their collars turned up and hats pulled down, the men and Lark were mounted, waiting for a train. Their horses huddled close behind a boulder. The railroad was reported to be carrying a shipment of newly printed currency from the US Mint and a load of well-to-do European passengers coming west to shoot game and view the

Yellowstone Canyon. It was Bobby Midgette who got the information from a friend of a friend. He had slipped into Oklahoma City to buy corn liquor for Clarence, who was getting very morose, and scout up a promising job of criminal work.

"Have you got a counting pony? Really?" Billy Midgette asked Lark. She nodded. "Who are all them others, Ivy and so forth, your brothers and sisters?"

"No. They're my performing dogs. Ralph's a terrier, good ratter, walks a tight rope, and jumps a rope, too. He rides on Pumpkin. The two Russian wolf hounds are Ivan and Alexander. They can course a wolf like nobody's business, but they don't get much chance. Usually they sit right up on big Min with me, at the finale of our act."

"The crowds go wild, I'd guess, over three beautiful blondes atop a Clydesdale." Logan grinned. Cumplin scowled.

"Sounds like you used to put on a real good show, but that's all over now. Now you are a wanted woman, and there's no turning back. You're hearing that from — ha — the horse's mouth, from a man who knows where of he speaks." Clarence had a faraway look in his vicious eyes, what could be seen of them. They were squinted down narrow, his face smeared with grease and gunpowder to protect him from the snow blindness he was prone to. The sun had been just warm enough, the day before, to melt the white surface which froze into crystals during the night and now glared brightly. Pale as he was, Clarence suffered worse than most in the dazzling, interminable white blaze. His lips and nose had already begun to blister.

"Where would you go back to, Clarence, if you could?" Lark asked, rolling her own eyes at the sky. The outlaw chief was getting on everyone's nerves with his irritable complaining.

Just then, Satan, breathing puffs of steam in the cold air, kicked out at Logan's waggish dog. Max, who got away unscathed, was inspired by his success to run circles around Satan before, in an exuberance of high spirits, he raced off. He plunged into what was for him neckdeep snow, leaping from drift to drift like a rabbit. "I swear that canine is laughing fit to be tied." Lark laughed herself, a contagious sound. The men joined with her, all except Clarence.

"I envy that old spotted Loosiana hawg dawg. He's always having a right good time. For me, life's been one unending crisis since I left my home on the edge of the Great Dismal Swamp," Clarence whined.

"Where's that at? It doesn't sound like someplace to be homesick for, any great dismal anything." Mose croaked.

"It's half in Virginia, half in Carolina. It straddles the line. It's a real dim, shady place, full of juniper, wild camellias, snakes and bobcats. No snow. Not too many men. Good place to hide. Runaway slaves knew that. Escaped convicts still do. That's how I first met up with Skeets, when he was on the bolt. Talk about missing folks? Know who I miss? Skeets. I never would have thought I'd hear myself say so, but ain't nothin's gone right since the old swamp Skeeter got gravelled."

"Will you stop feeling sorry for yourself, Clarence?" Mose rasped. "I cain't talk right and likely never will again, and do you hear me complainin'? I am just lucky to be alive, is the way I see it. Now, let's try and look sprightly and get on with this train robbery."

"You always was a pathetic saphead, Moses Blakely. Things have come to a pretty pass when I, Clarence Cumplin, have to listen to a pep talk from the likes of you.

Well, I sure do hope this enterprise goes better than our previous forays. The last few times out been brutal," Clarence sulked. "Bobby and Billy back up into each other sneakin' round a corner, and their guns go off, right outside the telegraph office. That sure let the folks in Silverdale know we were there. So the citizenry gets alarmed and up in arms, we flee empty-handed and lose two more of my staunch men, Bland Blandford and Tuggwell, shot in the back." Clarence sighed deeply.

"That was just before Aubrie Banks fell into the mine shaft up near Peckham, wasn't it?" Logan asked, his tone facetiously mocking. Clarence was too self-absorbed to notice, but Lark did and smothered a giggle, fluttering her lashes at Logan. *I love you,* she silently mouthed, thinking he was the best-looking man she'd ever seen.

His hair, shoulder length now, flickered with gold sparks in the bright morning glare. His grin crackled like white lightning, and his tongue traced over his lips seductively. Lifting a brow, he gestured with a tilt of his head toward a stand of trees nearby. Sundance restlessly pawed the snow and exuded steamy breath like a red dragon. The resplendent Tennessee stud glowed a fiery, golden rust color against the white landscape. His rider's wonderfully wicked dark eyes flashed.

"You are just *daring* me to follow you, right?" Lark asked, wanting to do exactly that but not having intended to say right out. She felt her cheeks flame and the tips of her breasts rise hard, thinking about Logan's proposal. Logan knew. He nodded.

"What are you conspirators up to?" Clarence grumped.

"We are just talking . . . uh . . . about Aubrie Brooks falling in the mine, right after Jason's horse threw a shoe and Jason got his neck broken. *Right?*" Logan asked, adroitly covering Lark's lapse. It satisfied Clarence, who went on reeling off a list of their failures, woes and *faux pas*.

"We couldn't open the safe in Blackwell because someone — Alf Littleworth, may he be burning hell this very instant — forgot the dynamite. I had to shoot him, naturally, even if he swore he had the explosives with him when he left camp. When we did blow open the safe at Bartlesville, it was empty, like they knew we were comin'. And the bank job before that, when Lark and me tripped over each other? All we got was nickels. Then the saddlebags come undone and dropped off right in the middle of Caldwell's main street, and we ended up with nothing but a damn bank teller who can't add worth a fig."

"Yeah, but that Jesse Jaynes is a real good cook, for a bank teller," Mose rasped. "There's always a silver lining in a sow's ear, boss."

"If we don't get us some money, I am going to have insurrection on my hands, no matter how good the cookin' is," Clarence said and pulled his gun. "Moses, things are grim enough without I have to listen to more of your mangled pieties. I can't stand it."

Blakely would have been done away with on the spot if not for Logan's intervention.

"You'll foul up this job, too, if the men guarding that train hear any shooting. Come on, Clarence, take it easy," he said. "You're just having a run of poor luck. May I offer a constructive criticism?"

Cumplin nodded dubiously.

"If you had let each of us carry a money bag instead of loading the lot on the pack horse you were leading, we wouldn't have lost all the loot that time. Nickels *are* better than nothing."

"Logan, I am becoming the laughingstock of the badlands! The fallen women down to Ingalls giggle when they hear my name. Even my horse seems to be sniggering at me, most the time. Know what they're calling this gang now? Do you?"

Logan shrugged. No one answered. When Clarence was in one of his really dark moods, it was dangerous to converse with him.

"The Cumplin Gang is becoming popularly known as the Goldilocks Gum Ups. I am losing my awesome image, my reputation for meanness, my notoriety! I am feeling bad about that, so this job better go good, hear?"

"I told you, didn't I, this will go slick as a whistle, like a snap? Remember?" Bobby asked.

After returning from town several days before, with a newspaper and plenty of whiskey, he had enthusiastically described the project's possibilities at a gang meeting. Exchanging looks with Logan, Bobby had drawn the conclusion that it would be a foolproof operation.

"Well, that's a damn good thing 'cause there's sure lots of fools in this outfit," Herman Flicker had cackled in response to Bobby's plan, slapping his knee. The man's tan, pinched little face wrinkled like a prune when he smiled. The former peddler-turned-outlaw still wore the dusty black coat and bent stovepipe hat he'd had on the day he traded his rig to Dario Heyward for a wide-angle camera and several lenses.

Flicker had been attempting to take a picture with the contraption, something he'd had yet to succeed in doing, when the Cumplin Gang went racing past him through town, pursued by every resident of Silverdale. When a bullet zinged into the hitching post near Flicker, he had jumped, reflexively clicking the camera's shutter and unknowingly capturing a picture on a glass plate of Lark and three of the men. Flicker had abandoned the heavy and, as far as he could tell, useless machine where it stood and gone after the bad guys and gal like everyone else in Silverdale. But the former peddler, who had run up substantial bills at the saloon and hotel, forgot to stop chasing. He had tailed the gang to their hideout and signed on.

"Hey, Clarence, what I said about fools? It was a joke" were the last words Herman Flicker ever uttered. He'd be best remembered in later years for the candid, head-on photograph he'd left behind. It would be displayed in museums and galleries as an outstanding example of frontier art and a testament to the pluck of one lone, dedicated photographer, brave enough to have faced death to get his shot. Tragically, it would be said, a great talent was lost. Herman Flicker was never seen again, but it was his snap that turned the Cumplin Gang into the Goldilocks Gum Ups and put Lark's half-masked face and long pale hair on every front page and in every post office in the country.

"This train holdup is going to add a link to the chain of bad luck Clarence has been suffering. I know this shooting and killing and chasing is hard on you, darlin'," Logan said to Lark later, after the meeting. Seeing her likeness in the paper had upset her, mostly for Charlotte's sake. "But just try to think of it this way; we're doing good by seeming to do bad. Like spies in disguise, we're fooling one very bad man into eliminating a lot of other very bad men. Clarence is whittling away at his own kind, diminishing his own strength and saving us and the law the unpleasant trouble." As he talked, soothing her, Logan and Lark were skin to skin under the soft warm bear pelt, and their hands were wandering purposefully.

"Sugar baby," he sighed, "next time we go into a town, you could quit us. You could go the sheriff and say you were forced to front for Cumplin. Let me snare Clarence on my own."

"Logan . . ." Lark sighed in turn, "are you trying to get rid of me—again? I am no quitter. I said I'd help, and I will see this thing through. We've got Clarence demoralized, shaken . . . teetering, half his men are gone and . . . and I don't want to talk about *him* now, Logan. I want . . . *you*."

"Some day, sweet girl, I am going to make love to you on the softest feather bed in the best hotel in Chicago. There'll be sheets almost as smooth and silken as your skin . . . soft lights in etched pink globes, pink French champagne bubbling, like your lovely laugh. There'll be a big, big box of Holland white chocolate, all sweet and creamy as . . . as this." He ducked his head under the cover and kissed the flat plain of her stomach. "And . . . mm . . . this." His lips moved to the inner curve of her thigh, and when he emerged from beneath the covers to lean on an elbow and look into her eyes, they were misty gray, full of promise and need.

"Chicago . . . sounds okay." She smiled, her eyes fluttering closed, her voice breathy. Her hand settled on his risen hardness, and she encircled and caressed. "You know what I want right now."

"Tell me you love me," he rasped.

"I love you, I do," she answered. "The more time that passes . . . the closer we get every day . . . every night that we're together, the more . . . the less . . . the harder . . ." She stopped talking and kissed his mouth, drawing his lips down to hers. They were ravenous.

"The more you want, the harder it becomes for you to

The Publishers of Zebra Books Make This Special Offer to Zebra Romance Readers...

AFTER YOU HAVE READ THIS BOOK WE'D LIKE TO SEND YOU
4 MORE FOR *FREE* AN $18.00 VALUE

No Obligation!

ONLY ZEBRA HISTORICAL ROMANCES "BURN WITH THE FIRE OF HISTORY" (SEE INSIDE FOR MONEY SAVING DETAILS.)

MORE PASSION AND ADVENTURE AWAIT... YOUR TRIP TO A BIG ADVENTUROUS WORLD BEGINS WHEN YOU ACCEPT YOUR FIRST 4 NOVELS ABSOLUTELY *FREE* (AN $18.00 VALUE)

Accept your Free gift and start to experience more of the passion and adventure you like in a historical romance novel. Each Zebra novel is filled with proud men, spirited women and tempestuous love that you'll remember long after you turn the last page.

Zebra Historical Romances are the finest novels of their kind. They are written by authors who really know how to weave tales of romance and adventure in the historical settings you love. You'll feel like you've actually gone back in time with the thrilling stories that each Zebra novel offers.

GET YOUR FREE GIFT WITH THE START OF YOUR HOME SUBSCRIPTION

Our readers tell us that these books sell out very fast in book stores and often they miss the newest titles. So Zebra has made arrangements for you to receive the four newest novels published each month.

You'll be guaranteed that you'll never miss a title, and home delivery is so convenient. And to show you just how easy it is to get Zebra Historical Romances, we'll send you your first 4 books absolutely FREE! Our gift to you just for trying our home subscription service.

BIG SAVINGS AND FREE HOME DELIVERY

Each month, you'll receive the four newest titles as soon as they are published. You'll probably receive them even before the bookstores do. What's more, you may preview these exciting novels free for 10 days. If you like them as much as we think you will, just pay the low preferred subscriber's price of just $3.75 each. *You'll save $3.00 each month off the publisher's price.* AND, your savings are even greater because there are never any shipping, handling or other hidden charges—FREE Home Delivery. Of course you can return any shipment within 10 days for full credit, no questions asked. There is no minimum number of books you must buy.

4 FREE BOOKS

TO GET YOUR 4 FREE BOOKS WORTH $18.00 — MAIL IN THE FREE BOOK CERTIFICATE TODAY

Fill in the Free Book Certificate below, and we'll send your FREE BOOKS to you as soon as we receive it.

If the certificate is missing below, write to: Zebra Home Subscription Service, Inc., P.O. Box 5214, 120 Brighton Road, Clifton, New Jersey 07015-5214.

FREE BOOK CERTIFICATE

4 FREE BOOKS

ZEBRA HOME SUBSCRIPTION SERVICE, INC.

YES! Please start my subscription to Zebra Historical Romances and send me my first 4 books absolutely FREE. I understand that each month I may preview four new Zebra Historical Romances free for 10 days. If I'm not satisfied with them, I may return the four books within 10 days and owe nothing. Otherwise, I will pay the low preferred subscriber's price of just $3.75 each; a total of $15.00, *a savings off the publisher's price of $3.00*. I may return any shipment and I may cancel this subscription at any time. There is no obligation to buy any shipment and there are no shipping, handling or other hidden charges. Regardless of what I decide, the four free books are mine to keep.

NAME _____

ADDRESS _____ APT _____

CITY _____ STATE _____ ZIP _____

TELEPHONE ( ) _____

SIGNATURE _____ (if under 18, parent or guardian must sign)

Terms, offer and prices subject to change without notice. Subscription subject to acceptance by Zebra Books. Zebra Books reserves the right to reject any order or cancel any subscription.

079102

GET FOUR FREE BOOKS
(AN $18.00 VALUE)

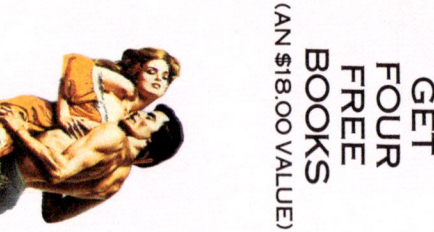

ZEBRA HOME SUBSCRIPTION
SERVICE, INC.
P.O. Box 5214
120 BRIGHTON ROAD
CLIFTON, NEW JERSEY 07015-5214

AFFIX
STAMP
HERE

think about leaving me?" he finished her sentence. She nodded.

". . . or ever wanting another man. What are you doing to me, Logan Walker?" she asked, delicious anguish and passion toning her voice, making it lush and mellow.

"I'm making you mine," he answered.

"How will I ever leave you?" Her eyes were half lidded, her lips parted.

"You won't." He was above her, a shadow against the star-studded sky, but full-blooded and real in her arms, with the brawn and muscle of a mortal man and the power of a god.

"I will . . . but not today."

"Not tomorrow, either," he answered. "Or the day after." He was right.

Two days later she was beside him, astride Satan. The gang waited for their train to round the bend and be brought to a stop by the ten-foot barrier of logs and stone with which they had blocked the tracks. Bobby Midgette was standing with one boot toe on the Atchison, Topeka and Santa Fe's steel rail.

"It's coming," he said, "I feel a vibration. It's pulling out of Newton now." And soon, they all heard the whistle heralding the approach of the mighty machine. It was a far-off lonesome sound on the snapping cold air.

Bellowing and screeching, the monster engine came to a sliding halt, its cow catcher just bumping the outlaws' barrier. Steam was huffing from the boiler, and black smoke came pouring out of the stack when Clarence and Billy, with Jesse the bank teller in tow, mounted the cab and began herding the engineer and fireman back toward the passenger cars.

"This here's Jesse Jaynes, so don't try nothin' funny," Clarence ordered. The trainmen reeled and stared.

"Say, what are you tryin' to pull? Jesse's been dead near ten years," the fireman said. Jaynes, smiling apologetically, tipped his hat.

"That's Jaynes, with an *n*. Don't pay him no mind. Clarence just does that for effect, thinks it's funny. Nothin' personal, gents," Jesse said.

Mose and Bobby, starting at the caboose, were to throw out the money box and any other valuables and work forward. The rest of the outlaws, clambering onto the train at random, froze when Cumplin's blood-curdling shriek of rage knifed the winter air.

"There's no new money and no gold!" he howled, stamping his feet and hurling away his hat. "There ain't no rich sportsmen dripping with jewelled watches, and there's not one fine English gun. Damn, how I had my heart set on a new Purdey or a Holland and Holland double-bore rifle, and now look! Look!"

There were half a dozen dogs, a goat and three soldiers unwilling to die for their cargo, four rail cars crammed full with Apache squaws and children, prisoners being shipped from Mount Vernon in Alabama to be resettled at Fort Sill in the Indian Territory.

"The braves will be brought out west later," Logan told Lark after exchanging a few words with one of the women. "The army captured these mountain people in the Southwest and held them in the malarial southern climate on the Gulf of Mexico where a lot of them died. Now they're being uprooted again."

"How do you know their language?" Lark asked, ruffling the dark hair of a small boy. She was disturbed by the child's glazed eyes and rattling cough.

"When I was in Washington about ten years back

with—" Logan hesitated, "with an aunt and uncle, I met a man there called Mickey Free. He taught me Apache. Mickey was part Irish, part Mexican, being raised down on the border with Old Mexico when he got stolen by Indians, along with some cattle. He was eleven or twelve at the time. He finished his growing up as a Chiricahua Apache. Later, he was an interpreter for the Army in the Sierra Madre Mountains before he was brought east. . . . Darlin', we'd best see to Crazy Clarence before he gets a massacre named after him."

Cumplin *was* so enraged, he would have slaughtered the lot if Logan hadn't come up behind him and knocked him cold with the fireman's coal shovel.

"I never saw any but three soldiers," Clarence said later, nursing a lump on the back of his head the size of an eagle's egg. In disgust, the gang had fled to their nearest refuge, a cave in the low hills that wasn't exactly cozy and homelike, but better than nothing. "Did anyone else see four soldiers? That fourth one, where was he hiding?"

"On the roof, Clarence," Lark said, holding a cold compress to his injury.

Lacking his hat during the get-away ride, his face had sunburned badly. Now it was blistered and swelled. His eyes were nearly closed, and his lips were cracked. Licking his wounds like an injured dog, Clarence was more dangerous than ever, and unpredictable.

"Yes, that fourth soldier was on the roof, securing a loose bit of iron that was banging so, it was giving him a headache, he told me. Sorry, sorry Clarence. I didn't mean to remind you of your own discomfort," Lark added, dipping the cloth in the pan of freezing water and ringing it out before reapplying it. "Now, if there had been someone on the roof of the fast freight that hit Jumbo the circus elephant, why, things might have turned out different for the poor critter. As it happened — say, Clarence, do you know about Jumbo the Elephant?" Lark asked.

The outlaw shook his head no. All the others, most looking glum, perked up.

"Want me to tell you about him, to take your mind off your own troubles?" She smiled.

All the men, cold, damp and hungry, nodded like children gathered for story time, and the fire seemed to glow a bit brighter.

Chapter Seventeen

"There has always been dazzle and danger in the circus world. It's the nature of the endeavor and makes it exciting—daring people risking life and limb, exotic wild creatures, canvas tents and ropes to be guarded against fire, tons of equipment inclined to topple, particularly travelling on unbanked back roads and 'specially at hairpin turns. We get stopped by covered bridges too low for the wagons, and sometimes, bridges splinter and collapse under the great weight of a wagon. It happens. Once, the big Howes Circus bandwagon tumbled right over a precipice, up in New York State."

"Must have been a great sight to behold," Clarence laughed wickedly. "Got any real disasters to tell about? The fearless flying trapeze man falling or the lions eating their tamers?"

"You are joking about my friends, some of the finest people in the whole world! You are twisted and awful, Clarence Cumplin!" Lark said, aghast and furious, for the moment forgetting all about Jumbo the Elephant. The color rose in her cheeks, and she got to her feet, her hand raised as if to strike him. After Logan tackled her and sat her back down, she was still fuming.

"I *know* it. You got it," Clarence boasted and tried to grin. "Ain't I the awfulest, though?"

"What you are is a sad case, like a real bad, mean little schoolyard bully-boy sassing the whole world. They do a lot of harm, some of those little yellowbellies, but sooner or later, they always get their comeuppance, like you'll get yours, Cumplin."

"Her tart tongue's going to get her killed some time, probably sooner than later, brother Logan." Clarence had gone pale with anger under his winter sunburn.

"I see her quicksilver temper as more of a problem from my vantage place, which is close enough to see no harm comes to her, ever." Logan's face was set in its frozen, dangerous expression. His eyes, fixed on Cumplin's face, were glazed. Some of the other men were unobtrusively moving closer to Lark to protect her if the not unlikely need arose.

"Your breeze and bragging doesn't work on me, Cumplin," she raged on, despite the pressure of Logan's hand on her shoulder. "See, you put me in mind of a timber rattler. I wouldn't want to step on one unawares, him hidden in tall grass, 'cause he'll strike; it's in his nature. But if you can see him, or hear him, he ain't nothing to fear. He's easy to scare — or kill. I'm not afraid of a back-shooting viper like you, either, not when I can look you in the eye."

There was a profound silence as if everyone in the cave was in suspended animation, like living things caught in amber. Moving fast, Logan put a few inches between himself and Lark and went for his gun but stayed his hand when Clarence didn't stir. The outlaw showed a cold displeasure as his tongue flicked over his blistered lips and he stared at Lark with beady reptilian eyes. In seconds, his look changed to bemusement and mortification. His gaze jumped from one man to the next, all of them lined up now behind Logan and Lark, any one of them in a position, and probably of a frame of mind, to shoot him dead. He backed up against a wall of the cave, his expression now blank and flat.

"If it was anyone but you, Goldilocks, who talked to me like that, there'd be at least one body on the ground by now. But . . . we are all devoted to you."

"Hell, devoted nothin'. We are all at least some in love with her, Clarence, same as the Doolin Gang is with the Rose of Cimmaron," Bobby Midgette explained.

"Rose belongs to one man, Bitter Creek Newcombe. Lark belongs to me, and none of you forget it," Logan cautioned, his words meant for Clarence. The outlaw smiled. It wasn't a pleasant sight.

"Bitter Creek? Now he's another bookish bandit like you, Logan. I know the whole Doolin Gang loves that gal. Next time we get to Ingalls, you ought to see to it our Goldilocks here has a chat with Rose. Rose knows the right way for an outlaw's woman to behave. She'll be full of tips and helpful hints.

"Now, Lark"—Clarence looked at her—"I gotta tell you, it ain't fitting or right, you saying to me all those things you just said. But I also got to say no one before ever explained things to me that way, about myself. I am fascinating, ain't I?"

"I could go on and on about you, Clarence. I ain't hardly started." Lark was still steaming with anger.

"Well, shucks. Do go on, but not about me. That's a subject we have to discuss private like. Go on about the big show, now, will you?" An audible sigh of relief went round the cave as the men slacked off into relaxed attitudes.

"Sure. Stuff always happens in the circus," Lark said,

more calmly. "I can tell about the time Barnum took his production to Australia and the ship ran into a storm. Half the animals were on deck in cages that broke loose and got washed overboard. His giraffes died of broken necks, but Barnum propped them up and went on with the show. He had a man hidden in their cage, a roustabout to move the giraffes' necks with a mechanical device. It kept the people happy."

"They should've stayed on land," one of the outlaws suggested.

"These days, the shows that can afford to pay the price are travelling by rail. That's sure got advantages, I suppose, over wagons, but still, thing's are not perfect. I worry. I never thought The Big Show was meant to move so fast as all that. After Jumbo's misfortune, I was even more convinced. I'll always be loyal to the old wagon shows, though I fear their days are numbered."

"I always have loved to see a circus parade march into a town, horns blaring, a lot of velvet banners and pageantry. My favorites are clowns, calliopes and bell chimes," Logan said, "and horses."

"The canvasmen who raise and lower the tent and the wagon drivers all do double duty in brass, playing their horns up on the bandwagon. A band wagon might just be the gaudiest, grandest, most beautiful thing any of us will ever see in all our lives." Lark smiled.

"I like the menagerie. I like the sideshow even more," Clarence groaned, wallowing in pain. He'd stretched out again and closed his burned eyelids. "I once saw Zip—The-What-Is-It, an odd lookin' man, and also JoJo, the Dog Face Boy. They gave me chills, them two. Where I come from, folks used to say circus people were witches, that they had conferences with the lords of darkness who gave them powers of enchantment and sorcery.

What do you say to that?"

"I've heard all about it — the cloven foot showing when a trick rider leaps over a horse and through a hoop, or does flip-flops. And there's that about the man dropping from a rope who comes to life again. What it is, is talent and sleight of hand and cleverness and perseverance and practice — mostly damn hard work — that make it all look so devilishly easy to people who want to see magic done before their very eyes."

"Sure. We got our own Mose, hung from a rope and come back." Clarence grimaced as he rolled a cigarette, but he couldn't smoke it. He hurled it into the fire. "I suppose you've been in parades, Miss Enchantress Bareback Rider?" His face contorted. It hurt him to talk or smoke. When Lark, mollified and sympathetic, kindly moistened the outlaw's parched lips, he almost smiled with gratitude.

"I've been in circus parades since I was born, small processions, though. With Mollie Bailey's show, my mama propped me on a pony and led me along any number of small-town main streets — under arching summer-leafed oaks, past feed stores and post offices and banks and whitewashed country churches. I saw all the children and their elders simmering with joyous excitement because we had come to their town.

"Professor Gentry always has a children's band. All the young ones of the performers and hands are put up on shetlands to play bells and drums. Mama and me, we lead the Gentry cortege. After us came the dogs and monkeys. Once, we had a monkey costumed up like Ben Hur. He was pulled in a chariot by our Russian wolf hounds, Ivan and Alex. My ambition now is to put a plume on my tough old Morgan horse, Satan, put on my spangled chaps and white hat and ride him between the snake den and the gilded lion cage, with elephants ahead of us, elephants in back. We'd prance up Broadway in New York City and hear people shouting 'Hold your horses, here come the elephants!' "

"Tell about Jumbo now?" Jesse Jaynes asked in a childlike, almost pleading way. As the gang's official cook, he'd managed to make a fair to middling stew of dried venison and jerky, flour and water. He measured out tin plates of the hot concoction, handed them around, put a coffeepot on the fire and settled down himself. Outside, the winter wind was howling. Inside, the cave, though a bit drafty, was nonetheless a decent refuge once the hissing fire, made from snow-sodden logs, had finally taken some of the dampness out of the walls. The men moved closer to the glow. Lark and Logan moved closer to each other, and back a little into the long, wavering shadows.

Chapter Eighteen

"Right. Jumbo. It's Jumbo we want to hear about," Clarence urged. Lark nestled against Logan, crossed her legs, and folded her small slender hands.

"Jumbo, the most famous elephant in the whole world, was only a poor, frightened, wild baby creature when he got captured by some Hamran Arabs in the North of Africa, in a place called Abyssinia, I think, maybe. The Arabs sold him to the French, who shipped him to Europe and put him in the Jardin des Plantes, a zoo in Paris. Well, this Jardin already had all the elephants it needed, so this forlorn and bewildered infant, along with two anteaters, was traded to the London Zoo in return for a rhinoceros. That little heart-broke baby, so sad and lonely and so far from home and his mama, was hurtin' bad. . . ."

"I know how he felt," Clarence said. "Go on telling." One of the other men, Moses Blakely, sighed deeply.

"The little elephant was real sick, near to dying, when he finally reached England, but there fortune smiled upon him at last." Lark smiled. So did her audience. "A kind animal keeper name of Scotty nursed that grieving baby back to health. It took months and months, but for-

187

ever after, the two, man and pachyderm, were inseparable.

"Well, soon as this little elephant got well, he got happy, and when he got happy, he got to eating and eating and *eating*. And growing. He grew a seven-foot trunk. It was said to be twenty-seven inches around. He had a twenty-six-foot reach at full size."

"No!" said Bobby. "Not really? I guess I'm about as interested in elephants as the next feller, but I never have seen one. I never thought . . . twenty-seven inches?"

"Shut up, Bobby Boy, and let the lady tell it," Clarence snapped. Lark was in the shadows, leaning shoulder to shoulder with Logan, and she felt his hand glide down her back and encircle her waist. She went on.

"Right, Bobby, twenty-seven inches of trunk and yet . . . he had a, well a wonderful, . . . delicacy of touch." Logan's hand was wandering. "Jumbo — short for Mumbo Jumbo because of the language they spoke where he came from — got to be twelve feet high to the shoulder. He weighed more'n six tons — some say eight — and he was sweet as a little lamb." Logan was mouthing the back of her neck, and she hesitated.

"Not sweet as a Lark. Yum." He laughed low.

"The only time Jumbo got upset and had little tantrums was at night when his keeper, Scotty, had to go home."

"Understandable, having a bit of a fit, when you don't get what you want when you want it," Logan whispered. Lark inhaled deeply.

"But those moderate outbursts made the Zoological Society people nervous. They got to worrying what their gentle giant might do when the mating urge came on him, so . . . Lo — gan!" she said softly with an admonishing giggle. "So . . . they sold Jumbo to P.T Barnum for ten thousand dollars. Now, P.T. already had elephants aplenty, but none so jumbo as Jumbo. That's where the word comes from. "Circus genius and attention-getter that he was, P.T. sent some of his publicity people to London to stir up a storm of protest among the English about losing their great elephant to the U.S. of A. Thousands of Britons flocked to see him. There were farewell parties. Little children wept. On his way to the boat, the elephant trumpeted, lay down in the street and refused to rise. Alice the Elephant, who Barnum said was Jumbo's broken-hearted true love, trumpeted in reply. This all occurred really, because Scotty, the keeper, who was going with Jumbo to America, gave the elephant a secret signal not to move."

"Like this hidden signal I'm giving you?" Logan murmured, his hand sliding up along Lark's rib cage to capture a swelled small breast. Her head dropped back against his shoulder. "Finish telling the boys their bedtime story so we can slip off on our own."

"You must be mad, talking of slipping off," she whispered. "The wind's howling like a banshee, the snow's up to your knees and drifting and there's no other shelter I saw."

"You don't see everything, sugar," he answered with a smile in his voice. She dared not look into his face just then and meet his fire-sparked eyes.

"Stop messin' with that woman, brother, and let her get talkin'," Clarence complained. The firelight was painful on his sunburned face and snowblind eyes. He, too, backed into the shadows.

Logan said, "Talk fast, honey." Lark tried.

"Barnum was sent a cable saying the elephant was fussing in the road, and Barnum cabled back, 'Let him lie there long as he wants. The publicity is worth it.' Typical

Barnum. It was all a setup, but it worked. The newspapers on both sides of the ocean had banner headlines, and thousands met Jumbo's ship at the pier in New York. Thousands upon thousands more all over the country came to see the mighty animal. He had his own railroad car, Jumbo's Palace Car, painted gold and red, with a bunk for Scotty, and Phineas T. made money hand over fist until . . . one terrible night up to Canada, in 1885, tragedy struck.

"Twenty-nine of Barnum's elephants had finished their act and were loaded on the circus train parked in the rail yard near the tent. Just Jumbo, the biggest one, and a dwarf elephant, the smallest — name of Tom Thumb — after the famous midget who had died not long before — were being led along a railroad track of the Grand Trunk, of all things, to their cars. A westbound express, engine number eighty-eighty, came racing along a downgrade, whistling. When the engineer saw what he thought, but had trouble believing, were elephants on his track, and they weren't even pink, he blew the three short blasts that signal real trouble. It was too late.

" *RUN JUMBO, RUN!!!*' Lark cried out in an urgent voice, in imitation of Scotty, startling her mesmerized audience. "The great mammoth did run, taking time to get up some speed, and Tom Thumb, the dwarf elephant, ran behind him. Jumbo got up to his fastest speed, but the train, even with its brakes locked, was screeching after him, still gaining speed on the downgrade. 'Turn, Jumbo!' Scotty wailed in desperation when he came to a passageway between two cars on the near track, but a gigantic running elephant can't turn on a dime, you all realize. Jumbo tried but —" Lark hurled herself into Logan's arms, so moved she couldn't go on for a minute.

"It's okay, darlin'," he soothed, holding her tight.

"The train hit the littlest elephant and hurled him aside. He survived, but Jumbo . . . he was hit hard. His skull was smashed. One of his tusks was driven back into his brain.

"The express derailed. Jumbo died. Scotty . . . well, he was wild with grief, especially when souvenir hunters came and cut pieces off Jumbo, the most terrible a big slice of one ear."

"Like I collect scalps, sort of?" Clarence mused. Angered again, Lark just gritted her teeth this time.

"Barnum had Jumbo preserved, as I recall," Logan commented soothingly, "and showed his big skeleton around the country and his so-called elephant true love from England, Alice."

"Jumbo and Alice were never a couple, but Barnum never missed an angle. After the accident, he wrote that Jumbo had picked up Tom Thumb, hurled the little elephant to safety and tried to face down that freight train. Jumbo died a Barnum hero. Later, Barnum gave Jumbo's skeleton to the Museum of Natural History and the carcass to Tufts College. Barnum was a trustee of Tufts, before he became the mayor of Bridgeport in Connecticut, his old home town."

"What happened to the trainer?"

"Poor Scotty never really recovered. He toured with the preserved Jumbo and then took up residence at Tufts where he was often seen dusting the stuffed creature and talking to his old friend."

"That is as heart-tugging a tale as I've ever heard." Jesse Jaynes was wiping a tear from his cheek. "Got another story, Miss Lark? Like that about Jumbo?"

"Another time, Jesse. I . . . I'm taking a stroll now, boys. Go on off to sleep 'cause you never know what tomorrow'll bring, probably nothing more than another circus story, but . . . who ever knows?" Feeling pretty emotional herself—thinking about Jumbo always made her sad—Lark pulled on her sheepskin coat and plunged out into the wintery air. Logan was right behind her. They stood close, trembling with chill and desire, in quavering silence, gazing about in wonder.

The cave was in a rise of low hills; the plain stretched out below. The sky above was streaming with stars. A lantern moon sat on the horizon illuminating the powdery snow surface, finer than diamond dust.

"This is a lovers' night and you incite a roaring in my blood, Lark McKay." Logan's voice was rough. "They're all in love with you. They'll do anything you ask, maybe even Clarence, too."

"Think so? Think he'll confess and absolve you just to please me? I think not. But I don't care to talk about him now, just about you. And me. Us. Where's this place you found?" she asked, almost shortly.

"Under heaven, anywhere under heaven, Lark, is our place. We're going to make angels in the snow down below, there on that virgin stretch of snow-drifted prairie. Is 'us' the right word for you and me, now . . . and always?" He pulled her to him, into his arms. His long, lean body radiated need. His lips were hard and cool, his breath hot.

"Us? Yes—us," she sighed. The small sibilant sound of her voice lifted on the wind and swelled, unfurled and dispersed to fill the universe. "But . . . it depends."

"On what?" His jubilation was clear in his voice. His impatience for her, which he was at pains to hide, wasn't.

"Logan, I love you. No matter what happens, it *is* us. It will always be. But I have to follow my dreams. I have to prove myself. My rainbow bridge spans east, the direction you've put behind you. Can you turn around and face the sunrise with me?"

"I can't promise but . . ." Logan began softly, his hand on her cheek, and Lark, loving him, wanting him, trembled with hope and impatience — and restrained herself, waiting. "But, I can try. We'll go your way first, cross your bridge. Then? . . . Then maybe you'll travel with me a way west, into the future. My future and yours have a lot, maybe everything, to do with Clarence Cumplin."

"It's horrifying, thinking our destiny depends on Crazy Clarence, but Logan, the men are all with us now. I saw that tonight, so tomorrow, let us take charge of our own future. Let's take Clarence in."

Chapter Nineteen

At a great distance, miles it appeared, across sparkling, blinding snow, a pair of shadow figures moved, a man behind a single horse. Across such an expanse, they appeared unattached in any physical way, disconnected from each other, yet moving together in perfect unison like separate pieces of driftwood on a single wave.

Half asleep and curled against Logan, Lark had her face hidden in the warmth of his throat. Leaning on one elbow stroking her hair with his free hand, he contemplated the approaching duo, almost as hazy as a mirage, waiting for it to get close enough to decipher, knowing he would understand how two seemingly independent figures, man and horse, were progressing as one so rapidly over deep snow.

"Skis!" Logan said with a laugh. "Look!" Max, who had come nosing out of his own night shelter, took off toward the new arrival, barking joyously. Lark sighed, moved against Logan, blinked into the pink-tinged, white glare of snowy dawn and kissed Logan's full mouth.

"Skis? A man on skis? Hadn't we better warn the others and run for it because—"

"Today is the day we're turning our lives around, remember? Anyway, I can see now it's that fat jolly mare, Divine, pulling Dario damn Heyward behind her on skis, no less. They'll be a little while yet."

"Is there time for us to make another snow angel?" she asked, a husky edge in her morning voice. All about them, frosted impressions in the crisp-crust snow documented their night's fun and games, and pleasures. There was the outline of long body and a littler one, side by side, lengthy arms outspread in one snow angel, folded like wings in another, broad shouldered, splayed-legged shapes enclosing the indentations of a smaller, rounder body. There was a big foot beside a little foot, hands, legs, knees and, finally, a single, deep blur-edged hollow, a snow fort, where Logan and Lark had nestled down and gotten to serious love.

That's where they found themselves, dug in, warm in a sort of lean-to igloo at sunup under a sky as big as the universe, their coats, hats, and wool shirts covering their naked bodies. They were wearing their gloves and boots and nothing else, watching the protracted approach of Dario and Divine.

"There is time, sugar, for one . . . two . . . maybe more snow angels. Or we could just stay right here and dig this one a little deeper, make it a bit more . . . impressive."

Lark laughed, the silvery sound carrying like crystal bells on frosty air. It must have reached all the way to the approaching rider. Dario's head came up suddenly, but there was nothing for him to see. Lark and Logan were lying down again, slightly reshaping their protected warm trench, rolling about. Soon, Lark was kneeling above Logan, looking into his hot, dark eyes. He readjusted their layers of cover and drew her mouth down hard, and she felt the surge of power when he went inside her, moving with sinuous urgency. His hands rested on the contracting muscles of her flanks, moved along the length of her slender legs, and his fine body coiled hard before it relaxed and he drew her down to him, her own body, as she stretched along his length, still besieged by the spasmodic consummation of the night — and the moment of love.

"A posse's only half a day behind me! A posse, hear, Logan!" Dario bellowed from a way off. Logan and Lark, side by side, dressed, muffled, wrapped, and clinging to each other, waved him on.

"Just in time for breakfast!!!" Lark sang out, jumping and waving both hands above her head. "Logan, I'll just go to the cave and see what Jesse, the cooking bank clerk, is up to," she told him, "and you can . . . explain things to your friend, how things are with you and me and what we're fixing to do." She slipped out of Logan's grasp and moved off, climbing toward the outlaw cave, then turning before going inside to watch the two friends greet each other.

There were shouts of real gladness and hand shakes and back slaps, all of which culminated in a great grunting bear hug. The tall, very thin Heyward was padded in a long buffalo robe half concealed by a colorful striped serape. His eyes were protected by big, round dark goggles while his balding head gleamed in the sun. *He looks like some prehistoric monster clown,* Lark smiled to herself before she took a quick look toward the cave entrance. There was no sound or movement. The men must still be asleep, and she hesitated to wake them. She stayed where she was, giving Logan and his friend, Dario, a chance to talk in private.

"I promised her mother I'd bring the girl home, Logan," Dario explained. "I keep my word, you know, or try hard to. This time, I'm trying damn hard. I promised Charlotte, swore to it on a stack of Bibles, her child would be safe, that the girl would be in good hands with you."

"You were right. On both counts." Logan took the thin cigarillo Dario offered. "I missed these. Missed you. Thought you'd have been gone by now."

Dario lit up, and cupped the match for Logan, and they both blew smoke rings for a while, which hung in the icy, still air. It was an ongoing competition to see who could puff the largest circle.

"You win. You got the biggest. Chalk it up. I thought so, too, that I'd be gone and you'd be riding with me, but—" Dario grinned, baring his big stained teeth—"I fell in love."

"She love you, this time?" Logan asked. "Or is she like all your other schemers, the ones who took your money and handed you back your heart kind of chipped and broken."

"This time, I have found a lady. I am competing for the hand of a *fine* woman. I do not know if she loves me now, or if she ever will, but I can dream with the best of them. I'll say no more for fear of putting a hex on the affair. That's only a turn of phrase. We are not, you know. . . ." Dario blew up a storm of smoke rings. "Now, about the girl . . . and the posse. What do you want to do?"

"Today, we were planning on turning around, coming back to start over."

"And . . . the past?"

"Lark's going to help me handle my ghosts. She has already."

"Matt January and Jake Chamberlain are coming after you, bringing judge, jury and hangman right with them. Ike Parker is no ghost. They're planning on swift retribution." Dario loudly blew his nose. The sound was like a goose honking.

"We are taking Clarence Cumplin in as a prisoner. He killed Rachel Blue. He can clear my name." Logan had grabbed up a handful of snow and was rolling it round, packing it hard.

"I know someone else who can clear your name. She didn't, so why do expect Clarence will, that snake in the grass?" Logan and Dario glanced up the hill toward the cave. "Clarence Cumplin has never done anyone a good turn that I heard tell of. And he's got—what—twenty men with him, and all of them wanted, too? Are they coming along for the ride, or what? I never thought you a fool, my friend, but now I'm beginning to wonder."

"Who's riding after us? The sheriff?"

"Worse. Vigilantes. Jake Chamberlain is leading them. It's meant to look like a party of gentlemen shooters out for some winter tracking, but that's not so. Jake wants to save the girl to impress her mother."

"Well, so do you. Jake's a decent man. I can talk to Jake." Logan was on his third snowball, lining them up at his feet in a row.

"True. It's who's riding with him that worries me." Dario's high brow furrowed. "Charlotte McKay's coming, a newspaper reporter from back east, a few hired guns belonging to Matt January, Matt himself and. . . ." Dario's cigarillo hissed out in the snow. He ground it down out of sight with his boot toe.

"And . . . ? Roe Ann?" Logan asked.

Dario took a deep breath. "You hit the nail on the head, my friend. Mrs. January. She's a woman who is not one to give up her creature comforts for a cold, *cold* ride, not unless she's after something. Now, you can bet it's not elk she's after. It's you."

"Lark knows there's someone besides Clarence who can give me an alibi. Lark knows why I've kept silent, but she doesn't know who I'm protecting. You're the only one, Dario, who does, besides the lady herself."

"Soon as Lark gets her first look at Roe Ann, it won't be any secret any more. A woman is funny that way. If she loves you, she can tell who loved you before her, who still does love you, just by . . . well, seeing it. It's uncanny, Logan, but in my experience, it's true."

Both men looked in Lark's direction. She was lounging at the cave entrance, putting her face up to the sun. "Except for her mama, that woman is about the loveliest thing I've seen," Dario said, waving. "What else doesn't she know?"

"Everything," Logan answered laconically.

"You going to tell her who you are, and all?"

"Soon as she — soon enough. I'm working on it. I want her to have me for who she thinks I am, a poor cowboy in difficulty with the law. But Lark and Roe Ann January together — that worries me as much as it does you. Roe doesn't love anybody. She doesn't know how. She's a devious woman, and given half a chance, she'll spoil everything Lark and I have together, just for the fun of it. Roe Ann is a life-wrecker, a spoiler. That's about all she really enjoys."

"I am not going to ask you again what you ever saw in her or why you're protecting her. I know you gave her a promise. And I know you southern gentlemen, to the manner born, can't go back on your word any more than a robin can fly north when fall starts to come on." Dario sighed. "It's my fault, I'm afraid, that she's riding with this gang of vigilantes. Here's how it happened, her coming along."

"Why don't you commence telling this tale at the beginning?" Logan said. By then he had made a dozen ice-packed snow balls to furiously hurl them away one after the other.

"Jake was having a little social gathering at the JAK Bar just when I was leaving to find you. He insisted I stay one more day, otherwise I would have had a longer lead on them, given you an earlier warning. It was at this dinner party Jake was so excited about that Roe Ann January up and asked how it was I came to know you, Logan."

"Just hold on. Lark may as well hear all this right now, except about Mrs. January and me, okay, Dario? Hey, sugar! Where's that coffee?" Logan shouted.

"No one's awake!" Lark called back, adding to herself in a lower voice, "but I bet they are now." She responded to Logan's beckoning gesture and slid down the hill toward the two men, bringing with her a few precious pieces of firewood from the dwindling supply at the cave entrance.

"Buffalo chips. Best fuel in this treeless country. I got

a saddlebag full, and a cooking pot. Miss McKay, my pleasure to meet you at last," Dario said, his grin as big as a mule's and warm as summer sun.

Chapter Twenty

Once they had a fire going and a panful of snow melting for coffee, Dario made his report.

"Jake Chamberlain's invited guests, as compared to myself who was never invited but not kicked out, either, began to arrive at the ranch about a week and half ago, supposedly for some good times and hard drinking before taking to sport — hunting plains game — though they never said what type of game, exactly, they were after. They were hoping to beat the early snow, but as you can see, they didn't quite make it.

"This safari was Jake's excuse and cover for organizing a posse without unduly worrying Charlotte . . . uh, Miz McKay, your . . . charming mother."

Lark recognized something in Dario's voice just then that caught her attention. It was love. She was familiar with the tone and timbre of it.

"The Cumplin Gang was back in the news by then. They were calling him Clumsy Cumplin instead of Crazy Clarence because his felonies kept failing," Dario continued. "Charlotte had already started to fret when you failed to appear, Lark, for your scheduled debut with the Ringlings, so Jake didn't let her see the papers with your picture and all. About that time, I happened along to the JAK Bar looking for my travelling companion here." He shifted a shoulder toward Logan. "I reassured her that with Mr. Walker you'd be fine.

"Then the Goldilocks poster turned up at the JAK Bar. My fault." Dario gritted his big teeth. "I tore it off the post office wall and made the mistake of bringing it back with me after a ride to town. So Charlotte got worried all over again, worse than before, but I was right, wasn't I? You'll tell her you were secure and unmolested all along?"

Lark's smile broke like a diminutive sunrise as she exchanged private looks with Logan. Dario took note but said nothing.

"Your choice of words, Mr. Heyward, may not be entirely precise, but yes, I'll tell her I was in the best possible hands and splendidly cared for," Lark promised.

He nodded with relief. "Well, Miz McKay, with all her gentility and grace, presided over Jake's long dining table, which has not been used in many a year. She brought the place to life and . . . *God* she's a fine woman. She charmed *all* the guests, even your grandfather, though he wouldn't admit it. Admit it, hell, he wouldn't even speak directly to her but always through someone else, Jake or myself, usually. There were Jake's trail bosses there, too, a half dozen ranchers and their wives, some of whom had travelled more than a hundred miles at Chamberlain's summons. Ike Parker, Doc Middleton, too, also an old army surveyor turned plains guide. That's Calvin Condon. Know him, Logan?"

Logan nodded, his mouth full of hot, thick, bitter coffee.

"There were a few eastern swells, cattle buyers, and a newspaper man who told me he had been feverishly sketching the goings-on when Cumplin spoiled George

Maledon's big hanging day. Oh, and George was there, too, and wouldn't you know, he tells one of his jokes. 'Why didn't the skeleton cross the road?' asks Georgie. 'Tell us, George,' the Judge says, laughing behind his napkin, 'why didn't the skeleton cross the road?' 'Because he had no guts. Haw,' says Maledon. Everyone else moaned, and we heard no more from him that evening. Feller next to me starts chattering.

" 'A sportsman who gets a three-pound trout with a light eight-ounce rod derives the most exquisite pleasure in the half-hour tussle to land the fish, though with sturdier equipment he might have caught more fish in less time.' It was one of those easterners. 'That right? Pass the salt,' I say. He does, and he goes on like that. 'It's the same delight, in my opinion, for the hunter who would choose to bag one black-tailed deer, after hours of stalking, rather than plow down a standing acre of dumb buffaloes.'

" 'That so? I wouldn't know,' replied I. 'I never have aimed a gun at anything but birds, for scientific purposes, and the only fishing I've done was with a stick, a string and a bent pin off a pier on the East River.'

" 'East of what?' Gideon Blakely says. He's a rancher, Miss McKay. He and his brothers, Samuel and Elijah, work a place near the JAK Bar."

"Our Moses Blakely must be kin to them," Lark said.

"Mose is another brother. Gone bad."

"Not *very* bad. Sort of sweet, if a mite inept, I'd say. Go on, please, Mr. Heyward," she said. Logan draped their bearskin about her shoulders. A cold wind was rising.

"On my other side there's sitting this Ethan Everet, the reporter for Joe Pulitzer's *New York World*. Everet hadn't done any big game hunting or spent much time in the West, either. In fact, he crossed the Hudson River for the first time on his way to draw the Fort Smith hangings. He's a tough little bantam rooster of a man, Everet, reddish hair, pleasant even features, small hands more proportioned for holding pencils than axe handles. Like everyone else I meet, he wants to know how I took up with that terrible killer of school marms and kidnapper of young girls, Logan Walker.

"Naturally, I try and control my temper, not wanting to make a display and ruin Jake's party which was starting to warm up nicely under Charlotte's delightful direction. People were having a good time. The only one looking moody, as usual, is Mrs. January. She keeps twitching her eye at me across the table. I ignore her, though. I turn to answer this Everet.

" 'I am a man of haphazard callings, sir,' I say. 'On my travels toward New Mexico, bringing a bell for the Penitentes in the desert, I've had to stop off now and again to earn my daily bread. That's how I met Logan Walker, who, by the way, is no killer.' The Judge, who never has cottoned to me, harrumphs. I ignore him, too. 'I met Logan when we were both working in the Chicago stockyards.' "

"Hard work," Lark commented.

"Yeah, but what I was doing was fairly clean work, killing cows—hitting them with a ball peen hammer at that curly-haired place on the forehead, you know, and pushing them down a chute to butchers and cutters. That's what I told this Everet. 'Cows are knocked out cold for killing, not like hogs. Hogs are hung up screaming, to be bled. They don't cut a cow's throat; they stab a vein near the heart and let the blood flow before the animal is split in half down the spine, skinned and quartered. Then, depending on the kind of cow—a boner, canner, or an old bull, it's dressed. Now, there is no fat at all on old bulls. They are pure muscle and every ounce counts. There are beef dressing contests among the stockyards' butchers that are better to watch than prizefights and with as good stakes and better, five thousand dollars and more.' Everet says, on his way back home he'll be sure to stop off at Chicago to sketch."

"What work was Logan doing there?" Lark couldn't keep from interrupting.

"I'm coming to that, young lady. It takes me longer than some to get to the point, but I always do," Dario explained. "Where was I? Oh, yes, I was telling that Everet fellow about butchering.

" 'There used to be a good market for fat, for making tallow candles, but now, with men getting rich in eastern Oklahoma taking oil out of the ground, and with this new electricity coming, fat's not worth much.' "

"Nice subject for dinner table conversation, slaughtering beef," Logan laughed.

"I never pretended I was the most poised of men, Logan, and most ranchers' wives aren't squeamish and delicate about killing cows, you know." Dario's feelings were hurt. He decided to change the subject. "Late-sleeping bunch you're running with. Sun's full up. Where's Cumplin?"

"Sleeping it off probably," Lark answered. "Yesterday was not a good one for Clarence what with his sunburn and another botched robbery. Let's let sleeping dogs lie a little longer. What *was* Logan doing in the stockyards?"

"You sound so like your mother, it's uncanny. She asked me the very same question just the same way. 'Logan was there trading horses,' I told her. 'He's a man who can turn a silver dollar on anything with hooves, but the high-bred, high-priced horse flesh, that's his specialty, originating as he does in . . . ?' " Dario looked at Logan.

"North Carolina cotton country is where I'm from. Didn't I ever tell you that, Dario?" Logan asked. Lark looked from one to the other, aware of something going on between them. It was more a feeling than a thought. She couldn't quite get hold of it, and Dario rushed back into his narration.

" 'He — Logan — 'spotted a particular horse about the same time I did, and that's when we got to talking. It was at a holding pen of killer horses. That doesn't necessarily mean horses that kill, though some of them are there for that reason. More often it's old, worndown animals ready to *be* killed, hard-working, gentle, loyal, creatures marked for the boneyard and the glue factory as soon as their useful days are over. Sad. But those horses were strangers to me, and I needed a subject on which to hone my recently acquired skill as a taxidermist. Among one lot of killer horses I was looking over, was this underfed stallion, ideal for my purposes because he was young and I could get him cheap. I didn't care that his dull coat was lashed and cut by quirt marks. I paid no mind to the obvious fact that though he was all bruised and battered, he was not bowed. Logan saw that.

" 'Logan and I both wanted that stallion, for different reasons, need I say. We asked around and found out he was a rogue. Lots of cowboys nearly broke his back trying, and he worked at breaking theirs; but not one had been able to gentle him.

"Logan did. The horse was an outlaw and a man killer, but Logan is tough. And he's kind. Which is what a man has got to be with stubborn horses and willful women.' " Dario showed Lark his mule-toothed grin. "Your mother looked at me when I said that same as you are now, Lark, adorably indignant. Well . . . to continue.

" 'Logan outbid me for that horse and nursed him to

health and beauty. Logan just won that stallion's heart, slow and steady, fair and square. He took an ornery bag of bones that was about to become stickum and turned him into proud, spirited Sundance, that one-in-a-thousand stallion a man dreams of, especially if he's of a mind to start ranching and building a champion stud of Thoroughbreds and Morgans. Once a man has got a horse like Sundance, and some rich grassland, the only other thing that man needs is the right woman, a good, broad-hipped, loving woman, and he can found a dynasty.'"

"Broad-hipped, did you say?" Lark asked.

"For birthing lots of babies. It's easier with wide hips," Logan explained, trying to keep a straight face. He couldn't. "Dario, you clod, most men don't confuse their wives with brood mares."

"Charlotte McKay intimated the same when I said to her what I just said to you. By then, everyone at the table has shut up and is listening to me. There's a hush. I have never been one to cringe from the spotlight, so, I continued talking. 'That's what Logan Walker wants, a dynasty, and he'll get it,' I say. 'He's determined. He could have become a rich stockman in Chicago. Eastern swells, like you, sir,' I told the man beside me, 'foreigners—French and English—with important money to spend were seeking out Logan Walker as purchasing agent. Soon as he started to attract attention, why, Logan was inclined to get out of town and on with his own business. He had every intention of traveling west with me to New Mexico . . . California, until he ran afoul of the law in Fort Smith—and then your lovely daughter ran off with him, Charlotte,' I said, and that, Logan my friend, is when all hell broke loose."

"What?" Logan asked, holding his head in his hands. "Tell it straight."

"Jake protests it's the other way around, that you ran off with her and you're using her as cover for your robbing and killing. I must say there's been no robbing and precious little killing, except of outlaws, since you and Lark took up with Clarence. Right then, Roe Ann's eyes open wide like they do when she's about to take a fit. Next, one of the Blakelys tells about an Indian he had met out on the range weeks before, how he gave the old brave the raised arm sign, imitating cow horns, so the Indian would know it was okay to take a steer, and then the Indian tells Blakely of seeing white men with a white girl, gagged and tied on a mangy black horse. Some one else asks about those two dead men I found strung up and brought to the JAK Bar. Apoplectic old Rufus McKay doubles his reward for both of you, and Matt January's hired killers have itchy fingers all of a sudden, are ready to ride right then. Only Charlotte stayed calm in that moment. 'I am going to get to the bottom of this,' she said, pushing back her chair. 'I will go after my girl myself.' We weren't about to let her go alone, were we?"

"How did you get to us first?" Logan asked, getting to his feet and offering Lark his hand.

"He travels fastest who travels alone, on skis in snow. What are going to do?"

"Ride back to meet them, hand over Clarence and ask for a new trial. Lark, sugar, tiptoe up to the cave and tell the boys to come on down. I'll explain things to them while you kindly see to Cumplin's sunburn."

A few minutes after Lark had entered the cave and no one had come out, Logan noticed one buzzard circling very high in an indifferent, lowering sky. He bellowed like a raging bull. His face going hard, eyes aflame, he took off running, cursing the deep snow that slowed him and the risen wind that was peeling the skin right off his face, most of all cursing himself. He was only half way up the rise when he heard Lark's scream.

Chapter Twenty-one

"Don't you go losing sleep or tears over them Midgettes, Lark," Clarence said after she stumbled over a body and backed out of the cave. "They weren't the nice, clean-cut mannerly cowboys they pretended to be. They were killers too, just like me. Oh, believe you me, miss, they *did* have their nasty side. You brought out the best in them, is all. I was not the only rotten banana in the Cumplin bunch. Listen, come in here and tell me, do you suppose maybe you could bring out the best in me, too?"

Lark stayed where she was. "Clarence, far as I've determined, there's no good to bring out in a loathsome scorpion like you. And I'm not coming a step farther in, which is what the fly should have said to the spider." Her eyes slated. "Why did you have to go and kill Bobby and Billy?"

"It was me or them, Miss Lark, ma'am. Survival of the fittest, that Englishman, Darwin, wrote. Rachel Blue told me about him. He was a sickly sort, always ailing; but he survived, and so will I. Rachel, she always liked to say 'we are all just strangers in a strange land.' I'd always said 'true' to that, 'but some of us are stranger than others.'"

"I'll say, and you are the most outlandish person I've come upon yet, killing these two boys." Bobby Midgette's body, back-stabbed, was just inside the cave, where it had probably been most of the night, close enough to the entrance to have attracted the first vultures.

"There was another Englishman," Clarence continued obliviously, "Frances Galton, who thought up something he called eugenics. 'Like produces like,' this Galton wrote."

"If that's so, you'd better not produce at all, you quirky, killing little tin tyrant." Lark was so furious, she forgot herself and asked, "How well did you know Rachel Blue?" She hadn't meant to put the words 'you,' 'killing' and 'Rachel Blue' together for Clarence. She could tell by the devious swing of his eyes, he had gotten a message she hadn't wanted to send—yet.

"Pretty well. I knew her petty well. She was always trying to uplift and edify me, to save me from myself, she said, and make me look to the future. Her favorite quote was something from John Adams, 'I must study politics and war that my sons may have liberty to study mathematics and philosophy. My sons ought to study . . . geography, history, naval architecture . . . in order to give their children a right to study painting, poetry, music . . .' or some such. There's more to it, but since I ain't intending on studying anything, I don't know the rest. I do know that Bobby and Billy were not the fittest or they wouldn't be lying there dead."

Bobby's brother, Billy, was sprawled beside him, with his throat cut, his wide-open, sightless eyes fixed on a stalactite pendent from the cave's roof. From the knife slashes on Mose Blakely's face and hands, it appeared he had put up a fight. He was still breathing but barely, and Jesse Jaynes, tied and gagged, was squeaking like a terrified rabbit caught in a trap.

"Oh, Lord, Jesse! What's he done to you?" Lark wailed, darting forward into the cave, only to be caught herself in Cumplin's snare. "Is there nothin' in you disposed to compassion?" she asked as Clarence got a firm grip, his arm like a tentacle about her waist, and pulled her into a dark, low corner of his lair.

"One step more, Walker, and your lady love here is done for," a voice sounded from the dark recesses as Logan stepped into the cave, guns drawn. When his eyes adjusted from snow glare to shade, he saw Clarence radiating menace like a python spreading its hood. There was a frozen look on the outlaw's face that indicated he'd really gone round the bend this time. His swimming eyes were those of a madman, his vacant stare something straight out of a vision of hell. He held Lark in front of him, a fragile butterfly in the grip of a scorpion, an arm about her neck, a knife at her face. The fifteen-inch Bowie blade had a coffin-shaped handle, and Logan knew better than to so much as flex a muscle.

"What do you want, Clarence?" he asked mildly.

"I want the lady's horse, Satan, saddled up along with my steed, Vamp, short for Vampire, you know. It's got to be more than coincidence, her and me having horses with kind of corresponding names. Oh, and get Sundance, too, Logan."

"There's a blizzard blowing up, Clarence. Where we going?" Logan took a step forward.

"We are not going anywhere. I'm planning on using that animal of yours, that damn arrogant son of the

morning, as a pack horse, Logan. I'll put him in his place or in his grave. Load him up. I want your wooly chaps, too, Logan, and the bear fur blanket that kept you two love birds so toasty. I'm taking everything there is and whatever money's left. Oh, and I need a mount for the quakin' cookin' bank clerk there. I am not going without my chef."

Jesse Jaynes squeaked, and Logan went to him, kneeling at the man's side.

"He's hurt, Clarence. Jesse's cut. He can't go anywhere, and you're still all sun blistered yourself."

"That's because I am the Prince of Darkness. Daylight's my enemy. It's clouding up, so I will prevail. Get busy packing or the dainty face of this . . . exquisite sorceress mightn't be so perfect for long. See, I'm going to make her my adjutant in the army of darkness. I plan on teaching her all I know about midnight, and beyond."

"Now, Clarence, you aren't feeling yourself. Lark will be more than happy to nurse you a day or two longer, isn't that so, sugar?"

"Yes," Lark said, not moving at all, knowing that if she so much as tilted her head, her face would be marked by Cumplin's knife.

"And we'll talk all this over again when you're feeling better, Clarence." Logan was squatting on his heels deftly untying Jesse. "Don't move until I say," he whispered to the nervous cook.

"No deal. Get moving. Do you think I didn't see y'all out there with that stranger, getting ready to turn me in? I figured it out, what you've been up to, getting me to kill off my faithful followers, one by one, until I was down to just your bunch. I am not as stupid as you suppose. I've told you that before, Logan. An avalanche don't have to land on me."

"But that's only Dario Heyward, the bell maker, Clarence. He's not the law."

"Ha, so you say." Clarence scowled. "I'll just take me a better look." With Lark still in his grip, he moved toward the cave entrance. He stumbled over Billy Midgette, and Lark gasped as his knife nicked her and a thin line of blood began to trickle down her face.

"Not for you to worry; it won't scar—this time. Ain't that what you told me, Walker, when you near severed my jugular? Of course, my old buddy Skeets got left with a *good* long-lasting scratch, didn't he?" Clarence laughed. "I'm learning a lot from you, brother." Cumplin stepped out of the cave and was blinded by the light just as Logan finished freeing the bank teller.

"Follow me, Jaynes, with a gun in your hand," he hissed and hurled himself out of the cave, colliding with Clarence, sending him sprawling in the snow. Cumplin rolled and slid downhill toward Dario, his hands, like talons, digging into Lark's arm. Fighting, she slid with Clarence, who had dropped his weapon. Now Logan had the knife, and with a roar like a lion's, he lunged and plunged down the slope after the outlaw.

Jesse Jaynes staggered out into the open, waving Lark's little Derringer. Dario held a primed double-bore, hair-trigger rifle in one hand and a steel mallet in the other as he moved fast toward Cumplin, who was caught between a rock and a hard place, as the former gang leader himself would later boast.

"Let her loose! You just let her loose, Clarence!" Jesse screeched. "If you hurt her, Clarence—" When Jaynes' little gun went off by accident, he was so startled, he fired it again, and kept firing. To get Jaynes under control and to throw a fright into Cumplin, Dario fired both gun barrels at the graying sky just as a big posse came into view,

215

riding right at them across the plains, hell bent for leather, their pistols going like fire crackers on the Fourth of July, sharp, short bang-bang reports in the icy air.

"Everybody, hands up! Now!" Logan called. The group was strung out in a nearly straight line, Dario at the bottom of the incline, Clarence and Lark a few feet higher, Logan next and, not far from the top, Jesse Jaynes, shaking with fright. "Don't give them any cause to feel menaced. Show them we surrender." Logan planted the Bowie knife up to its hilt in the snow at his boot heel and raised his hands, all the while watching Clarence Cumplin and Lark, who was still a prisoner. The outlaw's arm was around her now in such a way that he could easily snap her neck and so tight against her throat, he could cut off her breath with hardly an ounce more pressure.

No one moved in the fixed tableau as the riders bore down on them. Jesse Jaynes, too terrified to unclench his fist, still held the on to the small gun like a drowning man to a bit of flotsam. All he knew was that he wanted to be standing close to Walker when that the posse got there.

So he slid toward Logan. His gun went off. The posse held up, lined up and opened up. Their guns blazed. The three battle-hardened men—Logan, Dario and Cumplin—fell flat. Jesse Jaynes trembled and fired his last bullet and flopped down. Thinking all the men were hit, Lark screamed and screamed; she couldn't stop, as she started toward Dario . . . turned back to go to Logan, and hesitated, wavering and terrified when the bullets found her.

She crumpled, and went down where she stood, her blood spurting ghastly red on snow whiter than linen.

Logan's roar of rage and torment seemed to go on forever, to fill the very sky and hang in the gray air as he grabbed the knife and charged toward her. But Clarence was closer. He got to Lark first.

"She ain't dead, yet"—he grinned maniacally—"so just hand over the knife or she will be. I ain't got no more to lose, brother."

When the riders galloped up and surrounded them, gazing at the wounded girl dumb struck, horrified at what they'd done, Cumplin again had his knife at Lark's throat. By the time Charlotte and Roe Ann January, who had been ordered to hang back, caught up with the posse, the doctor was kneeling at Lark's side, taking her pulse, and a tall, erect, perfectly groomed, white-haired old gentleman was standing over them, tears streaking his ruddy face.

"Daughter," Rufus McKay said to Charlotte, addressing her directly for the first time, "I was correct. Your little girl always was a prisoner of these men." He opened his arms to his own daughter, who hid her face against his chest and sobbed like a child.

"She's hit in the leg and chest. Her pulse is strong, but if she loses more blood it won't be," the young doctor said. "I need a fire, shelter, hot water, blankets, now!"

"Uh, uh, Doc. No," Cumplin snarled. "I'm getting out of here, and she's going with me. She's kind of my life insurance. Besides, there's a reward out for her, ain't there? I want it. I'll send someone with instructions where to leave it and find her, after I'm *long* gone.

"Fetch the horses, Walker. Ain't this where we began a little while back? You could have saved us all a lot of trouble and grief if you'd done as you were told right off. Now do it." As Logan began to move very slowly away, evaluating the likelihood of success of any desperate action on his part, a thought occurred to him.

"You'll have another murder on your head if you move her. Take me instead, Clarence. The reward's a lot bigger. I'll be easier to travel with, too, not being shot up and all." There was a mutter from the men in the posse and then what seemed a measureless pause while Clarence mulled over the offer, looking back and forth from Logan to the inert form of Lark.

"You're right. I do not need any wounded woman to slow me down, and there *is* a bigger reward for you," Cumplin finally said, his grin quite mad. "Old man"—he turned to Rufus—"are you the one who put up them rewards?"

McKay stepped forward, one arm about his daughter still, as though he were afraid of losing something rare and precious he'd only just found.

"Are you still planning on paying, and if so, which one of 'em do you want now, him or her?"

"I did offer the rewards, sir. And I never"—he gripped Charlotte's hand—"never, with just one exception, have gone back on my word. I'll pay you every cent, only now I will call it ransom."

"For mercy sake, she is dyin' in the snow!" Charlotte gulped between sobs. Clarence didn't even glance at her. He was interested only in Rufus.

"You going to pay on Walker, the reward . . . ransom, whatever you want to call it, dead or alive, like this says?" He reached into his shirt and brought out the folded poster.

"I've told you I am a man of my word." The wind tugged at the edge of McKay's hat. Tears froze on his cheeks. He never moved.

"Your word as writ down here is 'alive or dead.' That right?"

The old man nodded. "It makes no difference to me one way or t'other how he's delivered. This man is going to die by shooting or hanging. This man kidnapped by grandbaby. Maybe he has got her killed, too, and I never told her—I never spoke her name."

"You are one gritty, tough old geezer, ain't you, Mr. McKay?" Cumplin mused. "I didn't have no father to raise me and show me the right path. If I'd had one, he might have been like you by now. Gray, sage, moral and principled. Then again, he might not. Like produces like, and I am none of those things I just mentioned."

"Son, that's the argument of a weakling coward. Growing up without a father is no excuse for going to the bad as you have. Now, don't make matters worse for yourself. This lovely girl's life blood is running out. Back off with that knife and let the doctor tend to her, *please!*"

But Clarence wouldn't, not yet. He was just beginning to enjoy himself, commanding a position of power among all these big, well-armed hired guns and important people who were all helpless before him, the scorned Crazy Clarence Cumplin.

"Having no daddy, I had to invent myself as I went along. You see before you, whether or not you admire the result, a self-made man. I was nothing but a scavenging swamp rat, and I climbed out of the slime the only way I could. My dear mother is an Old South lady turned loony bird, since the war. She spends most of her time in the booby hatch. She never liked me at all, and if she ever got the chance, she'd do to me what William Clark Quantrill's old lady did to him.

"Don't get any closer, Doc!" he ordered when the surgeon, black bag in hand, tried to approach Lark again. "See, Quantrill got back-shot, paralyzed from the neck down, and then he died. He was buried in Louisville. After the war, Mrs. Q., as his mother was called, had her boy disinterred to be taken home and laid to rest in the family burial ground in Ohio, she said. Only he never got there.

The ghoulish woman sold his bones as souvenirs. That's some mama for you, ain't it?"

No one answered. Jake Chamberlain's vigilantes, afraid to further jeopardize Lark, were, as one, very very slowly pressing in closer, forming a tighter and tighter circle around the outlaw and his hostage. Cumplin became more agitated.

"Old man, I'll take you up on your offer. I'll ride away with Walker instead of the girl, if he's tied hand and foot. I'll send to you for the reward later. There's another if. I'll do this only if you give me some guns and pay up now for Lark. You've got her, don't you?"

Rufus, who seemed exhausted all at once, reached imploringly toward the outlaw with an arthritic, crooked hand. "Be reasonable, I implore you, sir. I'm not riding with such a large sum of money on me."

"I am," Logan intruded, his voice tight. As he went down on one knee beside Lark, he thrust a thick wad of folding money at Clarence, who was as surprised as everyone else. "Lark honey." Logan leaned to whisper in her ear, his voice so low only Clarence heard what he was saying. "Don't leave me, please. Darlin', I'm coming back for you. We've only just begun and now —" his voice broke, and he leaned to drape the bearskin over her, wrapping it round her body which seemed so fragile and small under the prairie sky. "Live for me. Don't forget me, Lark!!" Logan added in a fierce whisper. He was bleary-eyed and blinking when he looked up. "Doc, please, help her now." Then, reluctantly, he turned to Clarence. "I'm ready. Let's get to hell and gone, you son of a bitch."

"You'll get no argument from me, brother." Clarence laughed. "I certainly am that, a son of a bitch. Mount up."

"Do you think we'll ever see either of them again?" Roe Ann January asked as the two men rode away.

Though she hadn't been able to hear a word Logan said, observing the heart-wrenching scene just ended told her all she needed to know. In seconds, her expression had changed from curiosity to shock to anger, finally to jealousy and sly vindictiveness. She was dressed in black, as always since Logan's trial and sentencing. The lack of warm color in her attire intensified the sallow cast of her face as she looked after the riders with nostrils flaring, her eyes wicked and angry.

"Logan Walker *won't* get away with it."

"Get away with what, Roe?" Matt January asked his wife. Though dressed in trail-stained gear and showing a three-day growth of mangy black beard, the man might have been considered handsome if not for eyes that were too small and of an unpleasant pale hazel color. They seemed not to be perfectly synchronized, the left pupil following the right after a fractional second's delay. It was just enough to make looking directly at him oddly disorienting. His wife rarely did, and consequently, she was unaware at that moment that he was regarding her with sinister suspicion.

"All I mean, Matt, is he won't get away with murdering Rachel Blue. Or taking advantage of that . . . that poor girl." Roe Ann looked daggers at Lark being attended now by the doctor, her mother and her grandfather.

"What makes you say that, Roe, about him taking advantage?" Now Roe Ann did look at her husband.

"Oh . . . I don't know. I've heard . . . gossip about Logan Walker—and women."

"Now you mention it, I've heard talk myself about him—and . . . *older* women."

"But . . . it don't matter any more. The crazy man, Cumplin, will kill that deceiver if a posse doesn't. If neither do, the prairie winter will. No one can survive out there, not in this hard, killing season, not even Logan Walker. In the spring, when the snow melts, all they'll find left of him is his splendid bones, frozen against a tree or in some gully, you mark my word."

"Don't be dumb, Roe. No posse'll find those two, and Cumplin ain't going to kill Logan Walker, not with all the links of history and blood they got between them. The winter won't harm 'em, neither. They'll head straight to Ingalls and see out the winter eatin' and drinkin' and whorin' at Squirrel Tooth Janie's hospitable establishment. Come spring, them two will be side by side, gazing at the blue Pacific Ocean."

Chapter Twenty-two

It was very early morning the day after Christmas, and only Lark and Dario were in the parlor, the others still asleep or in the dining room gratifying themselves on Aida's steak and eggs, fried potatoes, spoon bread and coffee. Wind was snarling around the house and booming down the chimney, hurling snow, which had been falling for several days, against the iced windows.

The blizzard had entrapped a houseful of Christmas Eve guests, invited to the JAK Bar for the express purpose of cheering up Lark McKay. It was apparent to all that something was terribly wrong with the girl, though only Charlotte and Dario knew the cause of her malaise, her yearning for Logan and her fear she would never see him again, not alive, anyway. The others, especially Jake and Rufus, were practically turning handstands to make her smile. To make them happy, she tried to smile. She mostly failed.

Dario Heyward, exchanging his peddler's stovepipe hat for his ornithologist's cap, had been attempting, in turn with others compelled by the storm to take up temporary residence at the JAK Bar, to distract Lark and stimulate her interest in something besides Logan, but every subject brought her right back to where she started.

"There are two types of meadow larks, eastern and western varieties," Dario lectured. "They look petty much exactly alike, both yellow-breasted, with yellow throats, but their songs are of different timbres. The western lark's is lower, and also unlike that of its eastern cousin in phrasing — syllabification. It is the single dissimilarity between them, yet, minor as it is, it makes all the difference. In Wisconsin where their territories meet and overlap, the two varieties never intermingle in choosing mates. It seems the little females will only dance to one melody even though both varieties of larks vocalize exquisitely. That's because they are Passeriformes oscine icterids — from the Latin, *icter* meaning yellow, *passer* meaning sparrow, *oscinis* meaning song, birds which have many pairs of syrinx muscles in the throat. Both kinds of larks have plaintive songs that pluck the human heartstrings and often bring a tear to the eye."

"Dario," Lark sighed, "it doesn't take any bird song to bring tears to *my* eyes. Tell me about skylarks. Logan called me his skylark, once."

"The courting male skylark," Dario pressed on, "has the most wonderful song of any bird on earth with the possible exception of the nightingale. He, the skylark, spends much of his time on the ground and suddenly, showing off for his ladylove, spirals upward, bursting into wildly lovely melody.

"You don't much care today, do you, Lark, about birds?" Dario asked. "Now listen here, my girl. I'm sure Logan is all right. I'm also sure that one day, he'll come acourting like the male skylark. He'll make a spectacular appearance and claim his true love — you. Whether he'll burst into song is another matter. Please don't look so sad."

Dario uncoiled his long thin body from its customary, now well-worn place on Jake's sofa to fluff Lark's pillows. She was settled in a big chair in front of a roaring fire and wrapped in an Indian blanket. "Did you know there's a lark-spit in every English kitchen?" he asked. Getting no answer to his question, he went on filling the silence. "The bird is considered a great edible delicacy. My father told me that. He came from there, the British Isles. My mother was from Italy. They met in Hell's Kitchen in New York City and—but that's a long story for another time. Where were we, Lark? Oh, yes, I was lecturing on larks. I'll continue.

"Colonies of skylarks have been taken from England, the land of *their* origin, too, and released all over the world, in the Sandwich Islands, New Zealand even in New York on Long Island. That was about ten years ago, 1880 I believe. It remains to be seen whether or not they will settle and thrive there.

"In the south of our country, meadow larks are called bobolinks sometimes, or rice birds, because so many were killed in the Carolina rice fields where they went to feed. Slaughtered in the thousands upon thousands they were, and sold, skewered, a dozen to the stick. Logan told me that. That's where he comes from, Raleigh."

"God! I hardly know anything about him! He never even told me where he came from. Or why he left home," Lark said, tears in her eyes brimming over.

She was recovering well from her gunshot wounds, Dr. Middleton, also a house guest, had assured everyone including the patient. But she knew that her heart, though untouched by anything but love, hadn't even begun to mend.

"Listen here, miss. I know your secret, and I also know that misery loves company; so I'll tell you woes." Giving up on birds to try a new approach, Dario pointed a long thin finger at Lark. "You, me dear child, are not the only one heartsick in this house."

"Who . . . else?" Lark asked. Her lower lip quivered. "I'm sorry, Dario. I've just got the weeps. Who?" She took a sip of hot milk thickened with raw egg, one of Aida's more conservative treatments for melancholy and the vapors. The cook was also doing secret and mysterious healing rituals in the kitchen with bits of straw, earth and a rooster.

"Me. I'm in love in vain."

"Who with?" Lark sniffled. "Why in vain?"

"With Charlotte." He hung his long head, which, angled at the end of his stick-thin neck, gave him something of the aspect of a scarecrow.

"But, oh, dear, Dario! Charlotte's in love with Jake." Lark looked up, alarmed.

"That's why it's been in vain so far, my secret love. And that's only the half of it," he answered, not going on to say what the other half might be.

"Does Jake feel the same way about Charlie, do you suppose?" she asked.

"For a while, I thought he did, but now I don't know anymore because—" Dario stopped himself just short of saying, *Because now I think Jake's in love with you, Lark*. "Well, let's just say I have some reason to hope that your mother will love me yet. You mustn't give up hope either, that your dreams will come true, not until all is lost for a certainty."

"But what about Charlie? If she loves Jake, and you love her, and Jake maybe doesn't . . . well, should she give up hope, or not?"

"Definitely! She must give up on Jake at once. She'd be much happier with me," Dario proclaimed, baring his big upper teeth like a mule getting set to hoot and honk. He clapped his hands once and doubled over with laughter, actually eliciting a small giggle from his audience of one, suddenly expanded to include most of the household.

"Ah, that's better! You've such a beautiful smile, Lark, you should show it more often," Jake said, striding into the room. Lark blushed when he kissed her cheek and his warm, dry hand rested on hers. Jake noticed the glow of color that came to her cheek and took it for a sign of pleasure, not distress, at his attention.

"Mr. Heyward, have you ever been told you'd make a great circus clown, even without makeup?" Al Ringling asked Dario, following Chamberlain into the room. "You have a very mobile face and an enormously endearing charm. Clowns, elephants, pretty ladies in fluffy gowns riding white horses—that's what the circus is all about. Interested?" The enthusiastic talent scout was always on the lookout for a new face whether it was beautiful, funny or bizarre. "I'm still trying to convince the McKays to join up with us come the spring. But my friend Jake here wants them to go into competition with me instead. He has offered to finance a Wild West Show of their own, like the one Bill Cody has been so successful with."

"If Dario Heyward were to go with any show, it would ours," Jake answered confidently.

"The man's not a clown, Al, and he's on his way to New Mexico," Charlotte said, making her entrance with Ivan, Alexander, and Ralph, who raced to Lark with a red india rubber ball in his mouth. He dropped it in her lap, waiting for a game. She threw the ball for him once or twice which pleased Charlotte no end. "Dario is taking a gigantic bell to some monks in the desert. Right, Dario?" She laughed, so grateful to him for making Lark smile, she kissed him on the cheek. Thin as he was, Dario quivered all over, like jelly.

"Brothers, not monks, aye, Heyward?" Ike Parker asked, following old Mr. McKay into the room. "Rufus told me about them years ago."

"When I was fighting Apaches in old Mexico, in '49, I heard about the religious fanatics and their *unusual* practices, though I never saw the ceremonies. I didn't know they had kept them up all this time," McKay said. "How did you hear of the Penitentes? Very few have, particularly back east."

"You see, sir, before I left home, I was shown a recent photograph taken by a Mr. Lummis. It is the only picture ever made of *los Hermanos de Luz*, Brothers of the Light, a secretive sect of Penitentes who still, now—today—in this modern era of the Iron Horse and Mr. Edison's electrical lights, go on being true to their ancient faith. I'm determined to learn for myself what really happens among them and the other groups who have dwelled in the isolated hamlets and deserts of New Mexico for hundreds of years. Regular churches wouldn't have them because of their . . . well, extreme customs of prayer, mortification, flagellation and . . . other excesses, so they have a secular clergy. They built their own adobe chapels, called *moradas*, which were decorated by *santeros*, itinerant artisans of inspired skill, I'm told, who carve extraordinary three-dimensional religious figures of wood, and others who paint on tin and wood.

"What I'm about to say may sound odd to you all, but hear me out. Though I am not myself a religious man, looking at those photos, I at once felt a strong bond with the wandering penitent craftsman. One day, months later, a strange thing happened to me." Dario paused, holding his audience, which now also included Roe Ann January, Dorsey Middleton, and Aida, who was holding a tray of coffee. All were spellbound. Even the little boy, Joachim, gazed at Dario with big, round awed eyes. "As I was passing a foundry in St. Louis, I was stopped in my tracks as if by a hand on my shoulder, one so strong I actually looked round. I saw no one, but yet, I couldn't proceed a step, so overcome was I with a passion to cast one large, deep-voiced and perfectly tuned bell to take west to the Penitente Brothers."

"Did you do that? Is it in your box wagon?" Aida asked, looking and sounding almost animated. Dario nodded. "I did, and it is, and despite appearances to the contrary, I am still on my way to deliver it. Anyone who wants to come along is welcome," he said, looking at Charlotte.

"I'm coming." Ethan Everet yawned. The news artist, a late sleeper fresh out of bed and rumpled-looking, meandered into the room and at once began to draw Dario. "When are we leaving?" he asked.

"After this winter hibernation. I plan to make it to the desert before Easter. Maybe that's where I really belong, in the desert. I've been to lots of other places now, but none of them caught me and made me want to stay."

"Every man must find his own right place in the world," Rufus said. Erect and dignified as always, his thick white hair brushed back, mustache and goatee perfectly trimmed, he drew a straight-backed chair up beside Lark's and placed his hand over hers. "I found my place, but it took time. My greatest goal, when I was young, granddaughter, was always to be someplace I wasn't, until I got to Oklahoma, and if anyone tries to bury me anywhere else, I'll kick the lid right off the coffin, I swear! When I came here, long years ago, it was a land bountiful with treasures — buffalo from horizon to horizon, fish so thick in the streams and rivers you could scoop them up with your hand and the skies darkened in spring and fall, with clouds of birds . . ."

". . . and hundreds of Indians, too, Daddy, who weren't at all glad to greet you," Charlotte reminded him. "Lark, your grandfather's feeling for the natural world was singular, almost uncanny. He could accurately predict when a mare would foal, when the first snow'd fall, when the moon would rise."

"I still can, Charlie. The only thing I wasn't good at predicting was my own unruly emotions that caused me to drive you away from me. If your mother had been alive, she'd have stopped me from doing such a thing, and there never would have been any breach in this family. Ah, your mother, Charlotte, brought serenity to the rash wild man I was *and* refinement and civility to this wild land."

"And it was really uncivilized here then, let me tell you," Ike interjected.

"We can largely thank you, Judge, for bringing us law order and my dear wife, your sister, Charlotte's mother, for giving us a measure of culture and elegance." Rufus smiled.

"Logan Walker told me he was looking for a lonesome place," Lark said. "Uncle Ike, I need to talk about Logan Walker. He is no murderer even if he can kill when he has to." There was a strength in Lark's voice that hadn't been there a few minutes before as she repeated the defense of Logan that she had maintained since her rescue.

"Listen, darlin,' he is still a wanted man, and that's dead or alive, remember; but if he turns himself in, presents evidence, speaks out about his alibi, I will hear him. He won't be lynched in *my* jurisdiction, but if he's guilty as charged, George Maledon will get him to hang legal. I believe in the law of the land. It works. I am as true to the law as a man can be. Don't you suppose I'd much prefer to be known as the Land Claims Judge or the Marryin' Judge instead of the Hangin' Judge? It is the property of fools to be always judging, that's what one of the old philosophers wrote. I agree, but there was a dirty job to be done here on the frontier. I have done part of it, ridding us of some of the worst of the lawless, anyway. We can all rest easier now that a lot of them are behind bars. The future is open before us. So, little Lark, if there's been a miscarriage of justice, you get word to this boy, Walker, let him know I am willing to rehear his case. . . ."

"Here here!" Jake Chamberlain cheered. "I can forecast what's to come, the land covered with cows, corn, farms and ranches. Fine, strong young women, who are the cradles of the future, will bear many sons and daughters and raise them up strong and unafraid, some to build here, some to gallop off on their own to claim and settle other wilderness lands! You are all invited to stay on for a big, *big* bash on New Year's Eve. We'll recall the past, celebrate the future—"

"Jeez, Jake, calm down," Roe Ann scoffed, sweeping into the room, still wearing black. She paused at a sideboard to spike her coffee with rye whiskey, took a deep gulp, sighed with pleasure and sat back in an armchair to listen to the conversation.

"Uncle Ike, if I had any idea how to get a message to Logan, I'd have done it. But I don't, I don't!" Lark sighed, not looking at Jake who, she was beginning to suspect, had spoken for her benefit about young women being cradles of the future.

"Well, I just might have an idea about how to go about finding Logan, little girl," Roe Ann said, her lips twisting in what was never meant to be a real smile. Her voice was thick with sarcasm. "Rather it's Matt, my husband, who perhaps could be persuaded to find Walker, that is if I can find Matt. He's the man who sleeps out in the bunkhouse with his boys or in the stable with his horse, or, preferably, in what ever bawdyhouse full of fancy women is closest. He might could find Logan. Matt's got friends in all sorts of places, including outlaw dens and lewd houses, all up an down this great land. If anyone can get to Logan Walker now, it's Matthew January, given the right incentive. You can bet on it."

When Roe Ann drank deeply and glowered with malevolence over the rim of her coffee cup, Lark suddenly knew she was looking at Logan's alibi. All at once, she began to feel much better, even hopeful that she could persuade the woman to speak the truth.

Lark might not have been quite so optimistic if she'd known just what the incentive was Roe Ann had in mind to set Matt January on Logan's trail.

Chapter Twenty-three

Champagne began flowing early, just past noon, on New Year's Eve day at the JAK Bar. There was almost continuous music from the spinet piano in the front hall, everything from Chopin nocturnes, Dario's contribution, to short bursts of barrel house rags, Aida's forte. Sitting tall, straight and expressionless on the piano stool, during short breaks from the kitchen, she pounded out the rollicking tunes in the style she'd learned in her younger days working as a barmaid in a series of frontier saloons.

Though the snow had finally stopped falling and the sky had brightened, most of the guests had stayed on at the ranch, pleased to accept Jake's invitation to see the old year out and 1892 in. More visitors, neighbors encouraged by rising temperatures and willing to hazard the snow drifts, kept arriving, among them three of the four Blakely boys, Gideon, Sam and Eli. Their brother, Moses, was in jail in Fort Smith awaiting trial.

There would be a bountiful spread at dinner. Aida's herculean efforts, abetted by Charlotte and the Blakely boys' wives, would yield stewed fowls, grilled steaks of JAK Bar beef three inches thick, boiled neat's tongue (ox to easterners), porcupine fritters, fawn haunch and other salted wild meats of the countryside. The *piece de résistance* was to be a roasted shoat—a young pig past the suckling stage and, until quite recently, something of a barnyard pet.

Lark, who was not only back on her feet but incessantly wandering the house, walked with a certain stiffness, great care and the help of a single crutch which Dario had produced from his peddler's wagon. Dr. Dorsey Middleton prescribed exercise to tone and strengthen her slackened muscles if she expected to perform again in the near future as an equestrian, and so, on doctor's orders, with the temperatures risen to near forty degrees, she paced the ranch house porch for more than an hour each day.

With foot-long icicles like sabres dripping in the warmth of the sun's glare and deep softening snow everywhere, the cleared porch was the only safe place for her to drill. She enjoyed it, and she always had company—the doctor or Dario or Charlotte but most often Jake, who was with her on that bright holiday morning. He was high-spirited, animated and as enthusiastic as a boy as he talked about how fine it felt to have the house full of people and how fond he was of her—and of her mother.

"Charlie told me a lot about you, while you were gone, Lark, what a great little trooper you were—are. She showed me a photograph of a little girl of maybe three . . . four, you Lark, in a smocked dress and straw bonnet trimmed and ringed with lace and daisies, the lace running down her back. The picture's a profile, you know, and that little girl, Lark, with her upturned nose and full, pouty baby mouth—well, a man would

be thankful all his life for a dainty daughter like that."
Despite the wind and cold, tiny beads of sweat stood on Jake's brow when he swept off his ten-gallon hat. It left a faint indentation on his forehead and in his gray-peppered dark hair.

"I never had a girl of my own like that—like you—to love, one with taffy curls and a freckled nose, eyes big as saucers. I'd have dandled you on my knee, taken you everywhere with me, taught you all of what I know about life . . . and about ranching. It's not too late for me to have a daughter, or a son . . . so. . . ."

Lark stopped still and looked up into his eyes.

"But, I need a wife. I think I've found me one, if she'll have me."

"Go . . . on," Lark said nervously, recalling her conversation with Dario.

"Well, we are something like a family already, the three of us—you, me and Charlie. I want you to know how well . . . fond I am of your mother, and I was thinking—well, wouldn't it be fittin' if we really were—a family, that is? So I am proposin' to ask her for. . . ."

"Yes, Jake? Go on. Asking Charlie . . . ?" Lark smiled relieved. Dario had been mistaken. Jake was proposing to propose to Charlie. Jake *did* love Charlie, after all.

"Well, she being both mother *and* father to you—she's all the family you got—before I spoke my mind to Charlotte, I wanted to hear it spoke aloud by you, hear you say you—"

"That I like the idea of becoming kin to you, Jake? I do, and so will Mama. Jake! It's wonderful." Lark laughed, her eyes dancing with gladness and gleaming with tears, happy ones for Charlotte, whose prayers were being answered, sad ones for poor Dario Heyward, a loser at love again, whose hopes would be shattered. "When are you plannin' on askin' Mama? This is going to make her real, *real* happy, Jake." Lark sighed. Then, in a rush of emotion, she hugged him hard.

"Tonight. Tonight Charlotte, and everyone else, will know! It's our secret surprise, yours and mine, until then. Oh, Lark, soon's you're up to it, I'm taking you and Charlotte skating on my pond. I've always imagined beautiful ladies in red velvet capes all trimmed with white fur—rabbit or . . . or fox, either is okay long as it's white—whirling and laughing down there in the winter meadow. Would you . . . like to do that?" he asked.

"A person has to walk before she can skate, but of course I would!" She glowed, imagining Charlotte's face when she actually accepted Jake Chamberlain's proposal.

He went on talking, but Lark didn't hear very much of what he was saying. She had her own prayers and preoccupations to concentrate on. She was expecting a caller and yearning so for a first glimpse of him that she just nodded each time Jake intruded enough on her thoughts to require some response. So great was her inattention, the man had probably been gone a good ten minutes before she even noticed he was no longer there.

The view from the ranch house porch was extraordinary. Lark could see for miles and miles, something that especially pleased her on that New Year's Eve afternoon because she had come wide awake at seven in the morning, with watery winter sun invading her room and the absolute certainty, planted in dreams, that Logan was on his way to her, that she would see his face before the year—and the day—ended.

The impression was so strong she had been tasting his lips on hers ever since. She felt the strength of his arms folding about her as her body opened to him, softened and moistened. The peaks of her breasts rose hard in dreams as her finger tips, working with perfect remembrance, seemed to trace Logan's long, lean torso from his narrow hips to the wide span of his shoulders. Awake, she had lush memories, explicit ones, of him moving against her, with her, into the warm, humid haze of her desire.

He would come to her that very day, he would!

If she had been pressed to explain the strength of her conviction that Logan was on his way, Lark couldn't have. Sixth sense, women's intuition, dream prophecy? She didn't know. She only *knew* he'd be there, and she was infectiously, wonderfully jittery with anticipation. She was so giddy with it, she would have danced if she could have. Butterflies were churning in her tummy, and a tingly tension in her every nerve ending made it impossible for her to stay put for long.

She was elated, and she was radiant and lost in a delightful world of her own, and if Logan didn't get to her soon, she might perish of longing!

It was during that day of restless meandering that Lark discovered to her surprise she liked the kitchen better than any other room of the house.

"We never had one, a kitchen. There was only the circus cooktent when I was growing up," she explained to Aida on her first call there of the day. "The best meal on the road, and the biggest, was always breakfast—steak, ham steaks, eggs and wheatcakes made at a mile-long griddle where the cook really kept the flapjacks flying."

"Mile-long griddle?" Aida, a literal person, questioned.

"Of course not." Lark laughed warmly. "It just seemed that way to me when I was a small child!"

Enlightened, Aida nodded and smiled herself as Lark, taking a donut, left the room to continue on her restless rounds.

The JAK Bar housekeeper, though continuing to be reserved with Charlotte, whom she regarded with slackening, always courteous, suspicion, had developed an easy fondness for Lark despite the fact that the daughter, like the mother, appeared to be exactly the sort of pretty female who brought trouble wherever she went. Somehow, the yellow-haired young one seemed different—maybe. Aida hadn't come to a final decision, but as Jake often said of people and things, there was always the exception to every rule, and that's what Lark was, probably. Aida not only liked the girl, she also trusted her.

That was not so of that January woman, far from it. Of all the guests staying at the JAK Bar, the only one Aida truly scorned and trusted not at all was Roe Ann January. Just thinking about the creature made the housekeeper's eyes narrow and the corner of her mouth twitch with contempt. Roe Ann was exasperating with constant demands for extra blankets, tubs of hot bath water, bottles of rye whiskey and new sheets every morning.

Aida was still ruminating about her least favorite

guest when her most favorite, Lark, returned to the steamy kitchen. With fewer than twelve hours to wait for midnight, the new year and Logan—the girl had been counting them off—nothing could shake her conviction that he was getting closer to her by the minute.

Shy smile flashing Joachim's eyes, dark as coffee beans, fixed on the girl whose flaxen hair fascinated the child. He'd never seen the like, but then, few had, the color was so rare.

"She gives not one thought to all the soaking, pounding, rubbing, boiling, starching, rinsing and ironing that don't get done by magic—Indian magic or white man's," Aida said out of the blue, just as Lark came tapping back into the room to observe the dinner preparations.

The housekeeper was prone to putting her thoughts into words, abruptly beginning in the middle of her musings, and Lark nodded, smiling, knowing some clarification might follow. Or might not. Aida handed her a cup of hot soup and went on with the monologue.

"Working over stains on table linen can't be helped. Use magnesia on food stains. Remember that when you have your own things to care for. Cover the soiled place with magnesia and paper and draw up the grease with a hot iron. Do it again and again and again. It cleans."

"That's good to know," Lark commented.

"For bleaching sheets, sun is best. There's not much sun here in winter. We used to use hogs' manure on sheets, for the ammonia in it and bluing, too, with indigo and ultramarine. Now Jake gets chlorinated bleaching powder at the general store in Fort Smith, and he buys store starch; but I still like my own starch.

I make it from potatoes. Jake bought me a methylated spirits iron, too. I use it. It makes its own heat inside, better than coals, better than putting an iron on a laundry stove. It's a help. After I iron, I use the linen press."

"Both? Why?" Lark inquired, knowing curiosity was expected of her.

"Because I like sharp folds and even edges," Aida replied. Lark politely went over to look at the linen press standing in a corner. There was a flat tablelike surface with a heavy board of the same size frame-mounted above it. The upper was fitted with a large wooden screw which, when turned, lowered it to the table top and whatever was placed upon it — sheet, cloth or napkin. The more forcefully the big screw was turned, the tighter the fit between the boards, and the better the result. It was a job that took strength, something Aida had to spare.

"January. Always treading on someone's corns, that one."

"So . . . the woman's troublesome, is she?" Lark asked, noticing that Aida, like some of the others at JAK Bar that morning, seemed happily churned up. The cook, Lark knew, handled rare moments of excitement by going on a talking jag, and the girl didn't want to cut this one short.

"January. Worse than troublesome. She has always been vexatious, carrying tales, plotting and scheming, setting one man against the other. That was her way even before she married Mr. Matt. She wanted Jake Chamberlain for a husband. He didn't want her for his wife."

"Oh?" said Lark, nearly bubbling over with the news that Jake had found someone he did want — Charlotte.

Instead of bubbling, she gobbled down another donut. Charlotte hadn't been able to stop herself from producing them in huge quantities since she and Rufus McKay had made their peace.

"Jake did not want Roe Ann Simpson. He had no interest in a pampered, lazy banker's daughter. Jake had *me*, after his misses passed, and ever since. I see to everything for him. I will always."

"You . . . you love him," Lark mumbled, her words hardly understandable. The tone of Aida's voice had turned the donut to sawdust in her mouth. She stopped chewing and looked with quizzical dismay at the cook, who shrugged, fleetingly showing a proud little possessive smile before she chattered on.

"Roe Ann settled for Matt January. She didn't want to, and so she went and turned a good man wrong. Turned him jealous and mean, drove him out to the bunkhouse. She is worse than ever since that boy left, the one killed the teacher and kidnapped you."

"Aida, he didn't kidnap me. I want to talk to you about that—him—because he didn't kill Rachel Blue, either, and he did have an alibi and I think he'll be here when—" Lark, on the brink of confiding everything, stopped short when Roe Ann, still wearing black, her face very pale, came gliding into the kitchen like a wraith.

"Don't let me interrupt. Go on, go on. You were saying?" she asked Lark, drifting straight to the cabinet where Jake kept his liquor.

"I was saying . . . ? Oh, yes, about when my mama and me had a piglet clown in our show act for a while. That's what I was telling Aida about. The pig's name was Rex. Cute as a button when he was teeny, but when he grew up big as all get out, Professor Gentry sold him.

"Uh, how do you cook up that stoat, Aida?" Lark asked. Not knowing how much Roe Ann had overheard, she began nervously limping about the large kitchen, annoyed at herself for talking about Logan at all.

"You really want to know how to cook a shoat?" Aida was skeptical until she realized what Lark was about—filling the air with harmless chatter for Roe Ann's benefit. "You strew fine salt all over a shoat one hour before you will put it down," the cook explained about the pig. "Then, slit it open like this"—she took up a long, very sharp butcher knife and cut with a fast upward motion, strong and precise—"just enough so you can fill inside, pack it with buttered bread, cut thick, to make the shoat look plump and round. More salt, marjoram and sage. Now . . . look. You mount it," Aida said, impaling the pig with a slow steady thrust until the point of the spit emerged beside the head. "Get rid of lower leg joints . . ." She deftly hacked them off with four fast chops of a small axe. ". . . put them in a kettle to boil with the liver . . . pepper . . . salt, to make the gravy sauce. Brace the upper legs to keep them straight and, ugh—" Aida grunted, hauling the pig to the open-hearth kitchen fire and settling it on the turnspit. "Catch the drippings in a pan under it. It is half done when the eyes pop out."

"Oh, gawd! I have always avoided the scullery." Roe Ann smirked and grimaced. "Listening to you, I know I done the right thing."

"What do you do with the head?" Charlotte asked, bustling into the kitchen rubbing her hands happily.

She was looking forward to baking pies and making more donuts. Aida had reluctantly agreed to that much trespassing in her kitchen.

"I'll leave you kitchenmaids to your domesticity. Too many cooks and all," Roe Ann said, exiting with her bottle, ignored.

"When the pig is done," Aida continued, "I rub it with butter. I cut off the head. I split it between the eyes. I take out the brains. I mash them with the liver and put them in the drip pan. For the gravy. The roast shoat is presented with its back to the platter edge, half its head at each end."

"Sounds *good*. I've always had them served whole with the head right on the pig." Charlotte rolled up her sleeves and got busy while Aida began to make a batter for flapjack fritters she would bake thin on a spider griddle just before dinner. She mixed sour beer, pearlash, rice, milk, and eggs. A busy silence settled.

Beans were baking, pots steaming, a neat's tongue stewing; Aida was mixing, Charlotte was humming and Lark was pacing.

"Charlie, this is going to be a momentous night," she announced. "I . . . I just *feel* it."

"I feel it, too. I have an inkling something very . . . very climactic and special is about to happen. I can't explain it. Maybe it's because Jake is real happy and sort of mysteriously nervous, too. I suppose I'm reacting to his mood, but besides that, he did mention there'd be big surprises before midnight tonight and—" Charlotte stopped short of saying she expected a proposal of marriage. She believed that talking about something you really, *really* wanted *before* you got it, would bring dire consequences.

There was no need, though, for Charlotte to express her thoughts aloud. Aida and Lark both guessed what it was she wasn't saying. The cook, betraying her own feelings about Jake Chamberlain, dropped the mixing spoon in her batter. Not knowing how to react after what she'd been told by Jake and what she'd read in Aida's face, Lark snatched up a half dozen donuts, gave her mother a quick hug and left to consult with Dario at once. Much as it would pain him to learn he had lost Charlotte, the bell maker had to be told of the latest turn of events. To keep a tender love story from turning into a romantic farce or, worse, a full-blown tragedy, Lark needed Dario's help.

"Aida!" she called over her shoulder, hobbling out of the kitchen with the little boy Joachim scurrying along at her side, "please call me when you're ready to do the pig's head."

But for the drip and hiss of shoat fat splattering in the pan, there was a silence in the kitchen again, this time an awkward one, until the three Blakely wives, Emma, Amy and Ethel, changed the atmosphere. They all at once filled the room with their pretty chattering voices, their rosy-cheeked children, eight in all, and mounds of fragrant, savory offerings for the evening feast.

"Ethel's pickled walnuts are famous," Amy said, kissing Charlotte on the cheek, undoing her bonnet strings and gathering up mufflers and knitted mittens of varying sizes as they were shed by the children. "Ethel soaks her walnuts in boiled and skimmed cold water, then covers them with ginger, boils them with whole pepper and mustard seed, adds garlic and clove and keeps them close covered for months, until a special occasion arises—or it's county fair time. She always wins a prize at the county fair."

"So do you win, Amy, for your potato cheese, and Aida wins for her fritters," Ethel added, "and so will Charlie McKay win a ribbon for her donuts and her pies." Charlotte laughed with delight.

"Think I'll still be around here, come the county fair?" she asked. "How *do* you make your potato cheese, Amy?"

"Boil the potatoes, cool 'em, skin, grate and pulverize 'em in a mortar, cover the pulp in sour milk and leave it three or four days in hot sun. Then I knead 'em, pat 'em and shape 'em, and dry 'em in cheese baskets in the shade. Store them in kegs. That's it. They'll keep a goodly while with nary a worm or maggot and grow better with age. Want a taste?" Amy asked, going off after a straying baby.

"What's that you have there, Emma?" Charlotte, nibbling, asked the youngest of the Blakely wives, a red-haired, dark-eyed mother of three-year-old twins, Houston and Abiline. She had set out a row of bell jars.

"Pickles. Firm ones. I can't stand insipid pickles. It's the fault of the vinegar if they go soft on you. You must throw it away and start over with new, scalding-hot vinegar, more horseradish, flag-root and alum. Pickles will last for years put up that way. I've always got some ready for special occasions—birthdays, Christenings . . . even weddings." Though they had just arrived at the JAK Bar, the Blakely wives had already been affected by the prevailing atmosphere of very high, very romantic expectations.

Chapter Twenty-four

"Joachim, you are more'n likely to trip me up, child, tugging on my skirt that way!" Lark said, trying, not too successfully, to get to the main room where Dario could usually be found in his customary place at the fire. When Joachim tugged at her skirt again, Lark stopped and placed a hand on the little boy's cap of dark hair. "Something wrong? I didn't forget to give you your ginger snap or something, did I?"

He shook his head no, raising his big, grave, brown eyes to hers and holding out one pudgy, tightly clenched little fist. When he uncurled his fingers, a piece of paper, folded and refolded very small, lay on his upturned palm.

"Something for me? That's real nice of you, Joachim. What's the occasion?" Lark smiled, hurriedly unfolding the wrinkled scrap. "Oops!" she exclaimed when a small object fell and rolled away to disappear under a chest of drawers. "Will you please go after it for me, whatever it is? I can't stoop down to—why, Joachim, where *did* you get this silver finger ring?" Lark asked, recognizing it as the one Logan had offered her, the one she'd so blithely refused. Now she slipped it on, struck to the heart at the sight of it and all atremble with elation. She glanced down then, at the scrap of paper in her hand and read

> 'Haply, I think on thee, — then my state,
> Like to the lark at break of day arising
> From sullen earth, sings hymns at heaven's gate . . .'
>
> I've only sleeping night owls and Satan for company, but a glimpse of a golden lark could turn my hellish darkness to dawn and rough wood portals to heavenly gates.

The quote from the Shakespearean sonnets and the addendum were written in perfect calligraph, each letter finely shaped, a small work of art in itself. The message was clear to Lark: Logan was waiting for her. She realized with some surprise that she had not ever before seen his strong, clear script. Thinking about how little she really knew of the man she loved, how much they still had to discover together, she forced herself to pause just long enough to fling a shawl about her shoulders and wrap Joachim in a thick blanket.

"I've decided to have another walk, a real one, perhaps as far as the gate . . . or the stables. Would you like to come along with me?" she asked the child. "Please come!" she implored. "I might need some help getting there."

"And getting back?" the child queried.

"Well . . . we'll see. I think I might be able to find

my own way home—alone," Lark answered with a trilling, joyful laugh before she crushed Joachim in a hug and planted a kiss on his brow. He laughed, too.

"The man said to bring you to where he was because it would make you happy. He was right. You are happy already. The man told me it was a secret, just for you and me," Joachim said, smiling proudly and nodding vigorously. "He gave me this to keep forever—for luck." When he showed Lark an Indian medicine stick beautifully worked with beads, she hugged him again, and they rushed to the front door, letting a gust of wintery air invade the JAK Bar, only as an afterthought remembering to close it behind them.

With immense effort, Lark compelled herself to move slowly and with great care through deep snow as she chattered happily to the delighted child, both burbling with excited laughter which hung in the dry air. The crutch, precisely placed, left a pattern of round holes beside deep parallel tracks of boot prints, hers and Joachim's, as the two, heads lowered against a rising wind and blowing snow, inched their way toward the stable. The fox terrier, Ralph, who had bounded out of the house after them, was in his usual pitch of excitement that was heightened by a walk with his mistress, their first together in weeks. The animal bounded and leapt like a jack rabbit from drift to drift. When in advance of his human companions he made his comically floundering way through a holding pen and came within yapping distance of the stable, he was joined in his snowy excesses by an equally peppy, noisy black and white dog.

"Joachim . . . Oh, Joachim, look!!" Lark said. "It's that crazy, wonderful, spotted Catahoula cow dog jumping about in excitement! And when Max is this excited . . . his master must be close by!!" The barn door swung open, and Lark, her heart racing, stood still. The tall figure of a man moved from shadow into glowing sunset illumination. Logan tilted back the deep-brimmed hat which had been hiding his eyes. He grinned.

Time missed a beat for Lark at her first sight of his strong-set jaw and wide, squared shoulders. She sighed with almost fearful delight, her heart swelled and danced in her bosom and she could hardly keep herself from darting forward. Only the fear of falling on her injured leg held her back, and she trembled with love and longing and wild impatience through what seemed a measureless time as, looking neither left nor right, Logan came toward her moving silent and swift as an arrow, the smile spreading over his handsome face to sparkle in his eyes, his arms reaching out, opening, their irresistible invitation finally drawing Lark forward.

She left her crutch planted upright in the snow beside the saucer-eyed, beaming little boy and, limping, took a few struggling steps forward through the deep snow. And then — they were together, Logan's arms enfolding her and drawing her gently to him as, with super-human restraint, he held himself in check for fear of crushing her. Her arms, encircling his neck, drew his lips down to her wide, laughing mouth.

That first kiss after so long and excruciating, so uncertain a separation was beautifully, infinitely tender.

"I was so afraid . . ." Lark whispered, "that I'd never see you again, never touch you, afraid you'd been hurt or killed or . . ."

"I didn't know if you were alive or . . ." Logan said, beginning to speak at the same instant, his voice low and dark, eyes hard-sparkle amber, like soft stones studded with gold. "I had no word about how badly hurt you were, if you'd pulled through, if I'd ever again hold you, feel . . ."

". . . and now that you're really here I . . . I'm almost afraid to see you, anywhere but in my dreams. Oh, Logan, that's where you've been this long, long time."

". . . feel your heart beating next to mine. . . ."

Their second kiss, which wrung a primal sob of desire from Lark and a moan of love and need and thankfulness from Logan, was even more splendid than the first—romantic . . . passionate, verging on mad recklessness—until they both remembered Joachim. Logan knelt in the snow, put his hands beneath the child's elbows and hefted him high in the air.

"You did real well, scout. You can be my outrider any time," Logan said, and their three laughs rose, mingling in the winter twilight. "Now, Lark and I have some . . . business to see about, just the two of us." Logan shot a sideways glance at Lark that changed her laugh to a ripple of a sigh. "So, will you go on back up to the house, Joachim, before your mother starts to worrying and comes looking for you?" Joachim nodded. "And will you keep on keeping our secret?" Logan asked, still holding the delighted boy aloft. When he nodded again, Logan set him down, and Lark wrapped the blanket more securely about his small body.

"What if Charlotte or Aida or anyone asks after me?" she mused in a husky voice. "I can't expect Joachim to lie. What's a boy to say?"

"Joachim, you tell the straight truth to your mama and to Lark's mama. Anyone else wants to know, just shrug. Now, that's not lying, is it?" Logan asked. He and Lark started the child on his way back to the warm ranch house and watched him safely home before, shivering, they turned to each other again.

"It's got real nice and warm today," Lark commented, smiling a little. "We've been real lucky so far, you and me, Logan, with weather, leastways. We got rain right when we needed it to cover our tracks, then a bit of Indian summer to romp in, a bit of chill and snow and all, just at the right time when we were gettin' cozy and. . . ."

"We're still lucky. If this had been a day of the sort of killing cold, zero and below, that's not unusual in these parts, well . . . it would have been a lot harder for me to get to you. I would have, though. It was like something was calling me, urging me on. . . ."

Lark's smile broadened. "It was *me* urging you. I had to set my longing eyes on you this day or die!" she said, near tears of happiness.

"It was as if you were a lost part of me I had to get back. I couldn't let another day go by, not seeing you, Lark, or . . . touching you." There was the fast flash of his glorious smile. "Now, let's get to some serious touching, sugar, in some warm place that's also soft and quiet and private and sweet smelling, like a hay loft, say?" His eyes danced with anticipation. "Well, would that please you?"

Lark's heart was pounding as she nodded and took Logan's hand, leading him to the stable. The instant they were inside, the squeaky door pulled shut after them, their bodies met and pressed close, and their mouths melded.

"I can taste cinnamon and sugar on your lips, love—" Logan sighed—"and I smell flowers in your hair."

"Sugar and spice yes, but not flowers, darlin'. You must be imagining things." Smiling into his eyes, Lark traced a caressing hand along Logan's jaw line.

"Imagining? Oh, just let me tell you what I've been envisioning . . . better yet, let me *show* you all I've been dreaming of."

"Yes, please show me now, Logan" was Lark's tremulous answer as he took her hand and led her to the hayloft ladder. They ascended slowly because of her weak leg, taking just one step at a time until they emerged into the loft where a lantern cast a soft cozy glow and the familiar, warm bearskin was enticingly spread.

"You've made such . . . such lovely preparations for love." Lark laughed, taking up a bouquet of everlasting flowers, their yellows and purples, though dried, still vivid. "They're smellin' of spring, love." She smiled as she sniffed them delicately.

"Now who's hallucinating?" Logan chuckled, taking the shawl from her shoulders and undoing the flaxen coil of her hair. He sank down on one knee, drawing her to him, enfolding her slender waist. Burying his face between her breasts, he moved a hand up along her leg, along the swell of her flank and hip. She undid her skirt fastenings and stepped out of it, still encumbered by the two layers of linsey-woolsey petticoats she wore over red flannel longjohns.

"I've hallucinated you again and again, Skylark, and always, your hands were filled with flowers, always you were waiting for me under a tree all ablaze with bright berries." Logan's seductive voice, indecently sensual and low, made Lark so weak with anticipation, she curved against him. "Sometimes your hair—" he raked fingers through yellow silk—"your hair would be coiled high, glinting with golden clips and combs. Sometimes it flowed like liquid gold . . . white gold, and I'd crown you with garlands of white star flowers, fine as lace."

Lark raked a hand through Logan's long chestnut hair, stroked his cheek, and sank down on her knees in front of him, her hands resting on his shoulders. she nuzzled at his throat like a kitten as she undid the toggle fastenings of his heavy shearling range coat. When her hand slid beneath his wool shirt and wandered along his rib cage, he gathered her inside the shearling.

"I remember you," she sighed. "Oh, do I ever remember." Her lids fluttered, momentarily concealing her misty gray eyes. They opened wide almost at once at the first adept touch of his fingers beneath her shirtwaist which brought the peaks of her breasts to stand hard against the soft flannelet of her winter chemise. Then they were flesh to flesh, finger tip to breast tip, and Lark felt streaks of heat piercing to the depths of her flat belly. Logan peeled away her longjohns, and she tore open her own shirt in urgent haste, then his, sending her buttons, and his, flying about the haystack. He had to help her with his belt buckle her hands were so shaky, and then, with their clothes in chaotic disarray, loosened, shifted and ripped but not, because of the cold, dispensed with altogether, their bodies brushed and touched and met as they sank down together, submerged in fur and wool.

Neither spoke or even uttered a sound. They clung to each other in a conflagration of hot and reckless carnality. Touching, tasting and stroking, they writhed isolated, alone in the world, together. Nothing remained real but their vibrant bodies fusing in the shared, desperate necessity to squander vast reserves of passion, both realizing in their nerve endings finally, and in their hearts and minds, what they had only felt for so long in longing dreams.

The wild profligacy of their lovemaking hardly tapped the garnered reserves of their desire until, much later, well after the sun had gone down, they paused. Deliciously tired, passion, like thirst, slaked, though not sated, they clung to each other in the soft circle of lantern light drowsing and dreaming.

"You carry my very life in your heart," Logan said softly yet with unbounded astonishment. His gold-sparked gaze smoldered as it slid lovingly over Lark's slim body, which was bare now at his side, all aglow, in their warm nest of fur.

"If that's so, you must tell me . . . who you are, why you and Clarence. . . . Why does he call you 'brother,' and you call him—where is he, Logan? Did you . . . ?"

"I didn't kill him. I couldn't if I wanted to. I made a promise. I'll keep it."

"Another one of your impossibly noble vows? He'd have killed you given half a chance. He's a murderer and a madman to boot." Lark shook her head. Obviously troubled, his eyes pained, Logan ran a hand through his long dark hair.

"He was always wild but not always . . . unbalanced. You see, he is my brother, in a way, my brother-in-law. Interesting phrase, isn't it, to use for an outlaw? He was wed to my baby sister when she was sixteen. He fathered her children. They were in love. It was losing Nancy and the babies that pushed Clarence over the edge."

"Nancy Walker . . . Cumplin. The initials on your belt buckle?"

"She made them for me, and painted my flask as well, the ones I traded for your ring. She wouldn't have minded. She believed in love."

"If your sister loved Clarence . . . why did she leave him?" Lark's eyes were the softest gray.

"She hadn't a choice," Logan answered. He turned away and gazed off into the shadows at the peak of the sloped roof above them that was weighted with snow. Below, horses shifted in their stalls and nickered softly, and sweet, warm stable odors rose to the lovers' loft.

"In a matter of weeks, in August of 1888—Nancy and the children were all taken from him by an epidemic of swamp fever. Little Mary was wanting eight days of her third birthday. The twins, Ben and

Stephen, were just past two, the baby, Nathan, three months. There is nothing on earth that twists the heart so as seeing the tiny coffins go into the ground, all in a neat row with their small white stones rising." Logan's voice broke.

> " 'This lovely babe so young and fair
> Called hence by early doom
> Just came to show how sweet a flow'r
> In Paradise would bloom.' "

"Soon after I had that sad inscription carved on the baby's little stone for poor Nancy, she took sick, too, and passed over, but on her deathbed, she asked me to look after Clarence as best I could. She knew there was violence in him just lying quiescent under her care and love. She was a beautiful girl who loved the world and he—when he was given the news she was gone . . . you'd not have known him for the man he'd been. I think if Nan had even an inkling how Clarence would change or that he might do harm to Miss Rachel—Nancy loved Rachel. So did I."

"Why did he kill Miss Blue?" Lark asked in a low voice.

"She was our cousin, once removed, a spinster lady school teacher. Nancy and I were her only heirs. She had come out to the frontier alone, as a girl, to gather wild flowers on the prairie, she said, and to roam free, but also to help transform the wilderness. A girlhood friend of Rachel's, Sophie Sheppherd, taught in the Indian school when the Apaches were prisoners in Florida and Alabama, and Rachel wanted to do that work in the West now that the tribes were being moved again. Nancy and I admired her work. So did the Massachuetts Indian Association. They supported her with money, though she put most of her own small wealth into her work. There wasn't much left for anyone to inherit, but Clarence didn't believe that.

"After Nancy and the children were . . . gone, Clarence and I came west to try and forget. Clarence went wild, turned to robbery and pillage. I was hurtin' so bad I turned my back on the world. I hid away in the hills for a time, then did a little herding and roping and trail riding for Matt January. I tried to keep to myself but finally, a fool, I took what solace Mrs. January offered. I'm sure you've figured out by now that she was my alibi. I must tell you true, sugar, I'll always be sort of grateful to her for bringing me back to myself. If she hadn't, maybe you and I would not have found each other and. . . ."

"Long as we don't lose each other again, Logan." Lark smiled wistfully. "Go on."

"It was just accidental I met up with Miss Blue at the hotel in Fort Smith, but soon as I did, I started visiting her regularly, to talk of Nancy. After a time, I brought Clarence to see her. I thought it might help him too, to talk to Rachel, as it had helped me. But by then, he had already taken to heavy drink, and one night . . . he killed her for the money that would have gone to Nancy. He never got one cent of it, never will. Me and the law will see to that. He's going to pay, I swear it. It won't be me that exacts the price. It'll be Hangin' Ike and his hangman, George Maledon."

"Where is he now?"

"Following my clearly marked trail. I wanted to lure him here. He's but a few hours behind. When I face him and Roe Ann January in front of Judge Ike, maybe our troubles will be over, darlin'."

"Maybe?" Lark tensed.

"Skylark, I can't stop myself thinking . . . it's all my fault . . . Rachel and Nancy and the little ones." Logan's eyes were flat and cold, his voice anguished.

"Your fault? How?" Lark demanded, her heart aching for Logan. He closed his eyes and let his head fall back.

"If I hadn't brought Clarence Cumplin home to Raleigh after I met him on a hunting trip in the Great Dismal swamp, he and Nan would likely never have met. If I hadn't brought him there to that hotel, Rachel Blue would be alive today. But she's not." The last sentence was a rasp of pain.

"Logan Walker, you ain't God, and it is real presumptuous of you to talk like you might think you are. You can't live no one's life but your own!" Furious at him and grieving for him at the same time, Lark let her own eyes drift closed as her calming hand began to play over him, lingering on his brow, on a burst of hard muscle, a convexity, a favorite slope or rise of flesh and bone, and soon, she had roused him yet again.

"I want you more," she said in her husky voice. She shifted atop him, kissing him and sheathing him in one maneuver, then moving languidly, though with purpose, as he draped her in sheltering fur. "From now on . . . I want, oh . . . I want to hear every breath you draw, Logan, day and night . . . every day

. . . every night . . . and I want, I want to watch . . . to see every glance of your eye . . . that's *all* I care to see, all! Logan, oh, Logan!" she moaned, throwing her head back in cresting rapture, draped only by her long flaxen hair now, yet oblivious to the cold. Her words came faster and faster, seeming to flow straight from her heart in tempo with the quickening rhythm of their young bodies until she was struck dumb by the tremors that rolled through her, strong yet delicate, and resonated through Logan, who, clinging to her at the climactic moment, was savagely tender.

"Tell me, are you still craving fame and fortune or can things finally be settled between us?" Logan rasped, after a time.

"Hm, yes, I'd say we could come to an amicable arrangement, like marriage, say, once your legal problems are cleared up. But that needn't rule out wealth and fame entirely, need it?" Lark asked, sweetly teasing.

"I don't ever want to share you, not with one man, or thousands." Logan scowled. "If I have to kidnap you again, I will. Be warned."

"Oh, well, seeing as how you are the very reason I draw breath, wealth and fame kind of dim in comparison to what I expect from you. So, if those expectations are met, I don't see why I couldn't give up — well, just about everything else I've ever wanted before. Or thought I did. That okay?" Shivering a little, she grinned, sat up and glanced about, then began to collect her torn and scattered clothes.

"Sure, okay. So . . . why are you going away from me now when I've only just found you?" Logan grumbled.

"If I'm not at the New Year's party, there'll be suspicions that'll lead to searches, and soon *you'll* be found. Unless you're ready to produce your alibi for Uncle Ike, or confess to murder, one or t'other, I better go now, hear?" Lark pulled on a boot.

"You're right, sugar," he relented, avoiding the subject of alibis. "Everyone's after me—the law, Clarence, Roe Ann, even Matt January. Come on. I'll help you up close to the ranch house, and I'll let loose of you, just for now, but keep your eyes open. Keep on the lookout for me later. I just might have a nice surprise for you, 'round midnight or shortly thereafter," Logan said, bestowing upon Lark his hard, glinting handsome smile.

"And I just might have a bit of a revelation for you, too, darlin'," she answered, her own smile tremulous but resolute. When they kissed, each was intrigued by the other's allusion. Each would have been more than a little surprised to know that Roe Ann January was the key to the success of both their schemes.

Lark kissed Logan hard and soft and lovingly, then grudgingly let him go just outside the circle of the JAK Bar's porch lamps.

"Logan!" she whispered, swept by a wave of fear before he'd gone two paces. "Let's just run—now, like gypsies!"

"And hide like maggots the rest of our lives? No," he

answered, the single word taking immense effort as he resisted his own impulse to gather her up in his arms and run like the wind. "You deserve . . . better," he added, turning away.

The night was so still, not a breeze stirred. Smoke from the JAK Bar's chimneys rose straight up. She watched him go, silhouetted against the sky. She waited until even the sound of his boots crunching snow had faded before she turned her thoughts to the house and its denizens. Like the light the lanterns threw, the voices and laughter drifting out to her seemed very small, almost feeble, in the immensity of the measureless prairie night, so still the whole world seemed to be holding its breath.

Chapter Twenty-five

"I should have got while the getting was good," Dario grumbled to Rufus at just about the moment that Lark and Logan were reluctantly parting. For the first time since arriving and settling in at the JAK Bar, the natural clown was glum. From his favorite place on the sofa, with troubled dark eyes watching the fire leap up the chimney, Dario perceived not cheery flames but impending havoc. "I could have been in the desert by now, in the warm sun, but instead, here I sit shivering in the Indian Nation on New Year's Eve on the brink of . . . disaster. I have bad feelings."

Sensitive to everyone's emotions, made privy to many secrets, Dario knew that certain expectations would be unfulfilled, and a lot of hopes, including, perhaps, his own, would be dashed for good before this night ended. It seemed to him the stage was set for catastrophe. His friends, to say nothing of himself, were facing heartbreak, and he was powerless to do anything about it. He slid lower in his place on the sofa and sighed dramatically.

"That's no way to face a new year, my man," Rufus McKay said, unfurling his newspaper with a flourish and rattle. "Where'd we be if we all looked at life as you are doing at this moment? Buck up, Heyward. Get off your duff. Get yourself a lantern and take yourself a walk in the brisk outdoors; let the wind blow the cobwebs off you, man, and get the blood started pumping through you again! Then stop by the kitchen. Perhaps the ladies will give you a plate of something tasty to tide you over to dinner." Mouth-watering odors were wafting through the house from the kitchen, and Dario scented the air like a large hound, his nostrils quivering, as he considered McKay's advice.

"Do anything but sit there opposite me complaining," the old man added in an annoyed grumble, and Dario sighed again.

"I can't argue with you, Mr. McKay. Right you are. A positive outlook is a decided asset, but I must decline to act on your suggestion to go strolling in the great outdoors. I don't like this climate, and I do not trust this climate. The mercury could drop any time. It's been known to do just that, and a man caught out in a plains blizzard ain't got a snowball's chance in hell. This is no fit habitat, Summer or winter, not for man nor beast."

Rufus harrumphed. " 'O, wind, if Winter comes, can Spring be far behind?' Ask yourself that, Heyward. You should have stayed back there in the East if all you were going to do was come out here and criticize Oklahoma."

"I had nothing to keep me in the East, sir, though I do on occasion recall with fondness the man-made beauty of the city—bridges, towers, flights of pigeons from tenement roof tops on a summer's eve, forests of masts on the rivers and such. Then I remember that men needn't build towering cathedrals in the wilderness. The bare land is awesome enough. It's the surging life of the city I do miss, particularly that area of New York that has come to be called 'Little Italy in Harlem,' a neighborhood resembling a picturesque European market village, at least to those who are not forced to abide there with no hope of escape from grinding poverty. Of course, as soon as you cross that imaginary line at Ninety-sixth Street and go north on Fifth leaving Millionaires' Row behind, you enter another world, where you will find Greeks, Cubans, West Indians, Spanish. . . . The locality I refer to in particular, where some of my mother's numerous relations lived, runs along the river on the east side of the Island of Manhattan. It's crowded with shabby tenements poorly built, fire escapes loaded with goods and furnishings . . . laundry fluttering across alley ways . . . streets lined with the stalls and carts of knife sharpeners, organ grinders, ice vendors, bootblacks. . . . Yet hope and a passion for life are found there, along with dark despair."

"Many's the woman who followed her land-hungry man west from such despair, Heyward, to face another sort of desperation — endless toil and loneliness on the frontier. And yet, those females made gardens in the wilderness. My wife, Charlotte's mother, was one such devoted stalwart, though I took her not from a city warren but from the ease of a moneyed home and the companionship of her sisters. If only I had it all to do over again, Heyward. . . ." Rufus sighed.

The two men lapsed into thoughtful silence until Dario looked up to see Lark, as radiant and beautiful as he'd ever known her, tiptoeing across the room. Standing behind Rufus, she winked at Dario and placed a finger to her lips for silence. Dario studied her, then blinked, realizing something was up. Not only was the girl elated, but her cupid's-bow lips were lusciously puffed and bruised. There was only one way that could have happened—kissing—and there was only one man in the world she'd let kiss her that way—Logan! Dario's melancholy eyes lit up for a moment before his face set again into an expression of worry and dejection. Happy as he would be to see his friend, on this particular day, Logan would be one more complication in the human drama about to unfold at the JAK Bar. Dario moaned and held his head in his hands.

"Now what is it, Heyward, you seek-sorrow, you?" Rufus demanded, stroking his white mustache. "I can't abide such an exhibition of gloomy emotion, not in a grown man."

"Guess who?" Lark interrupted in a sweet, high falsetto voice, covering the old man's eyes.

"Ah! No other than my lovely grandchild, a young lady with very cold hands. Your pessimistic friend here was just telling me he feared to set foot out of doors. What's your advice?"

"Depends. On if you've got a good enough reason to go and on what you're of a mind to go outside to do," Lark replied with studied nonchalance, meeting Dario's silent questioning look with a telling smile, completely confirming his suspicions.

"She is surely a sight to cheer the biggest bug-bear, even you, Heyward." Rufus smiled over his shoulder, reaching back for Lark's hand, drawing her to a seat beside him.

"Now, Grandfather," she began very seriously, "I must speak with you about Charlotte's future and mine and I—"

"I'll speak to that point myself, child, around midnight, on the eve of this new year that finds us together for the first time, you, your mother and me. I'll have a little surprise for you and your mama. Right now, there is just one thing I want to say to you, what I've already told Charlotte. I didn't always do what was meet and proper when it came to you two, and I deeply regret my mule-headed mistakes."

"Grandfather, the past can't be undone, so don't plague yourself, 'specially now that everything is coming out so . . . so perfect," Lark said with only the faintest hesitation. Dario moaned and rolled his eyes at the ceiling but held his tongue.

"Now, don't get me wrong, child," Rufus said. "You might's well try to make cheese from chalk or skin a flint as think I'll weep over spilt milk. I do not believe in nursing regrets; I never did as a young man. I don't now as a seasoned fellow with a white head and traces of too many old lies on my face. 'The mill cannot grind with water that's passed.' I do, though, intend to try and make amends for the wrong I've done you and Charlotte. As for the future, I could wish you velvet gowns and gold a'plenty, girl. Hellfire, granddaughter, I could give you all that—gowns and gold—but without love, my dear, a mountain of money won't mean much, especially when you are old and gray and lonely like I would have been if you hadn't come home to Oklahoma."

"I agree wholeheartedly with your outlook, Grandfather!" Lark exclaimed, sitting up straight in her place, happily surprised by his philosophical views. "If I never hear the roar of a crowd again or have another spangled satin dress or a coat with a velvet collar, I won't mind. I've found what I want, and it's not silver or gold, or fame or fortune. Love's all."

"All? All? It's everything!" Dario bellowed, springing to his feet. "And harder by a long shot to get and keep than gold, but if you've found it Lark, well, I might find love, too, before this day and this year's done," he said as Lark followed him into the hall.

"Dario . . . don't get your hopes up. Jake's going to propose to Charlie tonight."

"At the very look of you, Lark, hope springs in my heart anew!" He thumped his chest with both fists and bellowed like a circus gorilla before he strode toward the door. "And you're wrong about Jake. He may be up to something, but I just know it's not proposing to Charlotte. New Year's festivities are to begin in an hour. I'm off to get ready now, if you'll excuse me . . . ?"

"Dario, wait! You're just blinding yourself to a truth you don't care to hear. From what *I've* heard, it's going to be awfully . . . well, surprisin' around here around midnight for more reasons than one, and I want you to know—" Lark stopped in mid-sentence as Dario vanished around a corner with one more bellow and thump.

"An alterable fellow, isn't he?" Rufus commented with faint disapproval when Lark returned to the parlor.

"Dario is very . . . emotional and exuberant and self-deluding, and I'm afraid he's in for a rough evening and some serious disappointment." Lark frowned, gazing into the fire.

"Now, don't you start in to pondering and getting woeful on me, missy. I have put up with Heyward's somber mood most of the afternoon." Rufus turned a page of his newspaper. "Hmm, says here, right after the first of the year, the trial's to start for some of the Cumplin Gang—that's Mose Blakely and Jesse Jaynes. The law still hasn't caught up with Clarence himself or that young cowboy, Logan Walker. But they will be apprehended, I've no doubt, and Ike Parker'll see to it they all swing, after what they did to you." The old man bristled with indignation.

"I am going to come forward and testify for those two men. They tried to help trip up Clarence. There's good in them both and . . . Grandfather? There's good in Logan Walker, too. He actually saved my life by changing places with me and going off with Cumplin when I was hurt. And . . . Grandfather?" Lark continued, fixing the old man with her soft, silvery questioning eyes, "I know he is not guilty of murdering Miss Blue. Is there no hope for clemency? Better still, of a pardon."

"I will not sanction outlawry! I didn't when your mama was a girl, I won't now and I hope the past won't repeat itself, women in this family taking up with desperados. If this Walker hadn't absconded with you in the first place, there'd have been no need of him saving your life," Rufus bristled into his mustache. "And that you said about Miss Blue? If he wasn't the one who killed her, who was and why wouldn't he give Judge Ike an alibi if he had one? Answer me that, child, before chattering about pardons."

"Oh, Logan has an alibi okay, but because he's a honorable southern gentleman, he will not besmirch the reputation of a so-called lady, even one who was — and still is — ready to watch him hang without raising a peep on his behalf. In fact, I think she wants Logan out of the way so her sordid secret will die with him; but I am no gentleman, and if I get my way. . . ." Lark pounded a dainty hand with a small fist. "Well, for now let's leave it at this: I, too, have a midnight surprise for you, and everyone. It involves Logan, and it will make things clear as a . . . well, clear as Dario's bell with perfect pitch." In her excitement, Lark planted a big kiss on McKay's brow and left him, blushing pink with pleasure, to Roe Ann, who was dressed in low-cut black satin and dripping diamonds as she rustled into the room with a tipsy tread. She looked more ghostly than ever, thin and waxen with hollow, artificially colored cheeks, blood-red lips and dark circles under her eyes.

"I see that game leg's really improving by leaps and bounds," she said to Lark's vanishing back. "She's sure chipper about something, ain't she, Mr. McKay? Did I hear her mention Logan Walker?" Roe Ann asked with a sour smile. She had been eavesdropping and needed no answer to that question. What she did need was information about Walker's whereabouts. No fool,

Roe Ann, like Dario, had needed just one look at the elated girl to put two and two together: Only love could have fanned Lark's spark to burn so brightly. Logan had to be nigh!

"She did indeed speak of the scoundrel." Rufus nodded, grumbling. "She hopes to save the boy from his melancholy fate."

"That right?" Peeling off one fingerless black lace glove, Roe Ann took an unsteady grip on a glass full of amber liquid. She sloshed some over the rim as she brought it to her bright red lips. "Oops, spilled some tea. Good thing I'm wearing black," she said, forcing a laugh, but not fooling Rufus, who shook his head sadly. The spectacle of an intemperate woman was one he found particularly disturbing. "Say, uh Rufus, how does Lark plan on doing that, saving Logan?" Holding her right wrist with her left hand, Roe Ann managed to put down the half-empty glass without spilling any more of its contents.

"She didn't tell me that, Roe Ann, but I suppose you'll find out along with the rest of us, at midnight. My little Lark tells me there are going to be quite a few surprises to greet the new year. Aren't you feeling well? Shall I summon Matthew or the doctor?"

"No, no. All I need's a change of scenery. If anyone should inquire after me, sir, please say I went out for a little bit of air and perhaps a moonlight ride," Roe Ann said, rustling away again, paler, if possible, than ever, her rouged cheeks and kohl-dark eye lashes giving her the aspect of a wicked, feverish clown.

"Hell, do you think that's wise, Roe, looking poorly as you do, to go traipsing about the countryside apparelled like that? Just the sound of that dress is likely to spook the horses and—" His words fell on deaf ears. "The woman never did have a smidgen of sense. I'd best dress for dinner and mind my own business," Rufus grunted before he, too, abandoned the main room after adding a log to the fire.

Chapter Twenty-six

" 'He who is short of tin with rent to pay
's a great deal shorter than the shortest day,' "

Matt January intoned to Lark, trying, with little success, to ignore his wife, an oppressive dark figure perched like a bird of prey, a carrion crow, on the edge of her chair.

Seated at dinner between Roe Ann and Matt, Lark found herself a prisoner of circumstance as the couple pecked and picked at each other with growing ferocity in falsely sugared low voices, across her, behind her and over her head while also attempting to keep up appearances and participate in the general conversation.

The girl was finding both Januarys thoroughly disagreeable, though if her sympathies lay anywhere, they were with Matt. He had put aside his flannels and soiled denim trail clothes for a parson's tail coat and an almost clean white shirt. Out from under the shadow of his Stetson and the confines of a duster, Lark could see he was a beefy, red-faced man with a soft belly and a soft, damp mouth. His small, oddly unaligned light-hazel eyes drifted repeatedly in her direction, making her somewhat uncomfortable. But he was, at least, making an effort to muster what charm he could for her benefit, something that only made Roe Ann, who was intimidated by her husband, all the more nervously savage.

"If there's one thing you know about, Matthew dearest, it's being insolvent," Roe Ann whispered in a hoarse caw. *"If you hadn't married me, a woman with means of her own, I shudder to think what might have become of you. You never would have had the rent money, that's a certainty. Did you ever think how lucky you are, always having me to count on?"*

After her chilling ramble in the out of doors, Roe Ann was more hollow-eyed and thin-lipped than before. She had followed a set of new boot and dog tracks through the snow from the house to the stable. She didn't find Logan, only a single pewter button, one which had, at Lark's impatient tug, flown off, rolled and dropped from the loft to the dirt floor below. Though still not sure of the significance of her find but imagining with some accuracy the torrid scene that had recently been played by Logan and Lark, Roe Ann had glanced up, smiled to herself and climbed the ladder. When she reached the top, she found nothing out of the ordinary or even out of place, just a twitchy mouse that scampered out of sight. Ruminating, Roe Ann slipped away again, pocketing the button. It was her only real clue, if it *was* a clue at all, but it was enough to start her plotting.

Later, looking about the dinner table and musing on the vengeful plan she'd formulated, she pinched her carmine lips in a self-satisfied pout of disdain.

"Sure I do count on you, Roe dear. If I had steered clear of you, like I was of a mind to do, when we first met, you know, sweetums?" Matt stage-whispered back to his sullen wife, *"I'd likely have wound up just a hard-working rancher wed to a lady who might actually have loved him. I might have wound up with a simple, decent woman, even a real pretty one, like Miss Lark here, instead of a rich one like you. But I'd have missed a lot in life that way, your clever, acid tongue, for example. Anyways, what are you talkin' about rent for? My land's mine. You gave it to me as part of the marriage deal, and I never had no rent to pay, did I, dearest?"* he added in a puzzled voice before addressing Lark. "St. Thomas's Day is the shortest one of the year," he said aloud. "We've passed it. Light is already lasting longer," he continued, tossing down a whole glass of French claret.

Trying to ignore the hypocritical and quarrelsome pair, Lark politely smiled and concentrated on snippets of conversation from around the table.

". . . man who can read and write can always earn his living as a quill driver—that is, with a pen . . ."

". . . I'd as soon grovel in the dirt for gold as earn my livelihood delving after dimes. . . ."

". . . San Francisco . . . long after the gold rush days, I met a man who called himself Norton I, emperor of America, real name of Joshua Norton. He was a crazy harmless old coot who thought he was emperor of the United States. He went about town dressed up in a uniform rimmed with gold braid and peacock feathers, issuing proclamations and twenty-year bonds. I offered him a job as a comic ring master with my circus, but he took it amiss. No 'emperor' would get himself up to such shenanigans, he said. Poor Norton had arrived in San Francisco rich at the start of the gold rush. And wound up poor. Losing all his money—of which he'd had a considerable lot—in the rice market pushed him round the bend, he cared that much about wealth. He died on the street near Nob Hill . . ." Al Ringling was saying.

"He wasn't the only loon there in Frisco, either. Another fella called himself the Money King, and one swore he was George Washington II," Jake added. As he spoke from the head of the table, he glanced from Charlotte to Lark and back again.

The dreamy-eyed daughter was a tempting confection, dressed in a lace-collared, fitted, lush red velvet gown with a matching red velvet band coiled in her yellow hair. Another, encircling her throat, was held in place by a cameo. The mother, also exceptionally beautiful that evening, Jake noticed, was wearing low-cut blue velvet with gold at her slender throat and long golden earrings dangling and dancing in candle light. He marvelled at his own good luck in having two such women in his life after all the lonely years, and there was a happy, almost boyish enthusiasm in Jake's voice which Charlotte noticed and took credit for. Goodness, he was sure looking exceptionally suave and bright-eyed and vigorous, she mused proudly and possessively, glancing across at Lark to see if she, too, saw the change in Jake. But Lark was looking daggers at that January woman.

"*No other decent woman, no matter how wispy, desperate and dull she was, would have taken you, Matt, my sweet potato.*" Roe Ann leaned across Lark to tell him. "*You didn't have a spittoon to your name.*"

"What do you mean, 'decent woman'?" Matt responded. "You ain't a decent woman, my little lovey dovey. I mean, the word don't begin to do you justice. I never could believe my uh . . . luck, you choosin' an ordinary fella like me. What I don't know is, why'd you marry me?" Sitting forward and raising her soup spoon, Lark tried to come between the two and listen to the general table talk.

". . . I was raising turkeys back in Virginia, but I had no luck," Gideon Blakely said. "They drowned on me, just standing out in the rain looking up at the sky with their beaks open. Dumb birds, turkeys. Apaches hold them in such low esteem they won't wear no turkey feathers or eat turkey meat. They let little children practice huntin' on turkeys."

"*I married you out of spite, Matt.*" It was Roe Ann again, whispering to her husband, this time behind Lark's back. In company she was feeling bold, knowing he couldn't get at her.

"*I never done nothin' to deserve your spleen, not till after we was married leastways and then 'cause you was being mean to me. I guess I just didn't rightly understand a complicated woman like you, cutie.*" Matt scratched his head playing the baffled buffoon, but there was a sinister look in his mismatched eyes.

Lark sat back and sighed, impatient for the meal to be done so that she could escape the Januarys.

She was anxious for Jake and Rufus to make good on their promises of exciting revelations, and also, she was getting more nervous by the minute about dropping her own bombshell—producing Logan and obliging him to confront his alibi for murder, Roe Ann. The sooner she got it over with, the better, or else she might lose her nerve. Lark glanced slant-eyed at Roe Ann, who, engrossed in her snide exchange with Matt, seemed not to notice the attention.

"I married you to spite my mother, you silly old fool you," Mrs. January told Mr. January. *"Dear Mum was startin' in to call me an old maid. I told her I'd take the first dumb cowpoke asked for my hand. I never could believe my luck neither, but that was you, Matthew."*

While counting off the eleven chimes of the tall clock in the hall, Lark heard Matt grit his teeth.

"And to think, I thought I was just askin' you to dance one reel, you sittin' out at the church supper with the spinsters. I always thought I was smart enough to get by, Roe, but I sure was dumb about you," he said with an odd laugh. *"But I'm on to you now. You can't fool me no more. Miss Lark, please be so kind as to pass along the salt cellar."*

Roe Ann almost hurled it at Matt's head, then stretched an arm across Lark to grasp his sleeve. Her eyes had started to flame with fury as she literally shook from head to toe in her effort to retain her self-control.

"Oh, dear. Clumsy of me, Matt, getting salt all over you. But listen, lambkin, I can still fool you any day of the week and twice on Sunday. In fact, I could just make a real jack-

ass fool of you tonight by runnin' off with—well, a fella's been hidin' out in the stable who's been after me for a long time to run west with him. Anyone ever invite you to run west with him, Miss McKay?" Now Roe Ann stole a sneaky look at Lark. Lark's smile froze on her lips.

"What are you talkin' 'bout?" she asked Roe Ann in a snappish whisper, playing dumb.

"You been with Logan Walker today, same as me, that's what I'm talkin' 'bout."

On the verge of laughing uproariously at the absurdity of Roe Ann's claim, Lark looked down, struck dumb to find Logan's pewter shirt button in her lap.

"What am I supposed to make of that?" Lark, really agitated now, pressed Roe Ann.

"I know that you know there ain't nothin' 'bout Logan Walker that's ordinary, not even . . . well not even a button off his shirt." Roe Ann said, her stifled laugh thick with contempt, her inference clear. Lark flushed crimson.

"What on earth do you mean?" she demanded, forgetting to whisper, then dropping her voice to add, *"You are just tryin' to rile me, ain't you?"*

"Now, why would I want to rile you, do you suppose?" Roe Ann sniggered.

"Rodeo? Ro-day-o! That's the Spanish word for 'roundup,' " Jake was saying to Ethan Everet. "It came here with the conquistadors who also brought the first horses to the New World. You stay on at the JAK Bar until roundup time, Ethan, we'll show you a rodeo worth sketching."

"If you want to run off with another man, Roe, I'm ready

to help you mount your horse," Matt croaked in a too-loud whisper, dropping his congenial facade. *"I'm already feelin' sorry for any poor gullible sap who takes up with you."*

"Except for one sap, Matt, the one who made a damn fool of you and me. Right?" Roe Ann demanded, giving a mean twist to the word *right*.

"Better yet, Everet," Jake went on, "come to Chicago for the opening of The McKay's Wild West Show and Roundup, Featuring the One-Time Leader of the Goldilocks Gang!"

"Made a damn fool of me, right . . . Walker did." Matt snarled, sounding like a schoolboy repeating a half-learned lesson. *"I'm not supposed to feel sorry for Walker. I'm supposed to kill him soon's I get the chance, 'fore the hangman gets him. Right, Roe?"* On hearing this last exchange between husband and wife, Lark, who had just taken a sip of wine, swallowed wrong and began to cough, gasping for breath, her eyes watering.

"Why, Lark darlin', you need help, say a pat on the back?" Jake asked with concern, offering her his handkerchief. She declined with an impatient shake of her head and turned her attention back to the battling Januarys.

"Why are you supposed to kill Logan before *the hangman?"* she asked Matt.

"I've seen Buffalo Bill Cody. He puts on a good show"—Everet nodded at Jake—"but I sure would like to watch a reenactment of Goldilocks and the Gum Ups robbing nickels from the Caldwell Bank or . . ." Everet began to chuckle.

"Logan, he made a damn fool of me, cheatin' on me with

my dear wife while he was in my employ, and right when I was treatin' him like a brother and a friend." Matt shook his head, sounding almost sad. *"My loving spouse wants me to have that satisfaction."*

". . . or the Gum Ups getting their pictures taken in Silverdale by mistake by Herman Flicker . . ." Emma giggled as most of the others joined in. Only the Januarys, still locked in domestic combat, remained aloof from the increasingly festive high spirits of the gathering.

"Tell you though, Roe, I sure miss the boy." Matt and Roe Ann each downed a whole glass of wine and looked daggers at one another. *"It's not that I want to kill Logan, Miss Lark, I have to. I gave my word."*

". . . or Goldilocks not holding up the money train outside Oklahoma City." Aida guffawed, her deep laugh setting off a torrent of hilarity all around the table as, to general applause, she presented the browned suckling pig with its head split and juices flowing before taking her place.

"Now hold on! Hold on one blinkin' minute." Jake roared with laughter until his eyes ran with tears, too. "We are planning a real ro-day-o with roping and bull riding and bronco busting, not a Punch and Judy Show or a clown carnival! Ain't that right, darlin'?" he asked Lark, who, still aghast at what the Januarys were saying, didn't hear him.

"Well, just hold on a damn minute! How do you know it's true, what you've been told?" Lark asked Matt.

"I trust my source, my sweet wife there, he said sarcastically. *She admitted it her own self, wantin' to make a clean breast of things, she said, so she and me could start*

over, she said—after I kill Logan. She was really afraid I'd kill her too, right, Roe? I might. I don't want to start over, not with you. And I don't want to kill Logan. I know it was all your fault, Roe, you preyin' like a scorpion on a lonely younger man. Why don't you just run right off with the fella you got waitin' in the stable and save us all a mess of trouble?"

Lark, open-mouthed, looked from one to the other.

"We are living in strange times. It's been so cold in France, the Seine froze solid during this winter of 1891," Dario was busy expounding, clearly enjoying the sound of his own resonant voice.

"Well, Matt, you're a real mental giant, you are. Who do you think it is in the stable waiting on me now?" Roe Ann sniggered.

"Now, just hold on a damn minute here!" Lark repeated, loud enough this time to attract the attention of the judge, who was sitting next to Matt. *"Your wife is Logan's alibi for murder, Matt January. She can't go running off, not now."*

The judge was all ears as he stared from Lark to Roe Ann to Matthew.

"Walker cheated on me, too, with a loose little minx, Matt. I am your wife, and my honor is at stake. Are you a man or ain't you?" Roe Ann goaded her husband, unaware that Ike Parker was listening.

Matt shrugged. *"Don't you want first dibs on him, Roe? Don't you want to have the satisfaction of shooting him yourself?"* Matt suggested.

"Keep your voice down! If I go gunnin' for Logan, and kill him, I'll likely hang, but if you get him, there ain't a

judge or jury in the world, or at least not in Arkansas, would find you guilty of murder, being a cuckold and all," Roe Ann insisted.

"I'll be the judge of that," said the judge. *"What is all this about an alibi? I asked that Walker boy and asked him again, 'Son, what is your alibi' and . . . say, are you it, Roe Ann, his alibi?"*

Roe Ann's startled eyes flicked about the table before a smile began to play at her lips. *"Nope,"* she answered, grinning meanly and folding her arms across her hollow chest after dropping something in Lark's lap.

"She's . . . why, she's just out and out lying!" Lark gasped, truly and deeply shocked at the woman's outrageous duplicity. *"Now that Matt knows you're a faithless hussy, why not 'fess up, Roe Ann? What have you to lose now?"*

"Walker is what I have to lose. It's me he's running with, girlie."

"Liar!" Lark hissed. She flushed, paled and flushed again, then histrionically cleared her throat in a futile effort to catch Dario's eye.

Dressed up in his best and only jacket, a black frock coat in which he appeared uncomfortable as he kept fussing at the floppy bow tie at his throat, he had eyes only for Charlotte. "There's some people saying it's the turn of the century affecting the weather. The twentieth century will be upon us in under ten years. Strange thing happened a hundred years ago, too. There were odd goings-on. Lot's of worry about fire and brimstone."

"Fire and brimstone's one thing. A Noachian flood

is another. Don't forget Johnstown two years ago, 1889. Two thousand people drowned," Gideon Blakely reminded Dario.

"Freezin' is worst of all in my opinion. Forty below I've known it to get up north a way on the High Plains," Ethel Blakely said, shaking her head. "Before the blizzard of '88, the air got real still . . . like it done today. Then the wind came on sudden, sounding like a fast freight train and carrying snow thick as baled cotton."

"Say what you will, that ordinary button proves me right or I'm Queen of the May. If you want the scoundrel to stay alive, you stay put, honey child," Roe Ann simpered and grinned, her grip firm on Lark's arm.

"Let loose of me," Lark insisted, not sure what she really did want just then. If this loathsome woman was, by some chance, telling the truth about being with Logan, Lark would shoot him herself. She fumed in silence awhile until it dawned on her that she had no idea what Logan really had up his sleeve. He, too, had said something about a midnight surprise! Why, he could just come sauntering through the door at any second, flashing his sparkling grin and oozing charm only to find himself flat on his back, oozing blood, done for by one of any number of folks, some at that celebration, some not. With Matt January and Roe Ann and Clarence and the law all gunning for him, Lark couldn't take that chance. She had to get at the truth and quick. She decided to suspend judgment and try to warn him at once, but she'd need an excuse to leave the table — and the house — without raising suspicions and a

posse.

"To hell with suspicions!" she burst out, all set to bolt. "I'm going to ask him myself—straight out!"

"I beg your pardon?" Amy Blakely blinked at Lark, who just then felt another restraining hand, this one on her knee.

"Leggo now, I am warnin' you, Miz January," Lark now whispered furiously while smiling sweetly.

"So's you can warn that two-timer to run and hide? No way, dearie," Roe Ann whispered back, also smiling if not as sweetly, the two looking like a pair of conspiratorial little schoolgirls sharing a guilty secret.

"Don't you move, Lark. If Roe's lyin' and don't know where Logan's at, you'll give away his hiding place. Pay her no mind, have a good time, enjoy yourself," Matt gleefully suggested to Lark. *"That's the best way to get her goat."*

Lark tried to follow Matt's advice. Absorbed as she was with her own problems just then—how to warn Logan, the cad, maybe—she stared at Jake with unseeing eyes, and though seeming to hang on his every word, she didn't hear a single one until Jake rose, cleared his throat and tapped a wineglass with a silver spoon.

"The midnight hour fast approaches, my friends! The time is half after eleven, and before the clock strikes again, I've something to say! Aida, to the piano! I need a real drum roll and rumble of a prelude, but your ivory pounding will do. Better yet, wind up the Victrola and put on John Philip Sousa and the United States Marine Band playing the 'Washington Post March.' For an occasion like this—I can't think of a more fitting introduction!"

Chapter Twenty-seven

"Folks and friends, I am fixin' to expand my family and change my brand!" Jake announced. "After all my years as a lonely, single man, I'm hoping to take a wife—if the lady I've a mind to wed will say yes when I pop the question." Jake burlesqued a wink and let his jaw drop, to show that he already knew the answer. "Neither love nor a cough, they say, can be hid, so I've some idea what her response will be." Jake extended his hands with their well-cared-for nails, one to a beaming Charlotte, the other to a smiling Lark, who had put her own worries aside momentarily to savor her mother's triumph and joy. "This pair of glowing girls, mother and daughter, are also best friends, and I don't want that to change. Though I love two McKays, I can only marry one, but—"

"Jake, you are sure right about that." Ike slapped the table and guffawed.

". . . but when I do marry one, I won't be coming between them, I'll be joining 'em. When Lark and Charlotte allow me into their lives and hearts for good, we all will be together, three best friends, always. I am hoping that before the year's out, Judge

Ike will do the honors and make me kin to these two fine females."

"Nothing I'd like better, you know, Jake, than to get working on my new reputation as the Marryin' Judge starting tonight." Ike Parker nodded, removing his spectacles and closing his brass case with a sharp click. "Ready?" he asked.

"Hooray and hurrah!! Get to it!" Eli Blakely exclaimed, stamping his feet and tapping his own wineglass as his brothers joined in. "Best news I've heard in a long while!"

"Now, Jake, hold on a damn minute here. Are you sure you want to take up matrimony?" Dario asked, not in jest, but stalling for time. He usually trusted his own feelings, but after what Lark had told him earlier, he was in an agony of doubt as he tried to decide what Jake was up to. "I know a writer fella living in Austin, Texas by the name of Will Porter. Maybe you heard of him. He's a sketcher like Ethan and a writer. He signs his work 'O. Henry,' and he's got quite a bit to say about matrimony and its pitfalls, Jake, like 'If men knew how women pass the time when they are alone, they'd never marry' and on the subject of a sleeping woman, '. . . you know it's better for all hands for her to be that way.' Also—"

"Oh, Dario, do stop!" Charlotte laughed breathlessly, flushed with pure happiness untinged by any doubts or anxiety. She met Dario's mournful eyes with an uncomprehending expression. "A man on the verge of proposing is in a real risky position, same as a tight rope performer about to step off his platform. Neither must be diverted from the business at hand lest he tilt or fall or lose his nerve!"

"Charlotte, I am so sure that what I'm doing is *right*, nothin' could divert me now." Jake nodded.

"Stick to your guns, Jake, stick to 'em," Ethel Blakely encouraged to general cheers and applause, "no matter what that woman-hating writer has writ!"

"Now listen, you all, listen," Jake pleaded, grinning. "I got a mouthful to say, and so does the judge, before twelve o'clock. The mistress of my heart, the future mother of my sons and daughters, has only to say 'I do.' Now listen, listen! Both my future kin are female persons of great elegance and talent. Both these ladies have also got strength of character and shrewd brains. And, if that weren't enough for one man, the beautiful mama is proof of the mature loveliness to be prognosticated in the exquisite daughter whose nubile luster is itself evidence of the fine progeny that'll be arriving here at the JAK-KAY Ranch startin' in, say August of 1892." He had an arm around each of the McKays.

"Jake!" Charlotte blushed scarlet. "You are a man of many skills, but arithmetic is not among them. There'll be no babies here at least 'till September, that is if it still takes nine months to make one. Right, Lark?" Beginning to look bemused, Lark nodded and sought Dario's eye.

"*Bravissimo*, Jake," Dario groaned, watching Charlotte anxiously. "Every girl needs a sugar-daddy to give her ribbons and laces and lavender sachets and black georgette flimsies and velvet pillows. . . ."

"Sugar-daddy? Hell, Dario, I'm no fancy man, but I am feelin' like a boy again. I feel young and wild as Texas. I've been around some, sure. I know the score, and I know what I want. A wife and a houseful little ones. Now, I've always been a man of few wants, but one of my prideful things is this ranch I built. One thing I do want is to leave the land to my own sons and daughters. Now, the thing about raising up tykes to honorable manhood or to be young ladies is this; you got to have a good woman, a young, strong woman to bear 'em and teach them to survive in a tough world, to—"

"Jake, if you don't pop the question soon, I'm like to pitch a fit." Charlotte sighed, admiring him from head to toe. His hard physique was as lean as dried beef, she thought, and his rugged profile and steely-gray, dark hair made him about the best-looking man she'd ever seen, especially in his tailless evening jacket that was called a tuxedo, he'd explained, a style gaining great popularity back east.

"For the strong silent type, Jake, you are sure rattling on," Lark complained. Jittery as a kitten, she was desperate to rush off to Logan, but now, with Jake suggesting a wedding on the spot, she couldn't very well slip off until the ceremony was performed and the festivities underway. "If you don't get to the meat and potatoes of this happy event, midnight will come and go before the knot's tied. The way you're proceeding, so will Independence Day!"

"Darlin' girl, I won't keep you waiting another minute. Let's do it! Judge, get your book." Jake laughed, extracting from his pocket a black velvet box. As he flipped up the lid to reveal a large diamond set in platinum and a filigreed gold band nested within, there was a sudden crescendo of discordant notes from the spinet piano in the hall. Aida lumbered back into the dining room and stood, hands on hips, gazing hard at Jake.

"You have not spoke out the words yet, 'Will you marry me,'" she said. "Who you thinkin' of hitchin' with?"

Jake looked frowning at Aida and turned quickly away. "I will do the formal asking down on my knee. I'll say the actual words in a minute now," he answered evenly. "First, I'm saying this: I have built the biggest ranch and the grandest, most hospitable house in the territory. There's only one woman—and she knows who she is—who belongs at the head of my table, in my parlor and in my bed, one woman I intend to trot harness with for the rest of my days." There was a pause and in the freighted hush, Dario groaned again. Charlotte smiled tremulously, her adoring eyes on Jake. He went down on one knee and said in a strong loud carrying voice,

"Will you marry me . . ."

Charlotte took a step toward him. ". . . Lark McKay?"

There was a deafening silence in the room until Roe Ann began to laugh with more than a smattering of malice, and several gasps escaped the lips of the Blakely wives. Lark, appalled, took several steps backward, away from Jake. The Blakely brothers were uninformed about the JAK Bar love story and insensitive to the finer nuances of the moment, yet even so they sensed something was amiss. Not knowing what and sure some response was called for, they finally let loose a few feeble yippees and yahoos, tie-eye-ohs and various other cowboy cheers.

"Lark?" Jake said, still down on his knees, extending his hand to her.

"Give the girl a chance to catch her breath, Jake," Rufus, looking puzzled, suggested. Lark was staring open-mouthed at Charlotte, who, her face devoid of color, seemed on the verge of collapse. Dario moved to her side and took her elbow to steady her.

"Lark, don't do this to me! You already told me yes. Now tell them." Jake gestured wildly.

"No, Jake, I *didn't*. You said you were going to ask Mama to marry you!"

"Charlotte?" Jake asked, getting to his feet, his face going florid. "Sure I was going to ask her—for your hand, but I decided to ask Rufus instead and surprise everyone else."

"You sure did that Jake, surprised almost everyone else, except me," Dario said, trying to guide Charlotte from the room. She shook her head and resumed her place at the table.

"Congratulations, Lark," she said with icy reserve. "Jake Chamberlain *is* everything you've ever wanted in a man—he's rich, powerful, handsome and so smitten with you, he'll give you the world. But you could have told me. You should have warned me, though in love and war, I suppose, all's fair, even stabbing your own mother in the back."

"Mama, don't!" Lark wailed. "Jake, tell her it's her you really want! This is not a kind joke, Jake."

Jake sagged into his chair, his face crumbling, his boyish vitality vanished. He looked all at once, aged and tired. He offered Charlotte a bleak smile.

"I want to marry Lark. I'm sorry if I ever gave you reason to think . . . otherwise or if I ever behaved improperly toward you, Charlie."

"You gave me reason to hope when I first came to

the JAK Bar, but you were always the perfect gentleman, Jake. That alone should have made me realize I was playing a game of solitaire. I was lost in a waking dream." The others slowly began to resume their places at the table, the mood of the gathering somber.

"Will someone tell me what the devil's going on?" Al Ringling demanded. "Who is marrying who and why?"

"Al, I've made a jackass of myself and nearly spoiled the party for everyone, but don't any of you trouble yourself on my account. Hear me, Charlotte? Lark? Charlie, you are not wrong. I thought at first—well, you brought me peace and contentment, but you, Lark! Oh, Lark, the simple and terrible truth is, you made me feel young! You stirred me all up inside. You brought this thrilling turmoil into my life, and I got to thinking it was time I gave the girls a whirl again. I realize now it'll be best if I just stick to what I've been doing, riding wild horses in my dreams." Jake looked at the startled faces about him.

"Now, come on, everybody! This is a party! It lacks only ten minutes to midnight, and when that clock starts in striking the hour, I am going to kiss every beautiful lady in this house!" he proclaimed with almost convincing jollity. "Pop open that French champagne, Dario, and get ready to revel. Aida, back to the spinet with you and start pounding out some of those barrel house blues because I am going to drink myself pie-eyed happy startin' now, and then me and the coyotes are going to commence howlin' at the moon like lone wolves!"

"Jake's right! Jake's right! Water under the bridge and all." Dario's jack-o'-lantern grin split his face from ear to ear. He was stroking Charlotte's soft little hand which lay limp on the table.

"Mama, *talk* to me!" Lark implored—but Charlotte, for the first time in all her life, turned a deaf ear to her daughter. "Mama, you can't think I led him on. It was all a terrible misunderstanding. Mama, you know who I love and—" Lark looked away, and when her gaze fell on the window behind Jake, she saw something move past it in the dark, a face, a vague shape. Logan! she thought, about to put his own plan, whatever it was, into motion! It was all she needed just then, the final straw after a long, tense, longing, loving almost lovely day that had suddenly turned into a nightmare. What a fix she had gotten into—Charlie really, really mad at her, one man inside with a broken heart because of her, another one outside putting his life at risk, also because of her. She had to get away and warn Logan about the Januarys and the judge and Jake—now. She'd try anything. Lark burst into tears.

"Mama," Lark wept copiously to the great discomfort of every man at the table, "if that's what you think of me, I am leaving here now. You'll never have to look at me again!" she said, snuffling dramatically, struggling to stand only to realize Roe Ann again had a grip on the skirt of her dress. So furious she forgot to keep the crocodile tears flowing, Lark cursed a blue streak in outrage, boxed Roe Ann's ears soundly and got set to do it again, all the while trying to tug free.

Charlotte did not want to look at her daughter. She knew her vexation would vanish as soon as she did, and she was determined not to be mollified by anything—yet. She had a point to make first, but even so, she couldn't resist a peek at the squeaking Roe Ann. Just one fast look at Lark and the cowed victim put Charlotte on the verge of giggles. She managed, though, to keep her tone frigid and her nose in the air while chastising her child, something that given the circumstances, she felt it her motherly duty to do.

"Lark, many's the woman who has betrayed her best bosom friend over a man. I never supposed you were one of that sad lot. In future, keep in mind that the men are few and far between who are worth that. It might be best if we do spend some time apart." About a half hour was what Charlotte had in mind, but she stopped herself from saying so.

"Charlie, you're wrong about Lark," Dario said. "Lark, don't worry. Your mother's upset now, but things will work out fine, I know."

"I'm going!" Lark announced, paying him no mind and pulling harder against a yelping Roe Ann, whose ears were glowing bright red.

"You wait a darn minute there, girlie," the woman said, splotches of red also showing on her chalky cheeks. She firmed her talon's grip on Lark and anticipated the excitement with which her revelation of Logan Walker's whereabouts was soon to be greeted.

"Well, I'll be done up brown if those two ladies aren't fighting!" Dr. Middleton exclaimed as, with a furious little yell, Lark finally gained her feet. When she wrenched free, her dress, to which Roe Ann had been holding like a crazed killer bull dog to the throat of a bull, ripped, the skirt separating from the bodice with a long rending sound. Thrown slightly off balance, Lark flailed about, trying to steady herself, and clutched the first object that came to hand, the double strand of diamonds encircling Roe Ann's throat. Lark tugged. Roe Ann gurgled—then shrieked as her chair rocked, tipped, and crashed over backward.

"Oh, dear me, I do beg your pardon." Despite herself Lark chortled at the sight of her nemèsis on her back on the floor like a turtle struggling, her thick legs waving in the air in a tangle of petticoats, flannel stockings and white bloomers. Lark stepped free of her rent dress and, wearing only black satin pantalettes and a lacey bustier, sprinted from the room, leaving chaos and shrieks of both consternation and hilarity behind her as the others at the table jumped to their feet. Some followed her, and some helped right Roe Ann while others gave full vent to side-splitting laughter.

"Never you mind about me, *never mind*," Roe Ann insisted, getting to her knees and slapping away Matthew's helping hand. "They say you can't catch a weasel asleep, but you will, you will, if you go *after* her right now, damn you!! You'll catch Logan Walker, and soon's you do, you shoot him, Matthew January, or hang him, or both, on the spot."

The front door slammed after Lark, then after Matt, then after Jake. It slammed again after Aida and once more after the three Blakely boys.

"Hold on all of you! There ain't goin' to be no shooting and no lynching in my territory!" Judge Ike thundered, and the door slammed yet one more time.

Not ten minutes later, a winter storm, all the more menacing for being unexpected, struck with a howling and roar like a prehistoric beast loosed on the land. Dense snow was hurled against the house, striking it like boulders in an avalanche. Almost instantly the windows were thickly blanketed and impossible to see through. Wind wended its way inside to flutter lamp and candle flames and taunt the fire on the hearth.

"It's another one those storms, like '88, come sweeping on down from Canada at near fifty miles an hour. It could drop the temperature fifty degrees in a few hours," Dr. Middleton commented.

"At least it's late at night, and most people are tucked in safe somewhere, not like the blizzard of 1888," Emma Blakely said in awe. "That one was called 'the schoolchildren's storm' because it struck at mid-morning and caught so many little ones away from home. Lives were lost. Sixteen children perished, frozen to death, following their teacher on a short walk of a quarter mile to the nearest house. But lives were saved, too, by brave school marms. There was even a popular song, 'Thirteen Were Saved,' all about a young teacher in Nebraska name of Minnie Freeman. Our own Miss Blue, God rest her, was one of that group of selfless and dedicated women. She stayed in the school house with her charges, and before that storm blew itself out, they'd burned everything, even the desks, to keep warm. I give thanks that my babies are safe with me here, tucked in upstairs. But . . . Eli's—" Ethel kicked her under the table, and Emma shut up as tight as a clam.

"Oh, my God, my Lark's out there!" Charlotte said, bringing her finger tips to her mouth. "I drove her away from me into a killing storm. I've never done such a thing as turn my back on my child, not since the day she was born, and now . . . now I might never see her again and because of some silly . . . vain, self-important, selfish man." Charlotte stood, sat, then stood again.

"Charlie, don't fret," Ethel soothed. "The boys are all out there looking after her, big strong boys they are. They're all probably snug as bugs in the barn right now."

"I'm going after my daughter, and if I find her safe, I am swearin' off men for good and always. The pleasure they give just ain't worth the trouble they cause. Not a one of them has ever brought me anything else but, all my life long!"

"Charlie, wait for me!" Dario called as she, like the others, disappeared into the treacherous night, slamming the door after her.

Chapter Twenty-eight

The front door banged open again before anyone else at the table had a chance to so much as move, no less leave. There was a sound of boots stamping in the hall, then of more than one pair of footsteps approaching the dining room. At the same time that several snow-encrusted figures, brandishing drawn pistols, shotguns and rifles, joined what was left of the party, there was a crash of windows being thrown open from the outside and of the back door kicked wide. Wind roared into the house along with more armed men, some prodding before them the recently vanished Blakelys and Jake, Matt January and the judge, Dario, Charlotte and Lark, who was shivering, soaked to the skin in her flimsy black under garments, and clinging to Charlotte's hand. Faced with the more pressing problem of Clarence Cumplin, their tiff had been forgotten.

"Good evening, folks. Well, isn't this real nice?" Crazy Clarence grinned, his wild eyes roaming the inviting room with its furniture of aspen wood and weathered pine, straight-backed rush-seated chairs, crystal, china, and white linen, all lit softly by candles glowing in a wrought-iron chandelier and by oil lamps along the sideboard. "It gives me satisfaction to present the new and improved Cumplin Gang. Now you, Goldilocks, get the guns off the rest of these hombres and toss 'em out into the snow. The guns that is, not the folks." The ear-ringing roar of a shotgun blasted, followed by the ping of a bullet ricocheting off a tin spittoon.

"I was reaching for my pencil, not a gun!" the shaken but unhurt Ethan Everet blurted, his hands in the air. "I'm a newsman. I only want to get a sketch of you, Mr. Cumplin, for our thousands of readers fascinated by your um, career."

On hearing this, Clarence smiled again. "Fascinated thousands? Well, sketch away but watch yourself. Any sudden moves on your part could result in your sudden death. That goes for y'all, hear? Get the weapons, Lark."

"Get them yourself, Clarence!" she answered, all in a pique. "I am going to my room to change before I catch my death."

"If you don't catch it from the cold, you might catch it from me if you ain't more po-lite." Clarence scowled. "Go on up with her, one of you, and watch she don't try nothin' funny. Goldilocks has a real sassy zest about her; she is tough and smart."

As every one of the baker's dozen of Cumplin's new gang members stampeded for the door vying for the role of Lark's escort, another shot sounded, and an oil lamp exploded, bursting into flames which Clarence extinguished with the contents of an open, half-full bottle of champagne.

"Boys, behave. Cooney, the job's yours. Anything goes wrong with little Lark, you're a dead man, hear?" Clarence told a grizzled outlaw with beetled brows and a week's growth of greasy beard.

Cooney stepped up to Lark and, still holding a pistol in each hand, crushed her in a bear hug while attempting to plant a kiss on her lips. When she bit him, both pistols went off simultaneously and Clarence giggled.

"Patience, Cooney, patience. Your time will come, later. Now, go on, Lark, go on, and come back wearing something real pretty. After all, this is New Years Eve, ain't it? We are going to dance and frolic, right, all night long?!"

"Wrong, Clarence!" Lark snapped. She took a candelabra from the mantel and stalked off with Cooney, cautious now, behind her.

"You are not coming in here. Wait in the hall for me," she imperiously commanded on reaching her room, and the man, nibbling his nipped lip, shook his head no.

"You might run off on me. I can't let you out of my sight."

"Well, you'll have to. I am not about to stand buck naked in front of the likes of you." Merely hearing the word 'naked' spoken aloud was enough to make Cooney blush, but even so, when Lark pushed open the door, he doggedly followed her into the room. She set down the candles and stood, hands on hips, studying him.

"Cooney, only a dolt would give up the safety and warmth of this house to head out into a lethal blizzard. It would be suicide, and I am no dolt. Now, sit yourself down in that nice easy chair, put your feet up and close your eyes while I change. You won't see me, but you will be able to hear me. I'll keep talking or humming, so's you'll know just where I am, okay?" She began undoing the laces at her bodice, and Cooney, petrified, quickly sat at the edge of the chair, his eyes clenched shut. Listening to soft sounds of lacing faintly whistling through eyelets and the rustle of satin garments falling, Cooney became increasingly agitated. Hearing drawers open and close, he pictured the delicate articles she was probably fondling, never supposing she was frantically, wildly flinging about handkerchiefs and petticoats and nightshirts and gloves in a frenzied search for the little gun Logan had given her which she had retrieved from a shaken Jesse Jaynes before he was carted off to jail.

"Talk to me or sing or something," Cooney groaned, his imagination getting the best of him. "Please?" That was the last word heard from that source. The blow of a pistol butt struck Cooney behind the left ear, knocking him unconscious, and Lark, caught off guard, spun about to find Logan looking at her, his gold-glinted amber eyes devouring her. Unlike Cooney, he had been watching Lark's prancing performance, and now he just grinned at her as she stood before him wearing only the black pantalettes which perfectly followed her shapely, small figure. She was grinning back at him, joyful and amazed to see him, though not as overwhelmed as he at the lovely sight of her.

In candlelight her creamy skin was rose-hued, the rose tips of her breasts standing budded. "So *this* is where you've been hiding out while I was worried sick over you," she whispered. "I'm so *glad*."

She set about towelling her wet hair. Logan watched, fascinated, never having seen her in so feminine a setting as this room with its oval mirrors reflecting the cut glass and silver on the dressing table and bureau and a canopied bed dripping white lace and ruffles.

Unable to take her eyes off Logan, Lark watched him in her long cheval mirror as she brushed out the tangles in her hair, her round breasts rising temptingly with each stroke until flaxen silk flowed over her shoulders.

Logan had yet to speak when he knelt to tie Cooney's hands and ankles using the strong silk laces from Lark's bustier. He gagged the prisoner with a kid glove and blindfolded him with a scarf, then hoisted the man to his shoulder. Logan looked both ways into the hall, stepped out and returned a few moments later without his burden.

"Cooney's out of action, tucked up safe in the big hope chest at the top of the stairs" were the first words Logan spoke, and Lark, with a little laugh of triumph and joy leapt into his open arms, taking his lips and fumbling behind him to lock the door. Their mouths kept working as Lark's hands went to Logan's buttons and buckles, peeling off buckskin and flannel until the two were skin to skin, the tips of her breasts to his hard chest and her hands moving over him, molding and caressing. He took a few steps back and spoke in a soft, husky undertone.

"You are outrageously beautiful," he said, manipulating the pantalettes down over her hips . . . thighs . . . knees until she stepped out of them.

"Please take me to bed," she said, very softly, each word passing her lips a caress, a bouquet. "It will be the first time for us — in a bed, indoors. It will be as if we're startin' over, strangers, falling in love, again." Lark's eyes were their most perfect lavender gray-blue, her smile radiant.

With a stifled roar of pure animal high spirits, Logan tackled her round the knees, lifted her off her feet and deposited her in deep feather down of a real mattress. He was above her at once, kneeling over her, touching her first with his eyes, then his finger tips, then each long, hard primed muscle in his body pressed to hers. Her lithe legs parted, drew up, and he went into her slowly, taking his time, so much time that she surged upward needing to sheath him, to draw him to her and into her, her legs enfolding his hips, her head thrown back, her eyes never leaving his face.

But he wouldn't be rushed. He went on taking his own good time . . . and on, and on, moving sinuously, receding, recoiling, delving again, never completely relinquishing the wellhead of pleasure as each probe got stronger, came more hurriedly, went deeper and deeper until they both were lost in long, wild flooding eruptions of love and passion and need, of giving and taking in a union so encompassing, so complete, neither could imagine facing the world again except as part of the other, the two together, always.

"Don't ever go away again," Lark sighed.

"Won't. Couldn't," Logan rasped, pulling downy layers of quilts up over them, holding her close and hard and tender, too. Outside the snow was flying, drifting deep, the wind was roaring, and they were warm and alone in each other's arms, for the moment at least.

"In bed . . . with you . . . it's where I'd stay forever. . . ." Logan sighed, tracing the lines of her satiny body, tasting her lips, her breasts, then guiding her back to fold in against the sheltering curve of his strong body.

Drowsing, peaceful, close to sleep, they both were shocked bolt upright by the loud report of a shot fired below.

"Forever will have to wait until after we tend to Clarence Cumplin," Logan moaned.

"Logan, let me do it. I'll handle Clarence. You wait for me right here, safe and sound and comfy in bed.

Almost everyone down there is after you: Clarence, Roe Ann, the judge, even Matt."

Logan only kissed her fast and hard, then began to dress, first pulling on his britches and boots.

"With them all in the same place at the same time, maybe I can settle up with everyone at once, including the law; now is the time for me to settle up and get on with living—with you." Wrapping herself in a quilt, Lark pursued him across the room, enfolded him with her, and held him.

"Logan, don't go down there now. Do this for me this one time. You might not make it alive to the bottom of the steps." Her voice was so soft and sweet, like a child's, her eyes so imploring, Logan nodded, reluctantly.

"I know Matt's had men looking for me since . . . well, let's say since he came into possession of some information he need never have known, courtesy of his newly dutiful wife. I suppose it's best the secret is out even if she is hoping he'll kill me and save her the trouble. Somehow though, I get the feeling Matt's heart's not in the hunt." Logan pulled his bib-front shirt over his head, squared his shoulders and leaned to the mirror to rake the hair back from his brow.

"Let me, darlin'," Lark said. Picking up her brush, she stretched up on tiptoes and worked quickly at his long mane. "Oh, look, Logan, there's not a button on that shirt," she commented in an overly sweet tone which put him on guard. He delved into his pocket and came up with a handful of pewter.

"Your fault." He grinned. "You pulled them off in the loft. I found them all, except one that's lost in the hay."

"This it?" Lark asked, prodded by the tiniest nagging doubt in the back of her mind, one planted there by Roe Ann's insinuations. "Wait right here for me." She sighed, not wanting to distrust him, only to love him, yet needing to know for certain he was hers alone. "I'm going downstairs, but I'll be back."

"You damn well better, and soon"—he grinned—"or else you'll find me in the thick of the fray, protecting you and settling things my way. Go on before I change my mind."

In the dining room, Cumplin had commandeered Jake's chair, propped his dripping boots on the white table cloth and pushed back his hat with the barrel of a pistol. "You are not much of a host Chamberlain," he told the furious rancher, who had been jumped and disarmed and was now nursing a blackening eye. "I have been your guest for more than twenty minutes, and you ain't even offered me a drink yet. I been riding two days and a night to get here. Now, bring on the booze, and I do not mean that feeble French bubbly. I mean business!"

"What is it you're after here, Cumplin?" Jake demanded.

"Wine, women, song and Logan Walker. Where Lark McKay is, he is or soon will be. The chap skipped out on me. See, I'm still aiming to collect the reward that old man there has got on Walker's head. Is dead or alive, either one or t'other, still okay with you, old man?"

"Alive's preferable," Rufus answered. "My granddaughter favors this Walker. She says he's an innocent man, wrongly condemned. What do you say, sonny?"

"I say don't call me sonny, old man," Cumplin replied, his eyes going mean and narrow. He raised a bottle of sour mash whiskey to his lips and gulped it like water. "Call me sonny again—" he stopped gurgling to say, "I'll blow you to kingdom come, hear?"

Rufus nodded. "I am old, but I am neither deaf nor stupid. I intend to enjoy the years left me yet," McKay said. "But you—" he pointed a crooked, arthritic finger at the outlaw—"now, you're not old, and you never will be. Your days are numbered."

Clarence very slowly got to his feet, raised a pistol and levelled it at Rufus. "Numbered? Who's counting?" he asked.

"I am, sonny." Rufus nodded, bringing all his natural dignity and stature to bear. He was playing on what he perceived as the outlaw's greatest weakness—resentment of authority.

"Dario . . . Jake, somebody, *do* something," Charlotte whispered. "Pa, don't rile the man. Don't challenge him. Don't—"

"Mr. Cumplin, you're right, you know, about Logan Walker," Roe Ann broke in. "He's here alright."

"Is he now? Where at, you harpy?" Clarence demanded, the whiskey beginning to have its effect.

"I don't rightly know exactly where, but I do know—" There was another pistol shot, and as Roe Ann slumped in her chair, Dr. Middleton lunged across the table to catch her before she fell while the others, Matt included, looked on in shock.

"Make a practice of shooting women, do you, Cumplin?" the doctor demanded.

"Well . . . I don't kill 'em, not as a rule." Clarence laughed maniacally. "I just winged her. You fix her. Now, let's get merrymaking, damn it! Where's Goldilocks, and who's that I heard before from outside pounding on the piano like a bawdyhouse *musiker?*"

Not until then did anyone notice that Aida, who had

followed Jake out of the house, had not returned when everyone else did.

"Did she say anything?" Jake asked, looking from one worried face to another. "Did she, Miz Blakely?" Emma, Amy and Ethel all answered no. "I must go see if the boy's still here. Cumplin, I must know if Joachim is safe in his bed or out in the storm with his mother. If she came back and took him away, why, I might never see my . . . my son alive again!"

"Your son, Jake?" Charlotte shook her head in disbelief. "You were begging Lark to marry you with the mother of your child right here and listening to every word? If I was Aida, I'd be long gone myself by now. In fact I am getting out of here — now. I can't spend another night under your roof, and if I know my daughter, she'll be coming with me."

"Jake, this has not been your night," Dario said. "You sure have got a weird way with the ladies, panting after a girl half your age, one who is mad in love with another man, when all the while you had one fine woman, Charlotte here, on tenterhooks and another, Aida, already sharing your bed and your life." His reassuring hand squeezed Charlotte's shoulder. "Clarence," he added, "have a heart and let this damn old April fool go up to check on the child."

"Heartless is what they call me, Heyward, but as I'm on my way up to get Lark, Chamberlain might's well come, too. Nels, you and Martell keep these people covered."

Jake and Clarence found Lark standing quite still at the top of the stairs. Bound and determined to negotiate a settlement that would insure not only Logan's safety but put an end to his legal troubles once and for all. She was preoccupied, going over her bargaining chips, when she had come upon Cooney.

The outlaw was propped up in a corner of the open hope chest. His eyes were wide, his mouth was agape and twisted and the handle of a kitchen knife protruded from his chest, the blade buried to its hilt between his third and fourth ribs.

Chapter Twenty-nine

"It was a balmy day like this day, January 12th, 1888. When that storm hit, it did damage as far south as Galveston. It even put ice in the Sacramento River," Judge Ike said, lighting a pipe and peering out from under knit brows. "We got a problem, folks. Blizzard outside, killer inside."

"And a missing woman and child," Jake said, pacing, drinking now, too, like the outlaws, and sounding distraught.

"Midnight's come and gone. I didn't get no kissing," Clarence drunkenly complained. "No music, no dancing, neither. We are all going to go back and start this night over, except for old Cooney, of course. No starting over for him." The outlaws were all looking distrustfully at Lark. "Seems every time I get around you, I start losing my best men. How'd you do it this time?"

"Didn't." Lark shrugged with studied nonchalance, harboring her own suspicions. In her view, Logan was the most likely, perhaps the only, suspect in the demise of Cooney. Since no one but her even knew he was in the house, she decided, given the new circumstances, not to mention his presence. It made matters awkward for her, though. He'd said not a single word about homicide. "Out of action" was the way he had described the trussed-up victim and with no hint of a warning to her, he'd left Lark holding the bag.

"I had ninety percent stock losses from the '88 blizzard," Sam Blakely said, also looking warily at Lark. "Beefs and cows froze on their feet . . . near ruined the range cattle business for good, that cold storm. Killed folks, too, lots of them not found till spring thaw."

"But we're a tough lot out here in Oklahoma. We sprang back like prairie grass," Rufus added. "Aida and the boy are probably holed up safe somewhere, Jake. Try not to take on so."

"That same year you had your plains blizzard," Ethan Everet said, "New York City was hit by one, too, a couple of months later." Like Matt January, Clarence and all three Blakely boys, he hadn't taken his uneasy eyes off Lark since the discovery of Cooney's corpse. "Can I be of help to you, Miss McKay?" Everet asked, seeing a secret smile play at her lips, then a lovely flush come to her cheek. She had glimpsed a shadow in the hall, Logan's she reasoned, and she couldn't help thinking about their recent rendezvous. "It must have been shocking for you—finding the body?"

"What? Oh, his body! It's phenomenal, yes." She sighed. There was an awkward pause during which Everet, blinking, not believing what he'd heard, sat staring at her.

"Oh, Cooney? *That* body, you mean? An unexpected and most unpleasant phenomenon is what *I* mean, but I am fine, thank you," she answered, recalling herself to the demands of the present moment. "I *was* thinking we'd best negotiate a truce, with these bandits, as long as we're all obliged to wait out the blizzard together."

The whole group, including the dozen surviving gang members, had adjourned to the main parlor. One of the outlaws had brought the remnants of the roast pig from the table and was now noisily gnawing at the bones, then tossing them, well-cleaned, into the fire. The Blakely wives were sitting straight and rigid in a line of straight-backed chairs, and Roe Ann, her arm newly bandaged, was stretched out on a settee, groaning occasionally, her long fingernails digging into Dr. Middleton's hand like pincers as she begged him to lace her whiskey with morphine.

"Truce?" Clarence laughed. "With you, Goldilocks? Not damn likely."

"Suit yourself, Cumplin, but I'll state my terms anyway. All weapons—guns, knives, *all*—will be collected and locked up in Cooney's hope chest, if you'll be good enough to get the body out of it. We'll give the key to Judge Ike to hold until the storm blows out. Then you go your way; we'll go ours."

"Nice plan," the outlaw called Nels said. A young Norwegian immigrant, a sheep herder driven from his Montana land by cattlemen, he had in desperation taken to a life of banditry with Clarence. "I sure could do with some shut-eye."

"Keep your eyes open and your guard up around Miss Goldilocks McKay and the Hanging Judge," Cumplin snarled. "Now, I'll say this about a truce: If the old man was to be the key keeper, I might consider the deal. I trust him. 'Course, you will have to gimme a kiss for the new year, Lark. I'm likely to get mean and irritable, I don't get no new year's kiss."

"Clarence"—she smiled—"you're *always* mean and irritable. Maybe, in a while, with the guns under lock and key, we'll have us a little promenade and do-si-do you and me, but now, while you're thinking about my gun containment plan, I want to hear about the big city blizzard. Tell us how easterners cope, Ethan," she suggested. "It's likely to be a long, long night, perhaps a longer day tomorrow, if the weather doesn't let up. It's best we keep each other . . . well, entertained and distracted."

"I'm ready to be real entertaining," Clarence leered, ignored.

"The circumstances preceding both storms in '88," Everet began, "were similar—a rainbow around the sun, temperatures so warm that though it was only March, trees in Central Park were showing buds and Long Island potato farmers were starting their spring planting. Then it hit us, wham! It all began with rain on a Sunday night, and by Monday morning there was ten inches of snow on the ground, and it kept falling. People went to work, some of them, me for one, because they couldn't afford to lose a day's pay. On the way, I got bowled over by wind more than one time, but it was worth it. I was the only sketcher out that day. It looked like a bomb had hit New York—wires were down all over . . . signs, shingles, hats were blowing about, milk wagons were overturned. I was taken by surprise and nearly done for by the cold, but, by God, I got good pictures!"

"Didn't the government weather service give warning?" Ike Parker bristled, adjusting his spectacles. A federal employee, he disliked hearing about the government falling down on its job.

"The U.S. Signal Service? Nah, Judge, no help. They predicted fair weather. Their so-called 'prophet' in the city, a fellow name of Dunn, had contact with more than a hundred and seventy other stations and two thousand weather volunteers, to say nothing of his carrier pigeon backup. He closed the office for the weekend, promising fair skies, and nothing was heard of him again until it was all over."

"There was four feet of snow in some parts. Drifts on Long Island, at Gravesend, were fifty-two feet," Dario added. "I was stranded on a train of the Sixth Avenue elevated line along with many others. I myself climbed down to the street using the cross bars of the elevated's steel stanchion. It was slippery and treacherous. Some people were willing to pay a dollar to enterprising young boys for the use of a ladder."

"That's New York for you," Charlotte commented. Her voice was strident, her expression downcast as she struggled to cope with her heartbreak and disappointment over losing Jake even though she didn't want him any more. She wouldn't take him on a silver platter, she insisted to herself, not a fickle fellow like him, not for all his wealth and looks and charm. "I don't know though, Dario, if I'd call such a thing as charging for the use of a ladder in an emergency fair enterprise or unconscionable exploitation. What do you think?"

"I think you should let me tell you all about my home town one of these chilly days" was his answer. "In fact, perhaps you might let me accompany you there, you and your daughter, of course." When Dario glanced at Lark, he realized something was going on and, following the direction of her eyes, met Logan's fierce amber stare for so fleeting an instant, he could have thought he'd only imagined it. Dario blinked. Logan was gone, but there was a shadow sliding away into the darkness of the hall.

"You were saying, Dario?" Lark asked pointedly.

"Uh, I was just thinking. I'd rather deal with a city

storm than a plains blizzard any day. At least in the city you can find shelter from the cold."

"I have got to go find Aida and . . . and the child," Jake announced ruefully. "If my boy is lost, all my hopes for the future will be laid to dust, and it will be my fault, mine alone."

"Jake, it's wind, not cold alone, that kills. You know that and Aida knows that. She knows if you can get off the high plains and into bottom land thicket, better yet into a barn, there's a better chance to make it through," Dorsey Middleton said.

Jake shook his head. "The worst storm I've lived through, the one in '88, it went down to twenty-nine below. A woman and a child . . . anyone, can freeze to death in ten minutes at twenty-nine below with no fire to warm them even if they are inside."

"Jake's right." Ike Parker nodded. "Any blasted soul who must venture out for some good reason, to see to livestock, say, has got to walk very slowly so as not to breathe too deep. Cold like this can tear out your lungs."

"Clarence, I've got to find the boy and his mother. I'll go along with Lark. I'll lay down my weapons if you'll all help me search for them."

"As a rule, I ain't the helpful type, Chamberlain." Clarence pouted. "You care so much about this half-breed boy and a big Indian woman that you'll risk your own life for them?"

"I do," Jake replied.

"I'll agree to the weapons truce," Dorsey interjected, "and I'll help you search, Jake; but in my professional opinion, no one in his right mind should be going anywhere for a while. Aida has found a safe haven by now or — she has not. Either way, we'll be risking our own lives for no reason."

"My first winter campaign when I was still in the army," Eli Blakely began, "I was with a troop of cavalry out on the Republican River. We was after renegade Indians who had slipped off the reservation in summer and was raising hell come that winter. We was marching right into a terrific snow storm so bad you couldn't see your hand before your face. We was forced to lead our horses. Some of the men refused to keep on, said they'd rather lie down and die than keep on through that eighteen inches of snow and vicious wind. The captain had at them with the flat of his sabre or they'd have done just that, lay down and died right there. Now, Aida isn't about to do that, Jake, and—good grief, Miss McKay, you feelin', pardon the pun, under the weather? Emma, perhaps you and the other ladies should see to Miss McKay."

Lark seemed to have developed a sudden bad case of the fidgets which drew Dorsey Middleton's attention away from his tedious and demanding patient. "Have you ever suffered from nervous attacks, Lark, or cabin fever?" the doctor asked, his bemused, analytic eyes fixed on her.

"I need a little sleep is all." She yawned dramatically. "That, or something to wake me up, like a breath of fresh cold air." Not trusting Clarence, she wanted to get to Logan, whose shadow kept moving back and forth in the hall, and insist he keep hidden until she'd worked out the details of his pardon with Roe Ann and Judge Ike.

"It is part of the soldier's duty to face cold, is it not, Doctor?" Rufus asked, just to keep the conversation going and distract attention from Lark who, he realized, wasn't sleepy in the slightest, or daft. She had something up her sleeve. There was a bee abuzz in her pretty bonnet. "I'll gladly keep the keys to the gun chest. When the dawn arrives or the storm abates, which ever comes first, you and your men take back your weapons and go, son . . . I mean Clarence. That a deal?"

"It is the soldier's lot to put up with cold, yes sir, and with the heat of summer, even with the agony of fire at the Indian's stake. Here's *my* sidearm, Cumplin." Dorsey Middleton, to start things moving, set his gun on the floor near the hearth. Within minutes a small arsenal had accumulated until only a few were still armed, the outlaw Martell, Jake and Clarence Cumplin.

"Where's that tiny, cute little Derringer Logan gave you?" he asked Lark.

"I lost it, but I have got something nearly as useful. I will give up my weapon if you will give up yours, Cumplin," she teased, slowly raising her fringed leather skirt to reveal a tempting length of leg and a sheathed buck knife secured to her thigh, secreted in her garter before she had ventured out of her room. She shifted it from hand to hand, flirting with the outlaw. "Then I'll ask Dario to play a tune on the spinet, and you and me can get dancin'. What say?"

"I say this: Nels, dump old Cooney out in the snow and bring that box on down!" Clarence laughed maniacally. "I ain't leaving here until Logan Walker shows up, but I will lay down my gun while I'm waiting—that's if you and me can dance the rest of the night away, Lark."

She nodded, her calm smile masking her inner tension, her gaze on his gun.

"We all have to stay put right here together in the same room till I say otherwise," Judge Ike insisted. "Or else some one of those outlaws could sneak off and re-arm."

"There's honor among thieves, Judge. I give you my word. I vouch for my men. I personally will kill any one of them that don't follow the rules of the game."

"Honor among thieves is one thing, Cumplin," Martell said. "Lawmen and judges are something else again. I ain't never found them big on integrity. No way, Clarence, I'll give up my sidearm. No deals for Joe Martell."

Cumplin's pistol went off instantly, twice, and Martell's guns went flying. The Blakely wives made little screams in unison. Martell gasped out a swear word and fell to his knees, holding his two bloodied and shattered hands before his eyes.

"Martell, you can keep them guns if you want, but they won't do you no good now, or ever again. No one says no to Clarence Cumplin, hear?" Clarence said. "Hey, Doc, I know there's precious little rest for the weary or members of the medical profession; but will you see to that dimwit while I count to three, and Goldilocks, me and Jake will throw our weapons on the pile. Ready? One . . . two . . . *three.*" Jake set down his Colt. Locking eyes with Clarence, Lark reached out, dagger in hand, but didn't relinquish it. The grinning outlaw had, as she'd expected, held on to his gun. "We'll both drop them at the same instant and jump back, okay?" he asked, and Lark nodded. "Now!" Clarence exclaimed and jumped as planned. Lark didn't.

"The rest of the tools of your trade, please, Clarence," she said, and with the chagrined look of a bad little boy, he produced another gun from under his shirt. Lark still didn't move. Clarence drew a knife from his left boot, then a small tomahawk from his right, and finally a coil of wire from under his soft black hat. Only then did Lark add her knife to the collection. The sigh of relief that ran round the room turned at once to gasps of consternation when Clarence produced yet another pistol, one he'd secreted behind a picture on the mantel. He cut a swathe like a sword through the unarmed crowd to get to Lark's side.

"In the country of the blind, the one-eyed man is king, isn't he? I'd wager you were speculating there was a future for you in espionage or diplomacy," he said. "There ain't, because you ain't quite as clever as you think, darlin', just another silly, yellow-haired skirt. You thought you were setting me up real good for your boyfriend, didn't you? I told you I never do trust a woman, 'specially you. Now someone wind up the Victrola and put on that lively Marine Band march I heard playing earlier. These law-abiding gentlemen, except for the piano player, are going to double time it up to the attic, and I'll be keeping that key myself. Hands up and start trekking!"

"Hands up yourself, Cumplin," Ethan Everet ordered as surprised as everyone else by the command. Lark's lost little Derringer, which he held pointed at the outlaw, had just amazingly materialized beside his foot. "Now, you march."

"I always said never trust a lawman or a woman. Now I'm adding newspaper reporters to my list. A man can't trust no one these days," Clarence gritted, raising his arms, his hands dangling limp at the wrists but still holding his gun. "Let's dicker further. I wasn't really going to put you good old buddies up in that icy attic."

"As far as I can tell, you've nothing to dicker with, Clarence, you heavy thinker you." Lark laughed, slapping her knee.

"I'll go out into the storm to look for Jake's woman and child. I'll need a couple of my of culprits to help. Do I have any volunteers?" Cumplin asked. Nels' right hand, already raised, shot up higher. There was a pause and then another young bandit jiggled an index finger. Joe Butch Cozad was a boy with a mountainy untamed look about him, like a feral tom cat with transparent, clear blue eyes and a narrow pitted face.

"You, Joe Butch? One look at you is like to scare the wits out of any little child. But, okay, you're on."

"Clarence, what are you really up to?" Lark asked, her eyes on him narrowed with suspicion.

"I want a chance to make up for some of the bad I done in this world, is all. I know how it feels to lose young 'uns. Even if Chamberlain is a deputy sheriff and a vigilante at heart, he don't deserve that. No one does." Remembering what Logan had told her of Cumplin's wife and children, Lark found herself, against her better judgment, believing Clarence. Her doubting smile vanished. She nodded.

"For Nancy?" she asked gently.

Clarence reeled as if from a blow, handed his gun to Rufus and said, "Just let me try and do good for a change. Jake, I need rope."

"There's none in the house but clothesline, maybe. Who are you fixin' to tie?" Jake asked. "It's awful cold in the attic though, and anyone up there who can't move around could freeze."

"The rope's not for that. It's for the search party. I'll tie an end of the line to the porch stanchions and let it play out while we hold to it. That way, when we do find Aida, we'll also be able to find our way back to the safety of the house."

Chapter Thirty

Anyone standing off at a distance the next day, peering with superhuman eyes through dense swirling snow at the JAK Bar ranch house and simultaneously observing all its inhabitants, would have found them scattered over two floors and through many rooms engaged in activities both convivial and solitary.

Dario and Charlotte were as good as alone in the parlor, sitting side by side on the settee, sipping hot buttered rum while the storm raged on outside. They shared the room with only the dogs, who lazed about. The two golden wolf hounds lay on opposite sides of the hearth, their heads on front paws like living andirons, the fox terrier, Ralph, lay on his side, silhouetted against a colorful rug, snoring, and Logan's spotted cattle dog, who'd spent little of his life indoors, luxuriated in the deepest, softest chair, dreaming. Max ran in his sleep, his legs going, his lids twitching, and occasionally he emitted a growl or yelp.

Others—Jake upstairs in his bedroom suffering a crisis of conscience, Roe Ann in Jake's office downstairs tormented by anger and jealousy and steadily imbibing—could not have been described as enviably content, though they would have appeared safe and warm at least, to someone outside looking in, battered by the storm.

Lark was enjoying herself immensely with only two less-than-overwhelming cares in the world—cheering Charlotte and clearing Logan. She expected to do both with ease.

"Far as I care, we could stay snowbound forever, or as long the firewood holds out," she told Logan, untangling herself from his embrace to rise and add a log to the blaze. The cooing couple was cuddling and kissing on chaise in her room.

"The snow *will* stop, soon probably, so this is as good a time as any to talk about forever," Logan said, stretching and arching his back. He was so long and lean, his eyes on her so hungry that she flew back to him to be gathered in his arms. He looked into her eyes, his hands cupping her face before one drifted to the swell of her breasts beneath her sueded leather blouse, and her lucent dove-gray eyes went carnal and misty.

"During this storm, snowbound as we are, real life is in abeyance. Soon, you will have to show yourself and confront Roe Ann, talk to the judge, see to Clarence, all that serious business. But right now I want you to make sweet love to me, Logan. I'll want you again in an hour or so, and tonight, and every night from now on. That's forever enough for me."

"But where's all this lust and devotion to be perpetrated?" Logan asked, his voice smokey and warm.

"In that lonesome place you said you were searching for." Lark now stretched out to her full five-foot length on top of Logan and tasted his lips.

"Listen a minute, listen!" he implored. "I know you want to hear the roar of crowds and to see great cities, to live in a fine, big house on a hill and—"

"Yes, yes. That's just what I want, Walker, a house on Carnegie Hill on Fifth Avenue maybe, built of blood-red brick, all filled with things called Hepplewhite and Chippendale and Tiffany and Biedemier. I want Brussels carpets and damascened tapestries. I want egret-feather fans and swansdown puffs. I simply must have brocaded evening dresses—"

"They're yours for the asking," Logan interrupted, laughing. "But I'd rather live in Carolina amidst wild camellias, in the gracious languor of the South. That's when we aren't travelling, of course, to Paris, London, Buenos Aries . . . wherever you'll be performing, and I'll, well, I'll be taking care of business."

"Tell me another one, cowboy!" Lark giggled. "Josh and tease me all you please. Damn!" she said, feigning anger. "All I ever really wanted from the time I first saw you is you. Ain't that clear as a rat in milk?"

"It is clear. I knew it before you did yourself, and, sweet girl, you've got me. But you don't know exactly what it is you've got. I may not be what I seem."

"What you seem is the best-lookin', hardest-riding, sweetest-loving cowboy drifter in the West, one in trouble with the law, who's got nothing to his name but his horse and his saddle and his dog and me. If there's more I need to know about you, I'll wager it's something *real* bad, right?" Lark laughed.

"There's more. My father wore Confederate gray. He died wearing it. He was killed when I was a tyke of two, just before the end of the war, just before my sister was born, but not before he invested what little was left of his fortune, anything he hadn't donated to the Southern cause, in small-gage railroads in the Argentine and in a salmon cannery in California, among other things. Father chose well. His investments grew. I'm his only heir. I own . . . well, a number of properties including the Walker Plantation, which just happens to have a house made of blood-red brick, sitting atop a hill."

"If what you are trying to tell me is that you are a rich man and not a dirt-poor cowpoke at all, Logan Walker"—Lark peered hard into his eyes—"I won't love you one wit less. Now what?"

"Now, get on downstairs, woman, and get us food. I intend to keep up my strength, and yours." He leered.

"Love can be hard work, nice work, but demanding," Lark agreed with ribald seriousness, scrambling to her feet and darting for the door. At once vertical, Logan moved with his usual quick grace and then some to ensnare her in his arms and kiss her before she wriggled free and was gone.

From the dining room, where a poker game had been in progress for hours, she heard the slap of cards, the jingle of coins and the frequent monosyllabic grunts of the players.

"I must leave here, Dario," Charlie was saying. "I won't stay one instant longer than I must under Chamberlain's roof. It's terrible here for me now, like being an inmate in a prison!"

"The worst jail is one you can't see, Charlotte," Dario replied, "the one you make for yourself in your heart or your head."

"He's right, Mama," Lark said, poking her head into the room. The dog Max thumped his tail lazily at the sound of her voice.

"Lark, we are unlucky at love, both of us, falling for outlaws. At least Mark Larken gave me a baby. All you got from your bandit lover is that mangy spotted cow dog." Lark and Dario exchanged helpless looks. "Lark, you are reckless with your heart, like me," Charlotte, slightly tipsy, went on. "You should have accepted Jake's offer. You need the steadying influence of an older man. He'd have given you your own show, and made you a big star. Marry Jake, why don't you?"

"I don't love him, Charlie. Remember what you said, about fate and destiny and love?"

"Forget what I said. If you can't have love, get something else. That's what I am going to try to do now. I am turning my back on the past and the West, and I'm going after everything I never had before — a home of my own right on the edge of the eastern ocean where I'll sit peaceful on my own verandah of an evening, looking out and knowing that for thousands of miles there's no tumbleweed, no prairie grass full of summer locusts, no bone-dry dust waiting to turn to mud in the first cold winter rain. Mostly, there'll be no darn cowboys. I mean to have a settled life, the comfort of my own hearth and my own logs, all I'll ever need, just burning bright red and blue, and more logs piled in the woodshed so there'll be no more skimping and shivering in a drafty shack or threadbare canvas tent on the edge of some desolate cow town after a hard day's work."

"Charlotte," Dario began with infinite patience, "let me tell you about the time I was up near the timberline looking for birds and a huge white-tailed buck came out of the trees, a most beautiful sight. Soon, three round-eyed does joined him in the silence, all unafraid . . ."

Lark withdrew from the parlor unnoticed and went on her way to the kitchen.

The Blakely wives and their eight children, along with Al Ringling and the doctor, were gathered around the table enjoying a New Year's breakfast of Hopping

John—black-eyed peas and rice cooked up in a big cast-iron pot. The dish was considered good luck according to Ethel Blakely and Logan, two southerners, the only right way to start the year, and no one was enjoying it more than Joachim.

The boy, who now occupied the place of honor at the head of the table, had been found in the stable, safe but hungry. Clarence had come upon him on the third foray into the killing wind and snow. Gloved, draped, heavily cloaked and scarved, Cumplin had shown impressive bravery and persistence in the search. He had risked his life, losing hold of the guide rope once and nearly vanishing into the storm, to eventually find the little boy asleep in the stable. The child had been left well wrapped in blankets and nearly buried in the straw of Satan's stall, which was also occupied by Max and Ralph, all four sharing body warmth.

Joachim, the dogs trailing after, had been carried back to the house by Clarence, who'd slipped and slid and fought the wind every step of the way as it threatened to snatch the small burden from his arms. Joachim had been greeted with tears and cheers from everyone, even Jake, who was too choked with emotion to speak and worried about the still-missing Aida.

Jake, too, had come to the breakfast table to celebrate the return of the child, who was thoroughly enjoying all the notoriety, attention and something more, a changed manner toward him in everyone at the JAK Bar. He wished his mother was there to explain everything to him, most of all to explain why she was going away. Aida had told her son nothing except that he was to be courageous and behave like a little man when she was gone, and so far Joachim wasn't finding it all that hard to follow her instructions, not with everyone fussing over him, especially his favorite, yellow-haired Lark. She gave him an extra-big squeeze now, before hefting a tray heavily loaded with potato cheese, cold roast pig, bread and a tin pot of coffee.

"Need some help with that?" Dorsey Middleton asked as she staggered a little in an attempt to casually stroll from the kitchen with her sizeable burden. She was the strangest girl he'd ever met, and the most intriguing.

"I'll manage, thanks, Doc," she called over her shoulder, heading for the stairs.

"Hellfire, and damnation, it makes my blood boil, losing to the likes of you, sonny!" Lark, passing the dining room, heard Rufus explode. There was a low burst of rumbling laughter from the other players—Matt, the judge and the outlaws.

"Listen, pops, you have met your match in me, oh, yeah!" Clarence laughed, sounding half sane. "I *do* like winning. Pass them silver dollars on over!"

Logan was waiting for Lark halfway up the stairs. He relieved her of the tray and, deftly balancing it high on one hand, stroked the other over Lark's swaying hips and swelling undulant flanks ahead of him. When she stopped abruptly on the landing, he kept walking, and they happily collided. His free arm snaked about her waist, he pulled her back against him, and she felt the surge of his manhood where his hand had just caressed before she heard the whisper of his breath at her ear.

"We'll eat after I nibble on you a while, okay?"

"I'll have it no other way, cowboy" was her breathless answer as she tumbled into her room and closed the door.

She was wearing no lingerie beneath her sueded leather skirt, and when his hand slid up along the inner curve of her shapely leg, he found her warm and moist and ready. She began to undo the laces of her bead-glittered shirt but got no farther than the second eyelet before Logan, who had carefully set down the tray and undone his pants, came up behind her and raised her fringed skirt to her hips. Enfolding her slender waist, he entered her in one thrust, and when their eyes met in the cheval glass, hers were gray mist, his dark fire and gold flame. She lifted her arms to reach back and encircle his strong neck, her flaxen hair framing her face, and her breasts thrusting. His hand coursed up over her ribs and captured a breast peeking through the loosened laces of her shirt, his fine fingers strumming the sensitive tip as his other hand dropped over the plane of her belly and fine golden fleece to delve between her thighs, parted wide for balance. His hands and his thrusting body, his ragged voice in her ear, his lips at her nape all orchestrated a climactic crescendo that left them weak and clinging.

It had been a deliciously swift joining, just enough to keep them happy as they fed each other mouthfuls of food. Lark loosened Logan's clothes. He slipped off her skirt and lifted her shirt over her head. Naked as Adam and Eve, splendid and flamboyant as Eros and Aphrodite, they stood shivering and smiling for a moment before diving beneath the bed covers to hold each other close, at first for one sort of warmth, then for a another sort of heat entirely.

Logan sighed and yawned. "The time's come, I think, for me to get things under way, get Judge Ike and Roe Ann together," he said, and Lark giggled with joyous venom visualizing the scene.

"Can't we just take a *little* slumber first, Logan? I'm feeling real warm and relaxed, and you know, no one's going anywhere, not for a while." Before she got to the end of her sentence, Logan was breathing deeply and evenly, sleeping soundly.

Lark awoke to find that the day and Logan were gone. She was alone. The windows were black, the fire was nearly out, and there was an odd stillness in the air. She found it unnerving and eery until she realized the roar of the wind had subsided; the storm was ending. The whole house was silent, asleep, until a piercing howl shattered the midnight calm.

Chapter Thirty-one

"You say you're ambidextrous, Clarence? You really can shoot as well with your left hand as with your right? Damn good thing," Doc Middleton said mildly, trying not to further alarm his latest patient. "How on God's good earth did this happen, do you mind telling me?" Pale as a specter and tinged faintly green with pain, Clarence was lying on his back on the kitchen table. Two of the severed fingers of his right hand lay beside him, a third on the floor in a large, spreading pool of blood.

"Axe, Doc . . . or some kind of cleaver. Wham! I was standing there, leaning on the table and gnawing the last piggy rib, when it happened. I never saw nor heard a thing. What are you gonna do to me, Doc, what are you?"

"Relax. There's not much to do. I can just try and stop the bleeding." Middleton tied off Cumplin's hand above the wrist and raised it. "And try to see you don't get the blood poison." When the doctor poured a generous pint of whiskey on the stumps of the outlaw's fingers, Clarence fainted.

"Where's the judge at? We have got a murdering

ghoul among us," Rufus said, chewing his mustache. "I can understand cattle rustling, train robbing, even horse thieving, though I don't hold with that, but knifing a bound man and slicing off a shooter's digits just is not acceptable to me. Only a real villain would resort to such sardonic acts. You ladies best stay close to your young ones," he told the Blakely wives, who were standing in the doorway in their bedgowns and nightcaps, clutching candles.

"Amy and Emma," Ethel said, "go on back up to the baby biddies and youngsters. I'll see to this mess and tend the patient, poor man. Even he, bad as he is, doesn't deserve this, especially after he rescued Joachim. Scat, scat now, you two. I will do the nursing because I am the one knows Miss Clara Barton, after all." Two Blakely wives vanished from the kitchen and were heard taking the stairs fast to get to the youngsters, who were all in their beds, even those who had been awakened by the blood-curdling scream and had been firmly directed to stay put and out of the kitchen. Their fathers, very sound sleepers all three, could not be counted upon to awaken even with a killer loose in the house.

"It must have taken quite a tall, strong person, Doctor, to do that damage to Clarence in one blow," Lark said, feeling slightly sick. Middleton nodded, worrying over the patient's pallid icy brow.

"A strong person or a weak one with a very heavy axe, or both, did this," Ethan Everet speculated, sketching rapidly, not missing a detail.

" 'Nefarious Clarence Cumplin Loses Fingers to Fiend,' That's my headline. 'Is The Bandit's career over? Clarence Claims Ambidextrousness.' That's the sub head. What a story. Have you ever seen your boss shoot left-handed, Joe Butch?"

"I ain't never seen him do no such a thing, no sir," Joe Butch answered.

" 'I ain't never seen him do no such a thing, no sir' a Cumplin gang member, Joe Butch Cozad, says. Want your name in the paper, Joe Butch?" The boy didn't rightly know about that, Lark heard him saying as she left the kitchen wondering where Logan had gone and what he had to do with Cumplin's misfortune. She was uneasy now about several occurrences—Cooney, Clarence and the pewter buttons—but mostly it worried her that Logan seemed to have gone missing now and had been out of touch on the other occasions that things had gone wrong. He might well be part of the bloody goings-on, either as a perpetrator or victim, and she would find out if she had to search the house from root cellar to icy attic.

Lark decided to begin with Jake's office, a small room off the kitchen, on the first floor. Finding the door locked, she knocked, got no answer, rattled it, and proceeded to the bath closet, a small room containing a commode, a real porcelain tub, a kerosene water heater and a shelf full of jars, bottles and bowls.

On first glance, the compartment seemed empty. On second glance, she found that to be an accurate deduction, though not the whole story. There was a shadow on the window, a long narrow one, clearly outlined by an ice-white moon. Drawing cautiously closer, Lark realized that someone was pressed to the glass, peering in. Drawing closer still, she saw that the window was locked from the inside by a brass bolt. She also saw that the person outside was as still as a . . . corpse.

Lark's scream, not unlike the one made earlier by Clarence, sent a shock of fear through the household, and in only a few minutes she was surrounded. Her hands were being patted, her face cooled, her head raised and her mother weeping.

"You fell in faint, Lark, and if all this keeps up, I might do the same," Doc Middleton said.

Joe Butch and Nels peeled Roe Ann's frozen body from the window, breaking the fingers and tearing the skin off as they did. Her hands and face were waxy and frostbitten, the fine bones of the nose and cheeks jagged. Blood had congealed around the shrivelled mouth, on the fragmented brow and along the torn and ragged fingernails which had been scratching and tearing frantically against ungiving glass.

"Her head has been battered, but what killed her was freezing. Roe Ann was trying to get back into the house. The question is, what on earth lured her out into the storm?" The doctor was finding it more and more difficult to maintain his *sang-froid* as the injuries and fatalities piled up.

"We all must gather in the parlor now," a terribly shaken Jake told his house guests. "Whoever is perpetrating these outrages can't get us all at once. There's safety in numbers." He was holding Joachim, the exhausted child sound asleep against his shoulder. Like Lark, Jake was touched by a deep, frigid fear heightened by a sense of guilt. Lark thought of Logan, Jake of Aida, both hiding their suspicions, both thinking they should have been able to predict such aberration in their lovers, both determined to know the worst, or the best, just as long the mystery was solved.

Once Lark had regained consciousness and was carried to her bed, Charlotte let go, disintegrating into silent, wracking hysterics, and the devoted Dario helped her to her own room. Ethel brought tea and toast; Jake arrived with brandy but quickly departed. Charlotte sat shaking, staring into the fire.

First she was silent.

Then she got weepy. Finally she began to talk, and nothing could stop her until she'd said what she needed to say.

"How could I have so misjudged the man? Lord, I never was any good at all getting a right fix on a feller, and Lord knows, I've tried, over and over, startin' with Mark Larken. Dario, I thought Jake was wooing me, but I was wrong. How wrong can a girl be?"

"Charlotte, don't rebuke yourself. Love is strange. Anyway, you are a fine woman, not a girl. You were right about Jake wooing you, until he brought Lark home to the JAK Bar. He found you gracious and charming and calming. He found your daughter wildly exciting, so he made a dumb choice. He couldn't help himself. The man is at the frivolous and flighty, frightened age when the future ain't forever any more. Jake always was an opportunist, and winning a young girl like Lark, a real prize for a man his age, that would have seemed a triumph."

"Just at first perhaps," Charlotte said, "but not for long."

"Charlie, you're right. I don't have to explain all this to you because you already know it, but I will, just so you and me understand each other. An aging, lonely, childless rancher with a girl like Lark on his arm would feel young, and look it, to his friends. He'd feel as powerful as when he was a youth, but it wouldn't have been right or made him happy long. He'd have turned to worrying was she loving him or his ranch or his money or his power. Charlie, forgive him. Forgiveness lightens your load and your loneliness, and listen, you're as much of a prize, more of one than Lark, for a man Jake's age—or mine."

Charlotte looked up, thunderstruck. "A . . . prize?"

"Of course you are, but why hand it over to a man so vain and weak he can't—doesn't want to—understand that? At least make him win it! Damn, I'd go through hellfire for you and . . . never mind. Let's take a walk, a sleigh ride, look at the sky, see what the storm's done to the world. It can't but help make you happier than you are right now." Dario sighed.

"How did you get so damn smart, Dario? You may be the smartest person I've ever met. Where do come from, really?"

"I'll tell you about the Big City one day, and about my Irish dad and about my Italian mother who passed young, how I took to the streets—and got out alive. The thing about children, Charlie, is you want to make them strong enough to fly away from the nest and survive on their own. My mother did that for me. You did that for Lark. No one did quite right for you, so you are more needy of love than some—I'm sorry. I shouldn't be talking this way." Dario's jack-o'-lantern grin appeared, and he blushed, an odd sight; but to Charlotte, he was suddenly princely handsome.

"Why shouldn't you be? Talk more," she said, "I mean, if you want to." She took a sip of tea and one of brandy and undid her ash-blond hair, an unconscious seductive act that struck Dario to the heart.

"You must treat each day as if it's borrowed," he said. "Live it and use it. That's all I want to say now. Now, I have to go help Logan and Lark—yes, Logan's here at the JAK Bar—and from the look of Lark earlier, he's probably in trouble up to his neck. Lock your door after me, okay?" Dario's wide lips barely brushed Charlotte's. As she sleepily watched his long scarecrow frame slip away, she began to wonder about how it would look, and feel, unclothed, on a summer day perhaps, sun-warmed, damp with sweat, moving against her.

"Dario? I've long been looking for a love that would pick me up, carry me away like a tornado or roll over me like a tidal wave. But if I could just find a man to treat me right. . . ." She smiled. So did he. "I want a different kind of love now."

"There's the love you need and the love you get, and somewhere between the two there's happiness, maybe. You know, Charlie, a feather in hand is better than a bird in the air. Want to try loving me?" His long-fingered hand rested on the doorknob. His heart beat like a drum. It was happening faster than he'd dared hope.

"I've always had . . . men friends, Dario, even when I had nothing else." She looked at him straight and unflinching.

"I don't care that I'm not your first love, as long as I'm your last." He closed the door precisely and leaned back against it.

"I'm not real young, Dario." Charlotte shrugged.

"When a man loves a woman, she's always the age he wants her to be." He didn't move for fear she'd vanish, or change her mind.

"I don't think I'm in love with you yet, Dario." Charlotte set down her teacup.

"I will not shut an eye this long night unless I speak my mind. I know I love you, but it happens to some that what's really in your heart you best conceal from yourself." He took a step, then another.

"You might just be right about that. I never was any

good at all getting a right fix on a feller, and Lord knows I've tried, over and over."

"Try me," Dario suggested, taking the tea tray from her lap. When he turned back to her again, Charlotte was standing, undoing the tassels of her wrap. "Here, I'll do that," he said lovingly, his glowing grin breaking over them both like summer sun. She stood a bit rigid, then relaxed as she stepped into his arms for the first time. His mouth on hers was strong and exacting, his build powerful, the ridges of his tight muscles firm against her soft and full, aching woman's body. It expanded and enfolded him after they found themselves on the bed, and he touched her deeper and stronger, claimed her more completely, than she ever would have imagined any man could; and when they'd accomplished what they had set out to, and they lay together overwhelmed, Charlotte said, "Dario, *now* I know I love you." And she saw not the clown's grin but tears in his dark and tender eyes.

Chapter Thirty-two

"I have no alibi. My alibi is dead, Lark, and I'm leaving before the thaw and law trap me here. You can't change my mind, but you can come with me. Coming with me?" Logan, stood on the veranda of the JAK Bar, the collar of his shearling coat up, his hat pulled low, rifle slung over his shoulder and his dog at his side. His eyes were like stone, withdrawn and angry. Lark hovered at the intersection of chill night air and the fire's heat, prettily flushed and getting set to sob her heart out.

"So this is where the cowboy rides away, is it, to go on searching for that lonesome place? Well, this is where I came in Walker, and now, I'm getting out. If there was one good reason to run, I'd be at your side, but as it is, I'd rather go on the road with a clown and a tame bear and perform for thrown nickels."

"Suit yourself," Logan said. "But don't you *dare* cry. I can't stand it."

"You have the undaunted nerve to say that to me when you are breaking my heart? Don't you dare tell me what to do!" She did cry, almost silently, her lucent tears falling fast. Logan pivoted on his boot heel, facing away from her. She was too beautiful and too sad, and it was too dangerous looking at her, he decided. If he did, he'd give in and likely get hanged, now that Roe Ann had been done away with and the medical prognosis for Clarence was poor. The outlaw's fever had spiked and never come down.

"Don't go!"

"I *am* going."

"I'll remember you all my life!"

"I appreciate that. Lark, I really do!" Logan, at his wits end, growled, turning on her. "I talked to your friend, Hanging Ike, Lark. 'A conviction's a conviction unless there's new evidence.' That's what he said.

"There's no evidence now. Oh, Lark, come with me, *please*. I don't want to live without you." His jaw was squared, his lips drawn thin, and Lark could hear the sound of his heart breaking in every word.

"I talked to Ike, too, Logan. If we do this straight and legal, he'll bend over backwards for us. I want you so."

"I don't trust Ike or Jake now. All these mysteries to solve might prompt them to try to hang the Cooney and January killings on me, too."

"And would they be far from wrong?" Lark snapped, half serious.

"If that's what you really think of me, I *am* going, alone. Now you mention it, you never did tell me why you knifed Cooney. If you were jealous of Roe Ann, which you'd have been a little idiot to be, that's one thing, but a helpless man lying tied in a box? Why?"

"Logan, you might's well just add Clarence to your list of my crimes." Lark said icily, and he stared at her, incredulous and amazed.

"But . . . you couldn't have done such a thing . . . could you?"

"Could I have done any of those dreadful things you

accuse me of, do you suppose? If you think so, you sure don't know me very well."

"What the devil is going on here, you two?" Dario interrupted. He was looking exceedingly happy, just coming down from Charlotte's room. "I turn my back for an hour or so, and the children get into a squabble. Tell me all about it," he coaxed, putting one arm about Logan's shoulders, the other about Lark's.

"He is accusing me of murders foul and evil," Lark sobbed out.

"Let's get this straight. Who is accusing who here?" Logan asked indignantly.

"Both of you stop it. Clarence killed Cooney. He told me so."

Lark and Logan both stared at Dario, then glanced longingly at each other, neither willing yet to admit the error of their ways.

"Want to know why Clarence did it?" Dario asked. They nodded. "You'll have to ask him that yourselves, and I suggest you do it now. He may not be long for this world."

"I'm not long for this world," Clarence croaked as they hurried into his room. He appeared all skin and bones beneath the blankets and as white as his sheets. "Grant a dying man one wish, brother?"

Logan nodded. "If it's in my power, old son, I'll do anything you ask."

"Marry that girl right here and now. Go get the judge." Lark looked up at Logan and moved a step closer to him. He offered her his handkerchief, and she dabbed at her eyes; but neither said a word.

"They were just having a spat, Clarence," Dario explained, "but I'd be more than happy to get hitched here and now for your entertainment." The sickroom had been slowly filling so that now there was a small crowd gathered around the bed, grim outlaws on one side, somber Blakelys on the other, Lark, Logan and Dario at the foot and Ethan Everet everywhere, sketching the scene from every angle.

"Last Days of a Desperado," Ethan said. "Catchy headline, don't you think?"

"Uh, Dario, who'd marry up with you?" Clarence asked, laughing, then wincing in pain. His head hurt.

"Here's the lucky lady now," Dario beamed, all aglow at the sight of Charlotte, who took his extended hand, smiling gloriously. When she kissed him, a ripple of *ohs* and *ahs* went around the room.

"Mama, is it true?" Lark sniffled.

"It is true, Lark baby," Charlotte sighed. "I have found the love of my life, and here's the judge now. We could make it a double wedding, you know." Though they looked at each other with soft yearning eyes, still neither Lark nor Logan spoke.

"Logan, if you marry her, I'll give you a very special wedding gift," Clarence said, his voice fading. "Well? I ain't got forever."

"I don't know if it's wise to marry a woman who thinks I'm a murderer. What do you think, Clarence?"

"That wouldn't bother me none," the outlaw answered.

"Well, I don't want to get tied to a man who thinks I killed Cooney in the hope chest." Lark was indignant. "Did you really think that, Logan?" she asked very softly. He shook his head no, took her hand and led her from the room.

"Sugar, please marry me now. I won't go because I can't live without you," he said, settling his deep-brimmed hat on her golden head. The gesture so delighted Lark, she actually smiled at him for the first time that day.

"I will marry you, Logan Walker, and run with you if I must if you promise now to take me to a really lonesome place for our honeymoon."

"I know just the spot." He flashed his hard-sparkle smile. "A cabin on a rocky Caribbean coast swept by every tropical wind that blows. It will save us a lot of dressing and undressing, never having to wear anything at all."

"What's this wedding gift, Clarence?" he asked as the two, looking radiant, joined the others again.

"Just your life. I'm officially fessing up to you, Judge, in front of all these people—I killed Rachel Blue, and I am sorry I done it. Drink and the devil were in me that night and many another night as well, though not when I did in Cooney. I never much liked Cooney, and I detested Miz January, 'specially after she did me out of my fingers, the witch; so I hit her a few times and locked her out. Drink and the devil must have been in her that night—she sure got lost in the snow quick enough—and there I was trying to be a gentleman for once, asking her to join me for a late-night snack. It just don't pay, being too polite, I swear. Well, Judge, can I die peaceful knowing I done Logan here a good turn?"

"Boy, as a rule, I don't accept deathbed confessions," the judge grumbled and scowled, "but this once, I will!" He broke into a big smile, and another sigh, this one of relief, travelled from one Blakely to the next. "Did I hear someone mention a double wedding? That's a double fee for me, I hope you know."

"Make it a triple. They're all on me and so's the champagne!" Jake announced, arriving with Aida and Joachim in tow. "I have come to my senses," he added, looking better than he had in days. "I long ago found the woman I love—this woman—and she ran off and left me."

Aida nodded in agreement.

"It took me a while to figure things out, is all. But I missed her so when she was gone, I finally figured out what I was feeling had to be love."

"Jake is kind of slow, but I love him anyway." Aida smiled.

There were six silver rings, six "I do's" and "I will's," and a lot of laughter and tears. The party lasted all night and so did Clarence. Next morning, when the sheriff came to arrest him, he was gone. Lark and Logan hoped it was to the safe lonesome place of his dreams.

Epilogue

"Spring 1893

"Dear Lark,

"Dario, wearing his favorite white apron, is cooking up a storm of rabbit stew, and I am sitting here on the edge of a swamp in Mexico, nursing your little sister, baby Wren. Dario's rambling and unsettled proclivities are not unlike my own, and so our Wren cannot help but inherit from us both the rambling fever. Right now, she and I are protected from the buffetings of chance by the finest of men, my dear husband. Dario purchased a new Studebaker wagon with a spring seat before we began our journey, so we have not found the road as hard as we might have. For the time, we lack true shelter, as did so many westering women and their babes, but we plan to return to settle and build, one day, in Oklahoma.

'Before we parted from your grandfather and the Chamberlains, Aida, who has become real fat and chirpy, was expecting a brother or sister for Joachim. Like the hen in her barn that was raising up a litter of motherless kittens, with bottle help at feeding time, of course, Mrs. Chamberlain was already raising another woman's child. Poor Squirrel Tooth Janie, the outlaw moll from Ingalls, got the 'milk sick' and died in just two days, though Aida did try treating the fever with joe-pye weed. Dario thinks the deadly malady, which kills men, women and children alike, or leaves them weak and frail for years, has its cause in the drinking of milk from cows that eat snakeroot and get the trembles. This Janie did confirm before she passed. The unfortunate creature left a newborn, also called Janie, at the JAK Bar, so Jake has his little girl at last and by now may have another.

"We parted from friends and family in Oklahoma soon after you and Logan did, in the very early spring, to seek the company of coyotes, wolves and catamounts among the other species of the plains and mountains. Like us, some were transients, the northering herons we saw in a spring rain marsh. There have been quite settled creatures as well — great basin rattlers and whip-tailed lizards holding down their part of the desert. We have watched the crescent moon fatten, bats whirling in its white unearthly light, and thrilled to the slant of rising sun climbing the ladder of the latitudes toward summer's zenith. When gathering what I supposed were prairie chick eggs one day, imagine my startlement when, from one, out hatched a little snake!

"In New Mexico we roamed mesas and arroyos and stopped at the Taos Pueblo to await the arrival of baby Wren. Your new little sister, Lark, was on time to the day, and in retrospect, I know I could have predicted her debut to the very minute!

"Once on the road again, we located the Penitentes in the desert, and Dario delivered his great bell, which was received with wonder and thanks. Then we set off to add the birds of Mexico, sketches and specimens, to the collection Dario has been sending east to his museum. We have faced bandidos on the 'Path of Skulls' and alligators at the edge of swamps, and I now know more about bells, birds and the terrain south of the border than I ever expected to.

"Something else I never expected was to hear again of Clarence Cumplin, but his story, and yours, Lark, as written and sketched by Ethan Everet, carried far and near, and his reputation is quickly disseminating. There are reports of the pair of you having been seen in many distant parts of the far west and in more towns and villages than he or you could ever have actually been. What his true fate was we may never ever know just as I may never know when, or if, this letter ever reaches you, dear daughter. What I do know is that we will all meet again, as we planned, at the JAK Bar in January of 1894 to celebrate our shared wedding anniversary.

"Your loving mother,
Charlotte."

"Summer, 1893
"Dearest Mama,

"We are in Chicago, and I do not know if this letter will ever find you; but I am bursting with news, and so I must write it.

"Clarence Cumplin is dead at last, for sure. I saw his end. As usual, he leaves me perplexed in my feelings because he was a man who didn't really want to be bad and wicked but couldn't stop himself from doing wrong. Anyway, it is all over for him now, and it was a hero's death he died, once again doing me a merciful service which, had he lived, I could never have adequately repaid. It happened this way. . . ."

Before going on with her letter, Lark set her pen in the ink well and went to the window. She looked out over the Carolina acres that she and Logan now called home, remembering the fateful day, the outlaw's last, with absolute clarity.

A Concord-built stagecoach, drawn by six white horses all lathered and straining at their bits, laboring to their utmost, came careening around a bend. The driver, up top, cracked his whip furiously as the armed guard beside him turned to fire a repeating rifle over his shoulders at hostile pursuers who could not yet be seen by the passengers inside the coach.

The occupants of the stage, three women in immense feathered hats and a man in a bowler, all attired in the latest frothy eastern fashions, leaned from the coach windows, waving brightly patterned silk handkerchiefs and calling encouragement to driver, guard and laboring horses.

Within moments, mounted men, what looked to be more than a hundred, appeared, hot in pursuit of the fleeing stage. Gunshots filled the air. The guard dropped his Winchester, fell from his seat, toppled to the ground and lay motionless as the galloping horses, circling after the stagecoach, leapt his spread-eagled body. Suddenly, blood-curdling Indian war cries rent the air as a party of painted braves joined in pursuit of the stage. The ladies inside kept waving, their big hats flopping in the breeze, as the shouting driver repeatedly lashed out, cracking his whip over the backs of his straining equines.

The masked outlaws and marauding Indians were soon followed by a Pony Express rider, who was tearing along, bent low over his mount's withers, just ahead of a hard-riding throng of cowboys and a contingent of blue-coated cavalry, their bugler sounding a charge. When the Indians turned on the soldiers with whoops and hollers, cowboys and cavalry were joined by Mexican Vaqueros, Arabian Horsemen, Russian Cossacks, Argentine Gauchos, Chasseurs a Cheval de la Garde Republique Francias, the 12th Lancers of the Prince of Wales and The First Guard Uhlan Regiment of the German Kaiser. As the unique chase continued, doubling back on itself at break-neck speed until it seemed that the tail had begun wagging the dog, that hunters became hunted, the breach between them was filled by a large man on a galloping palomino. There was a rider at his side, a slender, almost elfin figure in a ten-gallon hat, astride what could, in the excitement, have been taken for a fire-breathing hellion of a black steed.

The massive man was more than six feet tall, not counting his Stetson, from beneath which thick, curling gray hair flowed to his shoulders. He was attired in a hunting shirt of beautifully dressed and tanned deerskin, fringed leggings, moccasins and a wide leather belt. The small person riding beside Colonel Buffalo Bill Cody and dwarfed by him also wore buckskin breeches trimmed with long, brightly colored fringe and a soft buckskin shirt decorated with shining, shimmering glass beads, porcupine quills and spangles of sequins. When standing in the stirrups the slighter rider took careful aim with a Winchester and shot off an outlaw's sombrero, her own Stetson went flying, and Lark McKay's waist-length flaxen hair cascaded down her back snaring sunlight. Her radiant smile flashed as a great roar went up from a flag-waving, foot-stomping, whistling applauding crowd.

"GOLDILOCKS!!!" they cried, over and over, more than twenty thousand strong, gathered to see and to cheer "Buffalo Bill's Wild West Congress of Rough Riders" performing in a horseshoe-shaped amphitheater near the grounds of the Columbian Exposition, the Great World's Fair being held on the edge of Lake Michigan in the City of Chicago in the year of 1893.

It was part carnival, part celestial megalopolis, actually called "The White City" for the design of its buildings amidst lagoons, pathways, plantings and promenades spread over seven hundred acres. Constructed of a plasterlike material and decorated with sculptures, vases, pillars and balustrades, the halls and palaces of the fair gave an illusion of white marble solidity and combined the high ideals of nature, design, beauty and progress in structures displaying the mechanical marvels to be expected in the new century — portable sinks and mechanical dusters, and such — all to be run by the power of the electricity that would miraculously flow to every home. Amidst the excitement, there was already a sign of nostalgia for a glorious past evidenced by the popularity of the Wild West show.

To open each performance, Will Sweeny's Cowboy Band of thirty-six men wearing slouch hats arrived in the arena on matched horses, mounted the bandstand and played a thrilling "Star Spangled Banner." Then came the Grand Review of the Rough Riders of the World before Buffalo Bill gave an exhibition of his superior marksmanship along with Buck Taylor, King of the Cowboys, and Annie Oakley, the Peerless Lady Wing-Shot. The extravaganza continued with a small herd of buffalo circling the arena, Indian boys riding bareback races, a dramatization of the Battle of the Little Big Horn during Custer's Last Charge and the foiled stage robbery during which "Goldilocks" made her first appearance of the show.

* * *

Lark McKay Walker, like the other members of her family, had become a Wild West Show star, a household name all across America, and her husband, when not horse trading for his own breeding stables, was a celebrity, too, billed by Colonel Cody as "The Most Celebrated Young American Horseman of the Decade."

With a crew of experienced cow hands and three rodeo clowns, men who were actually death-defying acrobats rather than buffoons, Logan exhibited for crowds of easterners, and westerners as well, so-called Cowboy Fun — leaning low to snag objects from the ground while mounted, lassoing wild horses, roping calves, riding saddle bronc buckers and, the most dangerous act in any wild west rodeo show, Logan's specialty — bull riding.

Staying atop a spinning, hooking, kicking two-ton bull, held on its back by a tightly pulled, braided rope passed about the bull's withers and wrapped about the rider's gloved hand, could be fatal. A big, heavy cow bell was also attached to the rope and dangled beneath the animal. It served to further goad the bull to leaping contortions of anger and also acted as a weight to pull the rope free of the rider's bound hand when he was ready to jump. Not many bull riders regularly earned such a choice. Most hit the dirt before they planned to, and for those who didn't, dismounting became the real moment of truth: If the rider did not free his hand fast, he could be tossed forward and hooked on the horns or thrown off still tied and have to run along with the furious animal, doing his level best not be stepped upon. A dislodged, tied rider might flap helplessly along like a rag doll or fall to be crushed and broken beneath jackhammer hooves. That's where the rodeo clowns came in.

It was their job to distract the animal from an endangered bull rider, who must run for his life and the safety of the fence, not daring to look behind him. It is then that the clowns, in garish makeup, flapping baggy pants or wooden barrels, distract a mad bull just long enough for a man to scramble to safety.

More than once, only fleeting seconds and a clown's antics had saved Logan's life. His bull riding was a celebrated, heart-stopping exhibition of skill and bravery, and the charming family performance that always immediately preceded it served to heighten the excitement, and the anxiety, of his audience.

With his beautiful young wife at his side, Logan demonstrated the finer skills of the art of dressage — riding Virginia style. For this event, Lark dressed "eastern" in a velvet side-split skirt with a high waist, a silk blouse with a black velvet ribbon and a rose at the collar and a rose-red, Virginia-cut riding coat with black velvet collar. Perched on the saddle in front of her was a beaming baby boy dressed in tiny jodhpurs, a tuxedo shirt, boots and a miniature custom-made Stetson hat. Robin Walker, the apple of his parents' eyes, had made his rodeo debut as soon as he could sit, and he had been basking in the attention of adoring audiences ever since.

With a deep sigh, Lark went back to her writing desk and took up her pen.

"Here in Chicago, Mama, fifty miles of streets and alleys run through the Union Stockyards. There are pens enough to hold two hundred thousand hogs, cattle, sheep, donkeys and horses. Huge drays drawn by the biggest horses, six to a team, load and unload incessantly at the docks and freight sidings, and millions of dollars change hands in the stockyards every day. It's a real rough part of town and draws, besides animals and legitimate traders, many of the tramps wandering the country wherever the railroad tracks lead. Apparently Clarence had hid among them to travel east undetected with a plan in his mind to make a huge robbery at the yards. He was broke and had been stealing what he could, like the 'Monday morning men' who grab drying clothes off lines when the circus pulls out of a town. To tide him over, once he got to the city, he took work as a rodeo clown, disguised by grease paint which he was never seen without. Clarence was a very talented clown of the variety called a bullfighter. He had been with the Buffalo Bill show a few weeks before he met death, but neither Logan nor I knew that.

"Everything in our show is genuine, right down to the least detail. Colonel Cody is real particular about that, but there's just one problem: Along on these Wild West Show jaunts are many genuine and actual cowboys, friends of the colonel's youth, old plainsmen now, using the tour as an excuse to go on an epic drunk, and Cody the biggest guzzler of them all. He is a hail fellow well met, all right, surely a courtly man with an eye for pretty ladies. Yet for all his world travels to London, Paris and Rome to tame in mere minutes the most unmanageable horses on the continent and show our frontier ways to the rest of the world, he is an easy mark, generous to a fault, just an open-handed, overgrown boy — and a drunkard.

"When he unintentionally let loose into the arena all our wild bucking broncs and three Brahma bulls — the worst kind of bull for its long horn — we had just finished the Virginia reel on horseback. I have taught Satan to jump in time to the music and to take a bow by rising up on his hind legs which he was doing at one end of the ring while at the other, Señor Vicente Orapeza, the rope artist, kept his spinning lariat leaping and circling so it seemed alive. Lamps and gas flares illuminated the action, and there was lots of red fire for the Indian dances when wild equines began springing into the air, and bulls to dart hither and thither. It was then I screamed out my terror on seeing my beautiful fearless child, your grandson, Robin, come toddling from the sidelines into the path of a big Brahma bull.

"Señor Opeza's spinning lariat, in a looped circle, snaked out and ensnared a bull horn, but that didn't slow down the wild beast one bit, just dragged Opeza right along. I was racing toward my darling boy from one side, his father on Sundance, howling with fury, coming from the other, and Annie Oakley, whose real name is Phoebe Moses, was taking aim when the valiant clown stepped in, gathered up baby Rob and lifted him to the safety of the hushed stands where twenty thousand pairs of arms were reaching out to enfold the smiling child.

"It was then the bull caught that clown against the fence. The man was gored and thrown, and he died, all in a half shake, in just the flutter of an eye. His own broken rib pierced a blood vessel, the doctor said later.

"I did not know that the great clown in the corn-shuck hat was Clarence until I knelt at his side and he opened those pale, madman's blue eyes of his. I thanked him. Logan did, too. I think he heard us, but we are not sure. I do not know, either, if he was one of the last of the old type of outlaw like Jesse James, or in the vanguard of a new conscienceless sort of criminal like that crazy killing boy they call Billy the Kid.

"Old Wild Bill Cody, though never an outlaw, was once young and reckless. In his early days, he would ride straight into a herd of buffalo, I'm told, a six-shooter in each hand, reins in his teeth, and bring down as many as eight animals before he'd quit. Now that the Indian Territories are being settled and our frontier is closed (or so the U.S. Census Bureau proclaims), the colonel, an older, wiser man, is all for protecting what's left of the wild creatures and our wild past. That will be preserved for us only in books, I think. Mama, I have been reading the dime novels about the colonel and others. Mostly I prefer the brave and resourceful women of the west — Keno Kate the Faro Fairy who made her way in the world as a gambler, Mustang Madge and Bessie Bond, the Border Beauty — and they were *grand* women, Mama, not to be forgot.

"It was my darling, unforgettable, loving man, Logan, who said that we were right at a great crossroad of history, we two and all the folks who came to Chicago, some of them, like us, from the heart of the true west, Oklahoma, to glory in our country's past, and to see its great future with their very own eyes.

"I will be jubilant when *my* own eyes set on my own dear mama once again, back at JAK Bar in a little more than one year from now.

"Your most loving daughter,
Lark Walker."